Merely a Miss

A Lord Rotheby's Influence Novel

CATHERINE
GAYLE

Night Shift Publishing

CATHERINE GAYLE

ISBN: 1495247376
ISBN-13: 978-1495247378

Dedication

To Grandpa, Uncle George, sweet Salvation Jane, and my Bailey Boo. I miss you all.

One

London, 1815

A SHRILL, FEMALE voice that could only belong to his mother demanded entrance just as a rather loud thud sounded against the door. "His Grace is not to be disturbed, ma'am," came the gruff, masculine response of his footman.

Peter Hardwicke, Duke of Somerton, could almost *feel* the commotion outside the doors of his library, not just hear it. Clearly unimpressed by the footman's response to her command, Mama pushed the door open and nearly burst it free from its hinges.

Forrester's jaw fell open from across the great oak desk. He stared at the dowager as she disrupted their business meeting. One look back at Peter, however, had the secretary snapping his mouth closed so fast he might have bitten off the end of his tongue.

The Dowager Duchess of Somerton might disregard her son's edicts, but no one would disrespect her and live to tell the tale. At least not if Peter knew anything about it.

Henrietta Hardwicke—lovely, still, with her rich auburn hair streaked with only a bit of white, and quite a lovely figure, despite having borne six children—pushed the doors wide as the bedraggled butler, Spenser, and Peter's baffled footman followed in her wake.

"Your Grace, I apologize," Spenser stammered. "We informed Her Grace that you required privacy, but she would not take no for an answer." His beleaguered butler looked ready to rip his hair out in frustration and, indeed, a few stray grays stood on end.

Peter could understand the sentiment.

He needed to sort out these matters with Forrester and send the man on his way. Then he could better focus on the day's true agenda: examining the ledgers from his various estates. Only that morning, he had held his quarterly meeting with Yeats to receiving his accounting. Peter's man of business held no small amount of concern over Carreg Mawr, Peter's Welsh estate. It seemed that Turnpenny might be losing his touch with the staff, at least if Yeats's hunch was correct.

Yeats was rarely wrong with his hunches. It was a seminal talent.

Peter's talents, however, lay in finding proof of his hunches by poring over the accounts. Doing so would require time, though, and a bit of silence in his house.

Neither of which was he currently being granted.

"That is correct, I will *not* accept no for an answer." His mother, ever forthright, smoothed the lawn fabric of her gown with her one free hand (the other being occupied with a note of some sort) and moved further into the library. "You may all leave now. I should like a word with my son alone."

All three servants waited for his signal before departing. At least *they* would respect his authority in this house. A throb formed behind Peter's eye.

He loved his mother—he truly did. In fact, he loved all of his family a great deal. It was because of that great love for them that he overlooked it when they treated him with somewhat less respect than his position in society demanded.

It was also because of that love that he needed to complete his current task. After all, one must always fulfill one's duty to those one loved. Peter's duty to his family was to assure their wellbeing. Doing so required the incomes from his properties. And maintaining such an income from said properties required his utter diligence and devotion.

He shook his head. Sometimes it felt as though no one else understood how great his responsibilities were. This was one of those times. He took a glance at the stack of papers toppling over his currently cluttered but normally tidy desk and awaiting his attention, then up at Mama's fierce determination—the firm set of her jaw and the slight rise of a single eyebrow. He tried to mask his annoyance as he waved the servants away and escorted his mother into a chintz armchair near the large and piteously over-cluttered desk.

His mother would always be granted his time, when he could make it for her.

Peter waited until the door closed behind the men before he asked, "What can I do for you today, Mama?" He said a silent prayer for patience.

She looked across at him with a deadpanned gaze. "To start, you can find a wife."

Good God. Again?

"I see." Of course, he plainly did *not* see. This was the last thing he had been expecting to come from her mouth. He pushed at the unrelenting ache in his temples, hoping the pressure might ease the pain. "A wife?" He had no time for this. Not this discussion, not this business with Carreg Mawr—none of it. The Parliamentary session would begin in short order. That's where his attentions needed to be. He needed to meet with a few of the other Lords so they could decide what to do about Napoleon. The man could only stay put on Elba for so long, after all, and Prinny was counting on Peter and his group to determine what, specifically, should be done with him. "And why, precisely, should I find a wife?"

"Why should you not? Peter, I want you to be happy. I want all of my children to be happy. Don't you want what Alex and Grace have found together? They are so very much in love." She gave him a pointed look. "You could be too."

Good Lord in heaven, why should he want that for himself? It was all fine and well for Alex, but Peter and Alex were hardly the same. He'd hoped that when Alex had married, Mama's matchmaking schemes would have come to a close.

They clearly had not.

"I already *had* a wife, or have you forgotten? Mary was everything a duchess should be. She provided me with two children—two *beautiful* children." He walked to the hearth, rubbing his right hand absentmindedly over his jaw. "I couldn't secure happiness with her, so why should I expect a different result simply from taking another wife? Your expectations are unreasonable, Mama."

She let out a huge sigh. "Mary was a good woman, but she was entirely wrong for you. You and I both knew that before you ever offered for her. Even your father said as much."

Not that he had had any choice in the matter.

"And you think someone else could be a better duchess for me than she was?"

"I'm more concerned that she be a better *wife* for you."

He chose to ignore that particular remark. After all, if one was a good duchess, one must also be a good wife. The idea that the two were not interchangeable was simply unfathomable. "I see."

She huffed at him. "Enough with the 'I see' business. You clearly do *not* see, or you would have already put yourself back on the marriage mart and be well on your way to having more children in your nursery."

"You think you can find someone to replace her?" Mary had fulfilled every obligation of the station with elegance and ease. Not just any lady could have handled the position with her degree of finesse. "No. I have more than enough responsibilities to fill two lifetimes. I won't even consider adding to them in such a way."

"Responsibilities? I do love you, as I love all of my children, but you are not always the brightest, are you?" Mama softened her rebuke with a smile. "Can't you see that if you loved your wife, she wouldn't be another burden for you?" She reached across his desk and squeezed his hand. "I only want to ease some of your worries, not add to them."

He looked at the pile of paperwork waiting on his desk—two large stacks of the ledgers from his various accounts, another, equally large stack of correspondence awaiting his response, and a book of proverbs.

Those proverbs were his one diversion these days, the one manner he allowed himself for spending his rather limited idle time. He refused to see such a pastime as wasteful, since at least the proverbs allowed him to grow in wisdom. However, he likely wouldn't be able to study them again for weeks, at the current rate, and longer than that if he agreed to whatever harebrained scheme his mother was currently concocting.

"Another person to feed, clothe, entertain, and see to their happiness would not add to my duties? I wish I could see the world from your perspective, but the reality is I'm responsible for you, five siblings, two children, and five estates, along with seeing to my duties to the crown. When am I supposed to find time for a wife amongst all of that?"

Not to mention he had absolutely no desire for one. There were plenty of women prepared to satisfy his sexual needs who didn't insist upon the commitment a wife or even a mistress would require. Peter failed to see what purpose taking a new duchess could possibly serve.

"You could see life from my perspective if you fell in love. Try it." Her eyes didn't ask for his cooperation; rather, they commanded his obedience.

He felt like a little boy again, one who'd just defied his mother. Mama could always do that to him, even as a grown man, even now that he was the Duke of Somerton. He was one of the most powerful men in the entire kingdom, for God's sake. "And just how, pray tell, do you propose I try it?" Why had he even bothered to ask? He dreaded her answer. Of course, he didn't have to agree to whatever her plan was. There was always another option, even with Mama.

"Make it clear you're back on the marriage mart. Let the *ton* know you're looking for a wife. And humor me by following through with it and attending balls, going to the opera, and actually looking for a bride." She neglected to crack even the barest hint of a smile.

He groaned. "Mama, I attended a number of balls last Season. I found no one suitable at any of them." The docile debutante daughters of meddlesome Mamas always filled the blasted affairs. An unsightly combination of unhappily married ladies and lonely widows were continuously on the prowl, on their salacious hunt for male companionship. For some reason, *all* of these females typically marked him as their primary target any time he attended such a rout.

Who was he fooling? He knew precisely why they marked him as their sport.

Sometimes he wished didn't not carry any of his titles, that he was simply Peter Hardwicke and not the Duke of Somerton. Then, perhaps, he could prove their attentions hinged only on a desire for station and not on a desire for him.

That, however, could never be. Like it or not, he had been born with the knowledge that he was destined for this position. He had been brought up with this singular purpose forever in his mind.

One simply could not escape fate, no matter how hard one might try.

"You attended a grand total of three balls last Season," Mama countered. "I expect far more effort than that this time around." She pushed a stray piece of hair behind her ear before resuming her position, regal as the queen herself.

His eyes narrowed to slits. "How *much* more effort?" He doubted he could bear more than four or five balls at the most. The Season only lasted a few months, after all.

"Total." Mama raised a single eyebrow, daring him to defy her.

He groaned aloud. With that determination in her eyes, the woman would stop at nothing less than insisting he attend at least two or three soirees for every week of the Season.

She frowned across at him. "You and Sophia *will* each find an eligible match before the year is out, so help me. She's already on the shelf despite my best efforts, the stubborn girl, though she thankfully still has a number of gentlemen admirers. If only she wouldn't keep running them all off! I honestly have no idea why she can't find a single gentleman suitable. And you, my dear boy, are hardly better off than she. As such, I intend to have you escort your sisters and me to every ball of consequence."

"Every ball of...?" Peter raked a hand through his short hair, sending it into disarray. Good God, his mother was relentless. He knew her well enough to know she would never give in until she had her way. "Fine. You have this one Season, and one only, to find me a bride. If I haven't found a suitable match by the end of the summer, you'll leave me in peace as the widower I am."

Damnation. He really needed to keep a better check on his temper so he wouldn't be so sorely tempted to speak before he thought. Fiend seize it, had he truly just agreed to attend entertainments every night for months on end? He must be barking mad. They should lock him in an asylum and toss the key into the fiery pits of hell.

Mama smiled at him. "Excellent. But mind you, I intend to see to it you hold to your end of the bargain. You must do your very best to fall head over ears in love with some proper and eligible young miss? I'll hear of no less."

"And what, precisely, shall I gain in all of this, Mama?"

"Why, happiness and love, of course!" Her hands fiddled with the note she'd been holding since she first burst through the doors of his library. "Now, there is one other piece of business I wanted to discuss with you."

Wonderful. How could things possibly get any worse? "What might that be?" he drawled. Peter saw no reason to feign excitement over any part of this conversation.

"I've been corresponding with my third cousin, Barbara Matthews, do you remember her? The vicar's wife? I'm certain you must. She's really a dear, sweet lady. Anyway, she has a daughter with no dowry, and they've been so unfortunate as to be unable to provide her with a come-out either. I should very much like to invite her to stay with us this Season so I can sponsor her. Will you allow it?" Yet again, her tone challenged him with an order more than asked a question.

"So you propose I should have *three* young, unmarried misses in my home partaking in the marriage mart while you force me to participate as well? I can think of nothing I would enjoy more, Mama." He couldn't hold back the sarcasm. Not that he had tried, precisely.

First there was Sophie, who'd already been on the marriage mart for close to a decade. Now Charlotte was due for her come-out. With the addition of this long lost cousin, Peter thought he might drown in silks and lace before he could even contemplate doing what his mother had asked of him.

She narrowed her eyes at him for a moment but didn't comment on his rudeness. "Yes, that's precisely what I suggest. How else will Jane ever find a husband? The poor girl has no true prospects where they live. It's the least we can do for her. We *are* her relatives, after all."

"Since you will sponsor her come-out, I suppose you expect me to give her official debut ball, as well." He waited for Mama's nod. "Will you at least allow me to combine Miss Matthews's ball with Charlotte's? These balls will be the death of me," he said, grumbling the last bit beneath his breath and certain she would still hear it.

"That would be quite all right, sweetheart. I'm sure Charlotte and Jane will be quite content to share their ball." Mama stood and began to gather her belongings. "Splendid. I'll send my cousin a response today and leave to collect Jane tomorrow. Might I use your carriage for the journey? They live in Whitstable, you know, and I can't imagine traveling to fetch her in something less comfortable."

Tomorrow? They would be back within less than a week. How would he possibly get through his ledgers in such a short amount of time? But it would be almost impossible to sort out the problems with Turnpenny at Carreg Mawr once they returned and he began to fulfill his newfound societal obligations.

He needed Mama out of his library, and the sooner the better. Every moment he could spare would be necessary. "Of course you may take the carriage. I'll have a room prepared for Miss Matthews before your return."

"That won't be necessary. I've already ordered it done."

Why had she even bothered seeking his permission then, if she'd seen to all of the details? Clearly, she had already made up her mind, no matter his wishes.

"Is there anything else? I have a great deal of work to accomplish this evening and would like to get back to it if possible."

"No, dear, that's all." She stood to leave the library, but turned just before reaching the doors. "And Peter? Know that I only ask this of you because I love you and want what's best for you."

"Yes, Mama. I know." If only she would trust him to know what was best for himself. He had been the Duke of Somerton and the head of the Hardwicke family for over five years now. Yet still she treated him like a little boy, for Christ's sake.

"Good. I'll inform Forrester which of those invitations he should accept before tea." Mama rubbed her hands together with a broad smile. "We'll be quite busy this Season."

Too bloody busy for Peter's comfort. He settled at his desk and opened the first ledger for his Welsh estate before checking the clock on the far wall. There was no time to waste on Mama's distraction of searching for a wife, but what else could he do? If he neglected to follow through with it, she'd badger him for the rest of eternity. One Season—one silly, fussy little Season—would surely not kill him. It might make him itch to strangle a libidinous widow or two at times, after they had attempted to work themselves into his bed, or perhaps wish to jump from the window of the highest floor at Hardwicke House, but it wouldn't kill him of its own accord.

Mama returned to his library only a moment after she'd left. "One more thing, and then I'll leave you to your business. Jane's dowry. What can you do about that?"

Why would she not leave him be? "Her dowry?" he drawled.

"Yes, her dowry. She needs one. You have more than enough to provide her with one. And she *is* a relative, however distant. How much will you offer her suitors?"

"As much as it takes to unload the blasted woman as soon as possible and convince you to leave me alone, that's how much."

For the first time that day, Peter earned his mother's smile.

JANE SET ASIDE the gown she had been sewing and chose a book from Mrs. Zachariah's collection on the nearby bookshelf. "How does *Pride and Prejudice* sound for today? It's high time we start with a new book." She leafed through the pages, desperate to lose herself in the story. Of course, the village matron would agree to whatever book she selected—their reading sessions were merely a means to achieve Mrs. Zachariah's afternoon nap.

"Oh, yes. That sounds truly lovely, dear. Why don't you begin?" Mrs. Zachariah pulled a quilt high about her shoulders and struggled to keep her eyes open while the late afternoon sun warmed her gray, papery skin.

Jane wondered how much they would read before her friend nodded off from the lull of her voice. She returned to her seat near the lounging chaise where the older woman rested. A large ball of orange and white fluff leapt into her lap almost as soon as she was seated. "All right, let's begin. *It is a truth universally acknowledged, that a single man in possession of a good fortune, must be in want of a wife.* What a terribly odd sentiment." Mr. Cuddlesworth purred his agreement as he kneaded his paws against her bosom.

"Was that in the story? Jane, do please try to keep your thoughts to yourself. My feeble mind doesn't need any more distraction than it already has." Mrs. Zachariah coughed and cleared her throat, then settled in again.

Jane pushed the cat's paws away from their inappropriate behavior and tried to readjust him in a more decorous position curled up on her legs. Try as she might, she'd never managed to break her cat from drawing attention to her more-than-ample bosom with his antics. At least no one here cared how thoroughly unacceptable the Mr. Cuddlesworth's behavior was, whether they were in company or not.

"I'm sorry, ma'am," she said once he was resituated "I'll try to do better." After only a few pages, Mrs. Zachariah's all-too-familiar snores reached her ears, so she continued to read to herself. She could always read it again to the older woman tomorrow—and she likely would.

Several chapters later, she was fully engrossed in the tale and had lost all track of the time. The housekeeper poked her head into the drawing room. "Miss Matthews? Your mother will be missing you if you don't leave soon, ma'am."

Jane looked at the Bornholm clock by the double French doors. "Drat!" She was more than an hour late. Jane rushed to tidy the room and return things in their proper places. Mr. Cuddlesworth grumbled at her from his new position on the floor where she'd unceremoniously dumped him. "Thank you so much, for the reminder, Mrs. Dennison. You are most dear."

Mother would be furious at her tardiness. They had a guest arriving, some distant cousin or something. A *dowager duchess*, no less. One would think she was the blasted Queen of England herself, the way Mother droned on and on about the *Dowager Duchess of Somerton*.

Why should a title matter one whit? The woman only a relative, and one who had never bothered to visit before, at that. Nor had she invited any of them to visit. She probably looked down upon them, because Jane's father was merely a country vicar and he held no title.

With the room set back to rights and her sewing packed away, Jane carefully moved Mr. Cuddlesworth to his well-worn (or rather, so terribly old and used it was falling apart) basket. She wished he'd find something else to sleep in, but her sweet cat was very set in his ways. The basket had been his since the very first day she sneaked him into the house. She'd tucked him in her skirts when she was only nine years old to accomplish the feat. He didn't seem to care how it was too small to house his body or how hideously the wicker broke about him. It was his, and he would use it until the day he died. Jane rather thought he might tell her as much himself, if he could speak.

Or if she could understand his cat language.

Once he was settled, she gathered her belongings and rushed out the door, the cat's basket tucked snugly under one arm and another with her sewing notions in the other hand.

She trudged through the muddy lane separating their two houses. At least the rain had finally stopped. Mr. Cuddlesworth hated to get wet. They always fought an epic battle when he needed a bath, though it was usually quite unclear in the aftermath which of them had come out the victor.

As she turned the corner toward her parents' home, she realized things were far worse than she expected.

Double drat.

A huge, crested carriage waited before the front door. At least four men accompanied it, each of them at work caring for the team of six horses.

Six horses! Oh, dear Lord.

Jane rushed past the carriage on her way to the house, ducking her head as she passed the team so as not to draw their attention. One horse reared back and whinnied, and her heart palpitated. Breathing became almost impossible. She froze where she stood, so that perhaps the beast would calm down.

Only a few more steps to the kitchen door.

One of the men waiting with the carriage grabbed hold of the horse's reins and calmed it, and Jane took that opportunity to dart the rest of the way. Thank heavens. She hoped she could clean up before being spotted by anyone. Mother would be livid if Jane came in to be introduced to the dowager with a muddy hem and shoes. She threw open the door and scurried inside.

And ran straight into the lion's den.

Drat, drat, drat.

Mother's eyes dropped to the floor and her cheeks filled with color. Oh, dear. She hated to embarrass her mother. Jane had always hoped that, perhaps as she grew older, she would find a way to stop being so clumsy—that she could manage to behave appropriately more often than she behaved inappropriately.

Fortune had not been so kind as to grant her that favor.

She set her baskets down on the floor and brushed a hand over the wild mass of blonde hair falling out of place on her head. Nothing could be done about the state of her attire at this point, but at least she could try to straighten her hair. The damp air was causing her curls to run riot, though, and they quickly bounced back to their original position.

Blast, why had she worn the green cotton? It always made her skin look sallow. Not only that, but it had far more pulls from Mr. Cuddlesworth's claws than any of her others. She really ought to make herself some new gowns sometime soon. Her current dresses were all too worn, too faded.

Too late to do anything about that, at the moment.

With a sheepish grin, Jane tried to execute a proper and polite curtsy to the dowager, but her muddy shoes slipped on the hardwood floor and she fell forward. Thwack! Her nose smacked hard on the floor just beside the dowager's feet.

"Oh, that hurt." Her pride, more than anything.

Mrs. Childress, the family's maid of all work, rushed to her side and helped her to her feet. A tiny pool of blood pooled on the floor just where her nose had been, and a few droplets fell forward and landed on the dowager's gown as Jane straightened. She took a seat across the table from the two older women. That was not quite the elegant entrance she'd hoped for.

Mr. Cuddlesworth jumped into her lap and shoved his head into her hand repeatedly, forcing her to pet him just as he wanted, and entirely oblivious to the scene his favorite person had just caused.

"Your Grace, oh goodness, I am so terribly sorry," Jane's mother interjected. "My daughter is quite the clumsy fool at times." Mother's voice trembled with misery as she sprinted about to dab a wet cloth on her cousin's gown. "I certainly would understand if you've changed your mind after the behavior she has just displayed."

"Changed your mind about what?" Jane tried to ignore the hurt tone of her mother's voice. She pressed another wet cloth, brought over by Mrs. Childress, against her bloody nose with her unoccupied hand and hoped the flow would cease soon. If it didn't, she would likely get blood all over Mr. Cuddlesworth and then have to give the poor dear a bath.

A chore neither of them relished. She might end up bloodier than she started.

"Gracious heavens, girl, I've taught you better manners than that. I apologize for my Jane's impertinence, Your Grace."

Jane frowned. "Mother, I can certainly apologize for my own impertinence. There's no need for you to do so for me." She looked the dowager full in the face. A glint of amusement settled deep in the woman's eyes and the tiny upward curl of her lips intrigued her. "Changed your mind about what, *Your Grace*?"

She was a grown woman, by God, and not some silly girl still in leading strings. She would speak when she wanted to speak, and question when (and whom) she wanted to question, regardless of rank or station. Jane purposefully left the apology out of her question, choosing instead to simply add a *proper* styling for the woman's rank.

Mother's gaze hardened in outrage, but the dowager laughed outright. Her blue eyes twinkled with delight and soon her fair skin flushed to almost match the rich reddish hue of her hair. "Miss Matthews, I do believe I like you."

She turned to Mother and took the cloth from her hands. Then she took over the task of blotting the bloody spots from the fine yellow muslin of her gown. It was quite the fashionable gown, too, with subtle yet intricate stitch-work along the seams. It took every ounce of restraint Jane owned to keep from leaning closer and examining that gown down to the last inch. She wanted desperately to recreate it—only in a blue shade, something more akin to the sky on a sunny, spring afternoon.

"Your mother hopes I haven't changed my mind about returning you to London with me and sponsoring you for a Season," the dowager said with a faint smile. "She can breathe freely, because I most certainly haven't. I daresay you'll breeze into those ballrooms and clear the air considerably."

"A Season in London?" Jane ignored the dowager and turned to her mother. "But we can't afford such an extravagance. And is it necessary? I can't envision a reason to go to such lengths, when there is always so much work to be done here, and all of the boys have their own homes now, and wives and children, and can't help you with the gardens any more, and—"

"And nothing. You have no marriage prospects remaining in Whitstable, thanks to your silly ideas. That's unlikely to change in the foreseeable future. If you are to have any chance at a future other than being a spinster living forever with your father and me, this is what must take place."

Oh, heavens. She knew Mother had been horrified all those years ago when she'd refused Mr. Thornhill's pursuit. Whitstable didn't boast many other prospects in general, and the few that did remain at that point had all since married. None of which had bothered Jane in the least—but clearly it bothered Mother more than she'd realized.

"But why must I marry at all? What's so wrong with staying here with you and Father? You need help with the gardens and the cleaning. Mrs. Childress can't do it all, you know. I can earn a living with my sewing, and—"

"Enough with this foolishness of sewing! Jane, the Dowager Duchess of Somerton has made an offer to you that you simply cannot refuse. You *will* not refuse." Mother looked close to tears. "You'll go. You'll do everything in your power to be charming and to find a husband. You simply can't fail again." She stopped on a sob and took a moment to recompose herself.

The incident between Jane and Mr. Thornhill was most certainly *not* a failure, at least not in Jane's estimation. She wouldn't marry him if he were the last man in all of England. Not five years ago, not now, not in another ten years.

Not ever.

"Is that understood?" Mother stood with her hands firmly planted against her hips, the outrage which had colored her cheeks finally fading. "I can't live with myself if we fail to at least give you one more chance at finding a husband, Jane. Promise me you'll try. That's all I ask."

The dowager gave her an encouraging smile, and Jane couldn't bear to blatantly ignore her mother's request. Besides, she need only go to London and *try* to find a husband. She wasn't promising to actually *take* one.

Added to that, if she went along with her mother's request, she could even look around for a place to set up a shop—and take a look at some of the already established modiste shops there, to see what her competition might be. She hadn't yet worked out the logistics of having a storefront in London while working in Whitstable, but surely it would be easier to work all of that out in Town.

After giving marriage this one last opportunity, she might finally be free to do what she wanted with her life. She squared her shoulders, resigning herself to her decision. "Very well, Mother. I'll try."

Mother heaved a sigh of relief and Jane returned her attention to the dowager. "Ma'am, how soon will we travel? I'll have to prepare

Mr. Cuddlesworth for the journey and pack some food for him." He raised his head at the mention of his name and looked up at her with adoring, amber eyes.

Her mother's jaw fell open. "You *what?* Jane, you can't be serious. Leave the cat here. He'll be just fine. Your Grace, my daughter most certainly will not bring that ball of fur to your home, there's no need to worry."

Goodness. Her mother really needed to stop trying to speak for her. "I most certainly *will* take Mr. Cuddlesworth with me, or I refuse to leave at all. Mother, he's never been without me. And he is so old now, just a little old man, surely he wouldn't do well if I left him here, no matter how well you took care of him. He has to go or I can't. There can be no compromise on this point, I'm afraid."

The dowager eyed the cat purring contentedly on Jane's lap. "No, I can see there's no compromise at all. Cousin Barbara, I'm afraid Mr. Cuddlesworth will simply have to come with us." She reached a hand across and brushed it gently over his coat, coaxing him to roll over and bare his belly to her ministrations. "Jane, will he do well on our journey, do you believe?"

"Yes ma'am, I think he'll do quite nicely, so long as he's with me. He'll be no trouble, I can promise you."

Two

MR. CUDDLESWORTH'S BODY convulsed again, and a horrid, hacking sound emanated deep within him.

"Gracious. The poor little dear." Cousin Henrietta, as the dowager had insisted Jane call her, winced with each wracking heave until the cat finally relieved himself of the meager contents of his stomach.

Jane winced. "Oh, goodness. I'm terribly sorry. He has never traveled before, so I didn't know he'd become so ill." The vomit covered the other half of the upholstered carriage bench upon which Jane sat. She mopped at it with an already ruined cotton gown, all the while worried about her sweet companion. His eyes looked glassier than usual and his fur was becoming matted against his body.

He feebly returned to her lap and looked at her with huge, miserable eyes.

"I imagine cats are much like children in that way," the dowager said. "We must simply take these things as life gives them to us. There's no reason to be upset." She looked across the carriage at the two of them with an indulgent smile.

"But the carriage! Won't your son be furious?" The smell alone might be enough reason for him to toss them out.

Of course, that wouldn't necessarily be the worst fate Jane could encounter. She *would* be in London, after all. What better place to start her business, what with all the society ladies out and about, and always in need of new attire to keep up with the latest trends?

"Let me worry about Peter. Besides, he owns many other carriages. If his servants can't remove the stench, then he can use a different one. You just take care of your Mr. Cuddlesworth."

At precisely that moment, the cat left Jane's lap and leapt onto Cousin Henrietta's. He shoved his head against her hand until she began to scratch beneath his chin. Goodness. He had never behaved like that, at least not with anyone but Jane.

"Mr. Cuddlesworth! You naughty boy, you've not been invited to sit with her. I do apologize, ma'am. As you can see, he has a mind of his own."

He purred in contentment, with his head thrown back to give the dowager's fingers better access to his most sensitive spot and his eyes closed in pure feline ecstasy.

Cousin Henrietta laughed when he relaxed to the point of slipping from her lap to the carriage floor. "Why little fellow, you're quite easy to please, aren't you? I believe I might fall in love with you, Mr. Cuddlesworth, if you aren't careful."

Once on the floor, the cat spiraled between her legs, rubbing himself all over his newfound friend and trying to climb up the inside of her skirt. He left a trail of orange and white fur everywhere he touched, which stood out against the aubergine fabric of the dowager's traveling gown.

"He should return to his usual self once we arrive. At least I hope he does. Oh dear, what if he is still ill once we get to Town?" Speaking the thought out loud almost seemed to confirm Jane's fear. "I can't stand to see him so sick and not be able to fix it for him."

"There, there dear." The dowager reached across the coach to pat her on the knee. "I believe this is all just a bit of a change for him. He'll be perfectly fine once we're home. And if he isn't, he'll have more nursemaids at his side than he knows what to do with, all waiting to see to his every wish or desire. I imagine even Cook will fall head over ears in love with him and try to sneak him some cod on occasion."

The dowager was probably right. There wasn't any reason to worry. Jane tried to relax again. Over the three day journey, the two had become quite close. Jane even found she could speak openly with Cousin Henrietta about any number of topics she'd normally avoid at all costs with her mother.

As the daughter of a vicar, Jane must always conform to Mother's expectations of her behavior, and not discuss politics or the wars, or anything *interesting*. She must sit politely and act the part of a lady, which she rather felt anything but.

Even more surprising than the ease she felt in discourse with her traveling companion, she was in awe over the woman's outlook on life. Cousin Henrietta wanted all of her children to marry—not because it was what society expected—but because she wanted them to be happy. What a refreshing thought! If only her own mother shared such a sentiment.

Jane wondered how Cousin Henrietta would react to one of her offspring choosing to remain unmarried in order to preserve his or her own happiness, instead of following the path she would choose for them. She imagined it would be quite different from her own parents' reactions, even though she clearly wanted her children to find that perfect match.

It seemed their happiness was more important to her than their marital state.

"He's a sweet cat, Jane. Obviously you know how to share your love."

Looking across at the two, she realized Mr. Cuddlesworth had fallen asleep with his chin draped across Henrietta's knee. She smiled at the sweet picture they made. If she had ever become proficient with paints or drawing, like her mother had wanted, she would love to paint them as they sat. "Yes. He's well loved."

"We're nearing London. We should be at Hardwicke House within the hour. My girls will be especially pleased, I'm sure. They can't resist the idea of another female in our midst, even though my sons might think there are already more than necessary. I think Mr. Cuddlesworth might enjoy Peter's children. Though, I do hope they aren't too rough on him. Little Sarah is only four, almost five. She may not understand that pulling his tail or grabbing his ears would be unwelcome."

"He can handle children. He never seemed to mind me as a child. Of course, I wasn't quite as young as they are, but he loved me from the start. I daresay Mr. Cuddlesworth will feel at home anywhere, as long as I'm with him."

In all honesty, the cat had always accepted anything anyone wanted to do to him with no complaints. Not all cats in her acquaintance would be so calm and patient while having its eyes poked by curious fingers.

The true question was whether *Jane* would feel at home in London with the dowager's family.

But she would learn soon enough. The grand homes of Mayfair slipped into her view through the dusty windows of the well-traveled carriage. She could spare no more time worrying about Mr. Cuddlesworth. She had herself to worry about now.

MAMA HAD LEFT five days ago. Each passing day brought more rain. Peter couldn't be certain when she would return, alongside his newest charge, and still he'd been unable to settle the accounts for his Welsh estate.

Clearly, something was amiss. The problem continued to elude him. Debits and credits were all logged, and the balances seemed to be properly calculated and forwarded. But somehow, more money had been going out than was coming in, and he had yet to discover the cause.

His workers and tenants all reported ample healthy crops, according to the account Turnpenny had forwarded to Yeats. The steward's documentation relayed that the crops had received fair prices at market. His employees were paid a more-than-adequate wage for their services, but not more than the estate should be able to afford.

So where had the money gone?

He had hoped to solve the mystery before Mama returned and his home filled past overflowing with females flittering about, but his time for such pursuits was quickly running out. Once she returned reconciling these ledgers would become even less likely to take place, particularly if he kept his bargain with her. There would be few evenings, if any, that he could keep his own company.

Not only that, but she'd surely insist he pay social calls each afternoon.

Peter hadn't called on a lady in the afternoon since before Mary. The mere thought had him quaking in his Hessians. Heaven forbid if one of them should think he might actually be paying her court...that he intended to make her an offer.

Mornings would be his only refuge, his only time to accomplish anything of value and fulfill his duties.

He prayed that would be enough.

Peter rechecked the figures for the umpteenth time, wishing he would find the error glaring at him in the numbers but knowing he wouldn't. A throb formed in his temples, and he tried to will it away.

Then the trilling laughter of his sisters echoed through the hallway. The laughs grew closer. Blast it, they were going to interrupt him yet again. Why couldn't they leave him be?

Since Mama had left, his sisters had barged in on him at least two or three times a day. It was as though, without their mother present, they were unable to think for themselves or decide how to spend their days. Some days it was enough to make him wish they were still in the schoolroom and he could just send them back to their governess, Miss Bentley.

He ought to have kept the woman in his employ—hired her to act as Sophie's companion or something, since clearly Sophie had no intention of marrying any time soon.

But then again, Miss Bentley knew his sisters entirely too well, since she'd spent years in the Hardwicke home instructing them on how to be a lady and teaching them to enjoy feminine pursuits. Which, he might add, it could be argued she'd failed abjectly. At least Miss Bentley, herself, tended to behave appropriately on most occasions. If only she could have effected such a change on his sisters. However, having her around as a companion now might only serve to encourage Sophie to remain a singleton instead of seriously considering a gentleman's offer.

The female voices had virtually descended upon him. He tried to put his papers in order before they swooped in and wreaked havoc on his business affairs, building neat stacks and placing things just so.

Maybe Forrester would return soon and they could discuss important matters. Masculine pursuits. Anything to run the girls off. He loved them, but they would soon drive him to distraction. Just before they arrived, he debated slipping into the antechamber beside his library. None of the girls even knew it existed. He could hide there and they'd be none the wiser.

But he waited too long.

His footman pushed open the doors and led the two Hardwicke sisters and their former-governess-turned-companion into Peter's private library. "Your Grace, the Ladies Sophia and Charlotte." The man bowed and darted out the door so fast one might have thought someone held a pistol to his head. Indeed, he escaped before Peter could issue him a proper ducal glare for his act of cowardice.

His sisters, tall and lean, and sporting the hallmark Hardwicke red hair and slightly freckled fair skin, flounced in and took over his space. Sophie, the eldest sister, sat in an armchair across the desk from him. Charlotte, however, shoved his ledgers out of her way and seated herself directly on the corner of his desk. He could not avoid her if he tried. Their soft, feminine fabrics stood out against the rich woods and warm leathers adorning his library.

Peter almost wished that if he must be interrupted, at least he could have some male companionship involved.

Alas, his brother Richard was an officer in the army. He'd been home for a brief visit a couple of months ago, but Wellington was not appeased that Napoleon would stay put. As such, Richard and the rest of the army were still on the continent. His next brother, Alex, was now a married father, living contentedly in Somerton and pretending that life in London was nonexistent.

That left only Neil to save him from the feminine fluttering currently accosting him. But, being the youngest brother, Neil was content to spend most of his waking hours during those times when the rest of the natural world was asleep doing God only knew what. Certainly drinking, possibly whoring, and maybe gambling. None of which Peter could entirely hold against the lad. In fact, were he not in possession of the title and the inherent obligations attached to it, he might possibly follow the same path. As long as Neil stayed out of trouble, Peter resigned himself to let the sod do as he would. Sowing a few wild oats would not harm him in the grand scheme of things.

Still, that left Peter completely alone to face the women.

Charlotte, from her position atop his papers, sighed loudly. "When will Mama come home with Jane?"

"Miss Matthews, Char," Sophie admonished.

"Fine. Miss Matthews." She glared at Sophie before continuing. "She has been gone absolutely forever, and I am simply desperate to meet our cousin. Oh, I do wonder what she'll be like."

Char's exuberance typically charmed Peter, but today it rankled. "They'll be here when they arrive and not a moment sooner. Can you cease asking me this same question? I haven't been able to answer you to your satisfaction any of the other eight times you've asked in the last several days. With all the rain the whole of England has experienced over the last sennight, it's no wonder their travel has been delayed." His headache intensified. Blood pulsed through the veins in his head until it was a wonder they didn't burst.

Her exaggerated sigh set his jaw to grinding. "The rain has been absolutely dreadful, Peter. We've been stuck inside the house without anyone at all for company except ourselves. Mama at least would have arranged for us to make some social calls. Why, even Josh and Sarah are practically bursting at the seams to play outside."

"Why can't you two arrange your own social calendars with your mother gone?" he asked with a pointed look in Sophie's direction. She'd been out in society quite long enough to know how to move about within it, by God. "I imagine the Marlborough sisters are quite as bored with the weather as the two of you. And let Mrs. Pratt know she's welcome to take Josh and Sarah outdoors, so long as she is prepared to nurse them back to health after they catch the inevitable chill."

If they all left, maybe he could concentrate again. And maybe—just maybe—his blasted headache would ease.

"Why must we visit the Marlboroughs, Peter?" asked Sophie. "I should far prefer to spend some time with Lady Golding and her sister if we are to only pay one call."

"And why should you be the one to decide who we visit?" Char cut in. "I simply *must* see Theodora Marlborough this afternoon, or I'll perish." As if to further enhance her declaration, the youngest Hardwicke placed her hand against her forehead and fell backward until she lay across his desk, pushing the last of his record books to the floor in a single, loud thump. "We have so much to discuss, with our come-outs so close."

Somehow in the midst of his sisters' whining, Peter had missed the new sounds outside his library. The doors opened and Mrs. Pratt bustled in, pulling his two young children in tow.

The nurse spoke before his footman had a chance. "Your Grace, I simply do not know what to do with these two anymore. Lady Sarah has thrown four temper tantrums thus far today, and Lord Grovesend insists on exasperating the matter by taking her dolls away from her and taunting her with them. Much as you used to do to your sisters, I might add." She harrumphed for emphasis and nodded so hard that her usually tidy gray knot fell loose about her shoulders.

Who had neglected to inform him that the world was coming to an end that day? Good God. If he found out, he would have them sacked in an instant.

He was granted neither a reprieve nor a chance to respond to the nurse, however. Sophie chimed in, "Peter truly was a horrible brother when we were younger, Mrs. Pratt, wasn't he? I daresay he was the ringleader and the one most intent on leaving me behind whenever the boys went off to do something fun."

"Why, yes my lady, I daresay he was. I do sometimes wonder if he has learned the errors of his ways with leaving the females out."

She'd been his nurse, for Christ's sake. She'd been employed by his family since before the day he was born. It was one thing for siblings to squabble and pick at each other, but something else entirely for a household servant to pipe in with her opinions. Unwanted opinions, at that. "Mrs. Pratt, I wonder why you should so suddenly devalue your position in my household."

He raised a single eyebrow in her direction, which she met with a rebellious glare and two hands firmly planted atop her hips.

"Oh, gracious," sighed a desolate Charlotte. "How much longer must we sit and mope about? Either we should be off to visit the Marlboroughs or we should find out more about Jane." She deigned to pass him a hopeful glance.

He glared and she resumed her sulk. What more did the chit think he could tell her about Jane? He'd never met the woman either.

His daughter appeared to have been ignored for far too long. Sarah reached across her nurse's body and attempted to pluck her doll from Josh's hands with a wail. "Papa! I want my dolly. Josh keeps taking her from me."

Joshua pulled hard against the toy and fell to the ground, pulling his sister atop him and tussling with her to win the prize. The nurse stood back from the fray and allowed the children to scuffle, Peter's sisters rushed to their assistance.

Charlotte pulled the wailing Sarah to her chest, then sat on the floor and pulled the girl to her lap. "There, my sweet. I'll find one of my dolls for you to play with." The four-year-old girl's tears left wet stains upon the primrose lawn fabric of Char's day gown.

Sophie wrestled Joshua away and tickled him until a trail of giggles followed their path across the library. They knocked into chairs and disturbed a tidy stack of books waiting to be returned to their shelves, perfectly oblivious to the destruction they caused to Peter's neat and orderly sanctuary—one which no longer resembled a sanctuary at all, and could certainly not be confused with anything resembling *neat* or *orderly*. "Well, Your Grace, what do you propose to do about all of *this*? Hmm?" The insubordinate nurse had inched closer to the doors and further from the hazards caused by his family. Her eyebrows were arched in the exact manner she had always used on him when he was an unruly boy, finding himself in a spot of trouble and looking to someone else to sort it all out for him.

Blast the woman.

His head screamed. Patience. He must remain patient, calm, collected. He *would* regain his sanity. And he would take back control over his life.

He rose to command attention. "Enough." His voice hardly rose above a whisper. What point could there be in adding to the melee around him by shouting to be heard above everything else going on?

As expected, his tactic worked. Char and Sophie ceased their jabbering and even Sarah and Joshua looked up at him with large rounded eyes.

"Mrs. Pratt, take the children outside so they can run off their pent up energy." His words were quiet but firm, so as to brook no argument. "Sophia, take your sister and leave my home in peace. I don't care where you take her, whether it be to the Marlborough residence, or to visit Lady Golding, or the Queen of England herself, but I need quiet. Have I made myself perfectly clear?"

"Yes, Peter." Sophie stood and started to organize their departure. She handed Joshua off to the nurse and turned to take Sarah from Charlotte when yet another entrance interrupted her tasks.

"Your Grace, your mother and Miss Matthews have arrived." Peter's butler drew aside so the ladies could sweep past him into the overcrowded room.

A twitch formed behind his right eye, strong enough it would be visible to anyone near at hand. Devil take it, would he never attain order again?

Mama glided over to him, a huge smile lighting her eyes as she looked about to find so many of her family gathered together. "Perfect. Jane, sweetheart, come in so you can meet everyone. Best to just get these introductions over with so we can move on getting you settled and situated."

Good God. Had he known this cousin would be so—well, so long in the tooth?

Jane Matthews was no green debutante—not by any stretch of the imagination. She looked far closer in age to Sophie, possibly even older, than to Char. How was the woman not yet on the shelf? Mama had thoroughly lost her mind if she thought there was any chance of this woman finding a match on the marriage mart.

Her blonde curls looked like a giant ball of fuzz atop her head, tossed about in utter disarray. He couldn't tell the shade of her eyes because so much of her hair hung across her face all willy-nilly to the point that he almost couldn't see them at all. Her traveling gown, a faded blue of some sort, had seen many better days with pulled threads galore and odd, brownish stains all across the skirt. Come to think of it, Mama's gown bore many of the same stains. Thousands of tiny hairs covered them both, to the point they appeared to have rolled around in a field of cotton.

The fabric of her gown bunched around the woman's waist and pulled too tightly across her bosom, emphasizing her overall plumpness. Peter couldn't tell if it was simply too small for her, or if she had fidgeted around so much during their travels that it had become twisted and tangled about her body.

Even if it were clean and free from pulls, the gown was far better suited to someone working in his kitchens than someone attending the glittering balls of the *ton*.

Mama would have her work cut out for her with this project. Peter could think of no one less desirable than the cretin standing before him. Who on earth could he convince to take the blasted woman off his hands? He immediately doubled in his mind the dowry he'd initially set aside for her. She would need every last pound in order to find a husband.

Not to mention a great good deal of luck.

And perhaps a bribe or two. Bribes certainly wouldn't hurt her chances.

The room around him erupted into activity again before he could muster a proper greeting for the woman. His sisters surrounded Miss Matthews, gushing over her and pulling her into tight embrace after tighter embrace.

"Oh, Jane, we have been waiting so very anxiously for you to arrive."

"*Miss Matthews*, Char. She's not yet given us permission for such familiarity."

"But she's family, a cousin! You don't mind, do you, Jane?"

Sophie let out an exaggerated sigh of exasperation. "Fourth cousins are far from immediate family."

The woman in question laughed—a warm, bubbly sound—and moved back to set the half-broken wicker basket she had been holding down on the floor. "It's quite all right, ladies, I don't mind in the least. Why, your mother has insisted the whole way here that I call her Cousin Henrietta. I'll need your help in determining who is whom, though."

To that point she had all but ignored him, which was fine with Peter. If only they would all leave his library so he could return to work on his ledgers. But then Mama arched an eyebrow in his direction and gave him a rather pointed look. She'd never allow him to go without at least greeting the woman.

He cleared his throat and waited for silence. In vain.

The female chatter rose to an excited pitch as his sisters nattered about all of the dress shops and linen drapers they would need to visit to prepare for the Season, and how delightful it would be to have Jane along with them.

So he tried again, only louder this time. Slowly, the din dropped off to an almost imperceptible roar. Everyone in the room other than his children turned to face him and waited for him to speak.

"Miss Matthews, I pray you'll be comfortable at Hardwicke House. Should you wish for anything, I ask that you inform me immediately."

Before she could respond, Josh once again pulled the doll from his sister's grasp, and she bellowed her displeasure. Peter still had never deciphered how such a small child could produce such a great sound. Sarah's tears were ever his undoing, though, whether justified or not.

He moved to admonish his son and appease his daughter, but before he could take even a step, a giant, orange ball of fuzz darted out from Miss Matthews's discarded basket and dove headfirst toward his sweet Sarah.

"Mr. Cuddlesworth, no!" Miss Matthews called out. "Oh, you naughty, naughty boy."

The beast would kill Sarah, or maim her at the least. Peter dashed out from behind his desk to rush to his daughter's side. His only thought was to protect his little girl, his baby, one of the very few things in this world he held as precious and dear.

At the same time, Miss Matthews bolted across the room from in the midst of his sisters, but neither of them could possibly reach his daughter in time.

The orange monster pummeled her to the ground. Sarah caught it in her arms and rolled over with it. The damned thing was easily half her size, if not more.

He had seen the damage a rabid animal's teeth and claws could do to a grown man. It would decimate his little girl in no time.

"Drat! You naughty boy." Miss Matthews reached Sarah and the offending creature at just the moment he did.

Peter shook from head to toe, unsure whether fear or anger had won the battle over his nerves. Whatever creature that woman had brought into his home could have killed his daughter. As things stood, the damage remained unknown.

He prayed they had gotten to her in time.

They both reached for the pile on the floor but stopped short with the odd sounds emanating from Sarah and her attacker. Instead of cries, giggles and a loud purr rustled from them.

Peter took a step back to re-evaluate. "A cat?" Not a monster. But in his house. *On* his daughter. For the first time in his life, he feared he might strike a woman.

"Mama, please explain to me why you have allowed this...this...animal into my home without consulting me on the matter." He chose to speak to his mother about it instead of Miss Matthews, because he was uncertain he could restrain himself from delivering the audacious woman a blistering set-down and ordering her immediately from his home. Peter tried to extricate his daughter from amidst the mounds of orange fur while he waited for his mother's response, careful to avoid its sharp claws and teeth.

He fought the rage building in his chest down. How could Mama have done something like this? Her own grandchildren could be hurt, for all that she knew. But letting his temper get the best of him was not an option. He would never—*never*—allow that to happen before his children.

"Oh, Your Grace...er, Peter...er, I mean Your Grace, that is." Miss Matthews looked at him with a sheepish expression when he slowly turned his glare upon her form.

She *would* learn to address him properly.

"Um, well, you see, Mr. Cuddlesworth has been with me since he was a just tiny kitten, and he's quite old now and has never been apart from me, and I simply couldn't bear the thought of leaving him for months on end."

Obviously, the woman didn't know how to act in polite company. He had spoken to his mother—*not* to her. The fact that she was responding at all spoke of her idiocy. If she had any idea of the rage building within him toward her, she would run from the room without looking back.

Of course, he shouldn't be surprised about her display of gaucherie, based upon her appearance. He might need to suggest an asylum to his mother, instead of his home, as a suitable place for their cousin to stay for the Season. Becoming the laughingstock of the *ton* was not overly high on his list of priorities.

And she had brought an *animal* into his house. There could be no accounting for whatever else she might subject his children to.

No harm could come to them. Ever. He absolutely couldn't allow it to happen.

"Of course my parents...er, well, they do care for him, and they would take excellent care of him, but I don't know how he would react to not having me around. My cat goes everywhere with me, absolutely everywhere, and he becomes a bit destructive if I'm not with him for too long, you see. With his old age, there's just no telling what he might do without me. It might be rather unpleasant, I'm afraid."

The cat licked Sarah all over her face. She elicited another round of giggles and squeals while he continued to purr. They rolled together about the floor. Sarah's frock was soon covered with long orange and white hairs, just as Mama and Miss Matthews were. If Peter allowed this to continue much longer, she might well have those same disgusting stains upon her attire as Miss Matthews and his mother currently wore—whatever they were.

The urge to put her in her place became overwhelming.

"Unpleasant?" he drawled, returning his attention to the miscreant. "Might its behavior be more unpleasant than whatever has caused the unsightly state of your attire? More unpleasant still than the fright that creature put me through when it attacked my daughter?" He advanced upon the woman, hoping to cause her some alarm and not stopping until he stood toe-to-toe with her.

She feared him—the look in her eyes made that fact quite plain—but she didn't cower.

Peter narrowed his eyes and continued. Clearly, she didn't fear him enough yet. "More unpleasant than it would be to banish you both to the stables, where it obviously belongs, and I daresay you might as well? You look an absolute fright. And Mama, you hardly look better."

His mother's eyes flashed at him, but Miss Matthews spoke before Mama could cut in.

"Ah, my attire? Oh, dear me, yes. Well, Mr. Cuddlesworth became quite ill on our journey and we've had a few accidents."

Her hands pulled at a stray thread on her gown, and it was a miracle it didn't unravel before his eyes. The woman had no business amongst polite society. That much was plain.

"I'm certain he'll be more than all right now that he's no longer in a moving carriage and can settle in." She brushed her hands down the front of her haggard dress and tried to straighten it, but her efforts made no difference. "But you are certainly overreacting, Peter, about sending us to the stables. He'll clean up in no time, and I'm quite sure I can remove these spots from both our gowns. Your Grace, that is. Peter. Oh, double drat, what on the blasted earth am I supposed to call you?"

A chorus of feminine gasps and childlike giggles sounded behind her.

Obviously, her *faux pas* didn't even faze her, as she kept digging herself into a deeper hole. "This business with titles is a bit asinine, isn't it? I mean, you are only a man, like any other man. You were lucky enough to be born to the parents you were born to is all. Anyway—" she waved a hand through the air as though to ignore all of what she'd just said— "where shall I take Mr. Cuddlesworth, so we can freshen up? I should most dreadfully enjoy a bath. Why, I believe I have some remnants of his stains stuck beneath my bosom and it's bothersome, indeed. Cousin Henrietta, wouldn't you enjoy a bath as well?"

Her bosom. She was talking about her bosom. To him. In front of his children, for Christ's sake. Peter had never seen or heard the like in his entire life. This Jane Matthews was a disaster ready to strike the *beau monde* and take him with her.

She turned to his mother while his sisters, children, and servants all looked on with their jaws agape. Mama just smiled with the widest smile he'd seen on her face since the day his niece, Isabella, was born. Sophie's jaw quickly returned to its usual position, and her shock gave way to a smile that soon put Mama's to shame.

He should be furious with Miss Matthews for her impertinence. He should banish her to the stables like he'd threatened. He should throttle her until her teeth rattled in her head.

No one spoke to him like that. No one dared.

But instead of doing any of those things, he had to fight back a laugh. Still, he couldn't allow her to see the unreasonable and thoroughly irregular effect she'd had on him. He fixed his sternest glare upon her instead.

"Come along, Jane," Mama said. "I'll show you to your rooms and have a bath drawn. That sounds delightful to me. Sarah, will you come with us and bring Mr. Cuddlesworth so we can show him where he'll sleep?"

His daughter squealed with joy before he had a chance to counter. "Oh, Grandmama, can he sleep with me?" Blast it, now that confounded animal would be sleeping in his home. How had he lost so much control over his life?

With Miss Matthews's arrival, suddenly all of his family had something to keep them occupied, so they all filed out behind Mama.

He finally had the peace he sought to work on his books and ledgers...but no longer cared. What in bloody hell was he going to do now?

Three

COUSIN HENRIETTA LED Jane through the winding halls of Hardwicke House to what would now be her chamber. "I do hope you'll be comfortable here. You're so sweet to allow Sarah to play with Mr. Cuddlesworth. She is already attached to him, I fear."

"As he seems attached to her. I'm glad he's made a new friend. Especially since I'll have to spend some time away from him." Drat those balls she'd be forced to attend. "Sarah can keep him company."

The walls lining the hallways were so elaborately decorated and furnished, Jane feared she might trip over herself from gawking—it was all so garish. *His Grace* felt this was tasteful? Good lord, she would be living in precisely the lavish extravagance she had always so despised about the elite.

The dowager seemed to notice neither her shock nor her disdain. "Yes, they'll be quite good friends, I believe. Here we are, dear." She opened a French door into a huge suite of rooms, draped with chocolate and gold fabric over all the furnishings, exquisite oil and watercolor paintings in gilded frames, massive mirrors running from floor to ceiling, and a roaring fire in the hearth. Even more of the gaudy embellishments than she saw in the hall filled what would now be her own private rooms. To one side, a tub sat full of steaming water, beckoning to her. It, at least, was welcome.

"Will this suit? I chose this chamber especially for you. Of course I chose it before I met you. I do think it's one of the more pleasant rooms though, with a lovely view of the back garden outside your window. When the roses bloom in a few weeks, their scent will waft up to you."

The main room of the suite was easily as large as half her parents' home. Perhaps even larger than that. Good Lord, what would any one person need such an expanse for? "Oh, yes, ma'am. This will more than do. I'll almost feel guilty, staying in such a place with Mother and Father in their tiny house at the vicarage. It's all quite splendid, isn't it?" She hoped no sign of her distaste came out in her words.

The dowager admonished her with her eyes, and Jane feared she had been unsuccessful. "I'll hear nothing of this guilt, young lady. Have your bath and relax, and I'll send someone to fetch you in time for tea." Cousin Henrietta left her then.

Somehow during the brief span of her interview with Lord Somerton in his library, servants had moved all of her belongings into the suite of rooms, unpacked her clothing and placed it all in the bureau, and drawn the most luxurious bath she had ever taken, scented with fruity oils.

One of those same servants was even waiting in these mammoth rooms for her arrival. The girl wore a tidy, starched lavender servant's dress and apron, which caused her soft blue eyes to sparkle against yellow curls. "Hello, miss. My name is Meg. Would you like me to select a clean gown for you to wear after your bath?"

"Ah, hello, Meg. Call me Jane, please." Her life, clearly, was about to take a drastic turn, if a maid thought to help her with such a simple task as selecting a gown to wear. Not that the choice would be all that complicated. Her options were limited to the drab yellow cotton, the drab sea-foam green cotton, and the drab periwinkle blue cotton.

Everything else Jane owned had been soiled on the journey.

She would need to discover where she could launder her clothes, and the sooner, the better. Cousin Henrietta's gowns that had been damaged on their journey, as well. Perhaps after her bath and tea, Jane could explore this monstrosity they called a house and find where she could clean her gowns.

More importantly at the moment, however, her bath would grow cold if she didn't get started with it soon. "I'll choose my own dress, thank you." Hopefully the girl would leave her alone now. "I believe I'll take my bath now."

But Meg didn't take the hint and leave. The silly girl tried to assist her in undressing, which was beyond ridiculous. Jane had clothed and unclothed herself since she was a young girl. She could never envision a real need for someone to bother with that, when she was certain many more important things must need the young maid's attention.

"Thank you for your assistance, Meg, but I'm quite capable of managing this task on my own. You may leave now and see to whatever other chores you must have waiting. I'll be perfectly fine." She waved a hand, shooing the girl along.

Meg didn't take the dismissal lightly. Actually, she looked rather taken aback. "But I'm to be your lady's maid, ma'am." Lady's maid? Good God. What on earth did they think she would need a personal servant for? Meg kept talking. "My only chores are those which you assign to me. My job, for the duration of your stay at Hardwicke House, is to help you in whatever ways you need assistance."

Jane's jaw dropped. This was going to require far more adjustment than she'd anticipated. At her parents' home, she'd always done quite a bit for herself. She'd never allowed herself to imagine a life with someone waiting around to do her bidding at every turn. It seemed so frivolous. She frowned at the girl, as fiercely as she could muster, hoping to give the impression that she wouldn't need any assistance so that Meg would scurry along on her way.

The impertinent girl frowned back, just as ferociously as she had done. "Her Grace will be most displeased with me, miss, if I should neglect my duties." Meg didn't lift a single foot to move.

Jane sighed. "Oh." She couldn't very well be responsible for having the girl sacked. Somehow, the dowager would have to come to the understanding that Jane would not be waited upon by anyone. "I suppose I'll have to take the matter up with Cousin Henrietta then. I'm certain, in a household as large as this, there are plenty of better ways of using your skills. Please, run along, and I promise to visit with her as soon as I've finished with my bath." It wouldn't do to let herself grow accustomed to such extravagances, when she surely wouldn't be able to afford them as a modiste.

Finally, Meg left her alone. But she only went as far as the dressing room, after making certain that soaps, oils, scents, and ample towels were at her disposal, and even then, only after informing Jane that she need only pull the bell, and she would rush back to her side to assist her in any way possible.

That was not likely to occur.

Even after Jane agreed to Meg's terms, the servant sneaked into the chamber again, once Jane was good and wet, in order to remove her stained gown.

"Meg, do be a dear and retrieve Cousin Henrietta's soiled garments as well. I might as well launder them all at once." She chose to believe the servant's scandalized gasp was due to the fact that the dowager had a soiled garment, and *not* because she intended to handle her own laundry. Good Lord, she had started washing her own clothes when she was only a girl.

Once she was finally alone, she settled in to the steamy tub and tried to relax. Her mind, however, would not cooperate.

The journey to London, while full of traumatic moments with Mr. Cuddlesworth, had provided her with far too much to contemplate— and her arrival at Hardwicke House had given her even more fodder to mull over.

She'd agreed to the journey to set Mother's mind at ease. Yes, she was five-and-twenty, and yes, she had already squandered the one and only chance at marriage she had been offered. But a marriage to Mr. Thornhill was the last thing Jane could imagine providing her with a lifetime of contentment. She could never love the man. He bored her.

The entire time he'd courted her (a full three years ago, and not one man had even hinted at the possibility of an attachment since), he'd made it abundantly clear the kind of relationship they would have should she accept him.

They would live in Cornwall, somewhere near the sea and far from her family. There would be no affection, no tenderness—not even any friendship. He would expect her to stay at his home and care for his children (which she must also provide), and never leave, never visit with friends, never do anything of which he didn't approve, since he was to be a vicar and must maintain appearances within the village.

What kind of life would that have been?

Mr. Thornhill was not wealthy, which her parents seemed to think might be the true reason Jane had refused him. How very wrong they were. Money did not matter one whit to her. She'd always been a hard worker, and more than willing to do her share—and a good bit more on top of it. Why, she'd even earned a modest income for herself for well over a decade through her sewing.

Mother and Father had allowed her to use her earnings to pay for the education which they'd never been able to provide her with. And after she'd completed her schooling, she had stowed her money away.

They thought she'd saved it to provide herself with a dowry. How little they truly knew their own daughter. A dowry? Having a dowry would mean a having a *marriage*. What woman really wanted to be married to a man—to become his property, there to sate his needs and fill his nursery—but who cared nothing of her own wants and needs?

And now—now, Jane might actually be able to put her money to use. Much better use, if one should ask her. She could open a shop and earn her own livelihood! She'd never need to marry at all, nor would she be forced to rely on her parents for the remainder of her life as a (blessed) spinster.

Keeping her plans a secret was of the utmost importance, however. If Cousin Henrietta learned of Jane's plan or suspected anything was amiss, she would surely alert Mother. And if Mother found out what she was planning, she would throw a fit and order Jane to return to Whitstable immediately.

In order to keep the dowager from discovering anything, she had to be sure none of the Hardwickes knew what she was doing. For that matter, none of the servants could learn of her intentions either. Which was yet another reason, Jane brooded, that she would much prefer to have Meg settled into a different position within the household.

No, Jane would have to be cautious about finding a place to set up her business, so as not to alert anyone. But now she had a plan, a goal, a dream—and she was so very close to making it all become a reality.

She would become a modiste. She would achieve her independence. There could be no doubts now. There was simply no room for it.

But now, too, there was the new hindrance of Peter. The *Duke* of Somerton. And quite the hindrance he was.

The man was extraordinarily tall and muscular. Why, he absolutely towered over her, and she had never been short, even for a woman. His auburn waves were cropped impeccably close to his head. She was not entirely sure, because there had been so many new things for her to look upon, but she believed his eyes to be two different shades. Still, she was quite certain she couldn't tell anyone precisely which colors they might be.

For all his aristocratic hauteur, he was a sight, to be sure. If only he had Greek looks like the dark hair and olive skin, instead of his fair, slightly freckled skin, she would swear he were one of the gods of ancient mythology.

Not only that, but the boor seemed intent upon intimidating her. Such a bully! The duke would likely have insisted Mr. Cuddlesworth stay in the stables, too, if not for his daughter falling head over ears in love with the cat.

If that *had* happened—if he had banished her sweet cat to spend their visit in such dreadful circumstances—Jane would have stayed in the stables with him, whether His Grace ordered it or not. The bloody man would not separate her from her sweet boy, no matter how naughty the silly thing could be at times. But *really*. His suggestion that she do just that was beyond lowering, despite the fact that she would have done it for Mr. Cuddlesworth without it being ordered.

The nerve of him. She knew herself to be quite beneath him as far as society was concerned—there was no question of that. It seemed he adhered to all of the dictates of society.

She should've expected as much. His Grace was, after all, one of those very members of the elite who had placed such impositions upon the world to begin with. Why shouldn't he meet all of her ideas of what was wrong with the world, when one was considered to be better than another, simply due to the privilege of one's birth?

Jane abhorred the fact that she must stay in the man's house. What odious dreadful fate. If not for the fact that she would need far too many baths, she just might decide to move out to the stables anyway, just to spite the pigheaded man.

She refused to let him see that he *did* intimidate her. He could try as much as he liked, but she wouldn't concede and cower in fear of him. Oh, why must she suffer from such an affliction?

As though her life were not complicated enough from the fact that she feared horses, God thought he would amuse Himself by giving her the fear of large men, too.

This would all be so much easier if the duke were old and balding, short and pudgy. Then she could think of him as the lazy, profligate aristocrat she assumed all aristocrats to be.

No, instead he was a demi-god...a pugilistic, brutish, abominably rude demi-god, it was true, but a demi-god nonetheless. All right, fine. She had never seen the man come to fisticuffs, nor anything remotely resembling such a thing, so pugilistic might be a bit more than he deserved. Just a touch.

A knock at the door Meg had left through had her splashing the water out of the tub from the force of her jump. Drat, she must have been woolgathering while she bathed for far longer than she intended. The water had gone from steaming to icy while she sat and planned. "Just a moment." She jumped from the frigid water and darted to the stack of clean towels. After wrapping one about her body, she sidled up next to the fire in the hearth. "Come in, please."

Meg ducked through the doorway from the dressing room, carrying Jane's periwinkle dress. "You are expected downstairs for tea, ma'am. I didn't find an afternoon gown in your belongings, so I thought this one would suit the best."

Had she not told the girl she would choose her own gown? She would definitely need to talk with Cousin Henrietta about this. Sooner, rather than later. No one had ever served her in such a manner in her life, so why should they start now? But arguing with Meg would serve no purpose, though. She was merely doing as she'd been instructed by her employer.

Jane forced a smile. "Thank you. That will do just fine, I'm certain." She allowed the girl to help her dress, more because she couldn't stop her than anything, before another knock sounded at the outer door.

The dowager appeared there when Meg opened it. "Jane, are you ready? I feel very much better now that I'm clean. Do you as well?" She swept inside the room with the elegance of a queen, wearing a gown in a peacock blue silk that was far more fashionable in its styling than anything Jane had ever owned. She could sew elegant gowns—but what would be the point, with the way Mr. Cuddlesworth always damaged them? "Oh dear, don't you have anything more suitable than that? Never mind that, we aren't expecting any guests today. It's only family, and we'll rush you off to the modiste to have them begin work on your wardrobe first thing tomorrow. My girls and I also need to visit with Miss Jenkins, so we can make a day of it."

Why on earth would Jane need someone else to sew her garments for her? Surely, after looking through some fashion plates and seeing more of the styles in fashion, she could manage to do the work as well as, if not better than, any seamstress in London. "Oh, no, Cousin Henrietta. It won't be necessary to have someone else make clothing for me. I am more than capable—"

The older woman stopped her with a simple, raised hand. "You are my guest, Jane. You'll allow me to spoil you rotten while I have you here, and that's all there is to that. You are quite competent at your sewing. Your mother showed me some of the gowns you had just finished for your friends Lady Rhoades and Mrs. Slaughter. They are just as well made as any you would find here in London. But, I don't wish to have you work while you stay with me. You are to be treated as one of my daughters. No more arguments."

"Well, if you won't allow me to make them, I can at least pay for them myself." The expense would eat through her funds—money that she'd already spent in her mind on other pursuits. Still, she would *not* accept any more of the woman's charity, irrespective of the spirit in which it was intended. Charity felt like pity—something Jane most abhorred.

Why, they were housing and feeding her for months on end, and taking her to countless balls, routs, and other entertainments. She simply couldn't stand for allowing the woman to pay for anything more.

"I'll hear of no such thing, young lady. You are my guest. Your mother and father sent you here to be under my guidance. You *will* indulge me on this." With that pronouncement, the dowager spun on her heels and fled the room, indicating with a very brief nod of her head that Jane should follow.

And Jane hadn't even managed to discuss her appointed lady's maid.

Drat, drat, drat.

Nothing was turning out the way she'd expected.

Jane refused to think about what would happen to her business if that trend continued.

PETER STRODE THROUGH his home, attempting to ignore the gnawing ache settled deep in his belly. Two days ago, on Tuesday, he had a prior engagement with Lord Harbridge. The earl was kind enough to offer to share his meal while they talked.

At least he ate that day.

On Wednesday, he took his tea and dinner in his library, thereby avoiding the newest addition to his household, alongside the rest of the inevitable female chatter that seemed to dog his steps at every turn, thanks to his sisters. It was handy to have business matters that could impede his ability to perform unpleasant familial duties, at times.

However, he'd neglected to order today's meal delivered to his library as well, and couldn't bring himself to put Cook out in such a way on short notice. He also couldn't convince himself to eat with the women.

So he would suffer through the morning's meeting with Yeats—where he hoped they could collaborate on the Carreg Mawr problems—on an empty stomach. Blast the woman for upsetting the normal order of his life.

When he arrived at the front hall, the lot of females were blocking the door and making an utter scene in front of his home. Good God, they were already drawing attention. A group of passersby out for a morning stroll stopped and stared from across Grosvenor Square. He would have to step in and do something about it, before his family became the laughingstock of the *ton*.

Of course, such an inevitability *could* make it easier to avoid the parson's mousetrap his mother was so intent upon forcing him into. What respectable father would wish his daughter married to a man who was a social pariah?

He pushed the thought aside and stepped inside the throng of feminine gasps and chatter to diffuse the problem—not knowing, of course, just what, precisely, the problem may be. Devil take it.

Some days he wished *he* could be a female and not have to think with clarity about a problem, but could just carry on, dithering about until someone else discovered a solution. Alas, he remained a man, and a duke, and the head of his family.

He brushed Char aside, as she was blabbering about something rather incoherent and quite likely unimportant. She was clearly not the cause of their delay. Mama and Sophie knew how to handle Charlotte and her silly banter. He would leave her to them. When he drew closer to the center of the group, the crux of the matter became suddenly clearer.

Smack in the center of their small circle, Miss Matthews stood as rigid as Peter had ever seen a body stand, with only the faint sign of tremors coursing over her frame. Her face shone as pale as powder and her eyes had turned almost completely black and were filled to the brim with fear. He was *still* unable to decipher their true color, even with her blonde hair neatly pulled away from her face and secured in a haphazard knot. At least, he noted with only a tinge of sarcasm in the thought, her attire today was not nearly as ill-used as what she had worn when she arrived. Though, admittedly, the sad shade of yellow did not suit her complexion in the slightest.

Her coloring in that gown looked more akin to the trunk of a birch tree than to a lady on her way out into society.

Sophie fished through her reticule for smelling salts, though Miss Matthews had obviously not yet fainted. Still, even Peter had to admit it was entirely too possible that it might come to pass, based upon her current appearance. Charlotte was fanning Jane's face with her hands for lack of a proper fan, and Mama held their cousin in her arms and was attempting to convince her to sit.

He didn't have the time to sit here and wait for Miss Matthews to faint, by Jove. "What, pray tell, is the matter here?" They were in Mayfair, for Christ's sake. It was not as though they had just been accosted by a salacious footpad in the slums of London.

Char gripped his elbow. "Oh, Peter, Jane has had quite the fright this morning on our way to visit Miss Jenkins. I daresay she'll recover quite soon, but the horses did startle her a good deal. Mama says not to worry, though, because nothing irregular is afoot."

His youngest sister pulled him away from the rest of the females, so he watched his mother direct Miss Matthews to a seat and brush away the assistance of Sophie's smelling salts, all from afar.

Charlotte's chatter never ceased. Which, of course, he expected. "Why, plenty of perfectly normal people are afraid of much smaller things, like spiders, you know. I'd think it not at all surprising to learn that far more people are afraid of horses than will admit to as much."

"Horses?" He swiped a stray hand across his chin. She'd caused this entire uproar over animals? She had a cat, for God's sake. Why should a horse be any more fear-inducing than an animal that would bite and claw if cornered?

She passed him a look of pure disdain. "Well yes, the horses. Do try to keep up, Peter. So we'll only be slightly delayed in getting a start to our morning. But as you can see, Mama has virtually revived Jane already! How delightful. And we didn't even require you to play the gallant gentleman."

Thank God for small favors.

Peter frowned. "I see." At precisely that moment, his barouche rolled around the corner. "I'll have to leave you all. Miss Matthews, I trust you're in good hands with my mother and sisters." Mama should be able to, but one ought not put too much faith in a woman who'd insisted on all of this. "Might you need my assistance for anything else?" Lord help him if she did.

Thankfully, she managed a brief shake of her head and Mama waved him on his way.

After he gained his seat, he took the reins from his groom and gave the horses a bit of head. One reared back and whinnied, and Miss Matthews's head whipped around to stare with wide eyes. Remarkable. How could the woman be so enamored of her cat, and yet so frightened of another animal at the same time?

He drove off toward his man of business's office, all the while trying to forget the look of fear on his houseguest's face.

Four

MISS JENKINS POKED and prodded at Jane as she took more measurements. How dreadfully annoying. But, try as she might, Jane had been unable to convince Cousin Henrietta to allow her to create her own wardrobe for the Season.

This Miss Jenkins had better do an excellent job of it.

Of course, if Jane were being honest with herself (and, dear Lord, she wished she would be more often, because lying to herself truly created more problems than it solved), she would have to admit that the work Miss Jenkins performed *was* rather exceptional—at least the work she had shown them. And she *had* created all of the attire that the Hardwicke women currently wore, all of which was terribly fashionable and immaculate and impressive.

If she could perform work of the same quality on even one garment for herself, it would certainly be the most fabulous piece she had ever worn.

"Ow!" Drat. The pin that had just lodged itself in her side might convince her to change her mind about Miss Jenkins's abilities, however.

"Oh dear, miss, I'm so sorry about that. We're almost finished now, and I promise it will be most worth the pain." The petite modiste pulled smooth peach silk tighter across Jane's bosom and placed a few more pins into position.

"Really, Jane, you shouldn't complain so much," said Charlotte from across the room, where one of Miss Jenkins's assistants was performing the same form of torture on her. "I daresay I've received ten times more sticks than you today, but have you heard me shouting about it?" The gorgeous redhead softened her rebuke with a cheeky grin.

"I suppose I'm just far more accustomed to giving the pricks than receiving them." And she would prefer to keep things in just that manner, thank you very much.

At least one good thing had come from their shopping excursion: the Hardwicke women had taken Jane to the finest millinery shops and haberdashery shops, where she was able to perform research for her future business. Looking through the ready-to-wear items and fashion plates at Miss Jenkins's shop had also proved helpful, having allowed her to learn some of the trends in fashions that her future clientele would wish to purchase.

Jane itched to try her hand at some of the new stitches she'd seen.

She had covertly purchased some fabrics for her own work while they shopped, without allowing the dowager to see what she was doing. A few lengths each of lawn, silk, and muslin would allow her to practice some of the more intricate stitches she had discovered. She'd stowed her secret purchases in her bags alongside the known purchases, until she could work on them at Hardwicke House without discovery.

If she were to do work that could attract the most elegant clientele, she would need to perform with a certain level of expertise on the most current, fashionable trends. Practice would be vital.

With the calendar Cousin Henrietta was beginning to fill for her, however, she wondered where she would find the time. Perhaps she would need to sleep a bit less than normal. Though, it was true, stitching by candlelight could prove disastrous.

While they were being fitted at Miss Jenkins's shop, Lady Warburton had come in, along with someone both Sophie and Charlotte had squealed in delight to see. Esther Bentley, apparently, had been their governess until Charlotte left the schoolroom, and was now Lady Warburton's paid companion. While they all giggled and tittered, Jane's eye followed Miss Bentley. The companion was a lovely woman, if a bit drab in dress, when compared to the finer ladies next to her.

While the modiste and her assistants fitted Jane and the Hardwicke women for the designs selected for their gowns, Miss Bentley sat by herself and looked through some of the older fashion plates and fingering the fabrics she'd apparently purchased at the milliner's—cottons in unpopular colors and prints, and a single length of a rich, mahogany silk velvet.

This, Jane decided, was a travesty.

As a paid companion, Miss Bentley was forced to accompany Lady Warburton to events where everyone else in attendance would be dressed at the height of fashion. She likely couldn't afford to pay for the seamstresses to sew her gowns—gowns which would already stand out for their lack of the nicest fabrics and newest designs. She would stick out like a swan among ducklings. Or perhaps more like a duck among swanlings.

Something would certainly have to be done about that.

Sophie reentered the main room of the shop and gasped, startling Jane out of her thoughts and plans. Apparently, it startled Miss Jenkins as well. Another pin found its new home in Jane's flesh. This one stung and bled just a bit.

Double drat.

"Oh, Jane, you look ravishing in that shade," Sophie said. "It enhances your complexion in such a unique manner. I daresay when that gown is finished, you will be utterly stunning."

Such effusive flattery was balderdash, to be sure, but a flush heated Jane's cheeks with pride, nonetheless. "Do you truly believe so? I haven't ever been so brave as to wear such a color. It tends to make so many ladies look quite sickly, you know." Much as she must have done earlier, when the horses set her heart to palpitating.

"True," cut in Charlotte, narrowing her eyes on Jane. "But you seem rather the exception than the rule, especially in comparison to us. Why, if a Hardwicke were to wear that hue, it would be absolutely ghastly. Gracious, Sophie, can you imagine it next to *your* hair?" She shuddered violently. "Putrid would be too kind a description."

"Which is why we would never *dare* to wear such a color," said Sophie. "But on you, Jane...well, I've never seen the like. Mama, are you certain she shouldn't use this fabric for her presentation to the Queen?"

Cousin Henrietta glanced up from her fashion plates. "It would be lovely, but we've already settled on an almost-as-lovely pink. Miss Jenkins already measured, pinned, and set that one aside." She narrowed her eyes in thought. "No, I believe we should leave that one be, and use the peach for a ball gown."

"Thank you, Your Grace," came the muffled reply of Miss Jenkins from her new position beneath Jane's skirts.

"You're quite welcome." The dowager returned to her fashion plates for a moment before: "Oh, and Miss Jenkins? Will you be able to have this one ready at the same time as her presentation gown? I believe this would be perfect for the first ball of the Season...the first time the *ton* lays its collective eye upon our Jane."

A chorus of delighted squeals and "Oh, yes, Mama!" responses came from the sisters. Jane flushed from all of the attention.

Miss Jenkins placed one final pin and removed herself from beneath the makeshift skirts of Jane's soon-to-be ball gown. "Of course. I'll have them all ready by then, Your Grace."

"Splendid." Cousin Henrietta packed away her fashion plates and the girls began to collect all of their day's purchases to return home to Hardwicke House. Their shopping trip was finally complete.

Jane now owned several ready-made morning and afternoon dresses, and even a handful of ready-made evening gowns. The purchases were delightful. An additional expense—one she had insisted on making for herself—came in the form of a handful of fashion plates to study (and, of course, the fabrics and notions she'd already stealthily secreted away beneath her other purchases).

Many more dresses, gowns, pelisses, and the like would soon arrive. Her exuberance to begin studying the newest techniques in fashion threatened to burst free, which wouldn't do—then she'd reveal her secret to all and sundry. She simply *must* contain herself.

The day had turned out to be quite industrious, if a bit on the extravagant side of things. If only it hadn't started in such a poor manner, with the horse incident.

Drat, drat, drat, why could she not control her reactions to the huge beasts?

The part that made it all worse was that the duke had seen the entire fiasco and, clearly, thought her a fool.

But perhaps his business matters would continue to prevent him from spending time with the rest of the family. Such an arrangement would be lovely, indeed. Jane could hope.

MEG, THE DEVOTED girl, would just not stop *doing* things.

Even as Jane watched with a full-blown glower, the lady's maid retrieved another of Jane's new gowns and placed it inside the armoire before returning to the small collection. "These are truly lovely, miss."

"Thank you," Jane said through clenched teeth. No matter how preposterous the idea of having a servant all to herself may be, Cousin Henrietta still refused to budge. The dowager insisted that if Jane was to be treated as one of her daughters in some respects, she would be treated as one of her daughters in all respects.

Meg couldn't be blamed for the conundrum, so Jane was desperately trying not to hold it against the poor girl, and to graciously and gracefully accept her assistance.

Which, at the moment, was growing increasingly difficult. Jane's fingers tapped at her side, searching for something to occupy them.

They clearly saw no reason they shouldn't be allowed to fold her gowns and put them away. Her fingers were accustomed to far more difficult work than this. Yet, because she'd been forced to find some task to assign to Meg, her fingers must remain idle. Watching someone else perform the simple task was almost more than Jane could bear. She felt lazy—a feeling she was entirely unaccustomed to.

It most decidedly did *not* suit her well. It was uncomfortable on her.

"This one is exquisite," Meg said, pulling the final gown off the stack: a lavender and silk afternoon dress with a cream lace overlay.

When this dress was removed, it revealed the lengths of fabrics Jane had purchased to work with on her own. Drat. She nearly cursed aloud, but managed to stop herself. Such behavior would have unequivocally alerted the lady's maid to something being amiss.

Thankfully, Meg was so enthralled with examining the gown that she didn't notice the fabrics left lying. When she turned to place the gown in the armoire, Jane snatched the material from atop the bureau and let it fall behind a chest of drawers.

A knock sounded at the door and Meg rushed off to answer it before noticing anything out of the ordinary, returning with Sophie and Charlotte following behind her.

"I hope you don't mind our intrusion," Sophie said and slipped into a chintz arm chair. "Char and I hoped to have some time alone with you, to get to know you." She looked at Meg and waited until the servant ducked out of the dressing room.

At least, if they were visiting, Jane wouldn't have to worry about what Meg was doing. The girl could go off and do whatever it was a lady's maid did while they waited for their next task. "Not at all. Come in."

"Sophie tends to do as she likes," said Charlotte, "despite whether anyone minds or not." Pulling a chaise closer to where Sophie and Jane sat, she smiled. "She intended to disturb you, without a care as to your thoughts on the matter. It's only one of the many less-than-desirable habits our governess was unable to break her of, much to Peter's chagrin."

Jane laughed. "I do much the same, myself. My mother is none too pleased about it." In fact, it might very well be part of the reason Mother had sent her here. Perhaps Mother thought the duke and Cousin Henrietta could set Jane straight.

If that were the case, she couldn't be further from right. A prim and proper lady, one who belonged in a genteel setting with servants waiting on her hand and foot, was something Jane would never be.

"We got that impression already. About you, that is," Sophie said. "I daresay I haven't laughed as hard as I did when you told Peter you had cat sick caked beneath your bosom. He looked like his head might lob off and roll across the floor at the slightest breeze."

"Oh, dear." She oughtn't to have said that. Actually, she didn't even remember saying it, but she must have done. Good Lord, would she never learn to think before she spoke? How mortifying!

"Don't be upset, Jane," Charlotte said. "We all rather enjoyed ourselves."

"At my expense," she countered. "But I'm not upset with you, only with myself. Your mother has taken on a task I'm afraid she can't master with me, Sophie. I'm a hopeless cause."

"Hopelessly perfect," Char said.

Perfect, indeed. A perfect pickle, more like. "Gentlemen will be swimming for the continent, once I descend upon the *ton*."

Sophie laughed. "You, my dear, give yourself far too little credit."

Char hummed in agreement. "They'll be beating down Peter's door to offer for you. We'll have to beat them off with clubs."

"Hardly," Jane replied. "I can't fathom any gentleman looking twice at me, if you're in the room."

Sophie Hardwicke had to be the most beautiful creature on the face of the planet, with her perfect ivory skin dotted with a light smattering of freckles, her intensely deep blue eyes, and the most striking rich red curls Jane had ever encountered. It was a wonder she had not already been swept off the marriage mart. And Charlotte could have been her twin, were she closer in age, save for her eyes being a more green shade.

"Oh, pish. None of them bother with me anymore. I've already rejected the suits of nearly half the *beau monde*." She brushed a stray lock behind her ear. "The rest are either too afraid to approach me, or too ignorant to realize I'm the best thing that could ever happen to them. Or the worst. Whichever the case may be."

Charlotte snorted inelegantly. "I think most would fall into that first category."

Jane couldn't imagine having turned away so many suitors. In her entire life, she'd only had one, and he'd been an overbearing imbecile on the best of days.

"Why did you reject so many?" she asked.

"I doubt I can recall my reasons for each of them, Jane. This *has* been going on for a good number of years, you know."

"Don't try to paint yourself in a better light, now," said Charlotte. She looked at Jane with a serious expression, nodding for emphasis. "They simply didn't measure up."

"Measure up to what?"

Charlotte and Sophie looked at each other, raising eyebrows in turn. "Well?" Char finally prodded.

Still, Sophie remained silent. She even bit her tongue—literally.

Char sighed. "They didn't measure up to her idea of the perfect man. She refuses to marry anyone who is less than what she wants."

"I'd say that is sound reasoning," Jane said. Why justify settling? Especially if, like Sophie, one had an ample fortune at her beck and call. Jane honestly couldn't fathom why more women of means didn't remain unmarried and happy.

"See?" replied Sophie, frowning across at her sister. "She agrees with me."

Char returned the frown. "And *she* is also well on her way to becoming a spinster."

Sophie laughed. "That's true. But that wouldn't be the worst thing that could happen to me. Far from it. It's a choice."

"It would be my choice, too," Jane said with a longing sigh. Her eyes widened when the ladies across from her each lifted a brow.

Oh, drat. She oughtn't to have said anything. Now they'd have questions and want to know why she desired no beaux. If she wasn't careful, she'd tell them absolutely everything without meaning to tell them anything at all.

Change the subject. She needed to change the subject. Now, before they asked her questions. "Sophie," she said, "do you think Miss Bentley would like me to make some gowns for her? I couldn't help but notice she wasn't fitted at Miss Jenkins's shop..." There. That was surely a safe topic. The urge to breathe a sigh of relief struck her, but she refrained through sheer determination.

"Of course," Sophie said with smiling eyes, clapping her hands together. "Mama told us you're quite the seamstress." She looked to Charlotte. "If Jane can sew Esther some gowns, she could possibly afford some nicer fabrics. I think that is a brilliant plan."

"Brilliant...stupendous...perfect!" Char said.

Jane grinned. "I even have a bit of fabric we could use to start with. They're just over...er...that is, they're behind the bureau over there."

Double drat. Why had she mentioned the fabrics at all? And even worse, why had she admitted to them being behind the bureau? This was not good. Not good at all.

Sophie moved across to the bureau, eyeing Jane all the while, and then peeked behind it. "Good Lord. This is not just 'a bit of fabric.' You have silks, muslins, lawn. This is quite the supply." She bent over and came up with the lot of it in her hands. "What were you planning to use all of this for?"

"Just a bit of practice," Jane replied, a touch too fast. "But it would be best to practice on something someone will actually use. So I thought...I thought I could sew some gowns for Miss Bentley with these fabrics. If she wants." She shrugged when Char and Sophie both gawked over at her.

Sophie narrowed her eyes. "Mm hmm."

"I'm sure she would be thrilled for your assistance," Charlotte murmured, mimicking her sister's narrowed eyes.

"Lovely." This whole secrecy plan didn't seem to be working as well as she had hoped.

"Lovely, indeed," said Sophie. She left it alone there, but didn't appear at all happy about it.

Jane would most definitely need to be more aware of what she revealed to both Charlotte *and* Sophie. She doubted either one of them would keep a secret from the other.

For that matter, she was beginning to doubt whether *she* could keep a secret from them.

GOOD GRACIOUS, THE duke seemed to be taking drastic measures to avoid Jane's company since her arrival.

Of course he claimed to have some dreadful business that kept him occupied and unable to spend a reasonable amount of time with his family. But Jane knew, without a doubt, that it was all a lie.

Why, she had caught him one day in the nursery, playing with his children when she went to check on Mr. Cuddlesworth, who had quite irrevocably attached himself to little Sarah since their arrival. On that visit, she had found His Grace on the floor, forming blocks into something that rather resembled a fortress, with his two children serving as assistants. She peeked further into the room to discover Mr. Cuddlesworth napping in his basket (which was carefully situated directly in a stream of sunlight pouring in through the windows, she noted) while Mrs. Pratt caught a bit of shut eye in an old chair in the corner.

Based on the elaborate design of the fortress, Jane would be surprised if the duke hadn't been with the children for hours at that point. And all the while, he claimed to be locked away in his library, poring over his ledgers. Balderdash!

Granted, he didn't realize she'd caught him in the act. Jane pulled the door closed as quietly as she had opened it—and the children were making a good deal of noise, as happy children tend to do. Her intrusion had gone entirely unnoticed by the lot of them, not the least of which being her cat.

Another time, a few days after that first incident, Jane had made her way through the halls of Hardwicke House to join Cousin Henrietta and her daughters for tea. As had become his custom, at least since Jane's arrival, the duke had declined and claimed he must meet with his secretary to go over these supposed "business" concerns. But how could that be the case when she'd seen Mr. Forrester, the duke's secretary, donning his beaver hat and coat in the front hallway and taking his leave just as the ladies had convened in the parlor for tea?

Jane thought it less than prudent to point out to his family the lengths to which the man had gone in order to avoid her company—because what else could be the cause of his sudden avoidance of all of them, if not her own attendance at those very functions?—so she just tucked those tidbits away for future use, should she need them.

While she had seen very little of the head of the Hardwicke family during her fortnight's stay in London, however, she had spent a great deal of time with the two sisters, Esther, and Cousin Henrietta. Even Lord Neil, the youngest of the brothers, joined them on occasion. On the day of their first meeting, he had strolled in to the breakfast room, still dressed from the previous evening, with longish, heavily tousled auburn hair and bleary eyes that struggled to remain open.

Lord Neil passed her a rakish grin and winked at her.

She liked him immediately.

He didn't, however, spend time with the females of the family on any sort of regular basis.

Actually, Lord Neil Hardwicke seemed to keep rather odd hours, coming when most people were going and vice versa. "Don't mind my comings and goings overmuch, Miss Matthews," he had told her upon one occasion, again giving her that devilish smile...the very one she had since discovered proved he was up to no good. "No one else does, to be sure."

Indeed, he seemed to be correct in that assumption. Much more import was placed on the frequent absence of His Grace than the far less frequent, though admittedly sporadic, absences of Lord Neil.

The duke's absences would now be forced to come to a close, however, as the dowager assured Jane and the Hardwicke sisters that her son would be accompanying them to all of their numerous and *infinitely important* social engagements.

Well, almost all. His Grace wasn't present for Jane's presentation to the Queen. Truth be told, she was rather grateful for that fact.

It had been nerve-wracking enough to be forced to wear such a dated and ostentatious design, however lovely the stitchery may be. And then to have to make her curtsy (without falling all over herself, she might add) to the queen, and back out of Her Blasted Majesty's presence (*still* without tripping).

To have that odious man present might have been enough to do Jane in.

As things stood, she made it through the ordeal without making a cake of herself in front of the queen, instead doing so before all of the other ladies waiting in the hall for their turn to curtsy to Her Majesty after Jane's turn had passed. The blasted gown boasted simply too many flounces, ruffles, and petticoats. They got all tangled with her legs, and she took quite the spill.

She would have been mortified if the duke had been present to see such a fiasco. It was bad enough doing it in front of Charlotte, who was also being presented to the queen, and Cousin Henrietta. In fact, Jane shivered even now thinking back upon it.

But her presentation to the queen had passed, and now she must prepare for her presentation to the *ton* at the ball given by Lord and Lady Bodham-Smythe at Turnsley Hall.

And *he* would escort them.

The idea of being surrounded by hordes of lords and ladies too high in the instep to take notice of her since she *was* merely a miss was bad enough, but when she must be escorted to such an affair by a man who clearly detested spending time in her presence—well, it was perhaps the most lowering situation she could imagine.

Jane hoped Lord Neil would choose to attend at least some of the events she would be forced to attend. Unlike his elder brother, he at least bothered to smile and speak to her when he saw her, usually.

She doubted that any of the other gentlemen at this ball, or any of them through the entire Season for that matter, would condescend enough to dance or converse with her. But Lord Neil would. Jane was certain of it. Perhaps even without being goaded into it by his mother, unlike his eldest brother.

Then she wouldn't have to feel like such an abysmal failure.

Not that she *wanted* to succeed on the marriage mart. Far from it. But being shunned simply due to her father's lack of title was not exactly her idea of a pleasant way to spend her evenings for months on end.

Jane supposed this evening *could* surprise her. The entire affair might not be as bad as she made it out in her head. She should go to Turnsley Hall with an open mind, with no ideas in her head about what to expect.

But that would simply leave her open for huge disappointment when everything turned out just as she expected.

Still—better to expect a pickle than to think one was biting into a peach.

Five

SITTING CROUCHED BEHIND a prickly bush in front of Bodham-Smythe's mansion was not exactly the manner in which Warwick Turnpenny, Viscount Utley had imagined spending his night. However, in order to discover exactly what he needed to know, he had few alternatives. Graciously, the cover of night and a smattering of clouds in the sky allowed him to remain hidden there far better than he could have done during the day.

After what felt like hours, he finally saw what he'd been waiting over an hour for: the Duke of Somerton's crested carriage rolled into the drive and came to a stop.

Utley had heard rumors that Somerton was rejoining the marriage mart this Season. Indeed, Phinny had even mentioned the possibility. He needed to see it with his own eyes, though. Rumor was not nearly enough.

The outrider came around and set down the steps, and then plain as day, Somerton stepped down. He turned and handed down the dowager and both his sisters.

But he didn't stop there. Somerton reached his bloody cursed hand back into the carriage, and down stepped a woman Utley hadn't seen before—a blonde with a few too many curves for his taste. Somerton placed her hand in the crook of his arm, patting it and keeping it snug, then held out his other for the dowager. He led the party up the steps into the grand townhouse.

His heart raced in his chest at the sight of her. Not that she was pretty or fair enough to cause such a reaction in him. Far from it, actually. But because of what she represented.

Vengeance. And maybe, just maybe, a solution to his financial woes. Phinny could only do so much, after all.

Once the damned Hardwickes were inside the doors and the carriage had pulled off down the road, Utley took another surreptitious look around to be sure no one was watching him. Then he straightened, stepped out from the bushes, brushed the debris from his evening attire, and darted around back to the servants' entrance.

"YOU WILL OF course reserve the first set for me, won't you?" The Duke of Somerton's rather awkward attempt at a request, at least to Jane's mind, came across more like a command. He wore an almost sheepish and quizzical look upon his face.

He wanted to dance with her? Cousin Henrietta must have orchestrated this. Jane couldn't imagine he would actually *want* to dance with her.

"Er...yes, Your...er, Peter, that is. I mean Your Grace. Oh, bugger it, what am I supposed to call you?" She ignored the looks of sheer curiosity and open incredulity upon the faces of some nearby onlookers—surely gossips desperate to spread news of her blunders to all and sundry at the first opportunity. Let them have at it. This would be the least of her mistakes this evening, she was certain.

The fact remained that if he were any other duke—anyone other than a cousin of some sort—she wouldn't be so confused. But the familiarity she held with the remainder of his family left her befuddled as to the proper form of address for Lord High-in-the-Instep.

"Your Grace is perfectly acceptable." Of course it was. She should have known he'd expect more formality than his siblings.

He glanced around, his eyes darting from one side of the grand ballroom to another. Finally, they settled in one general area before he turned to his party. "You'll excuse me, please. Miss Matthews, I'll return to collect you before the first set begins." Then he executed a perfect, if rather hasty, bow and walked away from them.

"Why gracious heavens," said Charlotte, "One would think it was *his* debut and not ours, Jane, if one didn't know better. I can't say when the last time I saw Peter so anxious might be. If ever!"

"What do you think that have been about, Mama?" asked Sophie. "He was all out of sorts. I've never seen the like of it." She narrowed her eyes in thought, then lowered her voice so no one could overhear. "He's always so...so...calm. This is highly irregular."

Cousin Henrietta followed her eldest son's path with shrewd eyes before turning them on Jane. "I haven't the first inkling what's going on in his head this evening." The dowager's denial was less than convincing, but Jane kept such thoughts to herself. "Now, Sophia. You *will* do your best this evening to secure a match, won't you? Excellent."

Sophie and Charlotte waited until the dowager was scanning the crowd before they simultaneously rolled their eyes to the heavens.

Unaware of their reactions, or at least unaffected by their less-than-enthusiastic responses, Cousin Henrietta continued. "I'll be quite busy this evening with introducing Jane and Charlotte about and being certain they're well received. Sophia, you'll have to see to your own affairs for the most part, of course. I have, of course, asked Peter to help me keep an eye on you both as well. It's quite an undertaking, I'm sure you understand, to have two debutantes to introduce at the first ball of the Season." With a rather pointed look at her eldest daughter, she finished with, "I should much prefer to have only had these two charges to look after, you know."

Before she could continue with her lecture, a handsome dark-haired gentleman joined their group. He bowed to them each in turn and smiled broadly. "Your Grace, Lady Sophia, Lady Charlotte. Might I beg an introduction to the lovely young lady in your care?"

"Why, of course, Lord Sinclaire. Meet my distant cousin, Miss Matthews. Jane, this is the Earl of Sinclaire. This rascal has ever been in and out of my home, since my sons were all just boys." Cousin Henrietta positively beamed as she spoke. "Miss Matthews has joined us for the Season, my lord."

His dark, almost black eyes smiled at Jane from beneath heavy lids. "Might I be lucky enough to beg your hand for the first dance?" He winked up at her before rising again.

What a Lothario. She had expected to secure only a very few dance partners for the night, instead primarily gracing the walls, but things were not turning out according to her plans. Jane nearly laughed out loud and was certain she hadn't concealed the amusement from her face. She'd never been able to, drat it all.

"Lord Sinclaire, I fear I've already promised the first set, but I would gladly dance the second set with you."

"Somerton?" he asked, furrowing his brow in a keen impersonation of displeasure. When Jane nodded, he continued. "The duke is a lucky man, indeed, to have secured the first to dance with the loveliest debutante in the room. I suppose I'll have to settle for the second set then."

Then he turned to Sophie, who was grinning from ear to ear at Jane with a wicked gleam in her eyes. "Lady Sophia, might I console myself in your arms for the first set, since your brother had the advantage over me?"

She nodded slyly as a swarm of other gentlemen moved in to request introductions and ask the young ladies to dance. Lord Sinclaire secured Charlotte's hand for the third set.

It was all becoming rather overwhelming.

Candelabras and chandeliers sprinkled a shimmer across the revelers throughout the ballroom, though it was not quite as grand as that at Hardwicke House. The scent of lilies and roses in full bloom assailed Jane's nostrils, from where they filled marble pots and dotted the floor everywhere the eye might rest. Fine silk and lace draped tables, filled with even more flowers and candles, flowing over until they almost showered down to the floor. And everywhere Jane turned, elegant ladies and handsome gentlemen strolled about, dressed in their finest and bedecked with more jewels than Croesus had a right to own.

This was all quite different from the quiet life to which Jane was accustomed—working in the vicarage gardens, sewing for the ladies of village, reading to Mrs. Zachariah. It was all so glittery and flashy and entirely unlike anything she'd ever in her lifetime experienced, or even dared to dream she might have the opportunity to someday come across.

Splendid, the lot of it.

Before she knew what was happening, Jane had been introduced to a dozen or more gentlemen and young ladies in likely double that number. She also had secured a partner for most of the nearly a half dozen dances before supper that night. Good gracious, she would certainly be footsore the next day.

Another gentleman, a dashing character with golden hair and brown eyes full of devilry, was making his way through the crowd toward them. He'd been standing near where His Grace was talking with Lord Sinclaire and a number of other gentlemen.

When he drew near enough, he pulled Cousin Henrietta aside and they talked in hushed voices for a moment.

Sophie motioned for Jane and Charlotte to draw nearer so they could form a closed circle. "Oh, goodness," she whispered, "I hope Lord Utley isn't requesting an introduction to you, Jane. And if he *is*, I pray Mama is shrewd enough to deny him. Why, he's an utter rakehell if I've ever known one. I don't know *how* Lady Bodham-Smythe could have granted him an invitation."

"Surely Mama wouldn't," murmured Charlotte, blue eyes as wide as saucers. "I can't imagine she could have forgotten all of the scandals the man has caused. He would be a most dreadful connection, to be sure."

"No one can be that bad, can they?" Jane asked, looking over her shoulder at the man. He looked rather innocuous, all things considered. Amiable, even. Agreeable.

But before anyone could answer her question, the dowager interrupted them. "Jane, I'd like you to meet Viscount Utley. It seems His Grace suggested he come to meet you, my dear."

Lord Utley oozed ingratiating charm as he bowed low before her. "How very charming, Miss Matthews." Perhaps she had overestimated him somewhat, if his sycophantic tone was any indication of his true character. He raised one of her hands to his lips and placed a kiss upon it, so softly she almost didn't feel it apart from the frisson of menace passing over her body, gone almost as soon as it arrived. She must have imagined it because of Sophie and Charlotte's warnings.

"The pleasure is mine, my lord." Jane executed a hasty curtsy, all the while doing everything possible to avoid glimpses of the shocked looks upon Sophie and Charlotte's faces.

"Might I request the honor of penciling myself in to your dance card, if I'm not already too late? I'd be devastated if I missed my chance at dancing with the most delectable Miss Matthews." His smile, while ever present, never touched his eyes, rather remaining only in the vicinity of his mouth.

After the Hardwicke sisters' warnings, she hesitated. But if Cousin Henrietta had introduced them, and if Somerton, himself, had suggested the introduction, there really couldn't be anything to worry about with him. Could there be? She tried desperately to convince herself of as much. But, after all, it was simply a dance. Nothing more.

"Of course, my lord. I would be delighted." She held out her wrist, and he selected his set, scrolling his name with a flourish.

Utley bowed again and backed away, a dodgy twinkle in his eyes that hadn't been there before. "Until later, Miss Matthews. I'll look forward to our dance." Then he was gone, as smoothly as he arrived.

"Mama!" Sophie whispered fiercely as soon as he was out of earshot. "Oh goodness, what have you done? I hope you haven't embroiled our Jane in scandal on her first night out in society."

"Well," Cousin Henrietta said, "Peter *did* send Lord Utley over for an introduction. Surely if he approves of the introduction, things can't be as bad with the viscount as the gossips would have us all believe. Something is not automatically a fact simply because Lady Plumridge and Lady Kibblewhite say it is, you know. You'd do well to remember that a bit more often." At Sophie's feigned pout, the dowager pressed on with an imperious brow lifted high. "They are rather correct on some other matters, however, such as your hazardous proximity to the shelf."

Sophie sucked in a breath and harrumphed as a few more young ladies joined their group. One of them—a refined lady with lovely blonde curls, no longer wearing the pastels of the unmarried—spoke first. "Your Grace, Sophie, Charlotte... And, may I assume, Miss Matthews?"

Sophie grasped the blonde's hand and squeezed, then winked at Jane. "Yes, this is our dear cousin Jane. And Jane, may I introduce you to one of my dearest friends, Lady Golding and her sister, Miss Lily Fairfax? And more dear friends, Miss Patience Marlborough and her sister, Miss Theodora Marlborough."

Ah, the famous Theodora. Jane had hardly ceased hearing of her from young Charlotte. "Yes, of course. It's lovely to meet you all." She smiled graciously.

Lady Golding took a look around the ballroom and then dropped her voice, bobbing her head over to Jane. "Was that Lord Utley I saw over here a moment ago? Pray tell me I was mistaken."

Jane groaned inwardly. Maybe Sophie was right about all of this. "Yes, that was Lord Utley." Dear lord, she must be in quite the pickle now. Drat. "Is there a problem?"

"Oh dear. We were afraid of that," said Miss Fairfax with serious eyes and a dour tone.

"Do tell us you haven't agreed to dance with him," Miss Marlborough feverishly whispered as her younger sister's eyes danced with devilry. Theodora Marlborough was a gossipmonger in the making, if Jane had ever met one. "It *would* be rather unseemly to back out once his name is on your card, but I fear it must be done, if you've agreed."

"I *have* agreed," said Jane sheepishly. Double drat. Why must there be so many complications with such a simple thing as selecting dance partners at a ball? "But I can't refuse to dance with the man now. Why, there's really no reason other than a bit of gossip, is there? And aren't all men entitled to a second chance—an opportunity to redeem themselves?"

Second chance for what, though, might be a good question to ask. For some reason, Jane had an inkling she might be better off without the answer to such a question.

Drat, drat, drat. This was only her first *ton* ball, and already she was becoming the center of gossip...and possibly scandal. "Well, I suppose there's nothing to be done but dance with the man. After all, it *is* only a dance," she said more emphatically than she'd intended. Might as well put on a good show of courage, even if she didn't quite feel so sure of things.

But nothing disastrous would come of a simple dance.

PETER WATCHED AS Utley, one of the most vile cretins in all of England, slithered across the ballroom toward his mother, sisters, and Miss Matthews.

Surely the bastard hadn't overheard the sum he was offering as Jane's dowry when he'd mentioned it to Sinclaire and the small group of eligible gentlemen gathered around him—eligible gentlemen who admittedly, at least for the most part, would be rather more than interested in such an advantageous match when a sum of that nature was involved.

Even if Utley had heard, it was unthinkable that his mother would grant the man an introduction. Mama knew as well as anyone that the lecher was a scoundrel in disguise as a gentleman, and she should keep all of her charges as far away from him as possible.

There was no reason to worry. Peter pushed the matter from his mind. Even if she didn't know of Utley's role in Peter's marriage to Mary, Mama knew of his reputation within the *beau monde*. She would handle matters with him with decency and decorum and send him on his way. She simply must.

Before he could return to his conversation with Sinclaire and the others, Lady Broederlet sidled up to his side. She wore a gown in a daring shade of red, cut entirely too low over her bosom to the point that her breasts practically spilled over the top. Her lips, somehow, came close to matching the hue of her gown as they stretched into a lurid and languid smile. A pink tongue darted out to wet them and spent far more time about it than necessary.

Blast it, he would have to at least speak to the woman. Not a task, he might add, that he was overly fond of accomplishing. "Lady Broederlet, I trust you're enjoying yourself this evening. Is Broederlet in the card room, then?" Please God, let the earl at least be present.

"Why yes, Your Grace, I'm having a sensational time. I'm afraid my dear husband has stayed abed at home tonight, however. He was not feeling quite the thing, and requested that I not stay at home fussing over him. He practically pushed me out the door, saying that it would be a shame to waste my assets on an evening at home, so I must be sure to share them with some worthy gentlemen." Her eyes narrowed to sultry slits that virtually undressed him right there in the ballroom. She continued with a husky, lowered tone. "I would be glad to share my assets with a man such as you." One long-fingered, gloved hand snaked up the sleeve of his coat, trailing fingertips along behind. "You would not want to disappoint me, would you, Your Grace?"

Thankfully, the discordant cacophony of the orchestra preparing their instruments on the dais came to an end at just that moment.

"Pardon me, my lady. I believe the first set will begin momentarily and I don't want to offend my partner." He backed away from the brazen woman and performed an elegant bow. "I must bid you good evening."

She cast a belligerent glare in his direction. Peter ignored it and slipped through the hubbub of revelers to find Miss Matthews, changing his course slightly, taking a circuitous path, when he caught sight of the Dowager Marchioness of Glanville slipping toward him. Blast it, this was turning into exactly the type of evening he had expected. And he had an entire Season ahead of him yet.

Mama must have put the word out already that he had resumed his position on the marriage mart, because everywhere he turned, the calculating, eagle-eyed gazes of lonely widows and mamas with lofty goals for their daughters followed him shrewdly about. He would far prefer to face the devil himself than to suffer through the attentions of all of these women who would soon be dangling after him. Good God, why had he ever agreed to Mama's plan?

Finally, he arrived at feminine titters surrounding his sisters and Miss Matthews. She was positively glowing in the candlelight. Her mess of curls had been tamed into soft, blonde waves. Her brown eyes—yes, he could finally determine their color—were warm and smiling. How had he ever thought her an antidote? She was about as far from it now as any lady had a right to be. For a moment, he stood and stared, even to the point of gawking.

Snapping his jaw closed and pulling his mind back where it ought to be, he bowed as their laughter subsided. "Miss Matthews, I believe this is my dance." Peter reached for her hand to escort her to the floor.

A rather becoming flush graced her cheeks as she smiled up at him. She ought to smile more often. Or perhaps she did, but not when in his presence. Hmm.

"Oh dear, is the dancing to begin already?" Miss Matthews asked. "You'll have to excuse me, ladies." She placed her hand gently on his arm and followed him into position as the lines formed.

Standing across from him, she beamed as she looked all around. With each new place her eyes landed, another twinkle formed in her eye, or an excited gasp came from her lips. She acted as though she'd never seen such a thing in all her life.

"Is this so very different from Whitstable, Miss Matthews?" Idiotic question. Blast, she'd arrived at his home only a fortnight ago. Of course such splendor would overwhelm her. Mama had performed nothing short of a miracle in preparing the woman for presentation to society in such a brief amount of time.

"Ah, yes and no, Your Grace." Her voice trailed off as the first strains of the opening quadrille filled the hall. She waited until they were within earshot of each other before finishing her rather odd statement. "We do have assemblies and other sorts of entertainments, but they are rather less lavish than this. I daresay only the Countess of Rhoades would have a gown as ornate as the ladies here all wear, and I'm quite certain she only has one that would be appropriate." The figures of the dance separated them again, and it was a few moments before she could continue. "And our assembly halls, while more than adequate for our needs, are not nearly so decadent. *Some* of the villagers might find such profusion to be ostentatious...a sign of pomposity, perhaps."

"Ha! And would you be amongst those who might find this to be a rather pompous affair?" A wry grin worked its way to Peter's features without his full permission. He couldn't seem to stop it from happening—an odd occurrence. This Miss Matthews was having a decidedly peculiar effect on him.

She lifted a brow and pursed her lips. "Well, yes, if you must know. It all seems a bit overmuch, especially when you consider how most of the people in the country live."

Such refreshing candor. They were separated by the figures of the dance again before he could muster a response. When they came back together, the swirl of air carried the most intriguing—and seductive—scent to his nostrils...musky and sweet, and somehow even a hint of peaches assailed him.

An image struck him, one of rushing her off to the nearest secluded alcove to taste her skin in order to see if her skin tasted as sweet as it smelled. Devil take it, he had to stop this at once. Why would he even *think* such a thing? But of course, he wasn't quite thinking.

"And how, pray tell, do the majority live if not in such splendor?" Of course, he *knew*. But he had the strangest desire to hear more of Miss Matthews's voice. Such a joyful sound.

Her delightful, lilting laughter met his ears. "Well, to start with, *Your Grace*, most of us are not addressed with such deference. Very few have titles, in the grand scheme of things."

Peter gave her a mocking smile. "So we're to be shunned because the unfortunate fact of our births requires a specific form of address to greet us everywhere we go?"

Again, the quadrille separated them for a few moments. He danced a figure across from a young lady he didn't even recognize, but whom obviously knew exactly who he was. Which just further emphasized his argument to Miss Matthews, but Peter doubted she would see things his way. He hadn't asked for his title. Nor had he requested the obligations that came along with it. Joshua hadn't asked to inherit any of it from him, either. It was simply the way of things.

Finally, he handed his momentary partner back to her true partner, and Miss Matthews's hand landed upon his arm with a feathery touch. Mischief lit her eyes, a warm, chocolate-brown that seemed to melt before him. "If the nobility cannot be blamed for the prestige entitled to them for their births, then how can anyone else be held accountable for their lack of high birth?"

Question for a question. Blast the woman. But there was something about her—an intelligence beyond her breeding, a touch of wit and humor. He yearned to discover more, which left him utterly befuddled. Had he not, only a mere fortnight before, been ready to banish her to his stables for her vulgar appearance and lack of social graces? A lady like Miss Matthews could never fit in with his life or meet the demands which would be placed upon her shoulders if she moved in the same circles of influence in which he lived.

But yet, here she was, at the first ball of the Season, seemingly at home amongst the highest sticklers of the *ton* and making quite the debut.

"Touché, Miss Matthews. I suppose the world imposes certain boundaries upon all of us, and we must merely determine how far to push against them."

Her eyes flashed and she elicited a rather indelicate and unladylike snort. It gave the impression she might prefer to smash the boundaries about her to bits. "So one should then submit to the limits imposed by society? Or were they put in place by God?" With a toss of her head, she scrunched her eyes together. "Why must one be forced into complying with an outdated social system when one might instead push to create a *new* order of things?"

Two could play her game. Peter stared at her with all the aristocratic hauteur he could muster. "And how might one go about creating a new order? Must one buck against all tradition and social order in order to achieve one's goals? Or are some social mores more acceptable than others, and therefore might one engage in them while creating a new order?"

Again, she swirled away from him, leaving a trail of that musky, peach scent in her wake. When she faced him again, their eyes locked in a heated gaze.

His body screamed to move closer to her, to pull her tight against him. This lust was damnably intrusive and thoroughly inappropriate. She was his charge, for Christ's sake—his responsibility. He should be protecting her from the unwelcome advances of rakes and rogues and not thinking about tossing her over his shoulder to carry her as far away from prying eyes as possible.

Besides, Miss Matthews would make a thoroughly unsuitable duchess. He couldn't allow himself to think of marriage with her, so he shouldn't think of her in that way at all. She deserved better than to become his mistress, and anything less than was unthinkable.

Thankfully, the set had come to an end. He escorted her back to his mother's side where she could await her next partner. "Miss Matthews, it was a pleasure." Peter bowed to her, and without waiting for her response, he fled to the card room.

A drink. He needed a drink.

And maybe a dunk in a basin of cold water.

Six

LORD POTTINGER, AN amiable and rather-too-eligible-for-her-comfort baron with light brown hair, escorted Jane back to Cousin Henrietta's side. Sophie stood beside her, flushed from dance and excitement.

"Your Grace, I do thank you for allowing me to dance with Miss Matthews this evening." After receiving a nod from the dowager, Pottinger gazed down into Jane's eyes. "I hope you might find it acceptable for me to call on you tomorrow, Miss Matthews."

Oh, blast. She didn't want to encourage the man, but how could she decline with Cousin Henrietta looking on expectantly as she was? Perhaps the baron would have more to discuss tomorrow than the soggy weather, though. She could hope.

But then again, perhaps he would not. Drat.

There was no graceful way she could envision to refuse, however, and Jane had already displayed quite enough social blunders and gaffes for her first evening in society.

She did her best to school her features into placidity. "Of course, Lord Pottinger. I'll look forward to your arrival." Then she prayed God wouldn't smote her down for such a tiny little lie.

Sophie grabbed hold of Jane's arm as soon as Pottinger strode away from them. Somehow, he bore an even wider smile than he had before leaving her. Jane wondered how such a feat could be possible before she brushed the thought aside. There would be ample time tomorrow while the baron was visiting to debate the finer intricacies of the insufferably kind man's inordinately large mouth.

Sophie tugged impatiently on her arm, commanding her attention. "Jane, do please pay attention. We only have a moment!"

"I'm sorry. What did you say?" Double drat. Hopefully Sophie wouldn't misinterpret her inattention to having developed any sort of tendre for the gratingly correct Lord Pottinger.

"I *said* that the next dance is a waltz. *And* it is the dinner dance. And in case you've forgotten, this is the dance you promised to Lord Utley. If you don't find some way to back out of this dance, you'll be forced to eat your supper with him. You need to pretend to turn your ankle or some other such infirmity. Goodness, you simply *can't* waltz with the man. And you absolutely can't allow him to escort you to supper. Your poor reputation will never survive this—not on your come-out."

"Oh, fiddlesticks. Supper and a dance with the man won't hurt anyone, least of all me." At least, she hoped not. "And what do you mean by 'my *poor* reputation,' precisely?" Gracious, had word already spread about all of the mistakes she was making? What a bind. But honestly, wouldn't it be worse to lie to the man?

"Your reputation? Er...well, since it *is* your debut, and you *are* virtually my age, there's been a good deal of gossip passing around about you from before the moment you stepped foot inside Turnsley Hall."

Drat, drat, drat.

"The gossip has been intensified by the rather large sum my imbecile of a brother has supposedly promised as your dowry. I haven't heard it from him for myself, but Sybil Pullbrook and Oriana Mollineaux suggested he's offering forty thousand pounds!"

Jane's jaw fell as low as the hem of her gown. "He is not. That's absurd." Surely he couldn't be so keen to be rid of her that he would go to such lengths as that. She was only a vicar's daughter, for goodness's sake.

A new thought struck Jane just then.

"Oh, dear." The blood rushed from her head and Jane reached out a hand for somewhere to sit. "The gossips must be saying I've been ruined. Why else would he settle such an amount upon me?"

Sophie pulled her onto a cushioned bench and held tight to her hand, offering the small bit of consolation she could give. She said nothing.

Perhaps Jane could work such a rumor in her own favor though. Then maybe she could avoid marriage altogether. Trying to keep the hope from sounding through in her voice, she asked, "Do you think most eligible gentlemen would turn away from rumors like those?" The corners of her mouth were inching their way upward into a damning smile. Jane struggled to contain it, but feared she was failing miserably. The absolute last thing she needed was for Sophie, or anyone for that matter, to discover she was trying *not* to end up married.

Sophie squeezed her hand and drew Jane's attention across the ballroom at where the duke was surrounded, yet again, by a largish group of gentlemen—all of whom were staring back across at them. A single auburn curl bounced against Sophie's shoulder as she turned her gaze to another corner of the room, where Lord Utley could be found striding purposefully toward them, his eyes locked on Jane.

"I'm afraid, my dear, that Peter's offer is having quite the opposite effect. It seems you're one of the few ladies in the room that every gentleman here wishes to meet." Sophie locked her shrewd gaze on Jane, surely discovering the dread in her eyes alongside a healthy dose of disappointment. "But the question I have burning to be answered is why does that scare you? Don't you want to marry? I'd think that would ease your worries, but it seems to be having the opposite effect." Sophie's eyes narrowed. "Quite peculiar, indeed," she murmured.

There was no time, however, for Jane to respond, as Lord Utley was quickly approaching them. Thank God. Blast it, couldn't she conceal anything from Sophie? Apparently not.

She pasted the brightest smile she could manage upon her face and hoped she wouldn't cause herself any more blunders or setbacks. Utley bowed to her and took her hand in his own, sending a course of shudders running across her spine.

"Miss Matthews, I believe this is my dance. I've been looking forward to this moment for the whole of the evening…" His fingers were cold, even through her gloves, and the way he trailed off left her feeling something had been left unsaid. The look in his eye was one she couldn't quite place, but it left her thoroughly unsettled.

Hopefully he wouldn't discover how uneasy she was at his proximity.

"Thank you, my lord. Shall we move to the dance floor then?" Looking over her shoulder, she caught Sophie's eye to signal she was fine and there was no reason to worry. Since another gentleman had already arrived to fetch her friend, they couldn't speak.

As Lord Utley deftly moved Jane through the throng of dancers, he placed a hand against her waist. His fingers curled toward her in a manner that gave her pause. Goodness, the man was indiscreet. She tried to maneuver herself into a position that would give her some distance from him without drawing his attention to her activity. She failed, however. Quite miserably, actually. His grip tightened and her entire side drew up against him. His heat radiated against her, and a sick roiling of dread built in her stomach.

Just before they came to a stop on the dance floor, Jane caught Somerton staring at her, his fury boring through her skin. On a second, more cautious inspection, she tried to decipher whether his rage was directed toward herself or toward her choice of dance partner—or perhaps toward them both. She couldn't really make it out, though, other than the fact he was furious enough to cause someone bodily harm, if the shade spreading over his ears was any indication. Drat.

But he had sent Utley to his mother to obtain an introduction, hadn't he? Blast the man. Sorting out *His Grace's* expectations would be the death of her, so she might as well just not bother trying.

She pushed all thoughts of the duke from her mind, or at least made an attempt to do so, and flashed Lord Utley a smile. She hoped it came across as rather sunny, but she feared it might look more like she had swallowed spoiled fish.

Utley drew her startlingly close to his sharp, angular body—too close even for a waltz. Such audacity! As he took her hand in his own and placed her other atop his shoulder, he leered down into her eyes with what could be mistaken for nothing other than lascivious intent. His other hand slid into place against her waist and pulled her even closer than before. "So lovely," he whispered close to her ear. His breath itched against her skin and sent a clammy prickle down her spine.

She could smell him—a sickening, sweet scent, unfamiliar and unpleasant, and altogether unsettling.

Blessedly, the music started before any more time passed, and he swept her across the floor, gliding along with the rise and fall of the steps. His eyes never left hers.

She prayed he could not feel her trembling, but when had she ever been known for such fortune? The candlelight swirled around, blurring in the fading background. The perfume of the flowers in the hall became strangling to her lungs. His arms felt like a vise about her, trapping her.

"Miss Matthews, are you all right?" His voice slithered across her, too smooth, bereft of any true concern or empathy. "Can I assist you in any way?" He slowed their movements and maneuvered them toward the outer edges of the dance floor, close to one of the open sets of double-doors leading out to the veranda and gardens.

Jane needed air. She needed...something. Perhaps it would be a good idea step outside so she could breathe a bit more freely. Oh, dear. Going out alone with Utley—with no chaperone—couldn't possibly her best course of action, but otherwise she might have a fainting spell. Certainly not what she had envisioned for her first ball of the Season. Double drat, and *why* could she not think clearly, when it was quite possibly the most imperative time in all her life to know exactly what she should and shouldn't do?

Before she answered him, he repositioned her closer the doors outside, almost leading her through them before she could gather her wits about her and decide what to do. "You must forgive my impertinence, ma'am, but I believe some fresh air will do you some good. I fear you're unwell." He slipped an arm about her waist to support her and virtually dragged her outside.

Her legs were moving beneath her, but she had seemingly lost all control over them.

Lord Utley directed her toward a bench and pressed her until she sat. "There you are, Miss Matthews. Take some air. You'll feel better in no time." He sat next to her, again closer than her comfort allowed. Her trembling subsided, but still, her skin crawled like thousands of tiny fingers were sliding over it at his proximity. "Your color is starting to return." His voice was merely a whisper. Then he trailed a finger along her cheek, brushing a stray wisp of hair back from her face.

Drat, drat, drat. How had she gotten herself into such a scrape? The man was entirely too close to her and touching her in a most inappropriate manner.

She squirmed away from his arm that was draped across the back of the bench, almost touching her shoulders and causing goose flesh to rise all over. "My lord, you've been most kind to see to my comforts. Thank you." She said all of this with as much emphatic force as she could muster, so as not to leave anything in doubt.

With her faculties about her yet again, Jane started to rise—only to have him grasp her arm and pull her down next to him.

She flashed a scowl at him. "I do believe we should return to the ballroom, sir, as my chaperone will be anxious if she cannot find me."

But he didn't release her. His fingers trailed up her gloved arm, up to the bare skin above the gloves, up still further to her shoulder to wander over her neck, leaving her a shuddering, convulsing mess as she fought to keep the roiling contents of her stomach under control.

"You are quite lovely, you know." His voice sliced through her like a sword, leaving the impression that he thought anything but what his words implied.

Jane ought to have listened to Sophie. She should have heeded her friend's instincts about this man and rejected him out of hand. Failing that, she ought to have found a way—any way—to stay out of his grasp.

Blast her naiveté.

Jane's eyes darted about the garden, hoping to land on another couple out for a bit of air, or a random gentleman strolling about alone who might act as her champion against this leering blackguard. But no one else was near. She looked back to the main house. Her voice would never carry far enough, not with all the hubbub of the revelries inside. No one would be able to hear her distress, should she cry out.

"We are quite alone, my dear." Utley's fingers continued to trail lazy paths along any stretch of bare skin they encountered. "But you must have realized why I brought you outside. Surely you recognize your own value, Miss Matthews. Of course, one might believe you to be beneath my touch—" he chuckled, looking at his fingers slithering over her skin— "but I can look beyond the unfortunate circumstance of your low birth when faced with your—ample—assets." His gaze slid to her bosom and held there.

She felt ill. Fully, truly ill. She'd walked blindly and willingly into a blasted catastrophe, and now she couldn't see a way out. Jane pressed her eyes closed and said a prayer for clear thought, willing her heartbeat to calm to a dull roar. "Oh, goodness. I believe I hear my chaperone calling to me." She extricated herself from his touch and pushed further along the bench, trying to put some distance between them. "You must excuse me, my lord, but I'm sure you wouldn't wish to detain me and risk the consequences. Her Grace would be most displeased." She stood and managed two steps before he roughly took her arm from behind, stopping her dead in her tracks.

"And we mustn't displease the dowager, must we?" His low voice sounded just above her ear and his grip tightened on her arm until it hurt. "If I'm not mistaken, however, her intention is to find you a husband. We could ensure such a match tonight, if you would cooperate with me."

Jane shook violently and her breath came out in short, desperate bursts.

His hands moved over her upper arms, holding them close to her sides, drawing her bottom against his thighs, where his protrusion pressed against her. "Of course, you've already performed your part rather well. I intended to coerce you to join me for a stroll outside where I could then seduce you, but no coercion was necessary. You played into my hands better than I'd planned."

Utley's strong arms forced her to turn and face him. Outrage warred with panic as she looked up into his eyes, hard and unyielding. The corners of his mouth turned up in a menacing grin before he lowered his head and claimed her lips in a painful, humiliating kiss.

One of his hands held her head captive to his assault while the other grasped her bottom firmly, pinching, prodding, and otherwise forcing her to move her hips closer to his frame until his eagerness pressed firm and hot against her stomach.

Once the shock dissipated, Jane pushed with all her strength against his chest and broke free from his kiss. Breathing heavily, she reached a hand up to slap him across the face, but held herself back. She had to think clearly. Striking him might have unintended consequences. "How *dare* you," she uttered. Then she backed away from him, inching toward the ballroom and safety.

Before she reached the doorway, Utley smirked and rubbed his chin almost as though she had struck him instead of holding herself back. "Quite easily, in fact," he called out to her, then turned in the opposite direction.

Of all the ill-advised things she had done in her life, this must top the list. Blast. And now she'd have to return to the ballroom alone. Perhaps she could slip inside unnoticed if she were very careful. If not, there was bound to be more gossip. It would be bad enough for her if anyone had noticed her leaving with the scoundrel.

Oh, who was she trying to fool? Doubtless, Cousin Henrietta would be watching for her, since she was *supposed* to be dancing with Utley. Already, Jane had proven to be the center of the rumor mill's focus for the evening, and it was still early.

She'd be lucky indeed if every eye in the ballroom didn't turn to see her in her shame.

How on earth could she get out of this newest scrape?

Jane frantically pored over various scenarios she could present to the dowager to convince her nothing untoward had occurred while she'd been outside with Utley, all the while scrambling through the winding pathways of the garden as the scents of blossoming gardenias and foxgloves wafted over her. Lost in thought, she didn't see the towering man standing directly in her way until she ran headlong into him, her nose bumping rather unnaturally against his well-toned chest.

For just a moment, she pinched her eyes closed and willed her breathing to calm. Then she slowly looked up, inching her eyes across his perfectly starched, white cravat and the snug black overcoat emphasizing firm muscles straining to be set free, hoping to discover anyone there—anyone at all, even Lord Utley again—other than the Duke of Somerton.

Her eyes traveled over his face, the smooth shaven square jaw, the furious scowl, and his hard eyes (eyes that were curiously multi-colored—how was it possible for one to be more green and the other to be more blue?) which glared down at her.

And of course, it was none other than the duke himself standing before, looking ready to rip her limb from limb.

Drat.

DEVIL TAKE IT. Peter couldn't decide who he ought to kill first.

He could start with the minx standing before him with eyes filled with a fascinating mix of fury, fear, and just a hint of shame.

He could strangle his mother for having introduced Miss Matthews to Utley in the first place, when she knew full well the man was a scoundrel of unequaled measure. It was bad enough that she'd instigated the entire charade by pushing Peter to take a new bride and by sponsoring her damned cousin for the Season.

If he were to do what he really knew, deep down, that he should do, he could follow Utley, the bloody bastard, to wherever he had wandered off to in the dark of the gardens and rip his head from his body. Not only had the bastard dared to dance with a decent, respectable young lady, in a decent, respectable ballroom, before legions of decent, respectable people, but he also had the audacity to take that very same young lady from the ballroom and away from the protective eyes of her chaperone and the rest of the *ton*. Not to mention his own eyes, but they were rather beside the point.

The lecher obviously was planning to do God-knew-what in order to ruin the blasted woman on her very first night out. Which shouldn't surprise Peter. He might have hoped Utley would someday change, but the bastard was clearly beyond hope.

And Miss Matthews had been bloody stupid to agree to any of it in the first place. Clearly, she hadn't been paying attention to the instruction his mother had given her or she would never have agreed to dance with the bastard, let alone leave the safety of the public eye to go somewhere alone with him.

Which brought him back to Miss Matthews. Blast it.

But damnation, he most certainly could not throttle her. At least, not at the moment.

Perhaps later.

In the meanwhile, she needed to be handled. Luckily, Peter doubted anyone else had seen her leave for the gardens with Utley.

He had followed them out himself as soon as he saw where the cretin was taking her, though the throng of revelers certainly didn't make the task of moving through them very easy for him.

And she *had* looked as though she needed a bit of air when he was taking her out, so any who had seen their departure would surely assume as much. She'd looked ready to fall over from the vapors at any moment. This little fiasco wouldn't necessarily cause her ruination. At least not immediately.

He took a breath to calm himself. There was no reason to lose his temper in front of Miss Matthews. Doing so once in his lifetime had certainly been more than enough.

But before he was entirely certain he had a firm rein over his anger, she interrupted his concentration with an imperiously arched eyebrow, tilting her head and pursing her lips. "Pardon me, Your Grace. I was just returning to the ballroom." The fear had fled her eyes, leaving only unveiled anger behind. Still, a slight tremor sounded in her voice. That likely irritated her to no end.

He deliberately kept his response low, cool. The last thing he needed was to alarm her further. "Were you? And might you also inform me of the reason you took it upon yourself to leave that very ballroom with Lord Utley only a few moments ago?"

"Why, no, I don't believe I shall. I have no intention to do any such thing." The anger in her gaze turned to a haughty glare. "I see no reason to explain my actions to you, sir."

"Don't you? And why, pray tell, is that?" Bloody infuriating woman.

"Because my business is my own. Pardon me, if you please." She tried to skirt around him to the right, but he shifted to block her progress. She rewarded his efforts with a disgruntled frown.

"I beg to differ, ma'am. You see, while you're in London, you are my mother's charge. And as I am the head of our household, you are therefore my charge as well, however much we may both desire otherwise."

Her eyes flashed. "Indeed. Nonetheless, you fail to remember that I've obtained my majority. I may certainly speak with any gentleman with whom I see fit, and even go for a stroll in the gardens of a night, should I so deem it appropriate. *Without* deigning to request your permission, Your Grace."

"And you call that scoundrel a gentleman, do you?" A raging fire was building in his chest, boiling like a kettle over a fire, and he fought to tamp it back down. Miss Matthews was becoming a devilish nuisance, causing reactions within him that no one had ever done before, damn it all. "Do you know who he is, ma'am? Do you know anything about Lord Utley at all? Or any of the myriad gentlemen present at the ball this evening, for that matter?"

She started to pipe in with a response, but he cut her off.

"No. You don't. And since you are so dreadfully unaware of anything related to these gentlemen's reputations, you have been relegated to my mother's chaperonage. For your own protection, ma'am." Peter's voice had risen so loud, surely someone within the ballroom would hear him soon. He deliberately lowered it again, taking a deep breath to regain control. "You're to do as she says in order that you don't make an unwarranted mistake. If left to your own devices, you'd likely ensure your own ruin if this jaunt into the gardens is any indication. You're most certainly not to take it upon yourself to accept a dance with one of the most notorious rakehells in Town, nor are you to then proceed to situate yourself entirely alone with said '*gentleman*' without the knowledge of your chaperone, or anyone else. Yet you thoroughly ignored her on this matter—"

"I most certainly did *not* ignore Cousin Henrietta on any matter," Miss Matthews spat out at him with sparks in her eyes. "She introduced me to Lord Utley, and she saw no harm in my dancing with him since *you* had sent him over for an introduction. We both complied with your guidance, *Your Grace*." Miss Matthews took the tiniest step forward until she stood only a hair's breadth away from him, wagging a finger in his face. "If anyone here is to blame for anything, it is you. You're the one who set this all in motion."

"You and my mother were both terribly mistaken if you think I'd have sent anyone like Utley for an introduction. How she could possibly think I would approve of such a thing, I'll never be able to fathom. But I'll deal with her later. You, on the other hand, must be dealt with immediately."

"Dealt with. *Dealt with?* Why, you arrogant popinjay!" She took another step toward him, stepping on his toes in the process and shoving him backward with no small amount of force—a fact that surprised him—and matching him step for step as he backed away. "I am not some green chit barely out of the schoolroom. Nor am I one of your siblings. You have no right to order me about in any way. You will kindly remember that in future."

Never in his life had he struck a woman before, not even one of his sisters when they were children, yet he found it difficult to restrain himself from that very atrocity at this moment. Her impudence stung.

"And you would do well to remember, Miss Matthews, that as long as you live beneath my roof you are under my protection and therefore must abide by my decisions."

"Well, perhaps I should not live beneath your roof any longer, then." She crossed her arms over her chest, which only served to plump up her already breathtaking bosom before his eyes.

"Perhaps not. Nevertheless, you currently do, so my word is law."

Her fury shone through in a great huff and a flash of her eyes. Dear Lord, she was beautiful when she was angry. Almost like a siren.

Peter shook his head, as though to rid it of such thoughts. Thinking along those lines would get him nowhere. "And my word is that you are to avoid all contact with Lord Utley from this moment on. For that matter, you'd better reject any attentions from Mr. Aldous Forster or Lord Tansley, should they attempt to pay you court. Maybe a few others as well. I'll let you know as I think of them. But I might never secure you a husband if some nefarious scoundrel ruins your reputation before you have a chance to make a decent match."

And the sooner she was married, the sooner he could set aside the way her ire bewitched him and move on with his life—without the chaotic wake that seemed to follow her everywhere that currently had his head in a twist.

"I see," Miss Matthews murmured with narrowed eyes. *Thank heavens.* "So I should avoid and blatantly ignore Lords Utley and Tansley and Mr. Forster. Would you like to add anyone else to that list, Your Grace?" Her heated glare could fell an entire army. But instead of sounding a retreat, Peter's only thought was to advance.

His eyes slid to her lips, which were darkened from the furious pinch she had kept them in for several moments. He wanted nothing more than to kiss them, to press his own lips against their angry pout until the heat in them turned to passion and promise instead of anger.

"Well?" Miss Matthews placed her hands on her hips in a posture much like an overbearing governess—which he found disturbingly alluring.

Christ, he ought to walk away now. But for some confounding reason, he couldn't. "Yes. There is one more."

"And? Who might this dreaded gentleman be?"

Peter advanced toward her, closing the small gap between them. "Me." Before he could stop himself, he leaned in and captured her mouth in a kiss.

Seven

HIS MOUTH LANDED on hers, hard, hot, and demanding. The golden flecks in his eyes—one blue and the other green—shimmered and came alive.

She blinked. After several moments, Jane still had difficulty fathoming what was happening. Even then, why he was doing it remained a perplexing mystery.

He drew her closer—one hand tangling in her hair, the other firm against the back of her waist. His clean, earthy, musky scent poured through her body and down to her toes and his warmth invaded her, leaving her feeling drugged.

When his tongue slid across the crease of her lips—softly at first, like silk, and then more insistently—she heard a low, ragged feminine moan that could only have been her own. Good God. What was happening to her? The animalistic growl that followed, however, unmistakably came from him.

When his tongue pressed against her lips with even more fervor, Jane succumbed and parted them for him. He swept inside, stroking against her, and a rapid, clanging series of tingles assaulted her stomach. She wanted to move closer to him. To feel more of him. Blast, what was happening to her? When he sucked, pulling her tongue into his mouth, an aching pang that bordered on pleasure built between her legs, alongside a fair amount of heat and moisture. Oh, dear.

And then his mouth left hers to trail wet kisses over her face, down her neck, across the exposed part of her bosom. Cool air danced over the wetness he left behind, and she shivered. Such a delicious juxtaposition, the burgeoning heat radiating between them and the shivery, shuddery moisture on her skin.

"So sweet," he murmured, his mouth hovering over the cleft between her breasts. Strangely enough, they were heaving with her frantic breaths, as though from some unexplainable exertion.

Again, the duke's mouth joined with hers. Her legs were weak and wobbly beneath her, and she fell into him for support, her hands taking up a feeble grip at his neck. If not for his arms wrapped around her like bands, she would undoubtedly be on the ground.

His pulse beat an erratic pace against the flat of her palm.

Just as suddenly as he had begun the assault against her senses, he broke off the kiss and pushed away from her. Jane stumbled backward, trying to regain her balance—not to mention her sanity.

He looked down upon her with an irate scowl that bordered on belligerence.

If he thought for even one second he could blame her for *that* encounter—

But then he spoke. "I'm sorry." His words were short, clipped. "That was inexcusable."

"Er...I..." Jane shook her head like a simpleton. Coherent thoughts were in rather short supply at the moment. Luckily, he didn't appear to care one whit.

His eyes darted about, scanning the darkness of the garden. Placing an arm about her waist, he guided her back toward the lights and gay sounds coming from the ballroom. He faced her, his eyes grave, almost ominous. "It won't happen again."

Then he opened the door to the ballroom, gave her a gentle nudge to get her feet moving inside, and closed the door behind her. No one seemed to notice Jane's entrance, which was just as well—she had no desire to explain how she had left with one gentleman, been gone for an inordinate amount of time, and reappeared with another, different gentleman.

Still, it would have been more appropriate for him to escort her back to his mother. She peeked through the window where he'd left her, nonsensically hoping for some sort of reassurance, but the Duke of Somerton was gone.

Bloody coward.

And he was a downright overbearing brute, to boot. To think he could order her about, to tell her who she could and could not converse with. She was a grown woman, and he was not her father or brother. The man had no claim over her to insist on any sort of behavior.

Well, to be fair, since she *was* staying in his home, perhaps she *should* conform to his requests. Or at least some of them. Well, she should if he had ever *requested* anything at all of her, instead of issuing terse commands.

But that was the whole problem—he hadn't made a single request. He'd done quite the opposite at nearly every turn. Any man with half a shred of decency would understand that issuing orders willy-nilly was no way to treat a lady.

Then again, Jane wasn't technically a lady, was she? Merely a miss. She was so far beneath his touch that perhaps he knew no other way of interacting with her.

Nevertheless, his kiss left her shattered. She had never expected to feel so...so...wanted. So beautiful. Especially not with him, a man who obviously thought so little of her.

For him to kiss her like that, to make her feel as though the world could end at that moment and she'd feel nothing other than intense pleasure (and—dare she admit it?—desire), and then to break it off with a callous shove and apology—it was the most demeaning thing she'd ever experienced in her life.

Jane wanted nothing more to do with him.

Why, if her mother wouldn't be so upset, she would hire a coach and return to Whitstable this very instant. Living under this man's 'protection' and facing his constant scorn and derision was almost more than she could bear.

But she couldn't do that to Mother. Mother would be devastated. Nor was Jane willing to upset Cousin Henrietta and her daughters in such a way. She would simply have to suffer the damned duke's condescension.

Drat. Now, more than ever, she needed to move forward with plans for her modiste shop.

The music came to an end and the crowd shuffled toward the dining room for supper. She slipped in amongst crush and forced all thoughts of the Duke of Somerton aside.

UTLEY DUCKED BACK behind his bush out in the garden as Somerton stalked past him.

He had to smother the chuckle that was threatening to release. Shaking his head, he reached into the inside pocket of his greatcoat and pulled out a cheroot, then moved back to the lighted path to light it with the flame of a lantern.

This was even better than he'd imagined possible—Somerton had feelings for the woman. Utley took a drag of his cheroot. He had never been prone to bouts of luck before, but perhaps his fortunes were finally beginning to change.

Adding her dowry, as generous as it was, to his coffers certainly wouldn't be a hardship on him. He might even be able to take up with a mistress on the forty thousand Somerton had boasted for her.

Why would the bloody duke offer such a sum for her if he wanted her for himself? Not that it mattered. The only part that really was a concern to Utley was that Somerton *did* want her. And Utley wanted her dowry, and a chance to take something Somerton wanted right from under the duke's nose.

Now he needed a plan. Something more concrete.

Utley tossed his cheroot to the ground and stubbed it with the toe of his boot, then made for the back alley and the hack waiting for him. He had revenge to plot.

A CHORUS OF female squeals and childish giggles coming from the downstairs parlor interrupted Peter's concentration. Yet again, he was attempting to settle the accounts for Carreg Mawr in his office. Each time he began to make some small semblance of progress, another shout burst through.

On the fourth instance, he glared at the closed door, wishing he could extend it through the panels and into the other room.

After the seventh interruption, he pushed his ledgers aside for a moment and stretched his legs, sure that clearing his mind would also clear the path for a return to work.

By the time the twelfth peal of giggles reached him, he had moved all of his materials from the library to Spenser's office at the end of the hall. Surely that would give him enough separation from them that there would be no more distractions from his task.

Obviously he was wrong.

Peter slammed his butler's office door closed. He'd make damned sure it was loud enough to alert the perpetrators of his displeasure. Then he stalked back to the makeshift desk he had created by pulling a chair close to an empty shelf. After all, he didn't want to disturb the stacks of papers Spenser had arranged just so.

When the fifteenth bout hit his ears, Peter threw his head back and took in a breath. Accomplishing anything of import was quite out of the question today. He set off to discover why his family felt it necessary to make as much noise as a room full of wild animals.

Upon nearing his drawing room, he was assaulted by more of the same, along with a myriad of competing floral scents warring with each other for domination. Peter's mother sat on a chaise in the middle of the room, surrounded his two sisters, his children, and

Miss Matthews with her furry, orange cat—not to mention dozens of bouquets of flowers in every variety and color possible.

None of them, he noted, paid Peter's arrival any attention at all.

He cleared his throat, but to no avail. Charlotte, who was carrying a large bouquet of yellow blossoms to a waiting vase near the hearth, continued to gush nonsense. "And this one is for Jane, as well. Very lovely, don't you think?"

"Quite, dear. And who sent those?" His mother looked like a proud mother hen.

Charlotte settled the flowers into their new home and then fussed with the card. "From Lord...Lord Eldredge! Oh, Jane. He's absolutely divine, and terribly handsome. I think he would make for a rather advantageous match, if you ask me."

Miss Matthews flushed rather becomingly, at least in Peter's estimation. "Might you remind me which gentleman Lord Eldredge is? I don't seem to recall."

At that comment, Sophie tittered with laughter and Charlotte gasped. "How could you not recall him? He's as handsome as a god, or at least as handsome as the devil himself."

"Charlotte, that's more than enough, thank you," Mama said, interrupting his youngest sister before she could make even more of a cake of herself than she had already managed.

The cat, up to that point, had been entertaining Sarah by following along under her legs as she toddled about the room and using its paws to swat at the underside of her skirts. Then it decided to cuddle with Miss Matthews. It jumped up onto her lap and proceeded to knead its paws—against *her bosom*. Her cheeks pinked even brighter than before and she shoved at the cat's paws. "No sir, Mr. Cuddlesworth," she whispered in a heated tone. "You know that is entirely inappropriate behavior in front of anyone."

The cat refused to be deterred, however, and purred its response to her.

"You naughty, naughty boy." Her look of sheer mortification was entirely too attractive on her for Peter's comfort.

A sudden desire to toss the blasted cat aside so he could resume its attentions to her bosom seized Peter by the throat. He had to fight for decorum to prevail. He cleared his throat again, a bit louder this time. "Good morning. I wager from the state of my drawing room that you all had some success in the first ball of the Season." He gestured toward the endless supply of fresh-cut flowers overwhelming his nostrils. "Perhaps, Sophie, one of the senders will suit you as a potential match? Or would that be rushing matters, since this is only your sixth Season on the marriage mart. Or is it your seventh?"

She only scowled at him in response, but then offered, "You did very well by Jane last night in securing potential suitors. The vast majority of these flowers are for her. I daresay she'll have a room full of gentlemen callers this afternoon. Well done." She clucked a tongue, and her tongue dripped with sarcasm.

"Do I hear a dash of jealousy, Sophia? Should I send more gentlemen your way at the next ball, so that you can then dash their hopes and give them the cut direct?" Of course, he was being forced at present to ignore his own jealousy, so he shouldn't give her such grief. Not that he really thought she was jealous. She'd had more opportunities to marry than he could count, and flouted them all.

Peter looked down at the orange fluff in Miss Matthews's lap again and forced his ire down. It was bloody ridiculous to envy a cat.

"Not jealousy at all," Sophie countered. "I was merely pointing out that you sent so many gentlemen for introductions to Jane, including some...shall we say, less-than-desirables."

"Really, Peter," interrupted Charlotte. "I could scarcely believe my eyes when Lord Utley came across from your group and begged an introduction to her. It was quite irregular, to say the least."

"I did *not*—" He couldn't finish his objection before Sophie cut in.

"Luckily for Jane, nothing happened when she danced with him. Granted, he *did* take her out for some air, *and then* he left her to rejoin the ball alone...but I daresay hardly anyone noticed so it doesn't really signify. I doubt her reputation will suffer overmuch from the gossip.

Surely they'll move on to something more scintillating—something *juicier*—in no time."

Through the entire discussion to this point, Miss Matthews had remained silent, listening to the arguments over her reputation—and the possibility of scandal—with an abashed look upon her face.

Finally, at this juncture, she entered the fray. "I'm unconcerned about the gossip mill, Sophie. And as I told you last night, I'm certain some sort of miscommunication must have occurred. Why, if Lord Utley truly has the sort of reputation you feel he has...well, then I'm more than positive that your brother would never have sent him over for an introduction. His Grace can't very well be blamed for a scandal which may very well not matriculate at all."

Sensible head on that one, even if she thought she knew more about what was good for her than he did. Still, it was rather charming to find a woman who could think so clearly. Most ladies of his acquaintance, his sisters occasionally being exceptions to the rule, couldn't make a decision about what flavor of ice they wanted at Gunter's on their own, let alone come to a logical conclusion to solve any sort of problem.

Blast it, why could she not be the dull, dreary, and uneducated, countrified mouse that he had initially thought her to be? He had a sinking suspicion that life as he knew it was soon to become overly complicated. And if there was one thing that Peter hated—truly, utterly detested with every ounce of his soul—it was complication.

He preferred his life to be neat and orderly, much like his office. Everything lined up in neat rows. Everyone knowing their role and position. Everything operating smoothly, without a constant need for his input or prodding.

But there was nothing neat, or orderly, or in need of merely a gentle prodding (not to mention having an understanding of her role, but he would have to deal with that later, when there was no audience present to eavesdrop on their discussion), about Miss Matthews. Nothing at all. In fact, she might just be the epitome of chaos itself.

So why on earth was he attracted to the woman?

She was everything he wanted to avoid, but at the same time, she had begun to consume his thoughts. Why couldn't she have been a bumbling fool when they had danced together last night? Then he would have been able to brush his budding lust for her aside and move on with his night, working to find her a husband before dancing with enough other young ladies to appease his mother.

Dancing with Miss Matthews, however, had only added fuel to his desire. She had proved her intelligence and wit while they danced, and he'd wanted to dance her away through the open doors allowing a cool breeze to waft over the party, take her under cover of the darkened garden, and do any number of inexcusable and dastardly deeds with her. Somehow he had restrained himself.

But then instead of fulfilling his obligations to his mother and dancing with other ladies, he'd allowed himself to stand to the side of the dance floor and watch her. Dangerous, that.

She had danced and laughed gaily with Sinclaire, and Peter's jealousy had only mildly surged. Then there was Eldredge and Pottinger, and a small contingent of other eligible gentlemen, all of whom would make rather advantageous matches for Miss Matthews, and whom he had sent over for introductions in the hopes he could hurry things along in that arena. Still, with each of them Peter had kept a tight rein over the envy threatening to dislodge whichever gentleman was on the receiving end of her smiles by clamping his jaw closed and glaring.

That tactic had worked rather well with keeping the undesirable women away from him, also—not an unwelcome effect, all things considered. He imagined he must have looked like a glowering lunatic for the majority of the evening.

But then Utley had come along, and the jealousy building in Peter's chest had turned to an erupting volcano of rage. That the bloody, licentious bastard had dared to dance with her was more than enough to send Peter into conniptions. As though that, in itself, weren't enough, the dance was not only a waltz—but also the supper dance. It took every ounce of Peter's patience, long honed through a lifetime of being groomed for his current station in life, not to challenge the scoundrel in front of everyone present, gossip and legalities be damned.

So of course, when the man in question had led his charge out onto the veranda, the very same thing Peter had imagined doing with her himself, there was nothing he could do but follow them. He'd been completely unable to stop his feet from treading the same path Utley's had taken.

Yet again. Peter loathed Utley more with each passing moment. Wasn't ruining two lives enough retribution for Utley? Why must he add a third?

Peter told himself (not to mention Miss Matthews when he'd confronted her in the garden during her attempt at escape) that his intention had been to protect her virtue. To make certain her reputation remained unharmed by spending time alone with a man of Utley's standing within society.

There *was* truth to that statement, though it was far from the whole truth. Was his tiny, white lie such a travesty, though, in face of the dangers presented by Utley?

Yet instead of protecting her, his own actions would have utterly ruined her, had they been caught. Blast it, why must he feel this inexplicable attraction to her? But that kiss—that one sinful and altogether-too-enjoyable kiss—had nearly been his undoing.

She smelled and tasted of peaches, sweet, ripe, and delectable. And while she was thoroughly inexperienced, her response had been eager and invigorating. Thankfully, she had fallen into him, serving to remind him, however painful such a task may be, that he must stop at once. Frankly, he ought never to have started in the first place.

Damnation, he was hardening again just from the memory of her curves, soft and lush, as he'd held her against his frame. This frustration would solve nothing, but what could he do?

But then his mother's impatient voice broke through his ruminations. "*Peter.*"

He looked to her, unable to stop the glower from taking over his features. Surely, he'd be hearing about that one later, as well. "I'm so sorry, Mama. What did you ask?" Or had someone else asked him something which he had then ignored? Good God, he had never been so scatterbrained in his life.

Mama lifted a brow. "I asked you nothing. Your sister, however, asked if you might be so kind as to take herself and the other young ladies of the house for a drive through Hyde Park this afternoon."

And so his torture truly began. He'd never have another minute to himself until the blasted Season came to a close, at this rate. He had agreed to it, however. And it was just this one Season. After this, Mama would finally leave him be. Peter gathered his wits and turned to the eldest of his sisters. "Of course, Sophie. I would be glad to take you."

"Really, Peter," piped in Charlotte. "Can you not tell your own sisters apart? I asked, not Sophie."

"What on earth has you so distracted?" asked Sophie. "You've been staring off into space with the most atrocious scowl upon your face virtually since you woke up this morning. And, I might add, you haven't the slightest inkling of what discussion has been taking place. If I didn't know better, I'd think you had your head in a twist over a female."

Char tittered with laughter and Sophie snorted inelegantly before trying to mask the action with coughing on her morning chocolate, while Mama gave them both a look full of admonishment. Miss Matthews said nothing, but stared fixedly out the front window at a tree branch blowing lazily in the breeze.

Apparently choosing to ignore their mother's unspoken warning, Sophie continued: "Of course, I know that could not possibly be the case, since the only lady Peter danced with the entire night was Jane. Why, he hardly even laid eyes upon another miss throughout the whole affair."

With that, Miss Matthews's face turned a delightful shade of pink all over. Peter had a sudden, keen desire to situate himself beside her and plant kisses all over that pink face, even with his family watching, just to see how much more splendidly red her face could become. He wouldn't mind kissing her any number of other places, as well, to see if they would flush such a charming hue—although he'd prefer not to have an audience for that.

But that sort of behavior was out of the question. If he followed through, he would be forced to marry her—and Peter could think of few ladies in his acquaintance less suitable to become his new duchess than Miss Matthews, even if she had caused him to stay up all night, in the grips of unfulfilled desire.

Before Peter could give his sisters any semblance of a response, Spenser entered and announced the arrival of "Lord Eldredge to call upon Miss Matthews." Then he bowed low before backing away when he received a nod from the dowager.

After only a few more moments, the drawing room was filled with nearly as many gentlemen callers as arrangements of flowers. Peter took that as his cue to exit.

He needed to find *some* time to settle his accounts, and now he would have to follow through with his promise to Char and drive the ladies through Hyde Park later in the afternoon.

And of course, there would be yet another entertainment to attend in the evening. He sincerely doubted he could manage another evening of avoiding all of the young misses desperate for a piece of his attention. At least, not if his mother had anything to say about it, which she was bound to do.

He pushed his way through the throng of admirers, gathered to fawn over his sisters and Miss Matthews, and stalked through the halls of his home. Once he collected his account records, Peter slipped upstairs to find a quiet room where he could work.

Any reasonable man had only a limited supply of patience. Peter's had long since worn thin.

THE WHIRLWIND OF Jane's first—and only—Season was blowing full force. After the first ball at Turnsley Hall, they had attended some new entertainment or another every evening. In the afternoons, Jane, Sophie, and Charlotte received their gentlemen callers, some of whom occasionally took them for a drive through Hyde Park or for an ice at Gunter's or strolling through the streets of Mayfair.

All in all, Cousin Henrietta declared Jane a smashing success. Somehow, instead of convincing the *beau monde* that she was hopelessly vulgar and backward, she was having quite the opposite effect. It was a mystery, that. At least as far as Jane was concerned.

Young ladies who were the at the height of fashionable society all wanted to be Jane's friends because, as Sophie was so fond of telling her, she had the audacity and the courage to say things that everyone else thought but never dared to utter. And gentlemen who were far more eligible than she had ever dreamed would want to associate with her had begun to pay her court. It was all quite overwhelming, to say the least. Not to mention more than just a bit daunting.

As she expected, the gossips quickly moved on to more exciting subjects after the grand debacle of Jane dancing with Lord Utley. He had disappeared after that night in the garden, and she had seen neither hide nor hair of him since.

Thank God. While she didn't particularly care to have anything more to do with the man, the preponderance of him giving her the same attentions again was enough to convince her she might need to seek some assistance from Somerton, of all people. She shuddered at the thought.

With him, as well, there had been no reoccurrence of that night's events. She couldn't say it had been an entirely *un*pleasant kiss—far from it, truth be told—but it had left her more than just a little baffled. The man had an uncanny ability to intimidate her. Jane was none too keen for him to see the effect he had upon her, lest he use it to his advantage—and her disadvantage. But at the same time she was drawn to him, as though some unknown force pulled the two of them together, as though they were meant to be together.

What a laughable thought! She, a mere country vicar's daughter, meant to be with the Duke of Somerton? If he hadn't been thoroughly and completely disgusted by her actions and still wanted some sort of connection with her, at most it would be as a mistress—something Jane would never condescend herself to become.

In all honesty, he'd made no indication that he intended to pursue any sort of connection with her since that moment, so Jane would do far better to push such thoughts from her mind and move on to more important and pressing matters—such as Lord Eldredge's continued attentions, which, at the moment, led her to believe he might soon be making her an offer.

Drat it all.

How had she allowed things to come to this? She never intended to lead the man along or give him the wrong impression, but somehow she feared she had done just that.

She *had* danced with him at a number of balls. But how many other gentlemen had she danced with at each of those balls? Far too many for her to count, to be sure.

And yes, she had spoken with him and sat next to him at Lady Kirkaldy's musicale Thursday last. But honestly, she would have done the same with virtually any gentleman in her acquaintance, and was forced to cut her attendance at the entertainment short when Charlotte had become a bit too animated during the intermission, knocking a glass of sherry over and spilling it over the front of Jane's gown. At that point, she'd been forced—or should she say blessed?—to leave so she could tidy herself up again.

Still, there was no attraction between them, or at least none that Jane felt. She was afraid—very afraid—that Lord Eldredge had developed a growing affection for her. Perhaps a tendre, even. She simply must find some way of convincing him she was unsuitable for him, and sooner, rather than later.

He had called on her every afternoon since their first meeting. At first, he would sit in the crowded drawing room at Hardwicke House and speak with her about the weather or the upcoming routs she might attend.

Then, he had started offering to escort not only herself, but also Sophie, to Gunter's for an ice or for a lovely, afternoon stroll through Hyde Park.

Each of these endeavors was perfectly acceptable to Jane— because she was never alone with the viscount. He was never granted any opportunity to speak with her more earnestly, more privately, because they were always surrounded by a chaperone or two, at the very least, or often (as in the case of the various balls) a veritable army of the same.

That had all changed now. Double drat.

When he'd arrived this afternoon, he had begged Cousin Henrietta for permission to take Jane for a walk through Hyde Park—alone.

Cousin Henrietta, thrilled with the progress of their "budding courtship," as she was more than happy to refer to it, had all too happily granted him his request. She'd not even seen the need to send Meg along as a chaperone, since countless others would undoubtedly be out at the park doing the same thing. No harm to Jane's reputation could possibly come from such a stroll through the park with a perfectly respectable and eligible gentleman, after all, so the dowager had practically pushed her out the door with him with a smile as wide as the English Channel.

"It is such a beautiful day, is it not, Miss Matthews?" he asked her as they ambled down Grosvenor Square, heading away from Hardwicke House.

Lord Eldredge was rather tall, though still stood about half a head below the duke. Drat, drat, drat. There she went again, thinking about that blasted man. Jane growled at herself beneath her breath and pushed the thoughts aside before she answered his innocuous question.

"Yes, my lord, it's quite lovely today. How very lucky we are to have the sun shining so brilliantly. I am a bit bored with the constant clouds and rain we've had of late." Not to mention the constant discussion with Lord Eldredge of the weather.

He smiled down at her, a smile that would easily dazzle Charlotte. Handsome would not begin to do the man full justice—he was downright gorgeous. Everything about him was utter perfection, from his white teeth all in a neat row, to his chestnut brown hair that fell *just so* across his forehead, to the manner in which he held Jane's parasol over her in just the precise position to block the sun from damaging her complexion while still allowing her to see for miles ahead without straining. He was everything any normal, reasonable young lady would want in a match—handsome, genial, titled, wealthy...

Clearly, Jane must not be normal. Or possibly she was simply unreasonable.

Or, perhaps, she was neither normal nor reasonable.

He patted her hand where she held onto his elbow, almost in the way one would pat a dog for fetching and returning a stick. "Yes, I'm afraid we've had far more cloudy days of late than sunny days. But all that rain has produced some of the most beautiful flowers I've seen in Town in years. Why, look at this lovely field of daffodils! They are quite vibrant, don't you agree?"

"Yes, quite." Dear Lord, must they discuss all of the flora and fauna of Britain on this walk? She might never survive a full day in his company without wishing to run screaming in the opposite direction for more invigorating conversation.

"I daresay, if I might be so bold, Miss Matthews, you would look ravishing in such a shade." When she didn't immediately respond, he rushed on, "Oh dear, have I overstepped my bounds with you? I had thought...er, well, I had *hoped* that we...that we might be ready to move into more familiar territory."

Drat. She'd been right in her assumptions, then. Jane really wished she had been wrong about this premonition, but this man, for some unknown reason, thought she held an affection for him which she absolutely *couldn't*, even if she *would*.

Lord Eldgedge certainly was a very kind man, and he would be a perfectly acceptable—even desirable—match for some lucky young lady. But why must *she* be cursed with such luck?

Everything happening in her life of late seemed to be having the opposite effect from what she intended. In all the time she had been in London, she'd still been unable to sneak out to look at potential storefronts for her future business, let alone do anything else in preparation for it. Cousin Henrietta had kept her so busy with social obligations that there'd been no time for Jane to do anything on her own.

But none of that mattered at the moment. Lord Eldredge was looking at her with a slightly pained expression, but one that he was desperately trying to hide from her. Hurting him more than necessary was out of the question. But she must make the man understand that there could be no future between them.

Double drat. "My lord—"

"Please. Call me Miles. I would really love to hear you say my Christian name."

Oh, goodness. She might have already made a bigger mull of things than she'd originally thought. "*My lord*, I believe it would be highly inappropriate for us to behave with so much familiarity at this point in time, sir."

"Is it truly too soon, Miss Matthews? Have I made some dreadful mistake, then? You don't hold me in the same affection in which I hold you?" He paused and stared out across the park they were nearing. "Because I *do* hold you in a certain affection. I think I might—"

"Oh please, sir. Do *not* say the words." Drat, drat, drat. How had she allowed this man to fall in love with her? And she hadn't seen it coming at all, even though Cousin Henrietta must have noticed. Why else would she have been so keen to rush Jane out the door with him, if not for the glimmer of hope she had for their future?

Dozens of fashionable ladies and gentlemen loomed in the not-so-distant foreground. Lord Eldredge stopped their progress before they were within earshot of any potential gossips and turned to face her directly.

"But I must. I believe I love you, Miss Matthews. I brought you out here alone today to ask you for your hand—to ask you to marry me." His earnest eyes bored holes into her. "To ask you to become my viscountess."

"Please do not ask that of me. Not now." *Not ever.*

"Then when? Oh dear...you aren't...is there another?" Anguish tore across his face.

"No, of course not," Jane all but snapped. Gracious, she needed to get a hold on herself. She took a moment and willed her voice to return to that of a sane, calm woman, not a raving shrew. "There is no one else in my affections. But—"

"But you simply need more time," Lord Eldredge cut in, breathing a sigh of relief. Blast and damn, why could he not understand? "Don't say no, then, Miss Matthews. Not today. I'll just have to increase my efforts to woo you, and ask you again when I believe you might give me the answer my heart desires."

Oh, damnation.

He resumed his position by her side and returned her hand to his arm. "Shall we continue to the park, then?" He pasted a false smile, betrayed by the hurt lingering in his eyes, upon his face and led her on.

When they had only walked a few more paces down the lane, the Duke of Somerton, of all people, pulled up alongside them in his curricle, heading the opposite direction toward Hardwicke House. He inclined his head in their direction.

Jane's attention, however, turned away from him and to the pair of horses leading his chariot. Her heart beat a frenetic tattoo against her chest and she found it terribly difficult to take a full breath, let alone hide her panic from anyone present. Instinctively, she pulled herself as far away from the beasts as she could, but Lord Eldredge placed a hand against her back and held her still.

"Good afternoon, Your Grace," he called. "Miss Matthews and I were just out for an afternoon promenade through the park."

"Eldredge," came the clipped response. "And Miss Matthews," followed, a bit more softly.

For a brief minute, Jane was able to pull her eyes away from the rabid beasts snorting and rearing their heads in her direction to look up at him. His eyes singed her with their intensity before they returned to her escort.

For at least that moment, she was glad for Lord Eldredge's support against her back. Her fear of the horses might have been enough to send her into a fit of the vapors of its own accord, but with the heat of the duke's anger added to it, she would otherwise surely be flat on the ground.

But why on earth was he so furious? Had she unwittingly broken another of the man's ever-changing rules? She was just preparing herself to ask him that very question when the horse nearest to Lord Eldredge, and therefore nearest to herself, reared back against the harness and whinnied. Blood rushing downward from Jane's head all the way to her toes. At any moment, she might disgrace herself before not only the duke and Lord Eldredge, but also the growing crowd passing the afternoon in the park.

Sit. She needed to sit.

And breathe. Breathing was an absolute necessity.

Jane waved her free hand toward a nearby bench. "I...I...think I should—"

But then it all went black.

"YOU SHOULD HAVE bloody well caught her," growled out a familiar masculine voice.

"And perhaps you should have controlled your horses," countered another. "Couldn't you see she was afraid? She was shaking visibly, you know."

"I might ask you the same question, Eldredge. You took her out from my house, away from my mother and sisters. You were responsible for her health and safety."

"If you thought me an unsuitable escort for her, you should have made your feelings known before now."

The arguing voices were causing her head to throb, and Jane had the uncomfortable realization that she was somehow perched between the two men blaming each other for her situation, one hard male body pressed against each of her sides, holding her upright.

"Keep your voice down. You're attracting an audience. The last thing she needs is more gossip."

Oh, good gracious. "The last thing I need," she said quietly, so as not to worsen the headache that was rapidly building, "is the two of you having a discussion about me as though I am not seated here between you."

She tried to open her eyes, but then fluttered them shut again when the blinding sunlight pierced through the slits. Jane must have flinched from the pain, because Lord Eldredge—having been lodged firmly against her left side—shifted slightly and raised her parasol into position to block the harsh rays of the late afternoon sun. At the same time, the duke jumped up from where he'd been settled against her right side to stand and block the light. Their combined efforts left her with little to support her, and she slumped over before straightening herself.

Somerton frowned down at her, assuming his usual, stiff bearing. "Miss Matthews, when you've recovered sufficiently I'll return you to Hardwicke House in my curricle." He scowled at Lord Eldredge, seemingly goading him to challenge his edict. "Mama will wish to look after you after your fainting spell."

"I can certainly escort her home, Your Grace. There's no need for you to go to such trouble." Then Eldredge apparently turned to Jane, his eyes wide as though he'd only just remembered she was present and could make her own decisions. "If, of course, you would prefer that, ma'am."

"You would have her walk so soon? I'd thought better of you than that. Clearly, I was mistaken in my impression."

She almost huffed in response, but thought better of it and decided to show a touch more decorum. "Why thank you, Lord Eldredge, but if it's all right with the two of you, I would much prefer to continue our stroll. It *is*, of course, the reason we are out to begin with, isn't it?"

The duke looked as though he wanted to argue with her further, so she sent him the same look his mother seemed to have perfected with him, an I-dare-you-to-challenge-me-on-this-and-promise-you-will-fail-in-your-endeavors sort of look.

After a short stare-down, he frowned. "Very well. I have more business to attend, as it is." He climbed up into his curricle again before giving Lord Eldredge the full heat of his glare again. "You are responsible for her health and safety until such time as she is returned to my home. I trust you'll give me no reason to call you out."

Call him out? Good gracious, what *was* it with these men? "*Your Grace*—" she couldn't resist placing the emphasis on the fussy title— "I'm certain that is the most asinine comment I've ever heard you utter." Jane ignored his slack jaw and kept going before she lost the little bit of nerve she'd mustered. "I'll be perfectly fine. Good day to you, sir." She punctuated her words with a brisk nod before turning her back to him and facing Eldgedge again. "My lord, shall we begin again? I do believe His Grace was just leaving us for matters of far more import."

When she regained the viscount's arm, he snapped to attention. "Of...of course, Miss Matthews." He inclined his head to the duke and then they were off.

The horses' hooves guiding the curricle down the lane sounded behind them within moments, and Jane finally began to breathe again. The *nerve* of that man. Ooh, he certainly knew how to rile her temper. Blast. She hated letting him see how he'd gotten the better of her.

In silence, she and Lord Eldgedge drew nearer to the others meandering through the wooded areas of Hyde Park. Before they came within earshot of anyone though, her companion finally rediscovered his voice. "Ma'am, do you think it was wise to speak to His Grace in such a manner?"

Jane's eyes nearly popped free from her head. Thankfully, he couldn't see her mortification. Gracious, what a bumbling idiot she could be. She had gone and firmly planted her foot in her mouth again, hadn't she? But it might be better to pretend ignorance, at least for the moment. "How do you mean, my lord?" When she turned to him, she batted her eyelashes in what she hoped was a passable impersonation of a disconcerted young miss.

His eyes widened in abject bewilderment. "Why, you called him *asinine*. I daresay, I have never heard a woman—nay, anyone—speak so plainly to the duke before."

"Oh, dear. Have I just proven my gaucherie?" Perhaps if she had, then Eldredge might forget his silly infatuation with her and find some more suitable lady.

"Well, no."

"No?" Jane's hope plummeted to bury itself beneath her feet and halfway to the Orient.

"No. It may have been...well...a bit rash to speak with him so, but I wholeheartedly agree with your assessment. I only wish I had had the gall to say so myself, rather than allow a lady to fight my battles for me."

Several riders upon horseback trotted along the walkway they were traversing, and Lord Eldredge gently guided her to the side so they couldn't come too close. He was being entirely too thoughtful, taking care of her fears before she had a chance to let them gain a head.

"I would hardly say I fought your battle, my lord. More spoke my mind when I would have done better to bite my tongue." She sighed. "I'm afraid it's a bad habit I've developed and cannot seem to break."

"There are worse habits you could have," he said with a laugh.

"Indeed." Oh, good gracious. She simply *must* find a way to divert Lord Eldredge's attentions, but it seemed everything she did only caused him to develop a more insistent *tendre* than before.

They walked along for several more minutes without speaking. Several groupings of fashionable people wandered around them, talking and laughing and gossiping in the warm afternoon sun amongst the landscaped walkways as canopies of trees draped overhead.

Rotten Row loomed in the distance, abounding with riders and carriages. Near the entrance to the Row, a young girl rode her mare alongside a gentleman, likely her father. The girl was riding sidesaddle, with her foot barely reaching the stirrup to keep her steady in the saddle.

"She is awfully young to be learning to ride, isn't she?" Jane murmured, turning her enquiry to her escort.

"What was that, Miss Matthews?" he replied, glancing about distractedly before turning to engage a group of passersby. He never focused his gaze in the proper direction.

His lack of attention was maddening, particularly in a gentleman so intent upon convincing her to marry him. Not that she truly had a right to be annoyed with him, since she often lost track of what he was discussing, but that was beside the point. "That girl. Over there." Jane pointed in the direction of Rotten Row where the riders all congregated.

Just then, however, the girl's horse was spooked by some unknown movement nearby and took off at a breakneck run. Lord Eldgedge was involved in a conversation with some other gentleman, and he didn't see the girl and her horse dashing wildly through the park.

"Oh, dear. Oh, drat, drat, drat." Jane removed her hand from Eldredge's arm and took a step toward the girl and her horse. Then she stopped. What on earth was she thinking? Jane couldn't do anything about that beast any more than the girl could.

"Goodness," Lord Eldredge said, finally coming up alongside her. "Someone ought to control that horse." He shook his head. "That girl's not ready to handle it."

The monstrosity turned in their direction. Walkers dashed to either side of the lane, hurtling themselves out of the way.

At the screams of the girl and various ladies scattered throughout the park, the gentlemen riders finally took notice. They headed neck-or-nothing toward her, but there was simply no way they could reach her in time.

The horse reared back and nearly threw its young rider from the saddle. Nearly and not actually, only due to her small, booted foot being stuck in the stirrup. She hung upside-down, flopping about at the side of the creature as it rushed onward.

Panic clutched at Jane's chest. "Oh, no. No, no, no." Someone had to help that girl. She would be dreadfully hurt if she wasn't helped down from that beast, and soon.

Lord Eldredge tugged at Jane's arm, trying to pull her off to the side of the walkway and out of the wild animal's path. "Come, Miss Matthews. We must move clear. Quickly." He gave her one more tug, more forcefully this time.

"But that girl!" She took another cursory look about the park, fidgeting with the folds of her gown. No one would reach her in time.

No one.

No one but Jane.

She wrenched herself free from the viscount's grasp and rushed toward the animal, even as it ran full-speed in her direction.

"Miss Matthews," Eldgedge called out. His voice seemed distant and hollow as he stayed where he was, safely ensconced behind a hedgerow.

But she had to ignore him. She had to do something. Bloody useless men.

The horse charged straight for her, but Jane didn't slow. In fact, she might have even gained in speed, in trying to reach the girl in time. Just when she and the horse were about to run headlong into each other, it stopped and reared back again, whipping its head back.

Its nostrils flared wide with deep, snorting breaths. Jane fought to catch her own breath while she raised her hands up for it to smell. "There you go, girl. It's all right. Calm down."

She could have been speaking to herself. Or perhaps she was.

Once it stopped prancing, she gingerly reached up and took hold of the saddle to hold the beast still.

"Sweetheart? Miss, are you all right?" Jane couldn't move around to free the girl's ankle until she was sure the horse wouldn't charge her again.

It sniffed at her, but seemed much calmer. So she moved to the side, smoothing her hands along the horse's sweaty flanks as she went.

The girl had fainted, likely due to fear. Smart girl. She couldn't imagine what had gotten into the child in the first place to convince her to mount the beast. Jane lifted her weight with one arm and used the other to untangle her ankle from the stirrup.

The horse nickered again. "We're almost done here. Do please cooperate with me for just a moment longer."

Drat, the buckle on the girl's boot was caught. It wouldn't budge. And the horse, while it had calmed considerably, was growing agitated with her attempts at freeing the girl. Once again, it pranced about and whinnied in displeasure at her awkward handling of it, whipping its head back and looking as though it was planning to rear back at any moment. Good gracious, what had Jane gotten herself into?

"Please. Oh, please just come free."

She almost had the ankle loose after untwisting the stirrup, when a thunder of hooves came barreling down upon them. It frightened the horse, and then it *did* rear back, ripping the young girl free from Jane's arms. The child flopped against horseflesh again.

"Laura!" called out a panicked male voice from somewhere behind Jane.

The horse grew continually more agitated by her awkward handling and danced about, making it ever more difficult to accomplish her task. Finally, Jane freed the girl's ankle and fell backward to the ground, holding the girl safe in her arms and landing hard on her derrière. Her tail bone stung like too many bee stings all in one place.

The girl's escort and his companion reached them, both men jumping down to the ground. One grabbed the reins of all three horses. The other took Laura from Jane's trembling arms and rocked her back and forth. "My girl. My sweet girl."

"I do believe she'll be perfectly all right, sir," Jane said as she tried to pull herself into a sitting position. "It only seems to be a bit of a fainting spell. There should be no permanent damage." *Dear lord, please let this child be all right.*

Somehow, a crowd had gathered all around them. A number of ladies fished through their reticules until one of them came out with hartshorn and pushed it forward amidst the none-too-hushed commentary swirling all around their small group.

"Did you see how she saved that girl?"

"Stopped the horse right in its tracks. Truly amazing, if you ask me."

"Miss Matthews, are you quite all right? Let me through please!" This last, of course, came from none other than Lord Eldredge. "I must see to Miss Matthews immediately, thank you."

Jane, however, was far more concerned about the health of Laura, so she neglected to answer him immediately. Some things were more important in life than rushing to answer a dandified gentleman who would allow her to do what he should have done instead.

Hence his next overreaction. "Step back, if you will. I say, allow me to pass."

A few muttered grumbles came from one side of the crowd, where bodies seemed to be parting in a less than comfortable wave. One gentleman lost his footing, Jane could only imagine from being shoved from behind, and fell into another gentleman.

"Miss Matthews! I am coming to rescue you, ma'am. Kindly let me through, please."

Finally, enough people moved to the side (likely in order to avoid being unceremoniously shoved about) to allow Lord Eldredge to rush through to her side and assist her to her feet.

"You've given me quite the scare, Miss Matthews. I'll return you home immediately."

She brushed the dirt and leaves off her walking dress and frowned at the small tear along the hem. She'd have to fix that before Meg caught sight of it. "That will be quite unnecessary, my lord," she said off-handedly. "I intend to stay until I'm certain young Laura will recover."

The girl had only just come around again and seemed to have no serious injuries. Still, Jane had no intention of leaving just yet.

Lord Eldredge took her by the elbow, however, and attempted to lead her away from the throng. "I must insist, ma'am. His Grace is counting on me to ensure your safety. You must be returned to your chaperone at once."

By this point, they had reached the far edge of the gathering. Jane pulled her arm free from the over-eager man's grasp. "My safety, sir," she said with far more force, not to mention volume, than she intended, "might have been better looked after if you had assisted me with rescuing that girl."

Several pairs of eyes turned in their direction, obviously making note of every word she uttered as fuel for the gossip mill. Drat, she had gone and made a cake of herself again. But she'd already built up a full head of steam, so there could be no stopping now.

"My safety would surely have been better ensured had you, a gentleman who has clearly had more experience working with horses than I have, been so thoughtful as to have done the rescuing yourself. But you did not, sir. You ran for cover and watched while I took matters into my own hands. I rather think my safety is quite fine without your assistance. Good day to you, Lord Eldredge." She spun on her heels and marched back toward the crowd around Laura, many of whom stood gawking at her.

"But Miss Matthews—" He put out a hand in an attempt to stop her progress again, but she shook him free and continued her forward progress.

"But who will see you home, madam?" His voice sounded weak, almost pathetic, to her ears.

Lord Pottinger stepped out from the crowd and bowed low to her. "My companions and I would be delighted to see you home at your convenience, Miss Matthews."

From the other side of the gathering, Patience and Theodora Marlborough moved into a clearing. "Miss Matthews, my sister and I were hoping to visit with Lady Sophia and Lady Charlotte this afternoon. It would be no trouble at all to add one more to our party."

Several others of her brief acquaintance made similar offers, thereby nullifying Lord Eldredge's arguments. With a crestfallen, dejected look, he stepped back from her and inclined his head. "Very well. I see you'll be quite well looked after, ma'am." He made an awkward bow to the group as a whole, and backed away, heading toward some bushes off to the side. "Good day to you."

How odd. The bushes moved, as though something had disturbed them, but there wasn't even a slight breeze this afternoon. Jane shook her head. She must have imagined it.

Well. Perhaps she had—finally—convinced Lord Eldredge to seek a match elsewhere.

Gracious, it had taken a lot.

Nine

YET AGAIN, DOWN the hall from Peter's library, something was causing a stir. Devil take it. As it was, he'd resorted to using trickery with his mother in order to accomplish some of his business matters. Only that very afternoon, in fact.

He needed to meet with Yeats again, somehow, in order to discuss the problems at Carreg Mawr. In all of the time Peter had devoted to poring over the books, meager as that amount of time may be, he had discovered nothing—nothing!—out of place. Not one crop had gone unaccounted for, not one wage seemed out of line. There was seemingly no reason for the discrepancies.

But still, there must be some explanation.

Carreg Mawr had always produced far more income than was required in upkeep. Even before he'd taken over the running of the old castle and estate from his father and introduced new crops to the home farm, it had proven itself quite profitable.

So Peter had gone to visit with Yeats at his London office to discuss receive a report from a new worker—or rather someone investigating matters for Peter, while under the guise of being a new worker—in Wales. He'd allowed Mama to think he was paying social calls to some unnamed females he might consider courting in order to gain the bit of freedom to accomplish his task. What she didn't know, after all, wouldn't hurt him.

It wasn't entirely a lie. But it was most decidedly an omission of the truth. Blast it. Something as relatively minor as neglecting to tell his mother the full truth, even at his thirty-two years of age, grated on his last nerve.

So he'd taken care of his business and allowed Mama to think what she would. At least he had until he ran into Miss Matthews on his way home, out for a stroll in Hyde Park with Eldredge.

Why was he so blasted envious of the man? Peter couldn't possibly want to spend more time with that woman than he was already forced to spend. There was no reasonable answer for the ugly mass of envy that had snaked its way through his body at the sight of Miss Matthews on Eldredge's arm. Jealousy had consumed every fiber of his body when he found them with her hand holding his arm. It had burned through him so fast, he was amazed his curricle hadn't burst into flame right there on the street for the entire world to see.

He had wanted to throttle the minx, too, when she'd refused to come home with him like a reasonable lady after she'd fainted. Damnably independent, that one was. He would be glad to be rid of her. Eldredge seemed to be eager to snap her up, so perhaps Peter would be rid of Miss Matthews sooner than expected. That should make his life a bit more normal at least.

If only the thought consoled him as it should, instead of making him want to rip Eldredge apart, limb from bloody limb.

But how could she be so afraid of horses of all things? He shook his head, remembering how she'd paled before him as she'd watched his pair, just before collapsing into a heap beside her escort.

An escort who *ought* to have caught her. Bastard.

Good lord, Peter needed to get her out of his head. Maybe he should take up a mistress, or at least avail himself of the services so freely offered to him by one of several widows about town. He merely needed a woman—any appropriate woman other than *that* particular woman—to slake his desires.

She was as thoroughly inappropriate as any lady could possibly be.

He should never have kissed her. Just the thought of what would have happened if someone had caught them when he kissed her was enough to send him into a mild state of panic. They would be well on their way to the altar by now, if not already married.

Honestly, could any female in Town be less prepared to become his duchess? Peter held serious doubts.

A peal of laughter rang through the halls again, so he decided to do what any reasonable man would eschew—he went to the drawing room to discover what could possibly have the females of his home so excited.

When he arrived, not only had Miss Matthews returned—sans Eldredge, he noted with a touch more glee than he ought to have had—but the Misses Marlborough had also joined the melee.

The elder Miss Marlborough was in the midst of recounting some delightful—or dreadful, depending on who was making the determination—adventure from the day. Not a soul in the room had noticed Peter's presence, and he had no asinine (to borrow Miss Matthews's term) desire to alert them of his appearance, so he leaned against the door frame and listened to her rapturous tale.

"And *then*—Sophie, I declare you won't believe this part, but on my honor, it is entirely true—then Jane dashed in front of the horse! The poor girl had taken a faint in the saddle and fallen from it, but her foot was trapped in the stirrup, and Jane somehow convinced the wild horse to stop long enough for her to work the girl's ankle free. No one else dared to go near the animal in fear they would be trampled."

A chorus of shocked gasps filled the humming air of the drawing room.

Obviously she must be speaking of some other Jane than Miss Matthews. Peter racked his brain to remember if there had been some other young lady at Hyde Park who might be a Jane, but he remembered no ladies at all save the one in question.

He must be even more distracted than he thought.

But it was impossible for her to have done anything of the sort. For Christ's sake, she had fainted dead away herself only moments earlier, simply from the sight of his pair.

He refrained from snorting aloud in derision and returned his attention to the young woman's tale.

"And when Lord Eldredge *rushed* to her side—long after any need for his assistance had long since passed, I might add—he tried to drag her away before she could ascertain that the girl was all right. Of course, our Jane let the odious man know in no uncertain terms that she could see herself home quite well, thank you very much, and then bade him good day."

Our Jane? But, how?

"You did not, Jane!" Charlotte said, clearly scandalized by the thought. "But he is sweet on you. Have you no care for his sensibilities?"

"What utter nonsense," Sophie interjected. "Why should Jane concern herself with *his* sensibilities when *he* clearly didn't care one whit either for her safety or for that of the poor girl?"

"Honestly," Miss Matthews said, lifting her hands as though to deflect attention, "I could not care less if the man is sweet on me, or if I have hurt his tender sensibilities, or anything else."

"Of course you care," his mother said. "He's quite eligible, Jane, you mustn't forget that. I do hope you've not ruined your chances—"

"Ruined my chances? Good gracious, if rescuing that girl is enough to 'ruin my chances' I think I'm far better off being ruined. Particularly if Lord Eldredge is the sum total of my chances!"

The orange ball of fluff that was so often planted upon her lap chose that moment to jump up and resume its customary position. The animal's purrs reached Peter's ears from across the room. Gracious that animal could be loud when it wanted to be.

"Jane," his mother admonished. "You *are* here to find a husband, you know."

"But must I accept the first man who makes an offer? Even if he is entirely unacceptable?"

Makes an offer? Peter perked up at that. Had the cad already proposed without first speaking to him?

"You don't think he's so terrible, do you?" a bewildered Charlotte asked. "He is rather handsome, I believe, and he would be a fantastic match for nearly any lady—quite advantageous."

"You feel that every gentleman you see is rather handsome," Sophie countered.

"Well, he *is*. And he is a viscount. His peerage is one of the oldest and most respected in the kingdom, too, and has been in the same line for an age. He could hardly be better respected. And he's dashingly handsome on top of it all!"

"There are far more important matters to consider than how good looking a gentleman is when choosing a husband," Sophie said cut in quietly. "*If* one must choose a husband at all."

"Which," Mama interrupted with a raised brow, "any reasonable young lady must. You might take note of that yourself, dear." She gave Sophie a rather pointed look.

And then received six pairs of eyes rolling up toward the ceiling in return.

"Well you must. It's simply how it is done. But," Mama said, allowing a pregnant pause to fill the room, "I suppose it *would* be best for you to still be available on the marriage mart when your come-out ball arrives, Jane. It simply would not do to immediately follow that with an engagement ball. Or, heaven forbid, to have to put on the engagement ball *before* your come-out."

Miss Matthews exhaled an audible sigh of relief. "Precisely what I was thinking, Cousin Henrietta."

Precisely, indeed. What on earth had Eldredge done to inspire such obvious aversion in her that she would be relieved at that answer, and that she would give him the cut direct in public?

And, even more perplexing, why was he so damned pleased with that result, when he desired to see her married off sooner rather than later?

He must have growled out loud, because every eye in the room turned to face him.

"Oh, Peter," Mama said. "How long have you been standing there? Come in, come in. Take a seat here beside me, if you please."

The side of the love seat she had indicated would place him next to Miss Matthews. He felt the desire to groan again rather too keenly, but few options remained. "Ladies." He inclined his head to the room in general. "I trust you are enjoying yourselves this afternoon." Peter directed his statement toward the Marlborough sisters in an effort to avoid looking Miss Matthews in the eye.

His mother chose to answer for them all. "Why, yes. We're having a lovely discussion on the necessity of marriage. You had wonderful timing, son. I was hoping to learn which lovely young lady has caught your eye enough that you paid her a call today."

"Er...well, truth be told, I met with my solicitor this morning." Why could she not have given him a bit more time to come up with a better response?—one where she would not discover that he'd neglected to tell her everything accurately earlier.

"Oh," she said, disappointment ringing in the single syllable. "Well, you'll simply have to pay calls to two young ladies tomorrow afternoon then, since it's nearly time to dress for the evening. We mustn't be late for Lady Kearsey's entertainment, you know."

Peter dragged a hand through his hair. "Mama, I promised you I would do my best to find a bride this Season. I am doing so. I won't stand for you ordering me about in my own home in front of guests, however."

She gave him an imperious look. "As long as you are my son, I'll order you about on any matter which I feel to be in your best interest, and that is all there is to say on the subject. I daresay the Marlborough sisters have heard me give the lot of you far more blistering set-downs than that was."

Well, that was the truth. That didn't make it any better, though. He was the deuced Duke of Somerton, and his mother was treating him like a simpleton. Damn, if he wasn't going to allow it, too.

Mama stood and placed her embroidery down on the table next to her, then turned to the Marlborough sisters. "I do apologize, ladies. My son has proven himself tactless, and I'm unwilling to listen to any more of his excuses. Will we be seeing you two tonight, Miss Marlborough?"

The elder sister nodded. "Yes, Your Grace. Mother will be there with us."

"Excellent. If you'll excuse me, please." And then she swept through the open doorway and out of sight.

Blast it. He'd have to pay calls to *three* ladies tomorrow just to make it up to Mama for that one. The thought of just a single visit was enough to sour his stomach at the moment...but three? His mood turned dark, black. He wanted to plant his fist through a wall, or better yet, through Eldredge's face.

Not that Peter could blame the viscount for his current temper. Well, not entirely. Good Lord, he never lost his temper. That seemed to have changed drastically since the arrival of Miss Matthews.

Miss Marlborough stood, her face a full blush as she stared at him. "Theodora, we truly must be on our way now. Why, look at the time! Mother will be wondering what's taken us so long. Come along."

The tension in the room had grown so heavy it would take three burly men to lift it.

Miss Theodora frowned up at her older sister, seemingly oblivious to the tension bursting at the seams of the room. "But she won't expect us for at least another twenty minutes, Patience. Charlotte and I have yet to talk alone."

"You'll simply have to wait until tomorrow." Miss Marlborough gathered her reticule and hastily put her gloves back on her hands. "We must be on our way. I'm truly sorry ladies. Your Grace." She executed a brief and clumsy curtsy, and half-dragged her younger sister behind her out the door.

Peter couldn't very well blame the chit for wanting out of his presence. In his current state of mind, he would much prefer not to be left in a room with himself, were such a feat possible.

His sisters and Miss Matthews said their goodbyes to the Marlboroughs, and then took their leave of him as well. "We really must dress for the evening, ladies," Sophie said. "And Char, do try not to sulk over the brief visit with Theodora. You see her nearly every day. It leaves you seeming rather petulant and missish when you pout like that."

"I'm not pouting. It isn't my fault that *he*," Charlotte said with a huff and a head-jerk in his direction, "is in such a foul mood to the point that we could barely speak with each other at all."

Peter bit his tongue. The last thing he needed now was to have his sisters band together against him. Was it not enough to have his mother scold him a troublesome child in front of people outside the immediate family?

"Nevertheless," Sophie said, "we should all be on our way." She shooed Charlotte into the hall with Miss Matthews following behind a bit more leisurely.

"Miss Matthews, I require a word with you."

Damnation. Stopping her had certainly not been his plan, but the words were out of his mouth before he could stop himself.

She slowed and faced him. "Your Grace?" He couldn't decide if apprehension or aversion was the more dominant feature on her countenance. Either way, she stopped.

Sophie sent him an accusing glance over her shoulder before slipping up the stairs and out of sight.

And now—now he needed to determine what on earth to say to the woman whose cat was rubbing figure-eights between her legs and pushing its head against the inside hem of her dress.

"You...you were quite brave to face a charging horse to save that girl today."

"Thank you." Her eyes squinted and flashed as she stared up at him and her hands fidgeted before her, clutching and shifting a fan back and forth between them.

Her nerves were enough to drive him to distraction. He wanted to take the fan from her and entwine his hands with hers. And *that* only left him annoyed with himself for experiencing such a bothersome reaction to such a thoroughly inappropriate lady.

"You will refrain from acting in such a stupid manner in the future," he snapped before he could think better of it. "Allow someone with more experience handling horses to see to them. You might have been hurt."

Oh, blast. Now he had proved himself a fool.

"*Stupid*, Your Grace?" She glared at him with a stare that would melt steel. "You dare to call me stupid? I'll have you know that while my parents were unable to afford to pay for my education, I was nevertheless educated as well as any daughter of any peer."

Never mind the fact that she'd called him asinine only hours previously. She had clearly forgotten as much.

Before he could retract her statement, she advanced upon him. Within mere seconds, she stood toe-to-toe with him, pushing a finger into his chest to punctuate her words. "No one—not even a *bloody duke*—calls me stupid, Your Grace."

"I did not—"

"You most certainly *did* call me stupid." She poked his chest again, causing him to take a step back toward the hearth. "And if it ever happens again, you'll be quite sorry. I'll be certain of it."

He narrowed his eyes. "You dare to threaten me?"

"Oh, you'd better believe I'm threatening you. I am *not* intimidated by you, no matter how hard you try."

Good God, her brown eyes had darkened so much he thought them fully black. What a bewilderingly sultry sight. The urge to kiss her again consumed him, deeper, harder than the first time. He settled for grasping her hand that was, yet again, poking him in the chest to stop her assault.

"You," he said, his voice low, menacing, "will do as you're told. Which means you will leave the heroics to someone better qualified for the task than yourself from this point forward."

The need to argue with him made itself clear in the fire blazing in her eyes, but she said nothing else when he squeezed tighter against her arm. Perhaps too tight. Devil take it. A single tear pooled in her eye but neglected to spill over.

At least she kept it from falling. He could handle virtually any situation, but a woman's tears almost always proved to be his undoing.

He loosened his grip but didn't release her. Not yet. He couldn't make himself break off that limited contact, no matter how inappropriate it was of him. "Have I made myself perfectly clear, Miss Matthews?"

"Yes, *Your Grace*," she ground out through clenched teeth.

"Good. You may go."

She tugged against him, but he still held her tight enough that she couldn't remove herself from his grip. "Kindly unhand me, and I'll be glad to do just that."

The look in her eyes nearly brought him to his knees—something between disgust and hatred, but not squarely on either end of the spectrum. He jerked his hand away from her.

She spun on her heels and fled from the room, racing up the stairs like her life depended upon it.

Christ above, he was everything she'd called him and worse. Never in his life had he been such a bumbling idiot. "Miss Matthews?" he called after her.

While she neither faced him nor responded, she did at least stop her progress, one hand clenching the stair rail so tightly that her knuckles turned white.

"I look forward to seeing you this evening."

A single, curt nod of her head was the last thing he saw before she disappeared up the stairs and around a corner.

DRAWERS STOOD NO chance against Jane's mood. She pulled them open with such force that one of them pulled completely free and fell clanging to the floor, spilling its contents as it went. Well, that was certainly one way of removing her belongings. Of course, there was the entire dressing room full of things which would need to be pulled free and packed.

Perhaps she should do more of the same. It had felt rather good, after all.

Moving to an armoire in her closet, she threw the door open and reveled in the noise as it banged against the wall. It was a good sound. Loud and violent, and just a touch jarring. Suited her at the moment quite well.

"Miss, is there something I can help you find?" asked Meg, who had just rushed into the dressing room with wide eyes. "I am certain that if you only ask, I'll know precisely where to find it, ma'am." The young maid scurried about behind her, putting pieces of furniture back to their rightful positions and refolding articles of clothing she had strewn about willy-nilly in her tirade.

Ha! If only the maid could find where Jane had misplaced her mind when she'd agreed to her mother's idea of sending her to Town for the Season. Then, perhaps, Jane might find a use for having a personal servant at her beck and call. Instead, now as ever, poor Meg was merely a nuisance. An aggravation. One more symbol of the *inferiority* of Jane's birth, or at least the inferiority a certain duke-who-shall-remain-nameless insisted to be in existence.

And he, of course, was perfect. High-in-the-instep. Superior.

A perfectly superior pain in the arse might be a better fit.

Meg placed a stack of neatly folded clothes back into the drawer Jane had just painstakingly unpacked. All right. *Fine.* She could concede that there had been nothing painstaking about the process. But she *had* just removed the dratted articles in the first place, and if she wanted them in the drawer, she would have left them there in the first place.

Calm down. Breathe. Meg was simply attempting to do her job. She did not deserve the blistering retort Jane had so nearly delivered.

That retort belonged to no one but Meg's employer.

"Meg, do be a dear and leave things as I have them, please."

"Leave them, miss? I don't understand." She continued to fold and stack the clothes into perfect, neat little stacks.

"I mean I don't want you to clean up after me. Please cease immediately." *Before I rip them from your hands.* Somehow, Jane kept that last little bit to herself. She prayed for patience. It simply wouldn't do to attack the servant for the sins of her master—the bloody man who had the audacity to call her stupid.

She would show him. He could not order her about, no matter how much higher he ranked within the ton than she.

"I'm terribly sorry, ma'am, but I'm a bit confused." Meg still held the shift she had been folding loosely in her hands, but at least she had stopped working for the moment. "Are you going somewhere? Might I help you to pack?"

There was a thought. "Yes, fine. Will you go and fetch a trunk, please?"

"Of course. But miss, where are you going? Her Grace sent me to help you dress for the evening—for the entertainment at Lady Kearsey's house. Are you not going?"

"No. I'm not." Not that it was any of Meg's business. "Please see to fetching a trunk immediately." The servant set the garment she was holding down and turned to do her bidding. "Oh, and Meg? Please don't mention this to anyone. Not yet, at least."

"No one, ma'am? But I'll need a footman to carry a trunk up the stairs for me."

Jane cringed at the headache building in her temples. *Patience. Time to exercise patience.* "No one but a single footman, then, and swear him to secrecy as well. Do please hurry."

Once Meg finally scurried away, Jane had a moment to think. If only she'd made more progress toward opening her shop. That would at least give her somewhere to go, a way to earn at least a meager living. But she had yet to even find a solicitor to aid her in the process.

Granted, she had done a good deal to learn about her competition, and she had studied the stitchery in the gowns Miss Jenkins had made for her. That was some progress, though not nearly as much as she would have liked.

But she needed a storefront. She needed a place to set up her business, preferably with living quarters attached.

Where would she go now?

Where *could* she go?

Only one thing was certain—absolutely certain, beyond any shadow of a doubt. She wouldn't stay one more night in the same home as His Grace, the haughty, repugnant tyrant who couldn't lower himself enough to cease looking down his nose upon her.

A commotion sounded at the doorway to her chamber. Good. Meg and the footman must be bringing a trunk in so she could finish her packing and leave before someone tried to stop her. Jane hated to hurt Cousin Henrietta, and she dreaded no longer having the companionship of Sophie and Charlotte...but what could be done for it?

"Pardon me. Let me through, please."

Oh dear. That was no footman. And it was definitely not Meg, either.

Drat.

Sophie burst through the door to Jane's dressing room and planted her fists against her hips, wearing a lovely blue evening gown and with her hair out of sorts, as though she had gotten up in the middle of having her hair coiffed for the night. "What, pray tell, is the meaning of all of this?" She gestured with one hand toward the mess about the floor, then looked over her shoulder at the footman standing behind her, sheepishly carrying a single, rather large trunk.

Good gracious, she did not have time for all of this. She sent a glare in Meg's direction, who refused to meet her eyes, then returned her attention to Sophie. "What does it look like?"

"It looks like you're running away, and I, for one, will have none of it." Sophie looked behind her at the two servants eagerly listening in to their conversation. "Leave us."

"Yes, my lady." They bobbed their bow and curtsy and slunk away, the footman taking the trunk with them.

"Whatever has gotten into you, Jane?" Sophie walked over to her, took one hand into her own, and pulled her down to a settee. "What on earth could have brought you to this?"

Jane studiously avoided meeting her eyes. "I don't particularly care to discuss it at the moment."

"Too bad. You'll tell me now, and that's all there is to it." She frowned when Jane didn't immediately respond. "It was Peter, wasn't it? I just *knew* he was up to something when he was eavesdropping on us in the drawing room earlier. And then when he kept you behind…well, out with it."

Jane merely shook her head. Sophie narrowed her eyes at her. Drat, she mustn't be hiding the truth very well. "You will learn, if you haven't already done so, that there can be no secrets kept from me. Not for long, at least." Sophie lifted a single eyebrow and inclined her head in a tell-me-or-else sort of manner. "I have my ways."

"Well, you'll just have to use one of your ways, then. I'm not giving in so easily."

"He kissed you."

It sounded like an accusation. "What? Really…" Had Sophie somehow seen them that night in the garden? And she had *thought* they were discussing the conversation that occurred only moments ago in the drawing room.

"I knew it! He did kiss you."

"No, no he didn't kiss me."

Sophie frowned. "He did so. Your eyes told me the truth, so it won't do you any good to try to lie to me. I'll see straight through you. He kissed you and you *enjoyed* it."

Jane knit her brows together and gave her friend the fiercest frown she could muster. Then she got up and started to pull items from drawers and closets again. "You have the strangest ideas, Sophie. If your mother knew what we were discussing..."

"But she won't know, will she? Besides, it's perfectly clear that you not only enjoyed it when Peter kissed you, you want him to kiss you again. Plain as day on your face."

"Humph." Jane shook her head to herself. Since when was that the best retort she could manage? "Whether your brother kissed me or not is entirely irrelevant. I'm leaving." The unmentionables in her hands were tangled into a knot, so she tossed them aside.

"Why?" Sophie shot back.

"What do you mean, 'why'?"

"I mean why? Why are you leaving? Why are you running away from him?" She stood and began to replace all of Jane's belongings in their proper drawers and cabinets, utterly ignoring the severe scowl Jane gave her for doing so.

"Would you please stop that?" Jane asked in an almost commanding tone as she pulled her garments free from Sophie's grasp.

"No. Answer me." The infuriating woman picked up another stack and tossed it into the armoire before slamming the door shut.

"Answer what?" Jane threw the door open and pulled the stack out again, tossing it onto the floor alongside the majority of the destructed dressing room's contents. "I'll answer you when you ask me a reasonable question and not a moment before."

"And I'll ask you a reasonable question when you behave like a reasonable person! You, my friend, are no coward. You proved that this afternoon. Why on earth are you behaving like one now?"

"I'm not. You're behaving like a shrew, poking your nose into my business." Jane pulled another stack of clothes from Sophie's hands, sending most of them falling to the floor—other than the dress that each of them had a hand fully grasping. "Let go."

"No. Tell me why you're running from my brother, when it is perfectly clear that you are madly in love with him." She tugged at the dress, pulling Jane closer to her.

Ha! In love with that rude, overbearing, condescending boor? Never.

"I most certainly am not," she said and returned the tug. "Unhand my dress. You'll ruin it."

"You can fix it later. We all know you're more than capable of that, even if you are incapable of giving an answer to a simple question."

"Why on earth would you possibly think I'm in love with him? I've never heard anything more ludicrous in my entire life."

"Then why are you nearly in tears? You love him, and you cannot stand it."

"I'm not about to cry," she said before she felt the sting of hot tears pouring down her cheeks. "Oh, drat!"

"I told you."

"You are most definitely not helping anything at the moment, Sophie." Could she possibly love him? Impossible. He constantly insisted on putting her in her place, he tried to intimidate her at every turn—and he hated Mr. Cuddlesworth! She could think of no man she wanted to love less than the Duke of Somerton.

No, it was out of the question. She was simply so...so...so mad at the man. Nothing more.

"Nevertheless, you are crying, and it is clearly about Peter. So what is it?" Again, Sophie led her to the settee to sit—but only after shoving piles of tossed about clothing off of it. "Tell me. Why are you leaving?"

"Because he's horrible to me. He called me stupid today, and I will not—*ever*—be called stupid. Not by any man. I won't stand for it, for the way he speaks down to me, the way he does everything possible to even avoid looking at me. It's simply more than I can bear."

"He would never intend to hurt you. I can promise you that." Sophie patted the back of her hand, calming and soothing. "Surely he's just unaware of his behavior. He's always doing things that seem to contradict what he really feels and wants. Terrible habit, that." Her eyes took on an almost wistful gaze, staring off into nothing.

"You only think that of him because he is your brother."

"Well—as you said, he *is* my brother. I love him. And because I love him and have known him my entire life, I can assure you that he's not truly a horrible man. Not at all. He loves his family and works very hard to keep us all happy and comfortable. Perhaps he is simply—a bit naïve about how he is making you feel?"

"That's no excuse," Jane mumbled, then sniffled and used a random garment to dry her tears.

"No. But it's also no reason to run away. Besides, whatever would you do? You are a single woman in London. There are only so many options, my dear, and none of them are acceptable."

"One of them is," she muttered beneath her breath.

Again Sophie's eyes narrowed into her shrewd, entirely too perceptive gaze. "What did you say?"

Double drat. When would she ever learn to keep her mouth shut when she good and well needed to keep it shut?

"Nothing."

"Stop lying. It is unattractive. You said one option was acceptable. Tell me what you meant."

"Er..."

"Don't you dare try to avoid this, Jane. Answer me."

"I could...I could open my own modiste business. I could sew to make my living." Please, let Sophie drop it now.

A moment passed in silence, then, "A modiste shop? Oh, that would be *perfect* for you!" Sophie's cobalt blue eyes sparkled with mischief. "But now is not the time. You need to face Peter instead of running away from him. Besides, your come-out ball is just around the corner. You couldn't disappoint Mama like that. Let us get through this, and then we'll see what's to be done. I'll help you."

"You'll help me? How?"

"Well, have you found a solicitor yet? I believe I know of a few gentlemen who could help. And perhaps you'll need a contributor—you know, financially. I can help with that, too."

"Oh, no. I could never take your money. I have enough on my own."

Sophie studied her for a moment and then nodded briskly. "Very well. And the solicitor?"

"I would gladly appreciate your suggestions in that area."

"Excellent. Then it's settled."

"Really? You'll help me do it. Why?"

"Because frankly, no woman should have to marry simply because that is the way of things. If you want to run a modiste shop, I'll do anything I can to assist you in that endeavor." Sophie stood and looked about at the massive mess in Jane's dressing room. "I suggest you allow Meg to help you dress. That is, if she can find something appropriate in all of *this*. We should be downstairs soon, or Mama will come up to see what's causing the delay."

With a grin as wide as the sea, Sophie left.

Ten

THE ONE MAN in all of England Jane most wanted to strangle was the one man who refused to leave her side the entire evening.

As expected, word of her misadventures in Hyde Park had traveled through the *ton* faster than one could sneeze. She was the talk of Town—quite literally.

Throughout Lady Kearsey's drawing room, interspersed groups of ladies and gentlemen stood whispering with their heads close together while pointing or passing a nod in her direction. Occasionally, their whispers rose in pitch and carried over the air to where she could hear. No one, it seemed, had anything to discuss that evening other than Miss Jane Matthews dashing before a mad horse—not to mention the tales of her rather public set-down of Lord Eldredge which followed.

Charlotte made her way with Lord Naismith, one of the many men of the *beau monde* who was currently paying her court, through the crush of the grand drawing room with a single glass of lemonade to where Jane was flanked on either side by Sophie and the blasted duke.

"I daresay if you hadn't already caused a splash with the *ton*, Jane, this would certainly be enough to manage the feat. Everyone I passed along the way was commending your bravery—and commenting a touch on your audacity, too, but not enough to truly worry about. That part will pass over in no time." Charlotte brushed a single lock of her auburn curls away from her face and tucked it securely behind her ear. "The gossips will undoubtedly have some new *on dit* to discuss by tomorrow, at the very latest, after tonight's balls."

"I suppose it's good I'm not counting on being the height of gossip, then, if they will move on so soon," Jane replied drolly. "But really, I wish they would not all point and whisper so. It makes me uncomfortable."

Somerton tilted his head to the side to stare more fully at her. "I would not expect you to care what was said about you, Miss Matthews. You always seem to do or say whatever is on your mind, irrespective of the consequences." He looked away from her and scanned the crowd. "If you did not want the attention, I'd think you might learn to act and speak with a hint more decorum."

"Is that so?" Jane lifted a brow. Two could play his game. "And if you intended to do as your mother expects of you and find a bride, I'd think you might expend your energies in such a manner instead of spending the entire evening in the company of your sisters and me."

"Obviously it *is* so, ma'am, as you've just shown everyone standing within earshot." He indicated Lord Naismith, standing with eyes wide next to Charlotte, whom Jane had thoroughly forgotten was there. Drat. The duke kept his voice low and gentle—misleadingly so, in fact. "And it's also true that you insist on turning the tables upon me in order to avoid paying any heed to your own flaws. You might consider spending some time on self-reflection. It would do you a world of good. And to answer your earlier question—or accusation, as that might be more appropriate, considering the nature of the words—I've decided that *someone* needs to protect you from yourself because of your inability to bite your tongue as you ought."

Oh, the nerve of the man. "It would likewise do *you* a world of good to remember there are other people in your life, people who have feelings and minds of their own and therefore do not need to be ordered about constantly." Unlike him, Jane made no effort at keeping quiet. It would serve the blasted man right to have a bit of scandal come down upon him. Maybe it would help him relax. "But why would you care about that? You are the *Duke of Somerton.* Everyone else in the world is too far beneath your touch to deserve even your notice. Heaven forbid you grant someone the unrealistic concession of thinking for themselves and making their own decisions."

During their argument, Sophie, Charlotte, and Lord Naismith had slowly backed away. Charlotte whispered something that sounded like, "Oh, dear, I've never heard anyone speak to Peter in such a manner," but Jane couldn't be entirely certain because of the fury pounding through the vein in her temple.

Sophie, ever clear-headed, interjected, "Oh, look, Charlotte. I believe Lady Rowland and her daughters are over there by the window. We haven't seen them in an age or two. Lord Naismith, would you be so kind as to escort us over to speak with them?"

Without waiting for a response from either of her companions, she took up Naismith's arm in one hand, grabbed Charlotte's hand with the other, and then led them away.

Even with the three of them gone, however, the duke and Jane retained an audience. A good quarter of the room were listening intently, peeking over their shoulders at intervals to see the display, and not entirely (or rather, not at all) trying to hide their attempts at eavesdropping. If the gossips would have moved on to something juicier by the next day, she and Somerton were clearly making certain nothing of the sort would happen.

"I'm a tyrant, am I? A dictator?" Somehow, his voice dropped even lower and he leaned in toward Jane, ensuring that no one could hear him but her. "And how could you believe yourself to be beneath my touch—you, whom I touched most inappropriately only a brief time ago? Or have you already forgotten my kiss?"

Heat rushed to her cheeks at the memory, and it only intensified at the thought that anyone might overhear their discussion.

She wanted to be anywhere but where she was at the moment, with him so close the heat of his body enveloped her like a cocoon. So close his breath against her ear fanned over her ear. So close his sandalwood scent invaded her and took root, like it had been burned for eternity into her nostrils. So close the passion building in his darkened eyes threatened to consume her. So close she couldn't form a coherent thought if her life depended upon it.

"Have you? Have you forgotten?" Somerton moved away again, far enough she could regain some small piece of her sanity. "Because I promise you, I have not."

His words poured through her and traveled straight to her most intimate places. Her body tugged and pulled, straining as though to betray her.

Jane shifted from foot to foot, trying to put at least a moderate distance between them. "You are behaving most inappropriately, sir," she mumbled. But gracious heavens above, she hoped he wouldn't stop. What a brazen thought!

"And you changed the subject yet again, ma'am." Disdain traveled from his tongue in rivers.

The clang of spoon against glass rang through the crowded drawing room, and Lady Kearsey's voice rang out above the crowd, requesting they all take their seats immediately. Thank goodness. The concert would finally begin, and perhaps she could remove herself from this infernal man's presence.

"Shall we?" he asked as he placed her hand against his arm and held it there in a manner which brooked no argument.

Drat. Perhaps not, then.

He led her to a position a third of the way from the front and slightly to one side, waiting until she was positioned before taking his seat directly beside her.

Jane looked about, searching for or Sophie or Esther's faces amongst the sea of London's elite. Even Cousin Henrietta would do, or perhaps Charlotte. For that matter, she would settle for one of the infernal gentleman admirers who so often plagued her with their attentions of late. Anyone to ease the discomfort of spending the rest of the evening in such close proximity to this particular man. For all she knew, he quite possibly would prove himself to be her nemesis, if tonight acted as a precursor for their future engagements.

Search as she might, she found no one to alleviate her discomfiture.

Oh, there were plenty of onlookers nearby, hoping (by the looks upon their faces) to catch any stray comments uttered between the two. She imagined they intended to rush off to the nearest gossip so hopefully they could be the first to reveal the latest tidbits. But when Jane looked to a few of them—women with whom she had at least an acquaintance—they all smiled condescendingly at her and turned away.

Double drat. She supposed now she was truly on her own with him.

If only the concert were nearly finished instead of only just beginning.

Jane looked down at the hand printed program for the evening and groaned. A pianist would start the evening, followed by a string quartet, and then an Italian soprano would close. Each of them would perform a minimum of five pieces each...with the soprano performing six. Including parts of *The Messiah*.

It would be an interminably long evening, indeed.

She settled in and tried to ignore the heat radiating from his leg, which he had positioned uncomfortably close to her own.

With no luck.

In love with him, indeed. That just went to prove that Sophie did not know everything, even when she thought she did.

IN THE LAST weeks, Utley had become quite the sneak. He'd skulked about Town, keeping an eye on Somerton and his Miss Matthews and learning of their comings and goings. He'd even spied on the other Hardwickes, as dull and dreary as such a thing might be. The only member of the family Utley had not been able to track handily was Lord Neil Hardwicke, but he was clearly busy sowing his wild oats and not doing anything of interest.

He hadn't stopped with his spying there, though. Oh, no. There were far too many things he needed to sort out in the midst of his planning.

And so, at the moment, he stood outside Lady Kearsey's townhouse (or crouched in the bushes, if one wanted to be entirely accurate), waiting for one invited guest in particular to step outside.

Surely, the biddy would follow her usual pattern and slip out before the close of the festivities—rushing off to spread her gossip as fast and as far as she could. Utley needn't wait much longer. Which was good, since his thighs were starting to burn from being in the same position for so long.

Finally, the grand doors pushed open, and the short, squat woman he'd been waiting for waddled down the stairs. She took off on foot down the street, not getting into one of the waiting carriages that had begun to reconvene.

Utley dusted himself off and started after her. They had business matters to discuss.

THIS SEASON, HIS first on the marriage mart in years, was quickly becoming an abysmal failure on his part, at least in Mama's opinion. Peter, however, thought the Season to be progressing rather swimmingly, if one should ask him.

Not that Mama cared for his particular opinions on the matter.

Her largest concern was that he was spending far too much time plastered to Miss Matthews's side and far too little time actually making any sort of effort toward finding a new wife.

Of course, he *had* promised to do the latter more so than the former, but one could argue that to be rather beside the point.

In paying his attentions to Miss Matthews, Peter was flabbergasted to discover that she was rather intelligent, interesting, and far more engaging company than the simpering young misses he would otherwise be required to dance with at the balls.

Which was why, on this evening at Lord and Lady Blacknell's ball, he had already danced with Miss Matthews once and had secured the first waltz with her, as well.

He had discovered four nights previously, at Lady Kearsey's concert, that he enjoyed antagonizing the poor woman rather more than he ought. There was something utterly fascinating about her when she glared at him, eyes full of passion and heat—which was invariably followed by the most delightful and ravishing blush he had ever seen.

It didn't hurt matters, either, that by staying so close by her side, Miss Matthews seemed to have fewer gentlemen callers paying her court. Not only that, but nearly all of the ladies (both eligible and otherwise) who'd been haunting Peter at these functions had ceased casting their looks in his direction.

He cared not whether this was due to the gossips assuming he and Miss Matthews were soon to have an arrangement or not. What the *ton* assumed meant nothing to him. He only hoped Miss Matthews felt the same about such matters.

If the onlookers at the Blacknell soiree weren't watching them so closely, he might even request her hand for a third set—but as things stood, that would be thoroughly out of the question. Doing so, he'd be forced to offer for her after such a show of preferential treatment—and clearly, neither of them wanted *that* to come to pass.

Even if they did, Mama would throw a fit of pique. Miss Matthews's come-out ball, for which his mother had been working tirelessly on the preparations, was to occur in only three more days. She couldn't have even a hint of a betrothal floating about.

As Mama said, it just *would not do.*

So he would have to settle for his two dances—with one being a waltz, where he could revel in the feel of her luscious curves pressed against his length, even if only for a brief span of time.

Thankfully, when they had danced earlier in the evening, she had maintained civility with him. That was a step forward. Actually, it proved they had traveled several steps in the few days' time since the concert.

Once the concert had begun, she had stared straight ahead at the performers and never once turned her head to look at him, not even when he spoke to her. During the carriage ride home, she had glared out the window to the darkened streets of Mayfair instead of allowing even a tiny glimpse in his direction.

Yes, being on speaking terms with Miss Matthews this evening had proven to be a vast improvement over their previous outing. One that he oddly desired to improve upon even more than what he already had done.

The upcoming waltz should give him just that opportunity—an entire set with her drawn tight in his embrace, where she could neither escape nor ignore him.

At the moment, however, he was dancing a quadrille with Lady Helene Fewster, an eighteen-year-old debutante and the eldest daughter of the Marquess of Oldham. The chit was everything Peter had intended to avoid as much as possible this Season.

He should have forced Neil into dancing with her, since the youngest Hardwicke brother had emerged from his cocoon of a bedchamber just in time for Mama to snag him and drag him along. It would serve Neil right to spend a dreary half hour in the company of this chit fresh from the schoolroom and practically still in leading strings—and an altogether dull chit at that. Why should Neil, who could almost never be bothered to show his face before the sun was making its descent from the sky—reveling in his life of debauchery, it seemed—be allowed to dance with Miss Matthews while Peter was stuck listening to such drivel?

She seemed to have nothing more in her head than a rather long list of gentlemen her parents deemed eligible, and therefore, worthy of her attention and pursuit. Frankly, it was rather lowering to discover himself placed on the same list as some of the halfwits she'd named thus far. When they turned another figure of the dance, Peter found himself face-to-face with Lady Helene again.

"Might you point out Lord Prescott to me, sir? Mother insisted I should find a way to obtain an introduction to him, even though it is usually done the other way around."

Prescott? Peter blanched. "Of course, ma'am. As soon as he makes his entrance this evening, I am certain you will recognize him immediately. He will be the gentleman gazing at his own reflection in every available surface."

Blast. It seemed he had caught Miss Matthews's penchant for speaking whatever passed through his mind without thinking first. But truthfully, the man was the biggest spendthrift in the *beau monde*, and an utter dandy to boot. How Lady Oldham thought Prescott should be even in the same league as he, Peter would never understand.

"Oh. I see." The figures of the quadrille sent them away from each other for several bars, so he was pleasantly spared from any more of her drivel for the moment.

Even after they came back together, Lady Helene remained silent. He supposed that if he must make an arse of himself, at least it had come to serve a good purpose. Perhaps he had done quite enough with that solitary comment to effectively remove himself from Lady Oldham's list of potential suitors for her daughter. He would much prefer to not be grouped alongside men such as Prescott—especially when said list-maker would encourage her daughter to go so far outside the realm of the genteel by seeking her own introductions.

Now, if only the music would come to a close.

Only a few (admittedly silent and uncomfortable) moments later, his prayers were answered as the quadrille trilled to a finish. Peter scanned the walls and found Lady Oldham right where they had left her. He escorted Lady Helene back to the marchioness's side, trying not to make his rush to be rid of her overtly obvious.

"Thank you, my lady," he said as he bowed to them both. "It was a pleasure." He pleaded with God not to smite him down on the spot for such an outright lie.

They merely nodded, Lady Helene with a look of displeasure floating in her eyes, so he made his escape and searched for Miss Matthews. Their waltz was next.

And from the state of his stomach, he was fairly certain it must also be the dinner dance. Even better.

She stood across the ballroom, near an alcove that jutted out toward the gardens, surrounded by his entire family—or at least, all the members of his family who were present for the ball. Her smile was radiant, and it quickly spread to all around her.

Montague, a widower seeking a new bride to care for his two small children—and a rather eligible one, at that, being a wealthy viscount with multiple country estates spread through the kingdom—had just made his way over to their group before Peter arrived.

Deuce take it, the man would be a good match for Miss Matthews. Not only that, but she would likely be just the type of female he would seek out. A touch older than a typical debutante. Familiar and comfortable with country life. Bubbly and vivacious. Good with children. Brave, even if a touch foolhardy.

Evidently, Montague agreed with his assessment. By the time Peter arrived at their group, Montague was saying, "Miss Matthews, I wonder if I might be so bold as to ask you to waltz with me. If, of course, you haven't already promised your hand to another."

"She has," Peter said, a bit more abrupt and menacing than he intended. "Miss Matthews will waltz with me this set."

The woman in question scowled at him for the briefest moment—so short a time, in fact, that Peter was sure no one else had noticed her reaction. It was intended solely for his eyes.

"That is true, Lord Montague," Miss Matthews said, with a hint of both consolation and aggravation in her tone. "However, if you can wait until the next waltz—the first after dinner—I would be most happy to oblige."

"I'll await my turn with much anticipation, then, ma'am."

Peter felt an intense desire to plant the man a facer for some undefined reason. Surely he was not *jealous* of the man. Envy over Miss Matthews? For what reason? The thought was ludicrous— almost laughable.

Almost.

But the fact remained that Peter was drawn to this woman, even if he had no understanding of why such a thing should be.

He must be suffering from an acute case of misguided lust. Nothing else could explain the sudden need to take her into his arms and whisk her away from any other man.

Finally, after what seemed ages but was likely only a moment or two, Montague inclined his head, first to Miss Matthews and the other females, then to Peter, and then he backed away.

At last, he could touch her again without worrying about who might see. He could hold her close and smell the faint hint of peaches and woman that followed her about, wafting in her path, leaving him aching to taste.

It would be thirty minutes of torture and pleasure, all combined in one thoroughly aggravating woman.

He held out a hand to her, ignoring his mother, sisters, and brother, and focusing only on her. "I believe this is my dance."

She hesitated for the briefest moment, but long enough that he worried she would change her mind and refuse him. Which, he must admit, she quite possibly could—he often thought she loved to goad him as much as he enjoyed pricking at her temper.

But she placed her hand in the crook of his arm and allowed him to escort her to their place on the dance floor. Something twinkled in her eyes, lending them a sense of mischief.

A very intriguing, even intoxicating mischief.

He took her into his arms with neither saying a word, and the music began. They swirled about the room, and everything but the two of them and that moment faded into the background.

"YOU WALTZ VERY well, Your Grace." Jane's heart beat a frantic pace as they traversed the ballroom. Between the music and the proximity of him, she had somehow lost control over her body's reactions.

"Peter," he said quietly. That odd look was back in his eyes—the look he'd been giving her since the concert a few evenings before. "Call me Peter."

"All right. You waltz very well, Peter. It surprises me a bit since it is rather a new dance, and your sisters tell me you haven't been to many balls in recent years."

Everything between them had been odd since that night, in fact. He had kept his promise—or had it been a threat?—of staying close to her. But the animosity between them had settled, at least for the most part.

Instead, a new tension existed. No—she had better be out with the truth of it. She was only lying to herself. This tension wasn't new. Far from it, in fact. It had been there since the very first ball of the Season. Ever since he had kissed her in the gardens.

Only now, it had intensified.

When they were in each other's presence, heat radiated between them and threatened to burn her at the core. She had the simultaneous desires in his presence to run as far from him as possible and to get as near as possible. The two ideas constantly warred with each other to dominate.

Right this moment, in fact, this tension took on new proportions. There was something about their nearness as they waltzed, with his arm about her waist and his hand holding her hand—with their bodies brushing against each other, his hard planes and angles firm against her softer, smoother curves.

It was a miracle she could breathe.

Then he laughed at her with his eyes. That joy in his eyes was such a lovely change from the hard, cold look they so often held when he looked upon her.

But, oh dear, she must have been woolgathering. Drat, why could she not keep her head about her when she was with him?

"I apologize. What did you say?" Heat rose in Jane's face, and she had absolutely no means to stop it. "I was woolgathering, I suppose."

"I can see that." He grinned, a wolfish, amused sort of grin with a sparkle in his eye. "I said that my sisters are correct. Since Mary passed, I have rarely gone to balls other than when Mama has dragged me. Until this Season, that is."

"Mary was your wife? Sarah and Joshua's mother?" Such a very sad thing for those children to lose their mother while they were still so young. Jane had grown quite fond of them in her time in London—Sarah, in particular. The little girl was a treasure.

"Yes. She was my duchess." Peter's eyes lost their laughter, and she longed for it to return.

"I'm so sorry. I didn't mean to upset you." Even his arms had tightened about her a little. "You must have loved her very much."

His eyes became vacant, a bit distant. Cold. "No. We didn't have a love match."

"Oh." Jane looked away. What else could she say?

"We married out of...out of necessity."

"She was with child?" Jane bit down on her lip and fought to hide the shock from her face, though it was a hopeless cause.

"No. Not with child. But she faced ruin." Peter's face had blackened with anger.

She wanted desperately to change the subject to something happier, something less painful for him. Her curiosity, however, threatened to eat at her until she discovered the part of the story left untold. Peter—the perfect, unfailing duke who never did anything improper—had caused his wife's ruin and was forced into a loveless marriage in order to protect her?

Surely Sophie would know the details, so Jane only said, "Oh." No need to disturb him further when she had other sources to ease her curiosity. Now she merely needed to contain it until she could corner her friend and wheedle her for everything she knew.

Several moments passed with neither speaking again, before Peter asked, "And where did you learn to dance, Miss Matthews?"

"Jane." If she could lose the formality with him, he should do the same. "I learned at home in Whitstable. We had some community gatherings with dancing and games and the like. Or occasionally, Lady Hinkley invited me to accompany her and her daughters to an entertainment in Canterbury or some other nearby village."

"You are friendly with a Viscount Hinkley's family? I would imagine very few peers live near Whitstable." Some of the anger had finally begun to dissipate from his face and he relaxed a bit against her.

"Yes. Lord and Lady Hinkley allowed me to do a great deal with their daughters as we grew up. I even took lessons from their governess alongside them."

He lifted a brow. "That was very generous of them."

"I paid my own way. It was not charity." She bristled at the defensive sound of her own words.

"I never assumed otherwise. And how, pray tell, did you afford to pay for your lessons? I imagine, based on the expense of my sisters' governess, it would be difficult for a country vicar's daughter to manage."

Could he truly be interested?

But there was nothing he could gain from such knowledge. No reason for him to ask other than his own interest or perhaps a healthy dose of curiosity. She might as well tell him, since no harm could come from it. "I sewed."

"Sewed? Well, of course. I assume it would be imperative for ladies of the gentry to have such a skill. But really, how could you afford an education through sewing for your family?"

"Well, that *would* be quite a feat, wouldn't it?" She laughed at the impossibility of the thought. "But I sewed for far more than only my family. Lady Hinkley hired me to sew garments for her and her daughters, since we lived so far from London and the modistes here. I sewed for Mrs. Zachariah once her arthritis became too painful for her to handle the needle and thread. Before long, word of my skills spread through the village and I had developed quite a patronage for my sewing."

"You are rather skilled with your needles, then. But if you have such talent, why on earth did you arrive in London in those...er...well, those rags?"

Jane grinned. "You may have noticed that Mr. Cuddlesworth tends to pull at my clothing with his claws. He doesn't mean to be destructive—not truly—but it's simply how he is."

Peter's jaw dropped a bit over that statement. "Your cat? You claim to know what your cat intends to do and what he doesn't?"

"Of course." Good grief, Mr. Cuddlesworth had been with her for years. She'd be a truly poor companion for him if she didn't understand him by now.

"But it's an animal. It can't speak."

"Of course he can't speak. But he lets me know what he's thinking and feeling—what he likes and dislikes." How obtuse could the man be?

"I see." The furrow of his brow told her the opposite of his words, but she decided to let that pass. At least for now. "But back to your sewing—after you completed your education, did you continue to sew for the ladies?"

"Of course, I did. The ladies in Whitstable still needed gowns. None of that changed just because I'd finished with my schooling."

Peter narrowed his eyes shrewdly. "So what's happened to the money you earned from that work? Have you used it to help your family? I imagine a vicarage in such a small village must find ways to stretch his income a great deal."

And just *why* was he so curious about that, all of a sudden? Her money was her own. A duke certainly had no need for it, not with his abundance of estates earning him more money than a man could ever use in his lifetime.

Jane shook her head to clear the suspicions from her thoughts. Really, there was no reason not to tell him. She needed to stop being so distrustful. "Papa would never allow me to use my money for family expenses. I've been saving my income for several years now…setting it aside, should I need it."

"That sum could provide you with a respectable dowry now, if you chose to use it as such."

Jane frowned at him. "That it could," she murmured. Was he trying to get her to offer it for a dowry? Would he rescind the offer he'd made to her suitors for a dowry and insist she use her own monies? And for what purpose? Perhaps his efforts these last few days at keeping her under a short rein were for some purpose other than what he suggested.

Still, maybe there was a suitor who'd spoken to him and Peter was attempting to protect her reputation from any of her usual social blunders.

Oh, drat. Thankfully, the appointment Sophie arranged for Jane with a solicitor was only two days away. She would finally be able to make some headway on setting up her shop.

"Well, there will be no need for that now, Jane," he said, a curious expression dusting his brow.

"No." If only she understood what that meant. Good Lord, she wished she knew what the man was thinking.

But then the music came to an end, and the dancing stopped. He placed her hand in the crook of his arm and led her from the floor in the direction of the dining room. "I believe supper is served."

"Indeed."

The next day couldn't arrive soon enough. Jane wanted more than ever to get to work. One meal seated next to Peter wouldn't kill her.

She hoped.

Eleven

THE NEXT MORNING, Peter awoke with a smile.

It might have been due to having spent a pleasant waltz and supper with Jane last night. Or perhaps it was because he had succeeded in yet again avoiding a dance—or even a conversation—with Lady Broederlet, who had been chasing after him about the entire Season instead of spending time with her husband. Possibly it was because he intended to have a picnic with his family in the gardens behind Hardwicke House early that afternoon to celebrate Joshua's birthday. Even Jane would be there, and likely her silly cat as well.

Any way he looked at it, Peter *would* have a perfect day today. He was determined to enjoy himself, even if Mama started in on him again about finding a woman to take to wife. No one would spoil his mood.

When he passed by the breakfast room on his way to his library, he did so with this very determination at the forefront of his mind and a smile on his face.

Until his mother called out to him from the breakfast room with: "Oh, Peter? You remember we've agreed to an evening at Vauxhall tonight with Lady Veazey, don't you?" She gave him a rather pointed, do-not-dare-to-come-up-with-an-excuse look over her cup of morning chocolate. "It's to be a small gathering—only a few guests. We do *not* wish to disappoint."

It was just his luck that he had forgotten. However, not even this would dampen his good mood. Not today.

"Of course I'll be there. I've been looking forward to it all week." Blast. That last bit was likely a touch too much, since she clearly believed he'd forgotten or else she wouldn't have reminded him in such a manner.

Mama didn't give his little slip any moment, though, and turned to admonish one of his sisters for some unknown offense. Peter took that opportunity to sneak out of sight and get to work before the picnic.

Yeats had sent him home with a report from Carreg Mawr the day before, and Peter wanted to see what it had to say.

When "A breakfast tray in my library," Peter said as he passed Spenser in the halls. "With coffee. As soon as possible, please." He waited only for the incline of his butler's head before barreling through the doors to his library.

Sparing not a moment, he grabbed the report from the bookshelf—the one designated for work yet to be done (which, he was proud to note, was much less full than any other shelf in his library)—and settled in at his desk.

He pulled the papers out and began to read.

And read.

And still read some more.

After finishing the entire stack, Peter cursed aloud. "Deuce take it, Phinny." Why had he been so blind? And how long had it been going on under his nose?

One thing was certain. The next time he saw Utley, he would be hard-pressed to refrain from planting the bastard a facer, if not strangling him. Phineas Turnpenny had certainly not acted alone.

SIX-YEAR-OLD JOSHUA, PETER'S heir and the reason for the day's celebratory picnic, flailed himself across the lawns with his almost-four-year-old sister Sarah following as close behind as her legs would carry her.

The orange cat, which Peter rarely saw anywhere other than either firmly attached to Jane or fast asleep in its ratty basket, was chasing behind the children, Sarah in particular, and largely ignoring the rather-less-than-exciting adults seated on blankets beneath trees. The animal was unexpectedly agile and lithe, considering that Peter had rarely seen it move, other than the day it had arrived with Jane and nearly mauled his daughter.

The cat's fascination with Sarah—and likewise Sarah's fascination with the cat—had only grown since that first day. From Sarah's recounting, "Mr. Cuddlesworth" often took naps with the children in the nursery both when they were napping and while they played.

He sighed as he watched his daughter collapse atop his son, and then the cat atop them both, eliciting the usual peal of giggles that only a little girl can produce. Having a cat in the house for a pet, he had to admit, had not turned out to be the worst thing Peter could imagine. It seemed none-too-inclined to bother him at all, and had left no permanent marks on either child.

And the joy on Sarah's face when she was near the animal certainly made up for the misgivings Peter initially held about allowing it into his home.

His mother interrupted his pensive mood. "Such a lovely day we're having today, with no rain. I do hope we are as lucky this evening to have such favorable weather. Vauxhall is lovely any time, but how could we enjoy the fireworks and explore the walkways if it rains on us?"

"Lady Veazey should have no concerns about her entertainment tonight, Mama," Charlotte said. "Why, there's hardly a cloud in the sky for miles. Surely it will hold up."

Then she turned to Jane. "This ought to be an evening for you to remember, for certain. I cannot think of the last time I was at Vauxhall Gardens and we had such lovely weather."

"Are they as beautiful as I have been told? The gardens, that is." Jane's eyes, Peter noticed, shone a lighter than normal shade in the sunlight, with amber flecks scattered amongst the usual, rich brown.

"Quite," Sophie said. "I daresay you've seen nothing to match the splendor of the pleasure gardens. And the fireworks!"

Jane flushed slightly before stammering out: "And what, precisely, *are* fireworks? I've heard them mentioned now countless times, but I honestly have no idea what to expect. I don't wish to make a cake of myself in front of the whole *ton*."

Peter choked out a laugh on a sip of lemonade. How could a woman who was already old enough to be considered a spinster have never seen fireworks before?

His choke was met with the most foul glare he imagined Jane capable of producing. "They are an extravagance to which I've never been exposed, *Your Grace*. I hardly think it's quite so amusing."

"I apologize," he stammered out, still attempting to calm the coughing in his throat. "It is not amusing—simply surprising, is all. I would have thought they'd have fireworks at least occasionally in the country."

She crossed her arms, which had been holding her up as she leaned back against the blanket, across her chest in a huff. "Well, you would have been wrong, then."

"Clearly." Good Lord, why was he so bloody attracted to the minx when she pouted at him with such an annoyed expression like that?

"You could explain them to me, to help me avoid further embarrassment, you know," she said.

"I could."

Several beats passed, with no one saying a word. His mother and sisters looked from one to the other, plainly waiting for one of them to sort their tiff out.

He was in no hurry. She was damnably intriguing to him, sulking the way she was.

"Well?" she asked and raised an eyebrow at him.

"Well, what?"

Her arms flew to the sky in exasperation. "Well, are you going to tell me what they are or not?"

Peter merely smiled.

Which was apparently not the reaction she wanted. She rose to her feet and stormed away after his children and her cat, who had moved off to a nearby oak tree Joshua was attempting to climb, while muttering something about, "Drat that bleeding imbecile of a man," beneath her breath.

All of which made him smile all the more. He was becoming quite a dolt. But what a lovely sight it was, to see Jane's hips swaying as she marched along the walkway, the fine lawn fabric of her afternoon dress swishing from side to side in time with her stride.

"Peter," Charlotte said, breaking his concentration on the sight slipping further away from him, "that was inordinately rude."

"Stop chiding your brother," Mama said to Char before turning to him. "But your sister's right. That was terribly rude. I should be appalled."

"Should be? Meaning you aren't?" How could he ever be so fortunate?

"I'm not," she replied, "but only because I can see there is something beneath the surface between the two of you." Her eyes narrowed at him. "You, my dear son, are developing a *tendre* for her."

This time, he spat the lemonade from his mouth in shock. "I most certainly am not." Ridiculous notion, that.

"You are," Sophie chimed in. "Denial won't change anything."

"Mind your own affairs," he growled. "You should be finding yourself a husband, shouldn't you? How many offers have you declined so far this Season, hmm?"

"Leave her be," Char piped in. "She's only stating what is perfectly obvious to the rest of us."

"Perfectly obvious to a group of unmarried hens, you mean? I think I'll trust my own judgment, if it is all the same to you."

"Listen to him growling like a wounded bear," whispered Char in fascination, oblivious to the murderous scowl he cast in her direction.

"What would you know about how a wounded bear sounds?" Sophie asked. "You've never seen a bear in your life."

"What does that matter?" Charlotte asked. "He's clearly only stinging because we can see straight through him." She took another scone and popped it into her mouth, not bothering to chew and swallow before she continued with: "Just like we always could."

"You all think you know so much about me, but you know nothing," he said. "Nothing at all."

"Stop berating your sisters voicing the truth you have no desire to hear," Mama said in a brook-no-nonsense tone.

Peter rose, prepared to deliver them all a blistering set-down and leave, when he heard the scream. A scream that threatened to rob him of all his breath and stop his heart from beating. Sarah. His baby girl.

"Sarah!" he called and rushed in the direction of the sound. Not seeing anything. Not realizing that his mother and sisters were right behind him, running as fast as they could.

She was around the corner of the house and off a distance further. The sound was slightly muffled, perhaps by tree branches.

He flew, brushing past bushes and tree branches. Her cries carried him forward. "Sarah?"

Then the sound changed. Was it squealing? Giggles?

Finally, he arrived where his daughter was, in a heap on the ground beneath a too-tall branch, buried in a pile of bodies. And she was laughing.

Because Jane was leaning over her and tickling the breath out of her, along with Josh and the damned cat, too. In fact, all of them were laughing, even if the laughter was coming through tears in Sarah's case. Well, perhaps the cat was not laughing. Could cats laugh? He doubted it. But it was squarely involved in the fray, nuzzling up against Sarah's chin while she squirmed and squealed.

Peter came to a dead stop, moving again only when Char and Sophie ran into him from behind and pushed him forward. After sending them a ducal glare, he asked, "Sarah? Are you all right? Sweetheart, I was so worried when I heard you scream."

But his daughter was in such a fit of giggles she couldn't answer him if she tried. Not that she tried.

Jane took pity on him, though. "She took a good fall from the tree there. Sarah thought that since Joshua could climb it, she should be able to as well. I wasn't fast enough to catch her, I'm afraid." She rose and straightened her gown about her legs, leaving the children and the cat where they lay. "But I've checked her all over, and there are no broken bones. I imagine she'll be fit as a fiddle again in no time."

"I see." But of course, he didn't. "And do you profess to be a doctor, then, Miss Matthews?"

"We're back to Miss Matthews and Your Grace, then are we?" she spat back at him. "No, sir, I'm nothing of the sort. But I know how to find a broken bone. You should just be thankful I was here to help her."

"Thankful? *Thankful!* I can promise you, ma'am, I shall be thankful the day you have married and are no longer living beneath my roof. And not a day sooner."

She leveled him with an icy stare. "Well, I'll do my best not to disappoint, then. Good day to you." The minx spun on her heels and marched back to the house, ignoring Sophie as she followed behind.

"Papa," Sarah said, "why are you angry at Jane? I'm not hurt." She looked up at him with wide eyes, still brimming with unshed tears.

"Never mind about that," he said and gently moved both the cat and Joshua off of her before lifting her into his arms. "Mama, please have Spenser send for a doctor. I want Sarah thoroughly checked over for breaks and bruises."

He waited for no response, and carried his princess back to the house, to Mrs. Pratt in the nursery. No expense would be spared when his daughter's health was at stake. And he would not trust the word of a silly spinster who treated a cat like a human and was scared of horses on such a matter.

Preposterous.

VAUXHALL WAS AN unexpected treat. Yes, of course Jane had known she would be going—that wasn't the unexpected part. It was the gardens. They were so lush and inviting, so green and colorful, so filled with vitality, she felt sure she would burst with the excitement she felt just from walking through the gates and traversing the walks until they reached Lady Veazey's supper box.

Even having Peter along would not spoil her mood. Not tonight. She simply wouldn't allow it to happen. There was far too much for her to enjoy, and she wouldn't allow anyone to ruin it for her.

The supper box slowly filled with the other invited revelers, all of whom Jane at least had an acquaintance. The two Miss Marlboroughs were present, as was Miss Lily Fairfax. Lord Sinclaire had joined the group, along with Lords Pottinger and Eldredge—the latter of whom passed Jane a kindly smile, but made no other effort at conversation, much to her relief, and Mr. Derringer, a kindly, older gentleman who remained unmarried. Of course, the elegant and petitite Lady Veazey was present, alongside her devilishly handsome husband. Finally, there were all of the Hardwickes and Jane. Somehow Cousin Henrietta had even wrangled Neil into accompanying them, as well.

Several matrons stood off to the side of the box along with the dowager, providing ample chaperonage for all of the unmarried ladies and gentlemen.

As the supper box filled to overflowing, Char brought two glasses of lemonade over to Jane. "I hope Lady Veazey is unaware of her *faux pas*. She has one more young lady present than she has eligible gentlemen. It just isn't *done*."

A cursory glance around the party proved Char's observation correct. But was it truly a mistake? "Perhaps an invited guest was unable to attend at the last moment," Jane murmured, keeping her voice down so she wouldn't attract anyone else's attention to the uneven numbers.

But then Lord Utley, smiling like the rogue she knew him to be, strode across the walk and stopped directly before the entrance to Lady Veazey's box. Drat. He must be the final member of the party.

"A lovely evening, isn't it?" he called out, inclining his head to their host and hostess and let himself inside.

"So glad you were able to join us, my lord," Lady Veazey called out to him, "and at such late notice, too. I was simply devastated when Sir Jonas Buchannan sent word he couldn't attend."

Before Jane could ponder the matter any further, Peter stormed across the box to stand beside her, the fierce look in his eyes enough to send her shaking to the corner, had the look been intended for her. "Charlotte. Jane." His brusque tone sent shivers across Jane's bare upper arms beneath the small capped sleeves of her gown. Thankfully, she could imagine his scowl to be intended for none other than Utley at that moment.

Peter's rather large frame was so close to her side, she couldn't move without brushing against him. He stood with his arms crossed over his chest, almost daring the newest member of the group to draw near.

Utley made his rounds, speaking briefly with each of the various smaller groups which had gathered in the supper box before moving on to the next. Sophie stood with Lord Eldredge and Miss Marlborough when Utley arrived at their group. Their voices were too low for Jane to make out anything they said, but Sophie's eyes never lit up, nor did she ever break into a smile as long as the cad remained with them.

Finally, after conversing with every other group, Utley moved to stand before Peter—who made no effort whatsoever to make the man feel welcome.

"Somerton," Utley drawled, his voice unctuous and ingratiating. "Pleasure to meet you, as always." His nose crinkled a touch, though he fought to conceal the action. "And of course, Lady Charlotte and the delectable Miss Matthews. It is always a joy to discover one is in the company of such lovely ladies."

"Utley," Peter clipped off, low and almost menacing. "I am almost surprised to see you out in company. Why, no one has seen you since the first ball of the Season, from what I understand."

"I have had to make a brief foray into the country to see to one of my estates. Sadly, at times, business must take precedence over pleasure. Of course you would know all about that, wouldn't you? But now I've returned, and Lady Veazey was delighted to discover my availability for this evening when we met on Curzon Street this afternoon."

"Is that so?" Peter asked, deceptively mild in his query. "Did you also, perhaps, visit your brother in Wales?"

"Wales? Egad, Somerton." Utley laughed, a nervous, fractious sound. "That is quite a trek, especially while so much is happening in Town. No, I haven't been to Wales in months. Perhaps longer." He passed a pointed look in Jane and Charlotte's direction. "But really, aren't we boring these lovely ladies with our discussion of business affairs?"

Before Peter could answer, and despite his obvious attempt to issue a response, with his mouth gaping open, Lady Veazey interrupted them all. "Dinner will not be served for another hour. I believe it would be lovely if we all broke into pairs or small groups and went for a walk through the pleasure gardens. Gentlemen, would you be so kind?"

Lord Veazey took up her arm and led her from the box. They paused at the gate and looked over their shoulders to be certain that none of their guests were left out.

Utley turned to Jane with a triumphant look upon his face. But before he could even open his mouth to ask if she would allow him to escort her through the gardens, Peter took hold of her elbow.

"Come with me," he muttered and tugged against her, practically dragging her forward.

She gasped, but was secretly pleased, not to mention grateful that she would not have to spend any time alone in the man's presence. With a quick look over her shoulder, she saw that Lord Eldredge and Neil were escorting Charlotte and Miss Theodora Marlborough out of the supper box, and Lord Sinclaire was only a few paces behind with Sophie. Miss Marlborough and Miss Fairfax promenaded one on either side of Lord Pottinger, leaving the matrons to form a group to take a leisure walk together—leaving Utley on his own. Lord Veazey gestured to him to come along and walk with himself and his wife—obviously not what the man wanted, but it suited Jane's mood just fine.

Peter was still tense as he held onto her arm, guiding her more than only a bit faster than necessary through the lamp-lit trees lining the various walkways. She wanted to say something—anything, really—but dared not upset him further. In truth, she wasn't certain why he was so intensely angered by Lord Utley's presence. Not that it mattered. Jane was more than all right with being whisked away from the man with all due haste.

Her last encounter with the man had been one she would have preferred to have forgotten...and almost had.

Almost. But not quite.

And because of that, she had no desire whatsoever to spend any more time in the man's presence than absolutely necessary. No time at all in his presence would suit Jane rather well, thank you very much.

Utley's arrival at Vauxhall left her unsettled, to say the least.

She must have been huffing for breath, because Peter suddenly slowed his pace and inclined his head to her. "I must apologize. I seem to have lost my manners."

By this point, they had outpaced the other revelers by such a distance that she couldn't even see them when she peeked over her shoulder into the distance. Peter led her through twisting walkways that were now less well-lit than the earlier ones—paths whose arch of trees overhead largely blocked the moonlight from illuminating their trail.

"There's no need to apologize."

Oddly, that was true. There wasn't. He had manhandled her and pulled her away without even a by-your-leave, yet she wasn't upset. Rather, she worried what had caused him such a great distress.

He answered her question before she could even give it voice. "Utley and I have a history. Not a very pleasant history, either."

"Oh. So you were displeased to see him this evening, then?" Perhaps, if they talked enough, he would relax again. She had so wished for a pleasant evening instead of the tension of the afternoon.

"I'm always displeased to see him," he growled. "The man is a scoundrel of the first order, a man thoroughly unfit to be in the company of ladies. Especially my sisters and those in my care." Peter released his grip on her elbow and smoothed his hand along her gloved arm, guiding her hand into place on his arm. The tension she felt there, while tangible, had begun to lessen.

"What did he do? If he is such a scoundrel, why doesn't the rest of society shun him as you seem to do?"

His pace slowed to almost a crawl and eventually came to a complete stop, staring off into the trees. "He ruined Mary." His arm shook beneath her, the tension building within him anew.

Jane stared up at him—at the silhouette of his face, at his thinned lips and the pulsing vein in his temple—searching for something unknown. "Mary was your wife?"

"Yes." His jaw barely opened to allow the word to escape.

"What—what did he do?"

Peter pulled his arm free and stalked away from her, rubbing a hand absentmindedly over his square jaw and shaking his head. His eyes were empty. She wanted to hold him, soothe his pain, but knew she shouldn't.

"He trapped her. Mama threw a ball at Hardwicke House, celebrating Sophie's come-out. Utley had been invited. We'd known his family for years—my brothers and I had played with him and his brothers as children. Utley had only just inherited the title from his father a few months before. He was the newest peer on the marriage mart."

Peter looked at Jane, as though he only then realized she was with him, even though she'd been there the whole time. "You should sit. We should sit." Trembling, he took her hand in his and led her to a bench beneath the trees and away from the lights.

"Mary attended the ball as well. She was the daughter of Lord Throckmorton. Mama had hopes that I might offer for her, even though we really had no attraction to each other. But I was the most eligible bachelor of the *ton* at the time, and Mary was one of the most respected candidates for marriage amongst the young ladies." His eyes closed for a moment.

"You...you did not love her, then?" Her hand was still fully ensconced in his, the heat radiating from him urging her closer.

"Love Mary? No." Peter's head dropped to his chest for a moment. "I wish I could have loved her. She deserved that, at the least."

"I'm sorry. I shouldn't have interrupted." Jane squeezed his hand, hoping he would continue.

"He lured her away from the crowd that night, out into the gardens. And once Utley had her alone, he—he put her into a very compromising situation." Peter looked up at her, as though calculating her reaction before continuing. "Sinclaire encountered them on their way back into the ballroom, and alerted us—Mama and I—to the circumstances. We rushed outside, but the damage had already been done. Utley had gone. He left Mary there, alone, crying."

"What did you do?"

"I offered for her. Mama sent Sinclaire to find Lord and Lady Throckmorton, and they arrived shortly after we did. Throckmorton agreed there was no better solution. He wanted retribution from Utley, but he wanted his daughter's happiness more."

"And she could never be happy with Utley," she said.

"No. I only wish I had been able to make her happy. She didn't deserve to be tossed into a marriage she didn't want, simply because of one man's vengeance."

Jane started at the idea of vengeance. She looked up into Peter's eyes, which were cold and hard. Now wasn't the time to press him. "But you weren't cruel to her, were you? You treated her well. I know your family must have adored her." How could anyone be unhappy living with the Hardwickes? Preposterous. They were as lively a bunch, and as loving, as any she had encountered. "And then there were the children. She must have loved your children."

"I suppose she did. But I didn't fulfill my obligation to her. I promised to love her, and I couldn't bring myself to make it happen."

"Peter," Jane said, her voice gentle, "you did all you could. You protected her from shame. You gave her a family, a home. You provided for her needs. If she was still unhappy, you can't continue to blame yourself."

"But didn't she also need love?" He choked out the words.

"Didn't you? Did she love you, Peter? Did she give you all that you needed?"

He shot up from the bench and spun around on her. "How dare you? Mary was the perfect duchess. She was an excellent mother to our children." Jane followed, placing a tentative hand on his arm. He pulled it away as though she'd scalded him.

"But did she love you?"

His eyes bored through her. "You could do no better. No one could fulfill her role in my life better than she did. Mary was born to be a duchess."

"No. I don't imagine I would be a very good duchess at all. Certainly not for you." The idea of being Peter's duchess was almost laughable. She could never conform to his expectations. Still, the scorn in his tone hurt.

They stood in the dim light of the garden walk, staring at each other, silent. Breathing. He smelled of firewood and soap, with the faintest hint of port.

"We should return," he said, his brusque manner fully returned. "Supper will be served any moment." Again, he placed her hand against his arm and started walking, leaving her little choice but to go with him. Her skin tingled everywhere he touched.

"You haven't answered me," she said as they hurried along the pathway. "Did Mary love you?" She might never understand why it was so important to her to know, but the need burned within her.

Minutes passed without a word. He likely would never answer her.

They drew close to the Veazeys' supper box, where most of their party had already reconvened, save a few stragglers. Lord Utley was amongst the missing.

Just before they entered the gate, Peter leaned down near her ear. "No," he said so softly she almost missed it.

Jane faced him, hoping the lighting of the box would illuminate his eyes enough she could interpret his meaning. The only thing she read in them was need.

Twelve

SOPHIE HAD BEEN right. Mr. Selwood, Jane's new solicitor, was the perfect man for the task.

On her first meeting with him, which, it should be noted, had been difficult enough to carry out without alerting Cousin Henrietta to any mischief being afoot, they had arrived at an agreement for the terms of their business relationship. They also arranged for a second meeting—one which Jane was altogether uncertain how she would bring about, seeing as it was to be held on Thursday afternoon.

Thursday, of course, being the very same day of Charlotte and Jane's come-out ball. Not the sort of afternoon Cousin Henrietta was likely to allow Jane to scamper off and do Lord only knew what.

But she had to find a way to meet with Mr. Selwood then, because he planned to show her a few storefronts which could possibly become her new modiste shop should she find the terms acceptable.

She couldn't very well open her shop without a shop to open, could she?

Somehow, she simply must find a way out of Hardwicke House without alerting Cousin Henrietta to the fact that she was gone. And then get back to the house in time to prepare for the ball. A minor snag in the plan—nothing *too* serious.

Thankfully, Sophie was fully committed to the entire plan. The two of them had stayed up quite late several nights, planning the best ways for Jane to accomplish her preparations for the shop without raising the dowager's suspicions, discussing what the décor should be and how the shop should be organized, debating prices and services and various other ways Sophie could become involved.

While Sophie was by no means a seamstress herself, the eldest Hardwicke sister had an excellent eye for fashion and was always ahead of the rest of society when it came to the current trends. Not only that, but she had a head for figures and loads of creative ideas for drumming up business.

It didn't hurt matters either that much like Jane, Sophie was in no rush to find herself at the altar. Marriage, while not an entirely unattractive concept, was not an area in which Lady Sophia Hardwicke ever intended to settle. Her husband would be perfect or he simply would not be.

Much to her mother's chagrin.

She had never told her mother in quite those precise words, at least not while Jane had been present, but both Sophie and Jane had every reason to believe the Dowager Duchess of Somerton had surmised as much.

And while Cousin Henrietta was currently spending much of her match-making focus on Jane and Peter (separately, of course), she consistently sent noticeable nudges in her eldest daughter's direction as well.

She'd made it abundantly clear: Sophie's prospects would not be overlooked.

Despite her mother's best, if misguided, intentions, Sophie would be quite content to remain an aging spinster. She had an ample fortune, so she need never work to support herself. Nor would she need to become a pariah to one of her siblings, forcing them to eternally provide for her, as long as she managed her fortune wisely.

Still, the prospect of working for herself, earning her keep, doing something with herself other than living the idle life of a *Lady* rather appealed to her. Indeed, as they sat in Jane's chamber after the rest of the house had retired, poring over their notes, she heaved out a sigh and set the sheet of foolscap she was studying down on the bed between them.

Jane glanced up and couldn't help lifting a brow at the look of sheer determination on Sophie's face. "Yes?" she prodded.

"You know, dear, having a solicitor to handle certain aspects of your business will not quite be enough. Mr. Selwood is a dear man, and he's rather more than capable, too. But will he be responsible for collecting payment for your services? For ordering materials and ensuring their delivery? I hardly think so."

"I hadn't thought of that," Jane responded. For that matter, she'd thought little beyond the actual work of sewing and designing gowns. Oh, dear. "I'm more than confident in my abilities to do the actual stitching, the designing...anything where I can get my hands on the fabric and create or decide how best to work a gown for a particular effect on my clients. But sales?"

Sophie winked at her. "That's why you need me."

"But what would your mother say? She would never in a thousand years stand for it. Even Peter would throw a fit if he thought you were going to *work*." It would be difficult enough to convince them to allow Jane to run her own business. How laughable—run her own business, indeed. She hadn't the slightest idea what she was getting herself into, at least in terms of London society and not simply selling her work to the ladies of Whitstable.

"I'm unconcerned about what they would say. Why, I'll be five-and-twenty in October. I believe it's high time I decide what I want out of life, if you ask me." Sophie pushed the pillow between them out of the way and looked straight into Jane's eyes. "You need me. I know who you want as customers, and I can convince them to give you their business. I can handle the bookkeeping while you focus on the creative aspects. Admit it, Jane."

And so she did. In fact, they decided to become partners in the business. Everything would be split equally. When she really thought about it, having Sophie working with her was a relief.

Then the conversation turned to how they could go about sneaking Jane out of the house to meet with Mr. Selwood again. The first time, Jane and Sophie had gone out for a walk through the park. Since they were together, Cousin Henrietta had not insisted upon sending a maid to chaperone, so they had gone alone. They'd met Mr. Selwood at Gunter's, and Sophie sat with some acquaintances and enjoyed an ice while Jane handled her business matters.

This time, however, would be far more complicated. Sophie had already promised to spend the afternoon with Charlotte visiting the Marlborough sisters. Jane was expected to attend the outing as well, but Char would surely ask far too many questions if she took off for a bit instead of remaining by their side for the visit. She wasn't ready for anyone else to know her plans. Not until her plans were more tangible, at the very least.

"It is time, dear Jane, to call in reinforcements." Sophie's pronouncement came after several moments of silence while both women forged internal debates. She winked. "Stay here. I'll be right back."

Sophie scurried off the bed and out the door of the bedchamber, then padded through the silent house in her bare feet.

Surely it was good that Sophie had an idea—wasn't it? Oh, drat, Jane hoped it was good. But the longer it took for Sophie to return, the more Jane's stomach churned and roiled, dreading what could possibly be in the works.

When Sophie finally re-entered the room, Jane nearly fell from the bed in shock. A fully dressed Neil, the handsome, youngest Hardwicke brother with his light auburn hair and rogue's smile, appeared by her side.

Jane pulled at her robe to be sure she was fully covered and glared at her friend for giving her no warning. This was highly inappropriate, and possibly the most devilishly and deliciously scandalous thing Jane had ever experienced in her life.

Well, at least the most scandalous thing she had experienced in her nightgown.

Neil merely grinned the way she imagined Mr. Cuddlesworth would grin at his prey before pouncing, which in turn sent a blush over Jane's face and down her neck. She pulled her robe up higher.

"What on earth is the meaning of this?" she whispered, hoping no one in the house would hear them and discover that a gentleman was in her chamber...even if Sophie was there, as well.

"I was hoping to have that very question answered, myself," Neil drawled. He didn't sound deep in his cups—at least she didn't think he did. Not that she had ever been in the presence of a drunkard before. Oh, double drat, how was she supposed to know such things? Times like the present made it abundantly clear how protected a life she'd lived, out in the country with a vicar for a father.

Jane shook her head as though to clear her thoughts. *Calm down. Breathe.* Sophie knew what she was doing. Didn't she?

"We need your assistance," Sophie said, facing Neil. "No questions asked."

He narrowed his gaze, looking at them each in turn. "Go on. I'm listening, but making no promises...yet."

"Tomorrow afternoon, Jane's going to feign illness—"

"I'm *what?* I'm never ill. Your mother will never believe that."

Neil chuckled. "I should have known Mama was involved in this somehow."

Sophie glared at Neil then turned the fullness of her ire on Jane. "She will. Stop interrupting. It's the afternoon of your come-out, and you are going to develop a bout of nerves." Sophie's resolve was enough to force even Old Boney himself into submission at that moment. Jane bit her lip so as not to argue further.

"All right. Jane is faux-ill. What does this have to do with me?" asked Neil. He wasn't behaving impatiently—that wasn't quite the right word for it. Jane thought he was rather objective and methodical, though, not playing around at all. She'd never encountered him before without seeing him make a joke of something or pull a prank. This change in his deportment was unnerving, to say the least. He acted as though he carried out covert operations on a recurring basis.

Sophie interrupted Jane's musings. "You're going to help her sneak out of the house—I would suggest through that window over there—and drive her in a covered carriage to Bond Street. She needs to meet with someone there and then return without being seen. By *anyone.*"

"Why, precisely, am I going to do something as asinine as this? And who is it she's meeting?"

"No questions. Either you do it for us, or you leave now."

Good Lord, Sophie had truly lost her mind this time. Sneaking out of windows—second floor windows, to be precise—and traipsing furtively all through London. No man in his right mind would agree to a plan as idiotic as this, certainly not without knowing more details.

Theirs was a lost cause, and Neil was sure to say something to either Peter or Cousin Henrietta. They were done for.

He stood there, immobile and silent, for so long that Jane was about to rip her skin free because it would not stop crawling about and was driving her to distraction. "All right."

All right? He was going to do it? "You can't possibly be serious," Jane said before she could think better of it, earning a glare from Sophie.

"I am. What time will this clandestine lover's meeting take place?"

Sophie glanced at some notes she and Jane had been going over with meeting times and business plans and fully ignored Jane's blush. "You should be in the carriage and leaving by two-thirty at the latest."

"I'll see you at the window at two-fifteen, then," he said to Jane and winked. "Anything else?"

A brisk shake of Sophie's head gave him all the answer he needed, and he left them as quietly as he had come.

"He's going to do it? Truly?" The entire idea that Neil would take part in such a ludicrous plan baffled her.

"Truly."

And that was the end of that particular conversation.

NOW, SITTING IN the drawing room the next afternoon with the other women of the house, Jane's nerves were taking control. A glance up at the large grandfather clock by the far window only intensified her unease.

Two o'clock. Almost time. Any minute now, Sophie and Charlotte would take their leave, and she would have to feign illness.

Although, with the current state of her stomach, there may not be nearly as much deceit involved as she had previously envisioned.

She stole a look at Sophie, who sent her a forceful frown. Obviously, her friend intended to follow through with her end of the agreement. But neither had yet seen Neil this morning, so how could she know whether he would make good on their arrangement? He might have only said he would do it, without actually intending to follow through.

Oh, drat, drat, drat.

And then he poked his head around the doorway. "Good morning, mother. Ladies." His roguish grin was well in place as he winked in Jane's direction, and his eyes twinkled devilishly.

"I would hardly consider this morning," Charlotte said. "Though, for you, I can see how it might be."

"Early to bed, early to rise and all that," he said in response, waving his hand airily. "You know how I enjoy watching the sunrise."

"True, but most of us are just waking when we see it. You often have yet to go to bed."

Cousin Henrietta quickly changed the subject, clearly having no desire to hear her adult children bicker any more than necessary—even if she did have a smile in her eyes that was struggling to work itself down into her mouth despite fierce resistance. "Neil, where are you off to this afternoon? You are dressed far more...well, *far more* than you would be to stay at home."

"Tattersall's, Mama. But only after a stop at White's. I intend to win some money off of Toby Shelton and purchase a new horse with it."

"Oh." His mother was unable to stop the frown from forming. "Well, do have a good time, then. And be responsible, please."

He waved and was out the front door without any further ado.

Jane tried not to snicker at Cousin Henrietta's continued mutterings which amounted to something similar to: "The day that boy ever learns to be responsible will be the day I drive a chariot in Rome."

Several minutes had ticked off the grandfather clock. Sophie stood and said, "Well, ladies? Shall we be off to visit with the Marlborough sisters?" She carefully set her embroidery work (which had noticeably not been altered the entire day, even though she clearly had made herself look rather busy with it) on the table next to her and straightened her lovely pink afternoon gown.

Charlotte rushed to do the same, with Char exclaiming, "Oh, I am so excited. It's been an age since I saw Theodora, I must say."

"You saw her only a week ago, silly," Sophie said. "That hardly signifies as *an age.*"

"Has it only been a week? Oh dear, it felt like far longer than that."

During their exchange, Jane remained seated—and Cousin Henrietta finally took note. "Are you not going with the girls, Jane?" The two Hardwicke sisters turned to her in shock (or in feigned shock, as the case may be) to discover what was going on.

Jane's stomach churned on the lie she was about to tell. "I don't think I ought to go, ma'am. I'm feeling a bit faint. Perhaps it would be better if I go take a lie-down for a bit. I would hate to be ill tonight and unable to attend my own ball." She hoped her face reflected the green she was feeling at the prospect of escaping through her second-floor window.

"Oh, dear. You do look a bit off-color. Ought we to send for a doctor?" Cousin Henrietta rushed over to feel her forehead with the back of her hand. "No fever," she muttered under her breath.

"Mama, I believe Jane is just feeling a bit nervous about the ball," Sophie said matter-of-factly. "It's rather overwhelming for her, you know. Why, the entire Season is so very different from what she was accustomed to in Whitstable. I think a lie-down is precisely what she needs to be in top form for the evening."

"Yes, that's likely all it is," Jane agreed. "Just a bit of rest will do the trick." Please let her accept that answer and drop the subject.

"Oh, but the Marlborough sisters will miss you dreadfully," Charlotte said. "We will assure them there's no reason for concern, of course."

"Do you need help getting up to your chamber, dear?" asked the dowager.

"No," Jane responded a bit too quickly. *Breathe. It will be all right.* "No, I can manage on my own, thank you. I'll just have Meg wake me in time to prepare for the evening, if that's all right with you."

"Of course, dear. And just ring your bell if you need anything before then. Meg will take care of anything."

Jane walked up the stairs as slowly as she could manage, until she was positive no one was watching her. She darted into her room and informed Meg she was not to be woken for a minimum of three hours (and prayed that would give her enough time to return to Hardwicke House without being caught), then shut herself into the room and looked at the clock.

Two-thirteen. Only moments to spare.

Before she had regained her breath and slowed her pulse from racing upstairs, a light tapping sounded at the window. When she pulled back the curtains, Neil stood before her on the tiny balcony ledge, a mischievous sparkle in his eyes.

Jane unlatched the window pane and pushed it up.

"Your chariot awaits, my lady," he said.

"You're rather prompt. But how did...how did you...?" Then she looked down at the ladder he had found God-only-knew where, perched against the side of the house. It ran down the length of the mansion and stopped directly next to an enclosed carriage. Or, to be more precise, next to the horses pulling the enclosed carriage. "Oh, my." She closed her eyes for a moment and tried to remember to breathe.

Neil winked at her. "Come along, sweet Jane. We haven't got all day, now, have we? Lucky for us, your suite is on the back side of the house, so we should be able to get away without being seen. Unless you've changed your mind, of course."

"I won't be changing my mind."

"Not even with the horses?" he asked with a chuckle.

She merely glared and gathered her reticule.

He held the window up while she climbed out, trying not to rip her gown as she hoisted her legs through the open frame, but also trying not to reveal too much of her stocking-clad leg to him. This was all highly irregular, and far more inappropriate than anything she had ever in her life imagined.

And maybe just the tiniest bit exciting.

The balcony was so small that in order for them both to stand upon it, they were almost touching each other.

"Will you be able to climb down on your own, or should I carry you?"

Her cheeks must have flamed at the thought of him carrying her. But to climb herself, she would have to look down at the horses the entire way so as not to lose her footing.

No, she was a grown woman. She could do this. "I can climb. Go on, get going."

Within seconds, he had leapt over the ledge and scurried to the ground. When she looked down at him again, he gestured for her to come along then held the wobbly contraption steady for her.

The banister was waist-high. Jane cringed, thinking of how high her skirts would have to be raised to get over the railing, but there was nothing to be done for it. So, she raised up her gown and held her skirts with one hand, then used the other to balance as she tossed first one, then the other leg over the side and steadied her feet on the rickety ladder.

A low whistle reached her from below, and she sent Neil her best scowl...then wished she had done nothing of the sort, since it put the horses back directly in her line of view. Blasted animals. If only they weren't so necessary for everyday life.

Before she could change her mind, she lowered her feet one at a time, grasping onto the rungs of the ladder with the one hand for dear life and still holding her skirts with the other, so as not to tangle a foot in them. Thankfully, she was at the ground in short order.

"I daresay, my dear, that was rather the prettiest sight I've seen in weeks. I can hardly wait to see it again when we return."

She had half a mind to slap the man for his impertinence before she thought better of it. They only had a few hours. She really must be on her way, and what would she do without his help? Even just getting back up to her chamber was an impossibility without his assistance.

Instead of striking him, then, she turned on her heels and stalked to the waiting carriage. Which would have been much easier to do had she remembered to let go of her skirts and loosen her grip on the ladder.

Since she did *not* remember to perform those rather pertinent things, the ladder came falling on top of her as she landed in a twisted heap on the ground. Drat. Not quite the haughty exit she had intended.

Even worse, Neil chose that moment to drop his roguish demeanor and play the gallant gentleman. He deftly removed the ladder from her person, placed it against the wall of Hardwicke House again, and then offered her his hand. "Might I assist you up, ma'am?" His voice held a polished, refined tone, even with a mocking twinkle in his eyes.

Why, exactly, had she ever agreed to Sophie's hare-brained idea?

Whatever the reason, it was irrelevant. She took his hand and allowed him to assist her to her feet, then straightened her skirts about her legs and climbed aboard the carriage—careful *not* to accept his aid this time.

And finally, they were on their way. When they arrived at Bond Street, Neil agreed to wait for her return in the carriage and not chase after her to discover her dealings.

She met with Mr. Selwood, who took her to visit three different shops. The first two were a bit too dusty and cramped, too poorly lit, and entirely unacceptable in almost every imaginable way.

But the third was about as close to perfect as Jane ever dreamed she would find. It stood on a corner, and had windows all along the front and the side, allowing ample daylight to stream in and light her work—and allowing plenty of room to display her wares for potential clients.

An area in the back would need only minimal work to suit as a dressing area, where the ladies who came for fittings could try on their new garments and Jane could work with her pins to finalize all of the stitchery. Off to one side, a countertop was laid out where Sophie could operate, dealing with all of the bookkeeping and such, and keeping an eye on comings and goings while Jane was busy with her sewing.

So of course, she said to Mr. Selwood after being shown this third and final shop on the tour: "I'll take it!" Her grin was so wide that the corners of her lips felt like they might crack, but she didn't care.

She was becoming a business owner.

They settled all of the details, but for its location and nicities, Jane believed she was coming out on top in terms of the rents she would have to pay. She had more than enough saved to pay for the first year's rents on the building, and still plenty set aside for buying her supplies. She could open her doors sooner than she had ever allowed herself to anticipate.

Well, there was still the slight snag of convincing Cousin Henrietta (and her parents, but they could wait) that she should be allowed to go about it.

Still, after the matter of Charlotte and Jane's come-out ball was in the past, then Jane and Sophie could work on buying their supplies and setting up the shop. She imagined they could be open for business by the middle of the Season—or the end of it at the very latest. Which would be in time to work on autumn and winter garments for her new clients.

This was all working out just splendidly.

She was still beaming when she returned to Neil in his carriage, but he kept his promise to her and asked her no questions. When they returned to Hardwicke House, she still had half an hour to spare before Meg would return to wake her from her nap.

She climbed the ladder to her chamber with a touch more decorum than she had displayed when descending. Neil spared her the humiliation of showing off her legs in their entirety again by providing her with the equally as embarrassing humiliation of scurrying up the ladder behind her and lifting her over the railing.

Jane was far too excited to be too upset with him, however, so she gave him a chaste kiss on his cheek and thanked him for his assistance.

"Any time, sweet Jane," he said, and rushed down the ladder to clean up the evidence of their excursion and be off.

Oh, she simply couldn't *wait* to tell Sophie the news.

Thirteen

"YOU LOOK SIMPLY divine, miss," Meg said as she placed the finishing touches on Jane's hair. Somehow, as usual, Meg had tamed the mess of curls into a smooth, bouncy coiffure that Jane would have never accomplished on her own. A few tendrils were strategically left out of the knot to frame her face and trail along the nape of her neck.

Her excitement from the afternoon had yet to wear off, and her skin was glowing back at her from the mirror, contrasting nicely against a peachy-pink silk. They had chosen (or rather Cousin Henrietta and Sophie had selected) this one because of its simplicity—no extra bobs or adornments tonight.

Jane would shine in her natural glory on this night. Her night. The night of this silly come-out ball thrown in her honor, which she would just as well skip in its entirety.

Oh, all right. She was not quite as callous as that. There was *just a hint* of excitement coursing through her over the prospect of a fete thrown just for her.

The rush of exhilaration over securing a storefront for her modiste shop, however, threatened to extinguish any frisson of emotion still burning over the upcoming ball.

She had yet to tell Sophie any of her news. There'd been no time, with the other girls returning from the Marlborough sisters' house and then all of them needing to dress for the evening.

Their celebration of impending independence would simply have to wait.

A knock sounded at the door and Meg hurried over to open it. Cousin Henrietta and her two daughters stood in the hall, beaming with excitement.

Three pairs of eyes looked her over, up and down, examining every detail.

"You're ready, then," Sophie said with a brisk nod. "Come along. Peter's already fuming downstairs about how long it takes the females of his family to dress."

"We must be downstairs before the first guests arrive," Cousin Henrietta said. She spun and hurried along the hall, her long, royal blue gown breezing behind in her wake. "Let's be going, then. It's time to form the reception line." The dowager didn't wait to see if they would follow her.

Sophie took hold of Jane's hand and led her along behind her younger sister, leaving a small buffer between them. "Are things settled?" she asked, quiet enough that no one else could hear the question.

The smile that built inside her bubbled over. Good Lord, she couldn't be expected to keep the news quiet if she had to answer. Instead, she merely nodded her head. Anything more might alert the servants that the house was afire if not something even more disturbing.

Sophie squeezed her hand in promise that they would discuss their new business venture more fully in the wee hours of the morning.

Now was certainly not the time.

EVEN WITH HIS house full to bursting with the quality of London, Peter could scarcely take his eyes from Jane.

She almost glowed tonight. Her smile—a true smile, shining clear through to her eyes and beyond—had never left her face, not even for a moment.

He had never seen anything more beautiful. Well, perhaps, his sweet Sarah on every moment of every day.

But this? This was different, by far. Jane was no child.

Somehow, the minx even stood out from the décor of Hardwicke House. The grand ballroom was filled with flowers and candles at every turn, the floral scent even somehow banishing the usual malodorous nature of town. The chandelier overhead and the wall sconces bounced flickers of gold over everything beneath them until the whole room was awash in their radiance.

After Peter's dance with her, Peter checked with Mama to be certain Jane would not lack for partners.

Mama looked at him without bothering to hide her disdain. "Heavens, of course her card is full."

The minx's dance card was plastered with names of nearly every gentleman present, and he couldn't arrange for a second set with her. Neither could he dance more than once with either of his sisters. So, Peter instead tried to fill as many sets as possible with contentedly married ladies of the *ton*. He had to congratulate himself on his success. Only two sets this evening would he be free—and for those he would scour the walls to find a wallflower and make her evening by asking her to dance.

Mama couldn't find fault with him. Not tonight.

At the moment, he was waltzing with Lady Fontaine, a newlywed fully enamored of her husband. He sincerely tried to converse with her, but realized he was doing a poor job of the task when she offered, "Your Grace, I do hope you'll have the opportunity to dance with Miss Matthews again this evening. She seems to hold your rapt attention." She trilled a laugh at his dropped jaw. "I daresay you are unable to fool anyone tonight about where your affections lie."

Deuce take it.

Sinclaire was waltzing with Jane, sweeping her through the throng so that her skirts swayed about her hips and legs in a decidedly enticing manner. A manner that drew Peter's gaze and held it firmly locked in its grasp.

"My affections?" He nearly choked on the words.

Lady Fontaine gave him a consolatory smile. "Of course. You do know how the tongues of the gossip mill tend to wag."

"But there's nothing for them to wag about, my lady, I can assure you."

"You, sir, are quite mistaken."

"Quite?"

"Quite." Lady Fontaine nodded and sent the plume over her head bobbing as though to emphasize her point.

Blast it, they'd send him to parson's mousetrap if they could. "Surely something must have been taken out of context, then. Or exaggerated. I can assure you, there's no reason for the gossips to be talking about me and Miss Matthews."

They spun around the floor and passed by Sinclaire and Jane again. He could almost smell the peach scent always present when she was in the room, even though several feet remained between them. His head involuntarily turned in her direction.

"And *I* can assure *you* that the way you look at Miss Matthews is more than enough to engage the gossip mill. Add to that how you walked with her alone for so long at Vauxhall on a recent excursion, and the rumors are compounded. And then one might also include the fact that she has been living beneath your roof for the entire Season in one's estimation of things, and what other conclusion must one draw? Such a thing only increases the voices speaking of the two of you tenfold."

"Yes, she's been living in my home—along with my mother and sisters, not to mention countless servants. Our association has been properly chaperoned at every turn."

"Nevertheless, there are rumors. Those rumors are only fueled by your fixation with the lady in question, Your Grace." Lady Fontaine fell silent for a moment, eyeing him with pity. "It would not truly be the worst future fate could hand you, would it? She is quite lovely, and rather refreshing. One could never meet a lady of the *ton* quite so unhampered by social dictates." She drew closer and lowered her voice. "Why, just the other day I was conversing with Miss Matthews and Lord Sinclaire, and she dared to talk about how constraining her corset was. It was shocking, to say the least. But really, why must we only speak of the weather and embroidery?"

"Indeed." No matter how engaging Jane might be, Peter didn't need rumors floating through the *beau monde* about the two of them. The thought of yet again being forced into a marriage—a marriage which clearly neither of them desired—was dreadful.

Lady Fontaine smiled, leaving only slits of her eyes showing. "Really, sir, you should not fight so hard. Love will take you, whether you consent or not."

LADY PLUMRIDGE, A chubby old harridan with hair as ugly and gray as her eyes, met him outside in the courtyard of Hardwicke House at the appointed time. "Well, Utley? I've not got all night, you know. You said you would make this worth my while."

He pulled another drag of his cheroot and eyed her. Blasted fussy woman. But he needed her. At least for tonight. Tomorrow she could crawl into a pile of horse manure and die if it would make her happy. He certainly wouldn't be bothered by such a turn of events.

"It will be worth your while. You'll have the scandal of the Season so you can finally best that twit, Lady Kibblewhite. But shut your damned mouth for two more minutes while I finish my smoke, and then we'll get on with it."

She huffed and snapped one slippered foot against the floor, but she kept quiet, at least. Rolls of fat jiggled and bounced at the movement. Disgusting.

Years ago, old Plumridge should have done himself a favor and suffocated her with a pillow in her sleep. Then he could have found some other young thing, a pretty chit at least, and brought her to his bed. Instead he was forced to lie with this pig of a woman, who'd been using his fortune to support her rapidly growing stomach, all the while doing her best to keep London's gossip mill afloat.

Utley took another long drag. Tonight, his fortunes would continue their recent change for the better. Who cared if his target might someday become as obese as the hag before him? Once he had the settlement Somerton had offered for her, he could send her to live in Surrey and never look upon her again.

Or better yet, he could suffocate her, much like Plumridge ought to have done.

Either way, he wouldn't have to look at her. He could simply put her dowry to good use.

In fact, the funds he would soon add to his fortune would be more than enough to fund a mistress, if he desired one. Which he did. Anyone would be better than that uncouth, vulgar woman, Jane Matthews. And with her fortune in his control, he could afford nearly any mistress he so chose.

He would simply get her alone and build a scandal, and his success would be ensured. As would his future.

Not to mention Somerton's downfall.

"Are you quite finished?" Lady Plumridge asked, interrupting his revelry. "I should like to return to the ballroom sometime before I catch my death from cold."

Utley tossed the cheroot to the ground, stubbing the embers with his booted toe.

"Excuse yourself from the ballroom at the end of the supper dance. Go above stairs to the family's apartments. You'll encounter your scandal there."

She narrowed her eyes at him. "That's all?" Her voice shook, along with the rest of her.

"That's all."

She turned and hurried back toward the warmth of the house, stopping only when he called out to her again.

"Lady Plumridge? You won't fail me, will you? The entire party must learn of the scandal you find this evening. I want it in tomorrow's society papers."

"You selected me and not someone else for just that purpose, didn't you? Trust me."

He inclined his head, aggravation etching his eyebrows together in a fierce knot, and she nodded before resuming her jiggling, bounding stride.

By tomorrow morning, Utley's mounting financial concerns would be gone, and his retaliation against Somerton would be complete. Rawden would finally be avenged.

"SHALL WE GO in to supper, then?" Lord Sinclaire tucked Jane's hand into the crook of his arm and started leading her without waiting for a reply.

With her smile from the afternoon still planted firmly on her face, she nodded. "That would be lovely. Perfectly lovely." Drat, would she ever not sound like an imbecile again? Nothing seemed to be coming out of her mouth the way she wanted any more, but she hadn't the slightest idea how to change that.

Ahead of them in the sea of hungry people, Sophie stood at Lord Pottinger's arm, gesturing to them with her free hand.

The crowd moved almost as one, herding them all toward the dining room.

A small voice, young and female, called out, "Miss Jane? Miss Jane?"

It had to be Sarah. "Sarah? Where are you?" But what on earth was Peter's little girl doing out of bed at this hour? Jane stopped and scanned the crowd behind her. How would she ever find the child in the midst of the large, adult bodies surging toward her like the tide?

Lord Sinclaire also stopped and helped her search.

"You heard her, too? Tell me you heard her." Jane pushed through the onslaught, ignoring the startled calls and surprised expressions her actions incited.

Sinclaire stayed close behind. "She'll be crushed in the middle of this," he said. "We have to get to her. Sarah?"

"Miss Jane," she heard again, much closer this time.

Four more bodies moved aside, trying to get past them and to supper, and finally Jane could see the little girl, reddish-blonde curls flopping about her head. Sarah's feet trod along the bottom of her nightgown, nearly causing her to trip over the fabric. Tears filled her eyes and fell in a trickle down her cheeks.

Jane rushed to her side and knelt to the floor. "What is it, sweetheart?" The little girl wrapped her arms around her neck and held on so tightly breathing grew difficult.

Lord Sinclaire stood behind them, presenting a large, immovable force to ensure no one trampled them.

"I had," Sarah said and sniffled, "a bad...dream." A hiccup followed soon behind. "Where is Papa? I want my Papa."

The poor, little dear. Jane took a cursory look across the ballroom to where the guests were headed for supper. She would never find Peter in the mess. Drat.

How on earth had the child made her way to the ballroom without being discovered and ushered back to the safety of the nursery by one of the countless servants about? Fat lot of good they were doing.

She rose and pulled Sarah up into her arms. "Lord Sinclaire, would you be so kind as to inform His Grace? I'll just take Sarah back up to the nursery and settle her in bed." And then once the child was asleep again, she'd pull the nurse out into the hall for a blistering set-down for allowing the little girl to wander about a house full of adult strangers...unless Peter took over that particular responsibility when he arrived. But Lord Sinclaire need not know *all* of Jane's plans.

"Of course. I'll send him along as soon as possible." He inclined his head before hurrying away.

Jane watched long enough to see that no one was paying them any mind, then carried her new charge up the winding staircase.

"Was it an awful dream?" she asked, hoping to get the child talking.

"Dreadful," Sarah answered on a sob.

"Terrible?"

The little girl's eyes widened and she nodded solemnly.

"Would you like to tell me about the dream, Sarah?" Surely it would help her go back to sleep if she could tell what had happened and then have it all banished away.

"No," Sarah wailed. "Please, he'll come back. Don't make me tell you."

"All right. You don't have to talk about it." Double drat. Now what?

They had reached the children's nursery, still with no sign of Peter or Lord Sinclaire. For that matter, there was no sign of Mrs. Pratt. What sort of nurse would leave her charges alone on a night such as this, with a house full with people the children didn't know?

Something would have to be done about that, to be sure. Jane would take the matter up with Peter first thing in the morning.

She turned to close the door behind her, but Mr. Cuddlesworth streaked past her and into the room at the last moment, nearly toppling Jane in his haste. She stumbled to Sarah's bed in the dark, carrying the child the whole way, then lay down beside the child and held her. Mr. Cuddlesworth leapt to the bed and shoved his way between them, purring contentedly.

"So you intend to spend the night with Sarah, then, do you?" she whispered in the darkness. "Very well. I imagine she needs you tonight more than I do."

Between the cat's purring and Jane's stroking of Sarah's back, the child was back to sleep in no time. Jane eased out of the bed, careful not to wake the girl. "You stand guard, Mr. Cuddlesworth, since Mrs. Pratt has gone missing."

Of course, her cat made no response other than to curl up closer to the warmth provided by Sarah and flick his fluffy tail in her direction.

Still, Lord Sinclaire and Peter had not arrived. Good Lord, what was taking them so long?

Jane moved carefully over to Joshua's bed, checking to be sure he was both present and asleep before she left. He was breathing heavily and tucked snugly into his sheets, so it was safe enough for her to leave. She'd find Peter and he could arrange for a servant to stay with the children. Or if she couldn't find Peter, she would fetch Meg from her chambers. That would be a better use for the girl, anyway. She should have thought of that long ago.

Jane slipped out of the nursery, struggling to see in the dim glow of candlelight in the hall as she pulled the door to a close behind her.

Really, the nerve of that Mrs. Pratt, leaving those children alone on a night like this! It was all Jane could do to keep from marching through the entire house right that moment to find the woman and tell her what for.

A familiar scent hit her nostrils—cheroot and whiskey, and a rather foul odor that smelled more like the streets of London than the inside of Hardwicke House should, what with all the flowers strewn about.

She squinted to find the source of the smell in the dim light, but couldn't discern anything out of the ordinary. Gracious, had it been so dark in the hall when she arrived with Sarah moments ago? She didn't think so, but couldn't quite recall. The footmen must be enjoying the revelry of the night, too, for them to have neglected the lighting. But then again, with Mrs. Pratt missing, too... She'd best proceed carefully. Lord only knew what was afoot in the townhouse tonight.

Taking a lit candle from its sconce on the wall, she turned to relight a few of the nearby candles. It wouldn't do for one of the children to wake again and be unable to see to find someone, and she could stand to see more clearly, herself, as she found her way back to the stairs.

Once two candle flames flickered back to life, that same foul scent struck her nostrils again. What on earth could be causing it? Jane held her candle up into the air, hoping to cast its glow upon the source of the odor.

"Looking for me, sweeting?" drawled a sickeningly familiar voice from the shadows. "How fortuitous for us both. I was looking for you, as well."

Utley. It had to be him. No one else in her acquaintance could make her want to scream and cast up the contents of her stomach at the same time.

Her eyes darted about the long expanse. Maybe Mrs. Pratt or one of the missing footmen would miraculously reappear in the hallway. She hoped. Probably foolishly, but she hoped, nonetheless.

No one came.

Drat. Drat, drat, drat!

She could scream. Hopefully, someone other than the children would hear her. Surely Peter and Lord Sinclaire were on their way up the stairs by now. Somewhere—perhaps somewhere on this floor—a servant must be at work. Jane's screams would be heard. Wouldn't they?

Or she could toss her candlestick at him and run. The flame wouldn't burn him much, so it likely wouldn't really slow him down. She might make it to the stairs before he caught her. If she was lucky.

Oh, lud, why couldn't she make up her mind, or have someone else around to make it up for her? It would all be so much easier to act if Sophie was standing beside her and telling her what to do.

What would Sophie do?

Jane's internal debates took too long. Utley emerged from the shadows faster than she could react, placing a hand firmly against her mouth, rendering it impossible to scream, and pulling her back hard against him.

Damnation, she had finally decided to scream *and* run. Now all she could do was kick.

Finally, two sets of footsteps raced up the stairs. It was about time.

"Bloody hell," Utley muttered, then yanked her backward, into a seldom-used study.

Fourteen

PETER'S STOMACH SETTLED in his toes as he rushed from the supper room. Sarah needed him.

The larger concern—the one that had him shoving Sinclaire aside and running, instead of walking—was that she'd come downstairs alone.

Without Mrs. Pratt.

With none of his countless servants seeing her and stopping her.

Something was very, very wrong in his home.

Without paying attention to whether Sinclaire was still following him or not, he raced ahead. All he knew was he had to get upstairs to his daughter. Now.

Peter took the stairs two at a time. The third floor, which housed his nursery, was almost completely dark. "Deuced footmen. What the blazes are they doing instead of their jobs?" A sparse two candles near the nursery door cast an eerie glow upon the hall in the absence of the usual lighting, providing just enough to see the doorway to his children's nursery.

He took one from the sconce and used it to light his path.

Slept. Thank God. He held the candle aloft in the room, checking both beds again to be certain that both of his children were in their beds where they belonged.

A heavy clomping of boots in the hall signaled Sinclaire's arrival. Peter took great care to silently exit the nursery, then closed the door behind him.

"You could stand to walk with a lighter touch." Peter glared upon his friend, even as another brash set of boots came up behind Sinclaire.

Neil skidded to a stop beside them. "I saw you two running off. What's wrong?" The excitement in his tone was impossible for him to hide, as though he were spoiling for an adventure.

"Sarah's all right?" Sinclaire asked, ignoring Neil.

"Asleep. Lower your voices or you'll wake her again."

"And Miss Matthews?" Sinclaire's voice echoed in the deserted hall.

The man clearly didn't understand how to follow orders. Granted, this was nothing new. Sinclaire and Peter's younger brother, Alex, had done as they pleased as boys.

Blast the earl for his impudence.

Neil looked back and forth between them. "What's happened to Jane?"

"Well?" the earl prodded, his tone a touch more reserved than it had been before.

"Well what?" Good Lord, Peter was supposed to be hosting a bloody ball. Neil and Sinclaire couldn't expect him to piddle around in the hallway answering inane questions all night. His guests would be waiting for him, and Mama would be furious if he was gone too long.

"Well, is Miss Matthews all right?" Sinclaire's glare matched his own. "Is she still in the nursery with the children?"

Christ, he'd forgotten about Jane in his worry over Sarah. "I am... She wasn't there."

Just like the minx to disappear on him. It was her bloody come-out ball going on downstairs, and now she was missing. As though he didn't have enough other concerns weighing on his mind at the moment. All of his servants had up and abandoned their posts during the ball.

"Something isn't right, here," Sinclaire murmured. "She wouldn't have left the children alone. Not with the nurse missing and Lady Sarah being frightened."

Peter sighed. Of course, he was right. Blast it.

"We have to find her, Peter," Neil said. "She could be in trouble. I should have—"

"She bloody well *is* trouble," Peter said, cutting his brother off without thinking about what he was saying. He punched the wall beside him, causing the candle still burning in its sconce to bounce around.

A soft moan sounded in the hall—feminine, afraid. "Blast, I just woke Sarah again," he muttered.

"That wasn't Sarah." Sinclaire's voice was low—so low Peter had difficulty making out his words. The earl jerked his head toward the unused study behind where Peter had just assaulted the wall, his eyes huge and black, and realization settled over Peter.

It couldn't be happening again. Not like with Mary. Not in his own deuced home.

Not with his family—his children—present.

But Jane's muffled whimper told him it was.

His jaw tensed and he held his arms at his sides, clenching and unclenching his fists. For a moment—only a moment—he tried to calm himself.

Peter strode to the study, Sinclaire and Neil close behind. He reached to wrench the door from its hinges, but it was already wide open, as though it was waiting for him.

He thrust his candle inside, sweeping it about. Even with what had happened to Mary, he couldn't have ever prepared himself for what stood before him.

Utley, the licentious bastard, had one hand covering Jane's mouth to stifle her cries. His other hand held her arms captive even as she struggled against him. Her eyes were wide and her legs shook. She had to be frightened out of her wits. Thank God she wasn't crying. Peter would lose the very thin veil of control he had over his sanity if she were crying.

"Somerton," Utley said, his voice high and shaking. "I had planned to be caught, but not by you." The Adam's apple in his throat bobbed once, then again.

What game was the bastard playing? Wasn't ruining one woman and leaving her to suffer the consequences alone enough? Peter narrowed his eyes at him, but faced him full-on. "You have precisely sixty seconds to unhand Miss Matthews and leave my home before I seek retribution." Which raised another question—how did Utley even get in to Hardwicke House, in the first place? The bastard was most certainly *not* on the guest list for the evening.

"Ha. Don't you see?" Utley asked with a cackle. "I've already won. Your *Miss Matthews* is ruined now. In moments, your guests will be coming upon us and she'll have no choice but to marry me. The scandal will be all over Town by morning."

Peter would allow Jane to marry that scoundrel about as soon as he would swim to France and join Napoleon's army, pulling his family along behind him. The man was daft. Which, of course, Peter already knew. Something in Utley had cracked back on that day...that day that haunted Peter's dreams since he was only a boy.

Losing one's sanity, however, did not give one leave to ruin countless other lives. Rawden's death, no matter the cause, couldn't be enough to justify ruining other innocents. "Forty-three seconds. I suppose you expect to receive her dowry as well? Is this about money, Utley? We all know you're well on the way to squandering the fortune you inherited."

Utley made no move to release her. "You've boasted quite a sum for her. Any gentleman in need of some...assistance, shall we say...? would be a fool not to do the same." He licked his lips and ran a hand over the sweat beading over his brow. "I'm no fool."

"Twenty-four seconds. And you *are* a fool if you think you'll ever again see even so much as a farthing from me, for any reason. You're an even greater fool if you expect me to believe money is the deciding factor in all of this."

A tic formed in Utley's jaw, and he moved his hand from Jane's mouth to her décolletage, wetting his lips repeatedly through his sneer.

Heat rose up through Peter's body and his head jerked involuntarily to the side and back. He felt, more than saw, Sinclaire and Neil both slip past him and closer to where Utley held Jane captive.

"You don't like that, do you, Somerton? You want her for yourself?" Utley laughed. "It matters not to me—I wouldn't bed her for the king's entire treasury. She can be your plaything. But I *will* have her dowry."

Peter's rage turned his vision red. He dove for Utley, reaching for his throat. Neil pulled Jane away just in time.

A rip sounded as they all fell, two in one direction, two in the other.

Peter held onto Utley's lapel and planted his fist into the bastard's face over and over. Peter reached back to send another straight through his nose when a hand pulled back hard on his arm.

"Stop, Somerton." Sinclaire tightened his grip and wouldn't let go. "Enough."

"Enough?" he roared. It would never be enough. He could never reclaim Mary's honor. And now, he could never reclaim Jane's honor, either.

He started to say just that, but Jane's quiet voice stopped him. "Yes. It's enough. Please."

She sat in the corner of the room shaking almost as badly as Peter was with Neil at her side. The bodice of her gown was held up only by her hands. Still, she didn't cry. Jane's eyes pierced through his, pleading with him. "Let it be enough."

One more. He only wanted one more shot.

But he couldn't do it and then look at her again. Not when she asked him to do otherwise. Peter let go of Utley's coat. A thud sounded when he hit the floor.

Peter's eyes followed the bastard, and landed on his own hand. It was covered in blood. Had he hurt Utley that badly? The memory already faded into the distance.

When Utley painstakingly rose to his feet and stood in the dim light filtering in from the hall, streams of blood poured from his mouth and nose.

"Leave," Peter said, his voice strangled, foreign sounding. "Never dare to step foot on my property again."

Utley's eyes were wild, but he said nothing. He turned and fled from the room, rushing for the back stairs only used by the servants. That must have been how he got inside Hardwicke House in the first place.

"I'll follow him," Neil said, just before Peter did as his feet impelled him to do and followed the bastard himself. "He won't return."

"I'll go, too," Sinclaire added and rushed out.

Peter didn't trust his voice (nor himself, in terms of actually allowing the man to live), so he nodded and remained where he was as Neil and Sinclaire chased Utley down the stairs to some unknown end.

Jane still sat on her chair in the corner, her eyes never leaving him, her hand holding the tattered remains of her gown to her chest. Her eyes were bright, unwavering. Focused on him.

Both of them were still trembling.

Peter took a step toward her. When she didn't flinch, he took two more. "I..." Thoughts left him faster than they arrived. Fiend seize it, what does one say at a time like this?

However, Jane seemed unconcerned about his inability to form a coherent sentence. She stood and walked slowly—meticulously slowly—to stand before him. With each step she took, he forgot to breathe.

How could she be so serene? So unruffled?

Peter was ready to rip limbs from the next man who stepped foot through the door—no matter who that man might be—if not worse. He wanted to bellow his agony from the rooftop for all of Town to hear.

He wanted to wrap her in his arms and assure himself no one would ever hurt her again.

"Peter?" she said, her voice a mere whisper.

He couldn't answer; he must say nothing, so as to avoid saying something wrong. Hurtful. Damaging.

To avoid doing something he would regret.

There were enough regrets already in his life.

She drew ever closer, her eyes searching him for something he couldn't give her. A foot away. A breath away.

A heartbeat away.

The heat radiating from her body would be his undoing if she didn't back away that instant. He should push her aside—force some distance between them.

But he couldn't move.

Jane examined him, her eyes scanning his face, his chest, moving down to his hand. He focused on her eyes as she studied his battered, swollen, bloodied hand. Utley's blood? Or his own? It hardly mattered at this point.

What mattered was that she took that hand—his hand—into one of her own and gingerly felt over it. Her touch was light as a feather.

It seared him.

"No," Peter said. He attempted to pull his hand free, to finally force his body to separate from her—her heat—but her butterfly grasp turned to steel. She wouldn't set him loose.

Once he stopped pulling against her, she trailed her fingers over the bones of his fingers, feeling for breaks. She bent to the ground and ripped a strip from her underskirts.

In the process, the hand which had been covering her bosom dropped away, and the torn fabric fell away with it.

He groaned and tried to look away, to look at anything other than the creamy, full breast bouncing below him. "We could have used my cravat," he said wryly.

If his sarcasm was returning, particularly in a moment like this, perhaps he was finally regaining his sanity?

"This was faster than undoing such a fussy knot." She tore the strip in two, then cleaned his hand with the first and wrapped the wound with the other. "This should do. The cut isn't deep."

After she finished her work, she stepped away from him—and finally remembered about her bared breast. Two hands flew up to cover her bosom, one clutching desperately at the remnants of fabric dangling precariously about her chest.

Too bad. It had been far too long since he'd seen such a lovely sight.

Good Lord, he was a cad. He was almost as bad as Utley, to think a thought like that at a time like this. Good thing the minx couldn't see into his thoughts.

"Thank you," she said.

Thank you. He certainly wasn't deserving of her thanks at the moment—not while he was thinking about taking her to his chambers and undressing the rest of her. Not while he couldn't remove his eyes from her.

"For...for rescuing me like you did." Her voice trembled.

Please, Lord let her not cry. He could handle anything—well, *almost* anything—but a crying female. He had to do something to keep her tears from falling. "Thank you," he blurted out. "For taking care of my hand."

Bloody hell. Something shimmery and wet slid down her cheek, barely visible in the faint candlelight. She was crying. He had to find some way to stop her.

He searched his mind, and came up empty. There was nothing to be done but to kiss her.

Peter closed the scant distance between them in less than a heartbeat. His good hand fisted in the loose curls falling loose from her knot. With his bandaged hand, he dried the tears falling from her eyes.

Then lip met lip and she sighed—a shivery, needy sort of sound that Peter devoured. He could drown in her. She tasted of peaches, and her warmth was like a drug.

His tongue parted her lips and Jane shuddered in his arms. Tongues stroked against each other, plunging then retreating.

Her hands left her torn gown and wandered over his chest and arms, pulling him closer, searching for more. Giving more. Everywhere she touched him, he burned. Feathery, fiery trails slithered across his abdomen, his neck, his back.

He felt greedy. She gave and gave, but still he needed more. Wanted more. It wasn't enough. It would never be enough.

Peter needed...he needed her. He loved her. Good God. The realization hit him like a careening carriage slamming into a brick wall. He needed to taste her. He left her mouth and trailed a wet path with his tongue over her chin, down her neck, to the swell of her bared breast.

"Heavenly," he said. "So sweet."

When he suckled the hardened nub, she gasped and lost her control of her legs, collapsing against the desk behind her. There was no choice to be made—he had to follow her there, because her hands were clamped into tight fists in his hair, pulling his head closer to her breast.

A tiny nip of his teeth, and she moaned.

A breath of air on the wet heat, and she sighed.

Hands were everywhere. His dipping into and kneading her soft, luscious curves. Hers running beneath his coat, stroking over his chest, arms, abdomen.

Footfalls sounded in the hall, moving closer to them, and Peter pulled back suddenly. Christ, what had he been thinking? "Straighten yourself," he ordered. It might be Neil or Sinclaire, but it could very well be any number of other people. His house was full to bursting at the moment, and Lord only knew where his servants were.

Jane looked up at him with fuzzy, confused eyes. Confound it. She was still lost in the haze of passion. She had no idea her entire life was about to change in the blink of an eye. Damnation, he should have killed Utley instead of letting him leave.

He pulled her to her feet and situated her hands on the torn fabric, holding it in place. "You must prepare yourself now, Jane." Peter made certain his tone was firm, not leaving any room for her to misunderstand his meaning.

Realization reached her eyes just in time, and she stood a bit straighter.

"And just *what* have we in here?" demanded a sharp, shrill female voice.

Devil take it. That was certainly not either Neil or Sinclaire. Who on earth had discovered them?

"I daresay you *wanted* to be caught, you did, since the door's wide open to the hall," the unknown intruder continued, coming closer into the room and holding aloft a candle—the last candle burning in the hall—to see their faces.

Lady Plumridge. Damnation. Peter used his body to block the old biddy's view of Jane, but it was too late. The damage was done.

Jane was ruined—and it appeared, at least to anyone in society, to have happened by his own hand.

The woman inched closer, surely trying to make out for certain who the victims of her vile gossip were. Blast, she wouldn't be able to hold her discovery in for even an hour, let alone until morning.

Another step closer, then, "Your Grace? Oh, dear. Why, I was expecting...er...well, this is certainly a surprise, sir."

Clearly, this had been Utley's plan. Only he intended to be the man caught with Jane himself, instead of Peter. Thank God *that* hadn't come to pass. He would never be able to forgive himself if Jane had to suffer such a fate.

"Well, step aside, Your Grace," Lady Plumridge continued. "It must be known who your little doxy is, mustn't it?"

"You will watch your tongue, madam, in the presence of my fiancée." He kept his speech velvety-smooth—dangerous.

"Fiancée?" said Jane, her voice filled with dismay. She pushed against his back in an effort to be heard. He refused to budge, even when she kicked him in the back of his knee. He would have to deal with her later. At the moment, he was busy protecting her honor and virtue as best he could, now that he'd effectively ruined the very same. Blast, he was an idiot, much like she'd once accused him of being.

"And you'll kindly refrain from ever referring to her in such a manner again," he continued, ignoring Jane's efforts behind him. "Remember that you are speaking of the future Duchess of Somerton."

"She most certainly is not," Jane said, much more loudly than the last time. She shoved herself to the side and awkwardly climbed from the desk, clutching her tattered gown to her chest with one arm while elbowing him in the ribs with the other. "Lady Plumridge, there seems to be a misunderstanding, ma'am."

Her desperation would kill him if she didn't compose herself soon. At least in front of one of the two biggest matrons of gossip in all of London. She could fall apart later and rail at him for hours when they were alone. But she had to understand the severity of their situation.

Lady Plumridge certainly did.

The gossipmonger couldn't conceal the burgeoning smile upon her face if she tried—and he doubted she'd made any such effort. "Miss Matthews, I'm quite certain there is no misunderstanding at all. Under the circumstances, you have no alternative. You two must marry, and frankly, dear, the sooner, the better."

Sinclaire rejoined them in the parlor. The combined looks of pity and fury he wore were a clear indication he'd heard at least the last part of the conversation.

"I agree with you, ma'am," Peter said, looking all the while at Sinclaire. "In fact, I was hoping my mother would soon join us so we could inform her of the happy occasion. I'm certain she would wish to make an announcement this evening. What a coup this will be for her, to be able to announce her cousin's engagement at the come-out ball she has given." And perhaps, such an announcement would diffuse the situation Lady Plumridge and her gossip-loving friends would otherwise cause.

Sinclaire took the hint and left, presumably to fetch the dowager and apprise her of the goings-on above stairs.

"You both," Jane said quietly, "seem to be misunderstanding me. I will not be marrying you, *Your Grace*."

Damnation, this was not the time. "You will," he ground out.

"I most certainly will not." Her glare was heated enough to melt a glacier.

Lady Plumridge giggled with mirth, sounding far more like his daughter than a woman quite so long in the tooth as she. Gossip of such magnitude had not been passed about all Season, and she had to be desperate to be the first to tell of it.

Blast it, he needed to talk to Jane alone—to make her understand the repercussions of what she was saying. "Lady Plumridge, might I have a word alone with my fiancée?"

"Oh, no, Your Grace. I don't believe that would be appropriate at all. Why, look at the trouble that's already happened, simply because the two of you were alone together?"

"Ah, but we're betrothed. Society does allow for some *brief* time alone for engaged couples, doesn't it?"

"Well…" The busybody seemingly searched her mind for any excuse to stay and hear everything that was said.

"We are *not* betrothed!" Jane said. "You haven't asked, I haven't accepted, and I might as well inform you now that I *will* not accept, no matter what your ideas on the matter may be." With each point, she poked her finger into his chest.

Lady Plumridge smiled in victory. "It certainly would not be appropriate for you to be alone if you are not engaged, Your Grace, and the lady claims you are not. Therefore, I simply *can't* agree to leave you."

He couldn't decide which woman he would prefer to be the first in his life he'd ever struck: Lady Plumridge for having the audacity to contradict his edict, or Jane for behaving like an unreasonable chit hardly out of the schoolroom.

Cross that off the list. He would never actually strike either woman, irrespective of how much they infuriated him. Instead, he settled with drawing a hand through his hair and coming away with a few strays.

Thankfully, before he thoroughly lost his temper with the two, Sinclaire and his mother rushed into the room, both winded from the exertion. They had arrived upstairs in the blink of an eye. Sinclaire must have put the fear of God in Mama. Peter would have to find a way to thank him later.

"Mama," he said, "I didn't want you to learn this way, but Jane and I will be marrying."

Jane opened her mouth to interrupt him—or perhaps more likely to contradict him—yet again. He put an arm around her waist and pulled her sharply to his side, glaring at her as fiercely as he had ever done as a warning to remain silent. Her mouth snapped to a close, and then she stomped on his toes.

Deuced minx.

"Quite soon," he added on a groan, hoping to further infuriate her.

She elbowed him in the ribs.

"Perhaps tomorrow. I don't particularly care to wait."

Jane huffed in response. Finally, she remained still and quiet. She really needed to learn her place—particularly now that she would be his duchess.

His duchess. His wife. Good God.

His mother beamed at them from just inside the doorway. "Oh, how splendid. We'll have to make an announcement this evening, of course. There won't be time for an engagement ball, it seems, but we'll plan a celebration for afterward, if that will suit you, Jane."

Mama stopped and truly looked at Jane for the first time since entering the parlor. "Oh, dear. You must go up to Meg at once and change into a new gown. Hurry along. There's no time to waste."

"But..."

His mother had joined them before the desk and now placed her hand where Peter's had been. "But nothing. You can't possibly rejoin the ball looking as you do. Go. Shoo."

Lady Plumridge had been creeping toward the door. The harridan likely wanted to be the first to return to supper so she could spoil the surprise or cause some other sort of uproar.

Mama, ever aware, took care of that possibility, as well. Once Jane was out the door and headed toward her chamber to change, Mama turned to Lady Plumridge. "Why, Sybil. I've not spoken with you yet this evening. Will you not be so kind as to sit with me for supper? We have an opening at our table." She firmly took hold of the other woman's arm and led her away, despite the woman's tittering and glancing over her shoulder.

Peter's head felt like Wellington's army was marching through it. Blast, how had this happened again?

"Will you please go down to supper, as well?" he asked Sinclaire. "Explain our absences as you will."

His friend inclined his head with a look of pity in his eyes, then went on his way.

Twice, women he had had no intention of offering for would become his wife.

Twice, Utley was to blame.

Devil take it.

Fifteen

MEG FASTENED THE buttons on Jane's lilac muslin much more quickly than she ever had before. "A quick brush of your hair, and then you'll be out the door and back to your ball, miss."

Sadly, Jane had no desire whatsoever to return to her own come-out ball.

As soon as she did, Peter would likely announce their *engagement*— an engagement she had never agreed to, and wouldn't ever agree to even if she felt it was necessary.

But honestly, why on earth should such a thing be required, when all she wanted to do was open her shop and make gowns for the ladies of society? Surely it wouldn't matter in the grand scheme of life if she'd been compromised. Nothing truly scandalous had happened. Not really.

And even if it *had* happened, her dressmaking skills should hold far more moment than her reputation, if all she was doing was sewing gowns, for goodness's sake.

In all honesty, a hint of scandal might draw more curiosity about her and cause some ladies to visit her shop that otherwise might not.

Let the gossips gossip. Jane couldn't care less.

But obviously, for some ghastly reason she had yet to decipher, Peter *did* care.

Drat.

Why had he suddenly decided to play the part of the gallant hero? To ride in on a white charger and rescue the poor, unprotected damsel in distress? To turn against everything she had come to know of him and to think of him?

Life would certainly be much less complicated if people would simply behave as they ought, or at least maintain a sense of consistency within their actions. How was she supposed to know how to respond to his ever-changing moods?

Bloody infuriating man.

"All finished now, miss," Meg said, returning the silver-plated brush to the vanity before Jane. "Hurry along. You mustn't keep Her Grace waiting."

This was one moment that Jane wished her assigned lady's maid were not so efficient. "Thank you, Meg." She stood and started for the door before coming up with a possible excuse to delay. "I don't suppose there is anything you need assistance with this evening, is there?"

Meg's fierce frown served as her answer.

"I suppose not." Jane sighed and reached for the door knob.

"Miss?"

A reprieve. Thank God. She said a silent prayer that it would keep her for a few hours and that the guests would tire of awaiting her return, even whilst recognizing the foolishness of such a prayer. "Yes, Meg?"

"I hope...I hope you'll consider keeping me on as your lady's maid once you are His Grace's duchess, ma'am." Meg flushed. "It has been a pleasure to serve you, and I know that it will all be quite an adjustment for you."

"Oh..." Goodness, she had no earthly idea how to respond.

"I should very much like to assist you in any way you need."

"I see. Thank you."

Double drat. Would Meg have to give up a coveted position in the house if Jane left? But she couldn't worry about that. She had to think of what was best for herself.

"Thank you, miss. Now be on your way, before Her Grace sends a search party up for you."

Leave it to Cousin Henrietta to do just such a thing. The woman was certainly determined once she decided something needed to happen. All signs pointed to her siding with Peter on this particular matter. Especially since she was so determined to see each of her offspring marry.

Jane opened the door and strode into the hall, almost running headlong into Peter only two steps outside her chamber. She let out a tiny squeak of surprise.

All right, fine. She virtually screamed, if truth be told.

He took hold of her upper arms to steady her, which kept her from toppling into him and kept both of them from falling to the floor in a massive heap of flailing limbs. Even after she regained her equilibrium, he maintained his grip on her.

Someone had come along and relit the various candles in the hall, casting a seductive glow in his eyes. For the first time, she recognized that they were two different colors—one an intense green and the other a deep, passionate blue. They bored through her. She wished she knew what his expression meant—the fierce eyes, clenched jaw, the pulsing vein in his temple.

Peter's hands were as taut and tense against her arms as he had seemed only moments earlier, when he'd discovered her in Utley's clutches. He'd looked like a lion, preparing to attack then. Stalking. Prowling. Dangerous.

"Are you all right?" His voice melted into the recesses of the hall, barely more than a whisper. It felt like a trembling caress sliding over her ears.

She nodded, unable to find her voice for once. His question held more moment than simply asking after her stability. That much was clear. But there was no time now—no time to sort it all out.

Tomorrow she would have to make him understand she wouldn't marry him.

His reputation would survive intact if she called off the so-called *engagement* after it had been announced—she held no compunctions about that. Only she would face the scorn of the *ton*.

From everything she had seen of the *beau monde* during her time in London, their derision would be fleeting, at most. In weeks, or even days, they would move on to the next *on dit* and Jane Matthews would be merely a passing memory.

Gradually, Peter released his hold on her and let his arms drop to his sides. "We should return to the ballroom. Our guests are expecting us."

"*Our* guests," she whispered beneath her breath. Drat, drat, drat. He was already speaking of them as though they were a unit, two halves of a whole. Perhaps she shouldn't wait until morning to disabuse him of this ill-advised notion.

"Yes. Our guests."

How could his voice be so calm? How could he not be as mortified about their current situation as she? He'd made it abundantly clear in all of their previous interactions that he found her to be as capable of fulfilling the role of his duchess as she was likely to spend the night rolling around in his stables. Peter could not possibly *want* this marriage.

And hadn't he told her only a few nights ago that he'd never wanted to marry his first wife either? That it had been far from a love match, but a marriage forced by Utley?

He would resent her forever if she allowed the farcical marriage to occur.

She had to stop him.

Before she could say another word, he took hold of her hand and placed it in the crook of his arm, holding it there with a touch more force than truly necessary, and pulled until she had no choice but to follow along behind him.

"Smile. Don't let them see...try not to show them how upset you are, Jane." His voice cracked slightly as he spoke, but he continued forward, guiding her down the stairs. Voices and laughter intermingled with the clinks of silver on china as they drew nearer to the formal dining room.

He stopped and faced her just as they arrived before the open French doors leading to the supper guests. "I know you don't want this. But I promise to protect you. I promise I will take care of you." Peter fixed her with a stare. "You'll never want for anything, Jane."

What nerve. Never want for anything, indeed. *What of love,* she yearned to fire back at him—but was too busy to speak, as she was forcing the tears stinging her eyes to subside.

Being short of words had never been an affliction Jane suffered before. The things this man did to her!

He resumed his position at her side and advanced again. As they entered the great hall, filled with more chandeliers, and wall sconces, and flowers in pots and vases even than it was with people, Jane prayed her face held a smile and not the greenish, sickly pallor her stomach suggested was more likely. All eyes followed them as they approached Cousin Henrietta's table near the dais. With each step they took, the gentle hush grew more pronounced until the silence was deafening.

They were all watching her—waiting for her to react, to trip and fall, to make some sort of social blunder. Little did they know, she was priming to make the biggest social blunder of all. They would have their laugh at her expense. Perhaps not tonight. But it would come.

When they arrived at Cousin Henrietta's table, Peter pulled her to a stop and his mother stood. The stillness of the hall threatened to rob Jane of her courage. She looked out upon the sea of faces, and they all blurred together into a riot of color.

Peter spoke. She knew he must have. But she didn't hear a word. Instead, she focused on keeping her knees from buckling beneath her, on pretending to be happy.

After long moments, the room erupted into applause. The crowd of faces rose, smiling at her. Sophie and Charlotte rushed over to embrace her. It was all she could do to stay on her feet during the ordeal. They must have said something to her—she didn't know.

She only knew she couldn't go through with this marriage.

The applause died down and the revelers returned to their supper. Another tug on her arm brought her to a seat at the table next to Peter. She sat with a blank stare at the plate before her. What was she to do now? Sitting was good. She didn't feel nearly so faint with a chair beneath her, where before, Peter's arm had been her only support. Perhaps she would not thoroughly embarrass herself tonight.

Perhaps she would survive the remainder of the ball and last until morning.

But then she would have to put an end to his ridiculous notions, once and for all.

Peter leaned toward her and spoke into her ear, softly, so no one else could hear. "Eat. You will be ill if you don't."

She might be ill if she did. Jane scowled back at him but took up her fork and made an effort to comply. Collapsing into a faint would certainly not be the best plan. After a few bites of roasted pheasant, however, her stomach responded with a ravenous growl; she ate with more vigor after that.

From across the table, Sophie caught her eye. Oh, how she wanted to sit and talk with her friend. That would not be possible for several more hours, at the least. Sophie already planned to come to her chamber tonight, though, to discuss the afternoon's visit with Jane's solicitor. Then they could work out a plan together.

Lord knew Jane's mind was not functioning properly at the moment. She desperately hoped Sophie's was. Someone had to be able to think for her.

Well, someone other than Peter, at least.

"GO UPSTAIRS. GET some rest," he said to Jane after the last of their guests had finally left Hardwicke House. "We have a long day ahead of us tomorrow."

She looked up at him with pinched-together eyebrows and pained eyes. Christ, the night's events had taken a lot out of her. Granted, she had taken it all relatively well, all things considered. But she was unhappy—probably devastated. Life had never prepared her for any of the things she was about to experience.

A vicar's daughter! How would she ever cope with becoming a duchess overnight? Simply being *out* in society was sometimes more than he felt she could handle with a modicum of decorum, given her escapades of late, but to be a duchess?

Not to mention becoming a mother.

And his wife.

He said a silent prayer of thanks that he had his mother and sisters with him, still. They could help her. They could teach her what she needed to learn. At least as far as her new role was concerned.

Mama would guide Jane through this.

And Peter would follow through with the promises he'd made to her earlier.

He may not be a man she loved, or even *could* love. But he'd damned well be certain she had everything she needed and wanted. She would be happy if it killed him. She would be honored. He would preserve her reputation.

This marriage would not be as cold and lonely as his first, by God.

Jane still hadn't moved; she stood staring up at him, with much the same expression she had worn since they returned to the ball. The poor thing was surely in shock. Her entire life had changed in a moment.

Mama and Sophie returned to the hall, still aglow from the jubilation of the soiree. He caught Sophie's gaze and gestured toward his betrothed.

A single nod followed. "Come along, Jane. Up to your chamber we go." Sophie took Jane's hand and led her away, leaving him alone with his mother.

They watched in silence as the two climbed the stairs.

After they had gone, Mama leveled her discerning gaze upon him. "You didn't want this."

A statement—not a question.

"No."

She studied him for a moment, then reached up and pulled his hand from where it was absentmindedly stroking his chin. "Was it...?"

The question floated in the air, hovering over the scent of newly extinguished flames and wilting flowers before falling between them.

"Utley, again." His own voice sounded strange to his ears—strangled, almost.

Her jaw dropped. "Again? Mary?"

Peter nodded gravely. "Mama, if I hadn't followed her. If I hadn't caught him when I did—"

"Hush." She drew him over to a nearby chaise and pulled him down beside her. "You did. You got to her in time. She's safe, and you'll marry her."

"I will." Whatever it took to keep her safe, he would do.

Mama squeezed his hand. "You're a good man, Peter. You make me very proud."

So why did he feel the need to punch his fist through something hard? His hand shook, even as Mama held it.

"Promise me one thing," she said, looking down at her small hand in his much larger hand.

"If I can."

"You can. Promise me you'll try to love her. Promise me you'll make more of an effort than you did with Mary."

"Mama..."

"You can. All you have to do is try."

She made it sound so bloody easy. He *had* tried before, with Mary, and had failed. But Jane? Lust he could accomplish.

Love was an entirely different beast.

"I know she deserves to be loved—"

"This isn't about her, Peter. This is about you. Try to love her, because you'll be a much happier man if you do. I told you that you are a good man, but you are far from happy. I want you to be happy."

"And you believe Jane can make me happy?"

Several beats passed without response. "No," she said, her voice weighty. "No one can make you happy but yourself. But if you're willing to try, she can make you love." Mama stood and kissed him on the forehead. "Good night. Will you be off to Doctor's Commons in the morning?"

"Yes. I'll take Sinclaire with me." He hoped the Bishop of Canterbury wouldn't delay with granting the special license. The sooner he could marry Jane, the better chance he had of avoiding scandal. Lady Plumridge could only be held off for so long.

Mama nodded and climbed the stairs, leaving him to his own ruminations.

He doubted he'd sleep that night. There was far too much to be done. First and foremost, he needed to talk to Forrester and arrange for him to travel to Carreg Mawr. It was high time he took matters there in hand.

There was no time to waste. Utley could already be on his way there after his quick eviction from Hardwicke House. No reason to allow him to reach his brother there first.

Peter sighed before turning to his library, calling out for Spenser and Forrester on the way. Haste was in order. And he needed a drink.

"I CAN'T MARRY him."

Jane sat across from Sophie on the foot of her bed, both exhausted. They were clad in their nightrails and wrappers after the ordeal of her come-out ball.

Sophie impaled her with deep blue eyes and frowned. "Why not?"

"You're supposed to be on my side, Sophie! You're supposed to help me figure a way out of this mess, not ask me why I can't marry him. I can't marry him because...because I can't."

"And you should answer my questions and not skirt the subject."

Jane fiddled with the brush in her hands, looking at it to avoid her friend's imploring gaze.

"Answer me. I won't sit here waiting all night, you know. I need my rest if you're getting married tomorrow. Otherwise my skin will look a fright."

"I'm *not* getting married tomorrow," Jane said.

"Well, you oughtn't to have agreed to it in the first place, then." Sophie reached across and took the brush from her hands, using it on Jane's riotous curls. "Now the whole *ton* is expecting a wedding between you and Peter. You simply can't break off the engagement."

"I didn't agree to it. And I can, too."

"You also didn't deny it in front of everyone at your ball when Mama and Peter announced it." Sophie's brush strokes were less forgiving than Meg's. "There were a good two hundred people here tonight. Maybe more."

"You aren't helping anything." Jane winced when her friend pulled through a particularly bad knot in her hair without pausing to ease the discomfort. "What am I going to do now? You know as well as I do that your brother doesn't want to be married to me any more than I want to be married to him."

Sophie kept brushing, perhaps even more forcefully than before. "I know no such thing. In fact, I think you're only trying to convince yourself of that."

"Now that's a piece of rubbish, for certain."

"What's certain," said Sophie, "is you're behaving like an utter dolt. It would be not only lamentable, but also ludicrous, for you to reject Peter now." She walked to the vanity and lay the brush down, then turned back to Jane with something of a pleading look in her eyes. "He's a good man, you know. He'll care for you well."

"I don't doubt that, but—"

"But what?" She threw up her hands and spun around to face Jane. "Is this about your shop? Because you can't possibly attempt to lie to me again and tell me you don't love my brother. It's as clear as the dawn to me how you feel. You're only fooling yourself if you deny it."

"Of course I love him!" Drat. Jane's eyes widened to the point she thought they might fall out.

Did she really? She couldn't possibly. Could she?

"Of course you do. So what's the problem?" Sophie took a seat facing Jane in the high-backed chair before the vanity.

"He doesn't love me." Oh good Lord, were these words really coming from her mouth? "He doesn't love me now, and I don't think he will ever be capable of it. Sophie...he's only doing this because of Lord Utley. And he already married a woman he never loved before. I can't allow him to do that again. I will not subject myself to a lifetime married to a man who wants anything other than to be married to me."

Sophie slid back into place beside her and pulled her into a hug, carefully wiping the tears away from Jane's eyes. Double drat, now she was crying—and all because of him. She wanted to plant him a facer now because of it. If only he was sitting there where she could reach him, she would.

"All right. Enough of this crying. Tears won't solve your problem, will they?"

She was beginning to think that nothing could solve her problem. Still, Jane straightened herself and dried her eyes.

"I suppose we'll just have to sneak you out of the house again, then, won't we?" Sophie asked. "You finalized your plans earlier with Mr. Selwood, didn't you?"

"Yes. The building is ready for me to use."

"I think it's time we set up your shop, then. You did say earlier that there's an apartment above stairs, didn't you? Somewhere you could sleep?"

Jane nodded.

"Excellent. Then we'll just wait until Peter leaves for Doctor's Commons in the morning and move you in to your new shop."

Her new shop. She was going to be a business owner—independent. She hoped.

"Do you think anyone will come to me after this? I mean, if I jilt your brother?"

Sophie laughed, a deep, musical sound. "Why, Jane, you'll be the talk of the *ton* tomorrow. You'll have a larger customer base in a few days' time than you could serve in a month."

She hoped her friend was right. If her modiste shop failed, Jane would have no option of staying in London. Not after breaking her betrothal to Peter, at least. She would have to return to her parents, and Mother would be terribly disappointed in her, to say the least.

"You're still planning to help me, then, even if I hurt your brother in this way?"

Sophie took her hand and squeezed it. "If you're right about him—that he doesn't love you and never could—then this won't hurt him. He should be relieved."

"And if I'm wrong?" Not that she could possibly be wrong. Not about that.

"If you're wrong, then Peter will take care of it."

Jane didn't know if that was a promise or a threat.

Sixteen

AFTER MAMA AND the girls went up to bed, Peter summoned Forrester and Spenser to join him in his library. Neil and Sinclaire were talking in hushed tones outside his library when he and his servants arrived, so he called them in as well.

When they were all inside and the doors were closed firmly behind them, Peter turned to Sinclaire and Neil, then sat behind his desk. "Utley?" Somehow, he couldn't get out any more than that. Even the one word had his voice breaking.

"He left down the servants' stairs and out the back door," Neil said. "In a hired hack. I followed him until it stopped at his bachelor lodgings. He went in…but I didn't get the impression that he intends to stay there long. I think he's planning to make an escape tonight."

Sinclaire cursed beneath his breath. "Where is he heading?"

"My guess would be Wales," Peter said.

They all turned to stare at him.

"Phineas Turnpenny has been siphoning funds from Carreg Mawr for months. I finally sorted it all out recently. I asked Forrester to plant a spy there as a footman to confirm my suspicions."

"Indeed, Your Grace." Forrester nodded with a frown. "Martin's latest report details how he caught Mr. Turnpenny adjusting the ledgers right after sending a suspicious looking package through the post to London. To his knowledge, Turnpenny is still unaware of his true function at the castle."

"So he's pilfering from you and sending it to his brother?" Neil said. "Isn't taking your money enough for Utley?"

"Clearly not," Peter responded dryly. Neil didn't know the half of it, but it was better that way.

"Now what?" Sinclaire asked. "He's headed there now, but—"

"But I can't very well leave Town, since I have to marry Jane with all due haste," Peter said, interrupting him.

Neil stood and moved near the hearth, cracking his knuckles. "I'll go. I can travel faster than he can, since he's injured. If I leave immediately, I can get there before him and have the magistrate waiting when he arrives."

Peter sighed. Neil was right, and his plan was probably for the best…but a part of Peter still wanted to be the one to settle matters with Utley, once and for all. For that matter, he wanted to handle things with Phinny. But the crown would have to handle Utley, and the magistrate could see to it that it happened—and he could lock Turnpenny up.

He nodded. "See to it."

Before Peter could change his mind, Neil was gone. Devil take it, how did his brother move so fast when he wanted to? Clearly, he was spoiling for an adventure. Town life had never really agreed with Neil. It gave him too much time to waste, so waste it he did.

Peter then sent Spenser and Sinclaire to gather up what servants could be found and to search the house for those who were missing.

They were found locked inside an unused drawing room on the third floor. Mrs. Pratt, several maids, and a number of Peter's footmen, after being rescued from their confinement, all confirmed that Lord Utley was responsible for the deed. He'd brought a pistol into Hardwicke House, so what choice did they have? Thank God they were all unharmed—however frightened they might be.

Finally, hours after the ball had finished, Peter's house was returned to something resembling normal. He went to the antechamber situated off his library, sat down in the leather covered armchair by the fire, and poured another tumbler of whiskey.

He only wished he could be with Neil at Carreg Mawr when the magistrate confronted Utley and Turnpenny, in order to truly taste the victory. Instead, he would be here, marrying yet another woman he never intended to marry.

Devil take it.

AFTER FURTHER DISCUSSION, Jane and Sophie decided it was better to wait until the house was quiet tonight, and then sneak Jane out to move to her storefront while the household slept. Even if the household servants didn't try to stop them or say something to Peter or Cousin Henrietta, surely one of the many members of the Hardwicke family would notice something afoot. Neil, in particular, seemed to somehow notice everything, even though he was rarely present.

No, Jane couldn't simply prance out the front door dragging a trunk of her belongings behind her. She also couldn't make it to Bond Street with her trunk on her own. A carriage was an absolute necessity. But not one of Peter's carriages. She couldn't risk waking the grooms and having one of them let information slip, or she'd end up right where she had started—being trapped into an unwanted marriage.

Sophie suggested hiring a hackney, which, after much hemming and hawing, they decided was their best course of action. Meg, having been sworn to secrecy, volunteered to go out in search of one—but only after enough time had passed that they could reasonably assume no one would wake. In the meanwhile, all three co-conspirators set to work packing those items Jane simply must take with her, with Mr. Cuddlesworth overseeing their work. He lay in his basket, which was situated on the four-poster bed beside them, with his head propped over the edge to watch their every movement.

"Anything that doesn't fit into your trunk," Sophie said, "we can arrange to have delivered to you later on. In fact, I'll personally bring it all to you—when I come to assist you in opening your shop."

"You're still planning to come then? Oh, but your mother will be murderous when she hears of your plan."

Meg chuckled and folded another of Jane's shifts. "Her Grace won't take the news well, but I hardly think she'll kill anyone. Least of all her daughter."

"Besides," Sophie said, "her reaction to me wanting to help you won't be anywhere near as explosive as her reaction to your leaving and denying to marry Peter. She thinks of you as her daughter already, you know, and Peter...well, she's *desperate* to see him married."

"You mean she's desperate to see *all* of us married." Jane grimaced. "Do you really think she'll be cross with me?"

"Cross with you?" Sophie lifted a brow. "Sweetheart, the only thing you need worry about more than her reaction is Peter's."

Jane frowned. "But I told you he wouldn't care."

"And I told you that you were wrong." Sophie rolled her eyes heavenward in Meg's direction. "Honestly, you'd think she would realize I know my brothers rather well after all of these years."

Meg fixed a pitying gaze on Jane. "Well, I believe I should be on my way to fetch that hackney coach. The trunk is about as full as it will go."

Sophie nodded at her, then turned to Jane. "You're certain about this?"

"Positive," she replied, despite the crickets hopping about in her stomach.

"Very well."

Meg started toward the door. "I'll direct your coach to the side of the house." Then she spun and was gone in the dark stillness of the mansion house.

"Meg asked me if she could go with you," Sophie said after several moments had passed. She reached a hand over and stroked Mr.

Cuddlesworth's head, eliciting a purr so loud it was almost a roar. "She can't stand the thought of you being completely alone there, with no one to see after your needs."

"I'm perfectly capable—"

"I told her she absolutely must. If Peter won't continue to pay her wages, I will. It would be a good use for my pin money…being sure you're well looked after."

Jane hefted a sigh. "If I'm going to have a servant, then I'll pay her myself. But I refuse to have a servant." Good gracious, had everyone forgotten that she'd lived her entire life with only a single servant for the entire family? She could manage quite well without any help, at least in that area. Jane threw the last few things she had been fiddling with into the chest and slammed the door closed.

"I'm afraid you'll be greatly disappointed, then. Meg and I refuse to allow you to leave this house if you don't take Meg with you." Sophie reached out and stilled Jane's hands, which were fumbling with the latches. "You need someone with you. Think of her as a companion, if you will. It isn't safe for you to be completely alone."

"I won't be alone. I'll have Mr. Cuddlesworth with me."

Sophie frowned and lifted a brow. "And what will he do to assist you? Purr at any intruders who try to accost you? Sink his claws into Lady High-in-the-Instep's gown, so she'll have to purchase a new one?"

Drat, Sophie was right. Jane took a deep breath to calm her nerves. "Fine. Meg can come. Perhaps I can use her assistance in the shop, too. She could take measurements and such."

Her friend smiled. "That's an excellent idea. I would feel better, as well, if you had a butler of sorts. A man to offer you some protection."

"Sophie…" She wished she had been able to better hide the irritation seeping through her voice. It sounded more like a warning than she intended.

"I won't take a chance with my luck tonight. We'll discuss it further when I come to help you set up your shop."

By this point, Jane knew that "discuss it further" coming from Lady Sophia Hardwicke meant she would arrive with a vast array of candidates for the position, and push and prod until Jane allowed one of them to stay.

Argument would be fruitless.

Lovely. And just *how* was she supposed to pay the wages of not only Meg, but also a footman? Yes, Sophie would offer to pay them. But that wasn't the point. The point was that this was Jane's shop, Jane's livelihood. Sophie could always rely on her brother to care for her if she needed it. Her pin money alone was more than Jane ever hoped to earn in a year from her dress making.

She wanted to prove she could do this on her own. To prove it to herself.

A carriage creaked by outside the window, pulling Jane out of her worries. She dashed to see if it was the hackney, but the driver kept going past where Meg would have stopped.

She held back a curtain and took a breath of the cool, fresh air. A hint of rain danced against her nostrils. Hopefully they would arrive soon. The thought of carrying her trunk alone had her worried, but doing it in the rain? It would be a farce of unparalleled measure.

Her thoughts turned to Peter again. Blast the man. Why must he constantly be at the forefront of her mind? "Why do you believe Peter will be unhappy that I've left?" she asked so quietly she was unsure if Sophie had heard.

"You may love my brother, Jane," she responded after a moment, "but you truly don't know him very well." She sighed. "He is a very proud man. The only things he holds in higher esteem than his honor are his family and duty."

"*Duty.*" He felt she was his duty—his responsibility. His charge. Had he not said that very thing to her at the first ball of the Season?

She would be damned before she would be his burden to bear.

"Yes. Duty. Admittedly, sometimes he is blinded by his duties." Sophie walked to stand beside her at the window and looked her plainly in the eyes. "Nevertheless, he now considers you part of his family, and therefore he sees it as his responsibility to protect you—your virtue. He would count it as a mark against his honor if he can't."

"I don't need his protection." And she bloody well didn't want it, either.

"By leaving—by rejecting his protection—you'll also prevent him from maintaining his honor. That's how he'll see it." Sophie turned her stare to the cobbled street below. "I believe your hackney has arrived."

"But...why are you helping me to do this if it will hurt your brother so egregiously?" Sophie's relationship with Peter had always seemed to be so loving, albeit in a provoking manner. Playful. Certainly never truly mean-spirited or hurtful.

With a single hand, Sophie brushed a stray curl away from Jane's face and tucked it behind her ear, a slow, gentle smile forming on her lips. "My brother is a good man, Jane. But there are many things he has yet to learn. Like it or not, I believe you're meant to be his teacher."

Meg stole back into the room then, flushed from her brief excursion. "Miss, we're all ready to go." She had already brought a valise in with them. Jane supposed it must hold some of Meg's possessions. "The driver wanted to come in and carry your trunk out, but I insisted he stay outside of the house. His boots would surely wake someone. We'll simply have to carry it ourselves."

Which they proceeded to do. Jane settled Mr. Cuddlesworth's basket on top of the trunk. Meg carried her own valise and one end of the trunk, while Sophie and Jane jointly lifted the other end .

They had a brief scare when Jane tripped slightly at the bottom of the stairs, but thankfully no one called out. They simply scurried along and got out the door where the hackney driver took the trunk from them.

"All right, I suppose this is it, then," Jane said. "Are you ready, Meg?"

"Yes, miss."

"I'll call on you tomorrow, if I can," said Sophie. "It may take a few days for Mama and Peter to recover from the shock, though, so don't be surprised if I don't arrive until later in the week."

"Sophie?" Jane said. The crickets in her stomach had just turned into frogs. She had thought she would be excited about her adventure. Not scared. Double drat. "You'll be all right, won't you? I mean, once they find out that you've helped me. And that you intend to continue helping me."

Good Lord, it sounded like she thought they might hurt her for offering her assistance.

"I can promise you," came Sophie's response. "No one will die over this."

How terribly reassuring.

PETER WAS SO tired when he returned to Hardwicke House after his visit with the Bishop of Canterbury that he felt ready to fall over where he stood. Despite how much he had accomplished last night, his day today was still far from complete.

Instead of even attempting to take a nap, he slipped back into his antechamber and poured himself another glass of whiskey and. He sat there before the empty fireplace, nursing his thoughts and his whiskey.

It wouldn't be so terrible to be married to Jane. True, she hadn't been bred to be the wife of a peer—indeed, far from it. But there was a lively glow about her. He doubted he would ever be bored with her. Annoyed, certainly, at least from time to time. Even perplexed, perhaps. But never bored.

He should be thankful Utley had chosen Jane as his victim this time, and not the boring Lady Helene, or one of the several widowed vultures who had been chasing after him since the beginning of the Season.

The events of late could certainly have worked out much less in his favor than they actually had. Still, it was a miserable fate he was now forced to drag Jane into—one she certainly had no desire to see through. She'd made her feelings on the matter easy enough to decipher.

He hated that she would be locked into a marriage, the thought of which so obviously repulsed her. But really, would she have been better with Utley? Hardly.

Peter would be a good husband to her. He would treat her well, and she would want for nothing. That was far better than a number of women in Society marriages could expect. She should be grateful.

Alas, he couldn't force Jane to appreciate his efforts at preserving her virtue. For that matter, he couldn't insist that she be happy and expect her to comply. He would simply have to do everything in his power to ensure her contentment within their marriage.

Spenser knocked at the door to Peter's antechamber and announced that luncheon was served. Peter merely nodded and headed that way, double checking the inner pocket of his waistcoat to be certain the license remained where he had placed it.

His footman (who had, blessedly, returned to his proper position) opened the double doors before him and announced his arrival.

Peter looked around the table and cursed beneath his breath. "Where is Jane?" Everyone else was precisely where he expected them to be. Trust his lovely fiancée to complicate matters, yet again. She certainly had a knack for it.

"She had quite an eventful evening, dear," said his mother. "I haven't had the heart to wake her."

The minx had better be well rested, if she was still abed at this hour. Perhaps she had managed enough sleep for the both of them. Of course, that would do nothing for his rapidly building temper.

Sophie coughed. "Sorry, so sorry. That bite went down wrong is all. I'm quite all right." She flushed and turned her attention back to her meal.

"Did you get the license?" Charlotte asked. "Mama and I made arrangements with a vicar of a small church nearby. He'll perform the ceremony this afternoon if you have the license."

"Really, Peter," Sophie interjected. "Can't you allow her a week to prepare? Or at least a few days. This is all rather sudden, you know." She took a bite of the cheese she had been holding for several moments and grimaced. "Oh. I thought this wouldn't be so sharp."

"You said that the last time you tried that cheese," Charlotte said, then turned to Peter. "She does have a point though. Why the rush? You announced the betrothal at the ball last night. I should think that would be enough to hold the gossips over, at least for a week."

Giving her more time would simply delay the inevitable. *And* it would give her more time to try to change his mind. Which he would not be doing. "We'll marry today. Mama, will you please come with me. I need to wake my bride."

Sophie rose so quickly that she bumped her knee on the table, then bounced around in a little pain dance. "Wait."

Peter closed his eyes and said a silent prayer for patience. "Wait? Sophia, she's had more than enough time to rest. Jane must get up and begin preparing herself." Could his sisters truly not understand the urgency of the matter? Good Lord. He turned to his mother. "Please, come with me."

"No!" cried out Sophie. She rushed in front of him and placed both hands on his chest, as though she could forcefully stop his progress.

He glared at her and removed her hands from his body, pushing her to the side so he could continue.

"What on earth has gotten into you today?" Mama asked as she followed behind him.

Sophie chased along behind them, squeezing her way past him on the stairs and yet again stopping directly before him. "I can't allow you to do this, Peter."

"To do *what*, precisely?" he growled. A twitch that had been forming since sometime the previous evening was now pulsing out a tattoo on his temple. "Are you attempting to save your friend from marriage? Or just from me?"

"Well, neither. Not exactly, at least." His sister, usually so calm and level-headed, was now biting her lip. He had rarely seen the like from her.

"Then what, exactly?" If she didn't give him a straight answer about her current antics in the next thirty seconds, he was liable to lose his temper and rip her head from her neck.

He never lost his deuced temper. Or rather, he never lost his temper until *she* tumbled into his life. *Jane.* Now it seemed to be happening on a recurring schedule—one that was intensifying in frequency.

And he was going to be bloody well married to her.

"I...er...well, Jane isn't up there. In her chamber."

Sophie's eyes widened as he glowered at her, advancing slowly up the next stair until he towered over her from the stair directly beneath her.

"In the house," she amended with a squeak.

"Am I to understand that you know where my betrothed is?" he asked as softly as he could manage.

Sophie nodded emphatically. "But I can't tell you."

Peter grabbed hold of her wrist, half-dragged her the rest of the way up the stairs, and pulled her into the nearest room, slamming the door closed after Mama came through. The last thing he needed was for his servants to overhear him bellowing at his sister in the front of the house, or for a visitor to arrive while he was in a full temper.

Peter shoved his sister into a chair and leaned over her. "You can't tell me? Or you won't tell me?" He neglected to even attempt to keep his voice down.

She bit her lip. "Both."

Impertinent chit. "Why?"

"Why what?"

"Why," he roared, "do you refuse to tell me the whereabouts of my fiancée? The woman I intend to marry today. The woman I compromised last night. The woman you've treated as your bosom friend these last months. The woman you've been virtually inseparable from, and therefore whose welfare you must care about a great deal."

"Because she asked me not to tell you."

He heaved a sigh and dragged a hand—a hand that was desperately itching to box something—through his hair. "And why did she ask such a favor of you?"

"You would have to ask Jane that question."

The urge to strike a woman had never consumed so fully him before now. Not ever. He took two steps back to be certain not to give in to his instincts. "I can't very well ask her if I don't know where she is, can I?"

"No, I suppose not."

He had to give Sophie some credit. Most men would have cowered in fear from him, the way he was bellowing and raging at her. But she sat there, unwavering. Her eyes widened a time or two, but she never even flinched.

Jane had clearly won his sister's devotion. While he was glad she had a friend so fully in her court, now was not the time for such antics.

"Peter, why are you so upset she's gone?" Sophie asked. "You ought to be relieved. She granted you a reprieve."

"A reprieve?" he roared. "From what?" Good God, Sophie was acting like an utter nitwit.

"From a marriage which, obviously, neither of you wants. Your first marriage was just that. Jane is simply making certain that you aren't stuck in the same circumstances as before—in a loveless marriage."

"It won't be a loveless marriage. It won't be the same as before."

She stood and faced him with shrewd, narrowed eyes. "You admit it, then?"

"Admit what?" Could she not give him an inkling as to what she was talking about? He would never understand how or why women felt the need to talk in circles instead of just getting to the root of the issue.

"Mama," Sophie asked, "did you hear him?" She turned to their mother, who had stood quietly and watched the scene unfold up to that moment.

Mama's face glowed with joy. Good God, how could she be happy now, when his entire world—everything he'd planned—was falling apart around him?

"Yes. I heard him." She moved toward them and took Sophie's hand in her own. "That is just splendid."

"What's going on?" The women in his life were determined to be the death of him. And if he didn't take care, they might just succeed.

"Calm down," said Sophie. "I'll tell you where Jane has gone. But we'll have to come up with a plan to convince her to return before I tell you, because I know you. As soon as you know where she is, you'll barrel out the door and try to force your way inside. And that, dear brother, will never serve your cause with her."

His head throbbed. "What have I done to change your mind?" Nothing made sense.

"Oh, nothing really. And everything."

"You love her, Peter," Mama said. "You love Jane."

"I..." Love her? Mama must be addled. There was no possibility he could love a woman who made him want to leap from a cliff with such regularity. But then, hadn't he realized just that last night? That despite her propensity to push him toward insanity, he loved her?

"Mama, we shouldn't push him. He'll get there in time." Sophie winked and tried to hide it from him, but did a poor job of the task.

"Enough!" Blast, now he was yelling at his mother and sister. "You said we needed a plan to convince her to come back. So, what will convince her?" This had better not take long. Devil take it, he still had to go to her, wherever she was, convince her to come back, and then get to the church so they could marry. And he still planned to do it all today. Why wait?

"She thinks you look at her as an obligation," Sophie said.

"She is one of my responsibilities. She will be even more so once we marry."

His sister frowned up at him. "Jane despises that. She wants to be able to take care of herself."

Take care of herself? Countless ideas began to course through his mind about how she intended to go about such an endeavor. Yes, she'd been raised in the country, and not in an aristocratic family. But she would never have to work as his wife.

He could only pray that she had not resorted to the worst of his many ideas. Surely she wouldn't.

Peter shook his head. "How am I supposed to use this to change her mind about anything, Sophie?"

"*We* need to convince her that she'll still be able to take care of herself, even if she is married to you. And that you look at her as more than just something else to add to your list of duties."

Sophie had likely filled Jane's head with all sorts of madcap, Bluestocking ideas and the like. She couldn't possibly have come up with her scheme on her own.

"If she is my wife, it is my responsibility to take care of her. To see that she never wants for anything."

"But for Jane, that's different than it is for most ladies bred to be part of the *ton*, Peter. She's been quite patient since she arrived here to stay with us, accepting the fact that servants would now do for her things she feels perfectly capable of doing for herself. Why, I even convinced her to allow Meg to go with her, and I intended to hire her a butler, as well. This all goes against her nature."

"Hire her a butler?" Good God, where had she gone? Peter shook his head. It didn't matter. "So what am I supposed to do?" He feared he would never understand his sister's rambling.

"You need to give her some responsibilities, as well. She needs to feel useful." Sophie put her hands on her hips and gave him a curt nod.

"Such as?"

She sighed dramatically. "You expect me to do it all for you. I told you what she needs. You figure out the specifics."

He scowled. "Fine. Now where is she?"

"Come with me. I'll take you to her." Sophie started out the door, then stopped to look over her shoulder. "Are you coming? And you should come as well, Mama. We might need you."

For the first time, he thought his mother might be on to something. Perhaps Sophie should be married. Soon.

Then she could be some other sod's problem, and no longer his.

Seventeen

"STOP THE CARRIAGE here," Sophie said.

The brief journey through Mayfair to Bond Street had commenced in silence. Peter had hardly been able to bring himself to look at either his mother or his sister the entire time, out of fear that he would once again berate them for this blasted secret code which he could not seem to break.

Once the driver pulled to a stop, Peter took a look around in dismay. Bond Street? This was no place for Jane to live. Yes, it was Mayfair. But these were shops, clubs, businesses. Not homes.

At least if she was here, however, she hadn't resorted to selling herself. Perhaps she thought to use a skill. She might have asked for a position with one of the business owners on the street, he supposed.

Not that Peter had any sense of skills that Jane might have. Or did he? She'd mentioned sewing before. Was she planning to work for Miss Jenkins or one of the other modistes? He truly didn't know her very well at all if he couldn't even sort this out. He only knew that she ignited his lust faster than should be physically possible, while at the same time making him want to throttle her.

He climbed down once the steps were set out and then assisted Mama and Sophie in doing the same.

"Where?" was all he could manage without losing the tight rein of control he held over his temper.

Sophie pulled a scrap of parchment from her reticule. She scanned it for a moment before scouring the numbers on the buildings. "Here. This is the one. Number Fourteen."

Number Fourteen was an empty shop, not an existing modiste shop like he'd expected. The uncovered windows revealed nothing inside but a couple of bare countertops and a handful of chairs. No sign that anyone was there at all.

"What in bloody hell does she think she's doing here?"

A gentleman Peter vaguely recognized Lord Raynesford glared at him from across the street, where he was escorting two ladies. He really needed to regain his composure. Cursing in public in such a manner was inexcusable.

"Jane has let this building," Sophie informed him. "For her business."

"*Her* business?" It was worse than he had ever imagined. What could have possessed the minx to think she could possibly run a business on her own?

"Yes, her modiste shop. She plans to make gowns for the ladies of the *beau monde*. I believe she'll be quite good at it." Sophie gave him a curt nod, as though to further emphasize her point. "If one should ask me, that is."

"Jane? The same Jane who came to London wearing tattered rags covered in stains? I hardly think fashionable ladies will rely on her for their fashion." She was delusional. And his sister was almost as bad. Yes, she'd mentioned she could sew—but making gowns such as would be required by Society ladies seemed far beyond her area of expertise.

"Oh, she does lovely work, Peter," his mother interjected. "She could do quite well for herself, judging from the gowns her mother showed me."

Perfect. This just served as proof that a severe dearth of common sense had recently afflicted the women in his life. "And she's living here, as well?" he asked. The thought of living in such a confined space caused him to shudder. While he certainly could make do in something smaller than Hardwicke House if necessary, this took the idea to an extreme.

"In the apartment just above," Sophie said.

It was pointless to continue standing around in the street, discussing Jane's intentions. Peter marched to the front door of the shop and tried the handle. It was locked. Thank God she at least had enough common sense for that.

But it would make his current endeavor all the more difficult.

Peter knocked loud enough that Jane should be able to hear him from above stairs and waited. And waited.

Then he waited some more.

"Do you think, perhaps, they didn't hear you?" Mama asked.

Coming out of a stairwell near the back of the shop, a bright orange ball of fur started toward them, slinking along in an arabesque pattern over the floor, and pausing to sniff at random intervals. *Mr. Cuddlesworth.* Jane was definitely here.

Peter sighed. "Jane heard." Grudgingly, he reached up and knocked again—louder and longer this time. "Open the door." His voice, while not loud enough to carry down the street, should still carry far enough to be heard upstairs.

Then they all waited again, almost as long as they waited the first time.

Almost. Sophie interrupted his musing. "Perhaps you should try again, Peter. It seems Jane and Meg can't hear. Maybe you should knock a bit louder."

This time, he glared. And growled. "They can hear me perfectly well." Jane was just willfully ignoring him. When she finally came down and opened the door to him—which had better happen soon—he promised himself to give her a good piece of his mind for keeping him waiting.

In the meanwhile, he pounded so hard upon the door that he thought it might break in, and he did not let up his pace. "Open the door, Jane! I guarantee you this noise will not stop until you let us in."

His fury grew by the moment. Finally, Meg emerged from a stairwell and walked to the door—Peter watched her through the windows—but she stood there without opening the door. Mr. Cuddlesworth moved to pace his figure-eights between her legs.

"Miss Matthews requests that you kindly stop pounding on the door of her establishment, Your Grace." The maid's voice trembled, but she didn't waver.

"You may inform Miss Matthews," he said with more menace than he intended, "I'll cease pounding when she deigns to speak with me."

"Oh," said Meg, with her eyes widening. "Well." Then she picked up the cat and scurried away up the stairs.

He waited two minutes for Jane to appear, then resumed knocking on the door—still louder, this time. "I only want to speak with you, Jane." Several passers-by stopped and stared. "You are causing me to create a spectacle on the street. Open the door."

Several moments passed, with neither sight nor sound of either Jane or Meg. Peter prepared himself to deliver her a blistering set-down when she finally appeared. The minx needed to understand she couldn't just leave without a word. She hadn't even bothered to tell him to his face that she was calling off their engagement.

This was simply unacceptable. And the idea that she could start a business? Laughable, at best.

After close to a quarter of an hour of him beating on her door and calling up to her, Jane stormed down the stairs with Mr. Cuddlesworth following in her wake. She threw open the locks and pulled the door open, issuing him a scowl that would melt an iceberg. "I beg your pardon."

"As well you should," Peter drawled, "for having the audacity to call off our engagement without informing me of such a decision."

He pushed past her and into the empty shop, taking her wrist firmly into his hand when she tried to push against him and block his progress. Mama, Sophie, and the cat followed him in. Mama closed the door behind them.

"Why, you arrogant—"

"Stop while you're ahead, Jane. That's a lesson you need to learn, I fear. You might also beg my forgiveness for your sudden departure from my home, without informing me of where you were going, since you are still my charge. And then there's the small matter of your mistaken beliefs." Peter continued to advance upon her, forcing her to back away lest he run her over.

"Mistaken beliefs? I'll have you know—"

Two more steps had her back pinned against the far wall, her wrist still locked tightly in his grip. "*I* will have *you* know that you'll most certainly and irrevocably not survive the blow to your reputation that the impending scandal will cause if you follow through with your silly plan."

"I most certainly will. Sophie agreed with me that the notoriety will cause the *ton* to be curious, and will only help me to grow and maintain a client base."

"Is that so?" He turned to look at Sophie for the first time since he'd entered the shop.

She nodded.

Fiend seize it, his sister was definitely not helping his cause. One might think she had even been plotting and scheming against him.

"That is most assuredly so," Jane said. "And she's right. Once word gets out in Society about the so-called scandal, ladies will flock to my shop in droves, eager to see for themselves the mere miss who had the audacity to jilt the Duke of Somerton."

"You are a fool. They will come, that's a certainty. But they'll come to gawk and make a mockery of you for your gauche idiocy."

"Jane, dear," his mother interrupted. "I'm afraid Peter is right this time."

This time. It was pleasing to know his mother had such confidence in him.

Jane looked back and forth between Sophie and his mother. "It doesn't matter. I will not marry him. And since he was so kind as to inform the *beau monde* of our betrothal—which, I'll have you all know, I never agreed to—I'll now be as good as black-balled for reneging on the arrangement. There's nothing to be done about it. I'll simply have to start up my shop and hope for the best."

"I can't allow you to do something so rash." Patience was preparing to abandon Peter completely, further exacerbated by the fact that the cat was now butting its head up against Peter's legs and rubbing all over him. "Your parents have entrusted you to my mother's care, which essentially places you in my care. Whether you marry me or not, you *will* return to Hardwicke House." Even if he had to drag her there by the hair.

The little halfwit opened her mouth to argue with him again. She didn't know when to stop. But then Jane whispered something that sounded rather like "Drat" to his ears. She stared up at him, fighting to keep the tears pooling in her eyes from falling. "I'll not marry a boor who could never love me." The conviction in her voice started to wane. "You can't deny that you see me as inferior—as someone unworthy to be your duchess."

At least she was allowing him to see the direction her mind was traveling. "I won't deny that I thought that at one point. But things change, Jane."

Her eyes crinkled at the corners and she frowned up at him. "What has changed?"

"For one thing, I remembered that my first wife was everything I expected in a duchess—but I still had a miserable marriage. I have no desire to repeat that failure."

Her frown softened somewhat and the tension in her wrist went lax. Hopefully she would give up her fight soon. They still had a rather full day ahead of them.

"Another thing is that I have developed a rather odd fascination with you."

She winced at the word *odd*, but refrained from interrupting.

"You see, I actually enjoy spending time with you...even if you do lack a few of the social graces most women of the *ton* are expected to master."

"You mean to say even if I'm an utter and complete disaster in the eyes of the *beau monde*."

"Far from it. There's something peculiarly refreshing about your tendency toward committing a *faux pas*. I look forward to discovering not only what you might do, but observing how the *ton* reacts to you. And they love you, Jane."

Peter specifically said *they* loved her—he hadn't included himself in the *they*. He probably should have. That might help things. But he wasn't sure he was ready to admit it to her yet. He needed to show her, because she wasn't one to simply take him at his word.

She stared off into the empty storefront for several moments before responding. "If I marry you..."

"Yes? *When* you marry me?"

Another searing glare. "*If* I marry you, will you treat me as a wife, or as a responsibility?"

She truly had some of the most ridiculous questions he'd ever heard. "They are one and the same. My wife is my duty. It is my responsibility to see to all of your needs."

Her frown intensified at that response. "And if I become your wife, what will be my responsibility? Other than the obvious, that is." Jane's eyes shifted to his mother and Sophie for a moment, then back to him.

"Other than sharing in the marriage bed, do you mean?"

She flushed a deep crimson almost instantaneously, and it took all of his concentration not to toss Mama and Sophie out of the shop and ravish Jane on the dusty countertop. He leaned in close to her ear, where the others couldn't hear. "And you *will* marry me, because as much as you may wish otherwise, you feel a need to finish what we started last night."

She shivered against the wall, her wrist pulling against his grip. Well. At least that had had the desired effect on her, even if nothing else had.

He had to get the conversation back on track. "I'll take that as a yes," he ground out, loud enough Mama and Sophie could hear. Good God, he felt like a green youth around Jane. "Well, apart from *those* duties, you must care for our children and stand at my side at any society functions where it would be required. Other than that, if you desire, you can be responsible for overseeing the running of my home."

"*If I desire it…*"

"Yes. If you wish. I won't insist upon it."

"Very well," she said with a scowl that would level a lesser man. "And what else would be included in my responsibilities?"

Christ, wasn't that enough? Mary had never wanted to have even half of that in her care. "You may also be responsible for organizing a ball or other entertainment each Season." The details of those always entailed a great amount of care in planning. Surely all of those things could keep the minx busy.

"Fine."

"Fine? Is that your acceptance of my terms?" He would never understand this woman. Not in a lifetime of trying.

"Yes." She picked up her cat and headed out the door to his waiting carriage.

Splendid. Now he would have that lifetime to try.

He only wished she didn't look quite so squeamish at the prospect.

AND SO SHE was damned for the next eternity. Drat, how had she allowed any of this to happen?

Jane stared out the window of the carriage as London passed her by. Or perhaps she was passing London by. She didn't know, nor did she particularly care.

What mattered at the moment was that she was on the way to her wedding.

To Peter.

The bloody Duke of Somerton.

Good gracious, what a pickle she was in.

"Are you terribly upset with me?" asked Sophie, seated next to her on the bench. They rode alone, making their way to Jane's wedding...though it felt more like a sentencing.

"You promised you would help me." Jane's voice sounded flat, emotionless, even to her own ears.

"I know you may not see it that way, but I really have helped you." Her friend—no, her sister-in-law—fiddled with the lace overlay of her imperial green gown. "Peter is right."

"Then why did you encourage me? Why did you tell me the scandal would pass over and no one would care?" She hated having such an accusatory tone. "Why didn't you stop me from leaving? You should have convinced me to stay."

"It was selfish on my part," Sophie said.

"Selfish. Ha."

"No. It was. Look at me." She waited until Jane finally complied with her request. "I wanted to believe that you could do it—that you could become a woman of independent means. Because if you could do it, then I could, as well."

"Why would you want such a thing? You have everything. You are Lady Sophia Hardwicke, the toast of the *ton*, the most eligible lady in the marriage mart. Gentlemen of means practically fall at your feet and beg you to marry them."

"Which is precisely what I don't want! Why should I be forced to marry some addle-brained marquess, just because we would make a good connection? Or because he has seven estates? Or because it would make Mama happy? What of my happiness?"

What, indeed? And what of Jane's?

The white kid gloves Jane wore constricted her hands, and she flexed her fingers to restore circulation. The gloves belonged to

Charlotte, whose hands and arms were daintier, more delicate than her own. But Cousin Henrietta had insisted she wear white to go with her white satin and lace gown and white slippers. White everything. It all made her feel like a giant, white cloud.

"I apologize," Sophie said. "I shouldn't upset you."

"Would you marry for love?"

Sophie sighed. "Yes. Or for..."

"Or for what?" This was certainly an unexpected response.

"Nothing. Never mind. But you—you are marrying for love, Jane."

"Fat lot of good that will do me," she mumbled. Yes, she could admit to loving the man. Actually, she loved him so much it ached in her stomach. But he said nothing of love—only of duty, responsibility. Would it be enough that she loved Peter without being loved in return?

Only time would tell.

That love—that inexplicable desire to be with him, even when he aggravated her almost beyond tolerance—had eventually convinced her to marry him. Now she had to make the best of the situation.

Maybe someday he would come to love her. If he could recognize that love meant more than obligation, that is.

The carriage pulled to a stop before the church, and Jane took a deep breath. Today, she was a bride. Today, she would become a duchess. Terrifying thought, that.

Peter climbed down from his barouche and moved to assist her to disembark the carriage. The time had arrived.

His strong hand held hers in a vise-like grip. "Ready?"

No tender words of romance. She shouldn't have expected any. The only response she could muster was a single nod.

He led her up the steps and down the aisle to stand before the rector. The Hardwickes filed in behind them, taking their seats in the pews. No one else was present.

Standing before the minister, the only thought in Jane's mind was how terribly odd it was to marry in the afternoon. Her father had not performed an afternoon wedding at the vicarage in Whitstable for almost as many years as she could remember.

And then they all stared at her until she said, "I will."

I will. She'd done it.

Jane Matthews was no longer Jane Matthews, but Jane Hardwicke, Duchess of Somerton. Mother would be ecstatic.

She, however, felt ready to cast up the contents of her stomach.

JANE SAID HER goodnights to the female members of her new family as they made their way up the stairs.

Earlier in the evening, Mama Hardwicke had told Jane that she and the girls would move to a new lodging as soon as something suitable was arranged. The newlyweds would need time to themselves. In the meanwhile, they would all make themselves as scarce as possible in the house.

Jane hadn't been worried about that, at all. Actually, she'd prefer they stay.

No one in the family worried about Neil. He was rarely at home any time they would see him, anyway. For that matter, he hadn't even attended the wedding ceremony. Jane was told he'd headed off to the country and likely wouldn't return for at least a week or more.

So Jane was now very much alone in Hardwicke House with her husband—at least it felt that way—and had no idea what she was supposed to do with the man.

In the library, Peter seemed content to continue sipping from his port in an armchair and reading the book he held close to the flame. She sat on the sofa near the hearth, running her fingers through Mr. Cuddlesworth's fur and wondering what she should do next. It would all be so much easier if he would simply tell her what he wanted, give her some direction.

After all, this entire marriage sham had been his idea.

He turned the page and read some more.

She cleared her throat, hoping to gain his attention. That tactic failed.

Her husband turned more pages, and still she sat.

The silence would soon drive her to distraction. "What are you reading?" she asked.

He glanced up momentarily. "A book of proverbs." Then almost immediately, he returned his attention to the book.

"Oh. I see."

But she really didn't see at all. Didn't he intend to bed her tonight? Drat the man, she had been both dreading it and anticipating it since the moment he mentioned her primary duty as a wife this afternoon. The least he could do was to get on with matters.

Perhaps he simply needed a stronger hint.

Jane let out a robust yawn and stretched her arms. "Oh dear, I'm growing quite tried. I believe I shall head up to bed."

"Rest well," he said with a cheery smile. "I've had your belongings moved to the duchess's suite. Meg will be waiting to assist you. I've already ordered a bath drawn for you."

"Of course. I see." This didn't sound like he intended to join her. And did he think her incapable of requesting her own bath? "Well, I suppose I'll be off then. Should I expect you soon?"

His eyes remained fully trained on his proverbs and his right hand stroked his chin. "No. I won't retire for a while yet. Good night."

Good night? "You will not...er, I mean won't you require..." Surely she was mistaken. Wasn't she?

"Jane, I'm not the boor you insinuated earlier. We both know you only married me because you were essentially forced into it by circumstance. You didn't want to be my duchess by any stretch of the imagination. I already have an heir, so there's no rush to fill my nursery." He looked her full in the eye. "When you're ready, you may come to me. But I won't bed you simply because I'm allowed to as your husband."

"Oh." Well. That was rather unexpected.

Peter set his book on the table and moved to stand before her. "Good night." With a hand gently against the nape of her neck, he pulled her close and kissed her. It was soft. Chaste. Teasing.

She wanted more. But she most certainly didn't want him to know that she wanted more.

"Good night," she said. She picked up Mr. Cuddlesworth's basket and backed away.

Halfway up the stairs, she tasted a faint hint of port on her lips.

He'd granted her a reprieve. How unexpected.

If only she was glad for it.

Eighteen

ALLOWING JANE TO walk away from him had nearly killed Peter. But it had been the only decent thing he could do.

Of course he was her husband—he could bed her at will, irrespective of her wishes on the matter. That was his right. Seeing her embarrassment earlier in her shop, when she'd asked him about such a prospect, had convinced him of her ill-prepared state of mind for nighttime activity.

Also weighing on his decision to give her time was the fact that she clearly abhorred the idea of being his wife. Christ, she'd gone so far as to run away in the middle of the night in order to avoid that very fate.

If they were to have any chance at a reasonably happy marriage, as he intended, then he had to allow Jane to proceed at her own pace. Coercing her into the marriage itself had already placed a blight upon her image of him.

So, until she was ready and willing to seek him out for coupling, he would wait.

Peter already knew he could survive in a near-sexless marriage. Mary had despised the act. She had only willingly agreed to it for the purpose of procreation. As soon as she was with child, she'd made it clear she wanted nothing more to do with him.

He could have taken a mistress—he'd thought about such a prospect on more than one occasion—but in his mind, that would mean he had failed.

Since the day Mary had informed him she was carrying a second child—his sweet Sarah—Peter had been all but celibate. There had been an occasion or two, after her passing, that he'd made use of the pleasures freely offered by a widow.

But there was never any sort of relationship. No expectation upon him. Just a mutual give and take.

With his wife, there would undoubtedly be expectation. And—he hoped—a relationship.

So, Peter would wait. He would give Jane time and space, and he intended to make himself as agreeable to her as he possibly could. He would grant her the independence she so desperately sought, by allowing her to choose. In the meanwhile, she wouldn't have to lift a finger in his home—servants would see to many of her needs, and he would personally take care of a number of others.

Jane would want for nothing. He had already promised her that, but more important in his mind, he'd sworn it to himself. Peter intended to work so hard at this marriage that she had no choice but love him. She must.

He couldn't fail. Not again.

Another loveless marriage was simply out of the question.

JANE FELT RATHER inconsequential in her new surroundings. Her new bedchamber was easily three times the size of her previous lodgings at Hardwicke House, and the attached dressing room would house an army of maids.

And that was just *her* part of the master suite. On the other side of the dressing room sat an enormous sitting area, which must be connected to Peter's dressing room and private chamber.

The sheer size of it all left her feeling more alone than ever before, particularly after the upstairs maids had removed her bath and vacated the chamber, leaving Jane alone with Meg.

"Your Grace, I'm glad we added the rosehip to your bath water this evening." They sat near the fire, and the lady's maid was brushing Jane's hair from behind. A silken wrapper was Jane's only covering after her bath. "It's a lovely scent, ma'am."

She'd attempted to tell Meg not to bother with such an extravagance; it wouldn't matter tonight, since Peter wouldn't be demanding anything of her. Jane's fate for her wedding night was to spend it alone.

"You needn't bother with formalities, Meg. The idea of being called *Your Grace* doesn't sit well with me." Just how, precisely, had she ended up a duchess? The events of the last twenty-four hours were all blurring together into a giant cloud in her mind.

"No, ma'am, I must. That would be most improper. His Grace would replace me on the spot if he learned I wasn't giving you the proper respect."

"Oh. Well, I suppose we cannot have that, can we?"

Her new life could be worse, she knew. If Peter hadn't arrived when he did last night, Jane could well be married to Lord Utley. That had been Utley's plan, after all—though Jane couldn't fathom why he'd plotted such a thing. Surely that was why Lady Plumridge had rushed up to catch them, though. What other purpose could the gossipmonger have had for being in the family's quarters? If things had gone to Utley's plan, surely Jane wouldn't be preparing to spend her wedding night alone.

She shivered. Her life could be *far* worse.

Marriage to Peter might not turn out to be as dreadful as she'd once imagined it to be. True, he was leaving her in a state of nerves with his unexpected decision this evening. Jane would almost rather have the deed done and over with. At least then she wouldn't wonder if there were some other reason (an aversion to her, or perhaps anger at the circumstances?) he wasn't insisting she fulfill this particular duty.

And everyone knew how highly her husband valued duty and responsibility.

"There now, that should do, ma'am." Meg stood and returned the silver-plated brush to the gilded vanity. "Lady Sophia sent a few things up for you, Your Grace. Since you don't have a trousseau, that is."

When Meg turned around, she was carrying a few colored gauzy articles—nightrails, most likely—and coming toward Jane with them.

"Thank you, Meg, but that will be all for tonight, please." The thought of having someone help her into one of those things, even if the girl had seen her before, didn't sit well. Maybe because she knew no one else would be seeing her in it. Certainly not her husband. Jane doubted she would see him before they broke their fasts the next day.

And by then, she intended to be fully dressed.

Meg placed the items on a dressing table and curtsied. "Yes, Your Grace." Then she slid out the door and padded silently away.

Jane dug through the armoire in her dressing area until she found one of her old, comfortable, white cotton nightrails. Once she had it on, she placed the new gowns where it had been.

After taking a candlestick from the dressing room, she slipped into her new bedchamber. The counterpane had been turned down. Yet another thing Peter must have ordered done, since Jane had finally broken Meg of that habit. Little things like that, she preferred to do for herself.

It was obvious he didn't expect her to visit his bed tonight—or at least not to remain with him.

Fine.

If he didn't want her, she certainly wouldn't force herself on him.

Jane brushed away the tear falling down her cheek. Drat. Crying was a highly inconvenient manner of falling asleep.

But by the time she slipped beneath the silken sheets, the dam had burst. Mr. Cuddlesworth leapt out of his basket and onto the bed, then curled up on her back and kneaded until she'd cried herself dry.

PETER SLEPT IN fits and starts that night. The knowledge that Jane lay in the opposite chamber of his suite burned at him. Nearly every time he woke, he was hard as steel and dreaming of her. Which, he noted, was not exactly the easiest manner of resting after his sleepless night last night.

Only a couple of walls separated them. It was torture.

When he awoke and discovered himself grinding his hips against a pillow, he questioned his own decision to allow Jane to decide when they would copulate. Celibacy with Mary had been entirely too easy. Restraining himself from touching Jane might yet kill him, if it went on too long. And if this self-imposed celibacy, even in marriage, neglected to kill him, he might resort to murder.

By the eighth time he woke, the sun shone through the picture window in his chamber, peeking around the edges of heavy drapes. There would be no more sleep for the weary.

PETER HAD SET his plan to woo Jane into motion the day after their marriage.

He arranged for Cook to send up a breakfast for them each morning, so they could dine alone together in the sitting room. He instructed Mrs. Wilson, the housekeeper of Hardwicke House, to assign an additional maid to see to Jane's needs, so that she would have one of her two available at all times.

Then he met privately with his mother and discussed which of the responsibilities that had previously fallen on her shoulders in the running of Hardwicke House would be transferred to his wife, since Jane should now be involved in such affairs. They also discussed which of those numerous responsibilities Peter would now take care of himself.

He scheduled time each afternoon to receive guests with Jane, so as to be certain everyone who came afforded her the respect her position as his duchess demanded, and so she would not feel overwhelmed by her new social obligations.

He escorted her to social functions in the evenings—to the theater, the opera, to various balls and musicales and the like—making certain to be visible at her side, to fetch her lemonade, to assist her in every way possible. Peter wanted there to be no doubt amongst the *ton* that he was enamored with his wife.

It was all rather exhausting.

And still, after nearly two weeks of catering to her every want or need, she had neglected to come to his bed.

His level of sexual frustration would soon reach epic proportions.

Spending this amount of time in her presence was certainly not helping matters any. He had come to genuinely enjoy her company. Jane's smile could light an entire ballroom far better than hundreds of candles, and her laughter could melt the heart of even the stodgiest of curmudgeons—as evidenced by her effect upon old Rotheby, who had come with Alex and Grace to visit his grandson and great-grandson in Town.

But while she smiled and laughed freely—and often—when they were with his mother and sisters or in company, her joy fled when they were alone.

Peter began to think he was doomed to fail, yet again, at creating a marriage based on love. Not from any lack of effort. Nor from a lack of love on his part. Deuce take it, somewhere along the way, he had gone and fallen head over ears in love with his wife. Yet she loathed being in his company and dreaded his touch.

A lesser man would forget about the promise he had made to her. But that wasn't Peter's way.

Instead, he chose to redouble his efforts at showing her of his love through his actions.

Eventually, he would wear her down. Jane would come to him. Peter had to believe it.

JANE'S NEW HUSBAND was driving her to distraction. Throughout the two weeks since they married, he hadn't allowed her to lift a blessed finger.

Take this morning, for example. They sat together in the downstairs drawing room, Peter on an wingback chair near the window, and Jane across from him on the brocade sofa with Mr. Cuddlesworth's basket at her feet. Before they married, Peter would have been dealing with his account ledgers and reports on his estates in his library.

But today? Today he had them spread out before him in the drawing room, so he could spend time with her.

And what, one might wonder, was Jane allowed to do while he did this? She would prefer to be meeting with the housekeeper and discussing the schedule of rotation for cleaning the various unused rooms of the house, or perhaps working with some footmen to move the furniture from one room to another, so as to make use of a different room.

Even if she couldn't be performing one of those tasks, she could be sewing a pretty new gown for Sarah, or taking the children for a walk through the park.

Instead, she was relegated to embroidery. *Useless* embroidery, she might add. One couldn't very well wear a swatch of embroidery to a ball, after all.

So much for his promise of giving her some of her own responsibilities, so she wouldn't feel so blasted useless. Every time she turned around, a maid or footman was rushing to assist her. Her responsibilities in overseeing the running of Hardwicke House had been reduced to conferencing with Cook each day about the menu for meals. Mrs. Pratt was still in charge of the nursery, so Jane couldn't even participate in rearing Peter's children without feeling like she was encroaching upon someone else's position.

Mama Hardwicke and her daughters had moved to their new lodgings at Number Seven, Curzon Street earlier in the week. Neil had yet to return from the country, but Peter assured her that the youngest Hardwicke brother would secure some bachelor lodgings as soon as he returned.

Jane wasn't even granted the responsibility of seeing after them and their needs.

The only thing she was allowed to do beyond embroidery, it seemed, was pour the tea when they had guests. Even with that, Peter would often rush to take the cups from her and pass them about.

If all of that wasn't enough, his lack of insistence upon engaging in the marriage act had gone on for so long she was certain that not only did he not love her, but he couldn't possibly even feel lust for her. The bit of lust she'd assumed he felt from their previous encounters had all but faded, leaving her with no alternative but to believe she'd only imagined its existence in the first place.

She was a dismal failure as a wife.

For all Jane knew, Peter felt she was just as dismal a failure at being his duchess—hence his insistence upon helping her with even the smallest of tasks, like passing around the tea.

If those worries weren't enough to keep her awake at night (or cause her to cry herself to sleep, as the case may be), Mr. Cuddlesworth had started acting rather peculiar.

From the day they'd arrived at Hardwicke House, her cat had latched on to Sarah. Jane didn't mind. He had always enjoyed children, so she was glad to see he had a new friend. He still came to spend time with Jane, particularly in the afternoons when she and the Hardwicke sisters would gather in the downstairs drawing room to see their guests. At that point in the day, the sun warmed the room, and cast sunbeams across the floor where he could sleep. But otherwise, he stayed with Sarah—even at night, on occasion.

But every night since their wedding, Mr. Cuddlesworth had been sneaking into Jane's chamber and stretching himself out across her back, much as he had done as a kitten. He would stay with her the entire night, and remain by her side or on her lap the entire day. This behavior had continued every day, without fail.

Sarah would occasionally come and fetch him. Then she'd carry him off to the nursery to play with her. But as soon as someone opened the door so he could escape, he would dart out and search the house for Jane.

She hadn't thought too much of it at first. Things in Mr. Cuddlesworth's life had changed drastically in recent months, after all—much as they'd changed in Jane's life. But now, she worried that his old age was finally catching up with him.

On this particular morning, Jane's spine bristled every time her husband "hemmed" or "hummed" about something in his records. She jabbed her needle through the fabric much harder than she intended, poking her finger in the process.

"Drat," she muttered. She pushed the fabric aside and looked down. Her finger was bleeding. She put it in her mouth so the blood wouldn't ruin her work or her gown. Mr. Cuddlesworth opened his eyes for a brief moment and purred at her.

Peter didn't even glance up at her. Good. With the way he'd been behaving toward her of late, he would likely send for a doctor if he knew she was bleeding.

Spenser poked his head in the open doorway. "Lord Neil, Your Grace." Before the butler could step aside and allow him entrance, Neil barreled through the doorway.

"Peter." He hurriedly inclined his head and struggled to catch his breath, as though he had just run from halfway across Town. Then he turned to Jane and repeated the gesture. "Your Grace."

Good Lord, would everyone in her life suddenly be calling her that? She supposed they would. Neil hadn't even stumbled over the title—he hadn't even thought twice about perhaps calling her Jane, as he had before. How aggravating.

Neil returned his serious gaze to Peter. "I need to speak with you. Urgently."

"About—er, about Carreg Mawr?" her husband asked.

Carreg Mawr—was that his estate in Wales? She couldn't quite remember. He'd gone through a litany of estates he owned one day as she sat doing her embroidery, telling her all about them and when they might visit each. The name of the place certainly sounded more Welsh than English though, so it likely was.

Neil lifted a brow, but didn't betray anything Jane could decipher. "Yes . There are a number of developments, shall we call them? that we should discuss."

Peter rose and carefully stacked his ledgers into a neat pile upon a table. "Come to my library. Jane, I apologize. I hate to abandon you, but I would be loath to bore you with business. Excuse us."

Bore her, indeed. Listening in on their discussion might actually provide her something with which to occupy her mind. Yet she waved the two men off. Let them have their silly business conversations. She would enjoy her time alone—which, she had to admit, was in rather short supply these last weeks.

Before she could settle into her solitude, however, Spenser interrupted her again. He inclined his head. "Lady Sophia and Lady Charlotte, Your Grace."

"Oh, do please send them in." She had only seen them twice in the last week, and even on those occasions they'd been unable to truly talk.

Her two friends rushed in and drew her into a hug, careful not to disturb the sleeping cat upon her lap.

"Is Peter gone?" asked Sophie.

"Not gone. He's meeting with your brother, Neil, in his library." Jane gestured for them both to take a seat.

Sophie picked up a scone from the nearby platter before settling in to the loveseat. "Good. Then we can have a real conversation."

"Are you settling in to married life well, Jane?" asked Char. "You look...you look like you aren't sleeping."

She had hoped it wouldn't show. But these two knew her better than anyone else. Perhaps no one else would notice.

"Are you?" Sophie scrutinized her thoroughly.

There was certainly no point in lying to either lady. They'd likely see through to the truth, in any case.

"Some. Not enough. And not well when I do sleep."

Sophie grinned. "Is Peter keeping you up at night? I remember when Meredith Ingersoll first married Lord Sainsbury, they both had circles beneath their eyes for weeks. And ten months later, their twins came into the world."

Jane frowned. "And what would you know of such things, being an unmarried lady, hmm?" Her attempt at a joke rang hollow, even to her own ears. Perhaps because, even as a married lady, she knew nothing of such matters.

Sophie failed to blush over the barb.

"But no. That's not why I can't sleep." Jane recounted her list of complaints against her husband. After all, if she couldn't talk to Peter's sisters about her concerns, who could she talk to? Certainly not Peter. However, she neglected to mention the parts involving their lack of intimacy. Some things were simply not suitable to discuss with unmarried ladies.

Sophie would not let her off so easy, though. "And how are things working out between you two at night?"

Charlotte blushed profusely. "Sophie! You can't ask her that."

"I just did." She gave her sister a look that clearly dared her to challenge her again. "Now answer me."

"I...well, there is...there isn't much to say." Jane could hardly believe she was having this conversation.

This answer clearly did not satisfy Sophie. "Why?"

Why? Oh, drat. She couldn't possibly admit that, in two weeks of marriage, she'd never been touched by her husband. Could she?

Her new sister wouldn't let the question go unanswered, though. "Is it unpleasant for you?"

"Oh, no," she said, perhaps a bit too quickly. "That is, I don't know."

"You don't know." Sophie stared at her, her eyes wide. "Peter hasn't bedded you yet? Good Lord, why ever not?"

Charlotte reached out and took her hand. "Did you deny him? Surely things aren't so bad you must resort to such measures, Jane."

"I've done no such thing." This was all dreadfully embarrassing to discuss. "He told me..." But the words seemed so terribly pathetic to confess out loud. "He told me that when I was ready, I should come to him. That he wouldn't require that from me—seeing as how he already has an heir." She took a deep breath before continuing. "He doesn't want me. Peter only married me because he had to, but he doesn't want me that way."

Mr. Cuddlesworth looked up at her with sad, amber eyes and pressed his head repeatedly into her hand until she scratched his ears.

"Fiddlesticks," Sophie said.

"What do you mean?" Jane asked.

"Our brother may have a number of things left to learn, I'll never deny that. But I've seen the way he looks at you. He watches you like a cat stalking a mouse. Trust me. He wants you very much."

"Then why? Why did he tell me he wouldn't require me to fulfill that duty?" She hated even thinking of it as a duty, but everything in Peter's world seemingly must be a duty, or else it simply didn't exist.

"Perhaps," Charlotte said quietly, "you're focusing on the wrong part of what he told you."

"Precisely," Sophie said. "Jane, dear. He told you to come to him when you're ready. That, to me, doesn't sound like something a man would say if he had no desire to participate in the act at all." Sophie knelt before her and forced her to look straight in her eyes. "Rather, it sounds like he doesn't want to make you do something you don't want to do."

"Oh, dear." Double drat. Blast her new sisters for being so very logical—so *right* about it all.

"So, sweet Jane, the solution to your problem is simple." Sophie rose and walked to the window, taking a look outside before facing Jane again. "It's time to seduce your husband."

Only that made it sound more like the beginning to an entirely new set of problems.

Drat, drat, drat.

Nineteen

PETER HAD TO travel to Wales. There was simply no way around it.

When Neil had burst into his drawing room that morning, Peter almost instantly knew. All of his suspicions were proving true.

Neil had somehow managed to get to Carreg Mawr before Utley did. His arrival had surprised Turnpenny, but Neil had explained it away. He claimed that Peter had offered to allow him to stay at Carreg Mawr for a time while he determined what he intended to do with his future. Very smart, indeed, since all of England and likely half the Continent knew how Lord Neil Hardwicke tended to sow his oats.

The next morning, though, Utley had arrived—and everyone knew the jig was over.

Good thing Neil had already enlisted the assistance of the local magistrate—and Peter's hired spy at Carreg Mawr, Roland Kirbye. When they walked into the study, they discovered Utley emptying the coffers into a purse and his brother, Phineas Turnpenny, tossing the true records into a roaring fire in the hearth.

The magistrate had arrested Phinny on the spot, but Utley had darted out the door and disappeared into the nearby woods. Phinny finally admitted that he had been raising rents, lowering pay, and otherwise filching money from Peter for years—and sending it all to his older brother, Utley.

Much as Peter suspected. He had thought very hard about replacing Turnpenny after what Utley had done to Mary. But, after much internal debate, he chose not to do so. Why punish a man for the actions of his brother? To that point, Phinny had proven to be a trusted steward over the castle through the years, even though there was still some lingering resentment between the Turnpenny family and the Hardwicke family after Rawden's untimely death.

Peter should have known that as soon as Utley had property and a small fortune to his name, he would proceed to dispense of it as fast as he could manage...and then he would have to turn to other means for an income. Now it all made sense. Particularly since Phinny had always been slavishly devoted to his brother.

But now Carreg Mawr was without a steward, and Utley was still missing. Peter needed to visit the property, sort out his staff, and hire a replacement, not to mention speak with the magistrate about the search for Utley. And he couldn't afford to wait.

The changes at his estate needed immediate attention, despite the fact that he had a bride who also needed his attention.

He'd have to leave tomorrow morning. And, since he really had no manner of knowing how long he'd have to stay, Jane would simply have to come with him. It would probably be best to take the children, as well, since the trip could last weeks, if not months. He couldn't leave them behind for so long.

Peter informed his valet and Jane's lady's maid of the need to prepare for the journey. Then he spoke with Mrs. Pratt, and let the children know of the holiday they would all be taking shortly. After dashing off a note to Mama, he called Forrester into his library and lined out tasks the secretary would need to see to for the duration of his absence.

There was so much to be done, he was unable to entertain guests with Jane that afternoon. She was always a charming and engaging hostess, however, so he held no compunctions about her ability to cope with the continual influx of well-wishers coming to offer their congratulations.

In fact, from the moment Neil had arrived that morning until supper, there hadn't been a single free moment during which he could spend time with his wife. He would have to double his efforts tonight. Thank God they hadn't accepted any invitations. He was ready for some time at home, away from the ever watchful eye of the *ton*.

Peter seated his wife beside him at the long, admittedly empty table. She glanced up at him, then her eyes darted away just as quickly. He thought she might even have a hint of a blush on her cheeks, but that seemed so unexpected and inexplicable that he was sure it was only his imagination.

Her cat scampered into the room and leapt onto the chair beside her. Normally, Peter would be disgusted that an animal was near when they were eating. It was happening far more frequently now, though, and he was growing used to Mr. Cuddlesworth's appearances. At least it didn't get on the table—it just crossed its front paws neatly on the very edge of the table and rested its chin on top of them, watching everything that passed by.

Peter had to admit, too, the cat was looking a bit scrawny. Scruffier than usual. It might be nearing the end. He doubted either his wife or his daughter would handle the situation well when it came to pass. He tried to prepare himself for the fact that they would both insist on the cat traveling with them.

"Have you had a busy day?" he asked, hoping to ease his way into informing her of their impending trip.

"Oh, yes. It's been lovely." Jane picked up her glass of wine, but it wobbled in her hand. She steadied it before any spilled. "Sophie and Charlotte visited this morning. And I received a letter from Mother and Father in the post."

Peter winced. He'd planned to take Jane to Whitstable sometime soon, since he'd yet to meet her family, but that would have to wait a bit longer now. "Splendid. I trust they're doing well?"

She lifted her fork to her mouth, but some of the food fell due to the jittering of her hand, landing securely in the midst of her bosom. Peter had to fight the urge to lean over and retrieve the piece of veal with his teeth.

"Oh, drat." The slight blush heated to crimson as she fished the piece of meat out with her fingers.

He couldn't have removed his gaze from her décolletage now if his life depended upon it. With each shaking breath, those lovely, full breasts rose and fell. If there was one reason to thank the French, it was for their exquisite influence in ladies' fashions—which currently lent him an eyeful of heaven.

Jane let her fork clang to her plate and dropped her hands to her sides, taking deep breaths with her eyes closed. "Yes, my parents are quite well, thank you. Their vegetable garden has been rather prolific this year."

If he couldn't regain control over himself, he might toss her over the table and take her right there.

And that thought sent a shock coursing through his loins. Blast it. He needed to calm down, focus. Vegetables. Her parents' vegetable garden.

"That must be lovely for them," he said, wincing when his voice cracked. "What crops have done well for them?"

"Oh, you know. Carrots, cucumbers…"

Peter coughed. So that particular line of conversation came to a close with him thinking of the shapes of those particular vegetables.

They each returned to their meal. The only thing on his mind other than consummating their marriage at the moment was their trip to Carreg Mawr in the morning—nothing else that might be able to assist him in broaching the subject.

He hoped she wouldn't be too upset. But the last time she'd been forced to travel, the journey had been a rather eventful one, with her cat being so ill.

"Neil brought me news this morning of my estate in Wales," he began.

"Good news, I hope," she murmured.

"I'm afraid not. My steward was taking money. He's been placed under arrest, but now there's no one caring for the needs of my property."

"Oh, dear. I suppose you must travel, then." She reached over with one hand to pet her cat, which was purring loudly beside her.

"Yes, I must. We'll leave in the morning."

"We? Will Neil be returning with you, then?"

"No. I meant you and me, Jane. And the children, of course." He hated the confused look in her eyes. "I simply have no way of knowing how long I'll be gone. You must come with me." Peter set his fork and knife down and took her hand in his own. "Perhaps we can think of it as a honeymoon."

She removed her hand from his and placed it on her lap. Her gaze turned to the cat beside her, and tears welled in her eyes.

"Of course, we'll bring Mr. Cuddlesworth with us. If you didn't insist upon it, Sarah surely would." He only hoped the cat would survive the journey. It might prove too much for the animal at this stage of its life.

"Very well," she whispered. A single tear streamed down her cheek and landed on her bosom.

For the first time in his life, Peter hated himself.

"Naughty boy," Jane said halfheartedly to Mr. Cuddlesworth as she picked him up and scratched his ears. "You were supposed to stay with Sarah tonight. In the nursery."

Only twenty minutes ago, she'd delivered him to Mrs. Pratt and asked the nurse to try to keep him there. If Jane was to have any hope of following through with Sophie's plan, having her cat watching matters—or worse, attempting to get in the middle of things—would not prove conducive to her state of mind.

But here he was. He'd pawed at her door while she was dressing in one of those dreadfully embarrassing, gauzy nightrails, and she'd let him in. She placed him in his basket and set it on the foot of her bed. "You must stay here, then. If you have to be near me tonight, this is as close as you're allowed to come."

He meowed in response. Hopefully that meant he would comply with her request.

Jane took one final look in the mirror. Good Lord, she could see everything. There was nothing left to the imagination. Hopefully this would work.

Hopefully Sophie and Charlotte *had* been right.

She bit her lip and tried to steel herself for whatever reaction she received. If only her mother had told her something—anything—about what would be involved in the marriage act. She felt ridiculous and terrified and eager, all at once.

Before another moment passed and she could change her mind, Jane stepped into the sitting room between their joined chambers and knocked at the door to Peter's dressing room.

When he called out, "Come," she nearly lost her nerve and rushed back to her own room. Instead, somehow her fingers gripped the door handle and pushed it open.

He stood shirtless facing an open armoire, carefully folding his superfine coat and placing it in a tidy stack. His Hessian boots had been removed as well and were situated neatly against the wall, waiting for him to put them on the next day.

Jane had never imagined the sight of a man's bare back could cause her breath to catch. Broad shoulders narrowed to a tapered waist. The muscles in his arms and shoulders flexed and tensed as he worked. Her pulse, already faster than normal, tripped to a stop and then raced ahead.

"What is it, Bradford?" he asked without turning.

"Peter, I..." She had no idea under the moon what to say.

It didn't matter. He spun around at the sound of her voice, dropping his cravat to the floor.

And he stared.

Devoured might be more accurate. His eyes roamed over every inch of her body, until she felt more self-conscious than ever before. She itched to cover herself, but somehow kept her hands at her sides.

She'd thought nothing could rival the sight of his naked back. She'd been wrong.

The planes and angles of his chest fascinated her, as did the sprinkling of dark hair covering it. His body looked so very different from her own. How might it feel to touch? Jane blushed at the thought—not to mention the heat in his eyes.

The buttons of his breeches were undone and the front flap dropped below his waist. Another line of dark hair trailed down his abdomen and disappeared behind the flap of his trousers.

She allowed her eyes to follow the path until she realized he was watching her reaction. Her eyes snapped back up to meet his.

Finally he spoke. "Do you need something, Jane?" His voice sounded strained, like he'd swallowed a hive of angry bees and was trying to keep them all inside.

She should make up a story—anything. She could say she'd been sleepwalking. Or just turn around and leave.

"You said I should come to you." Dear God, her mouth had turned on her. "When I was ready, that is."

"Yes." Peter didn't move. He hadn't moved since he'd first turned around and discovered her in his dressing room. She wasn't entirely sure he had even breathed.

She surely hadn't.

Was he just going to stand there and make her explain it all to him in explicit detail? Cruel, despicable man. If only she weren't so desperately in love with him.

"I'm ready," she said. At least she thought she said it. Perhaps not, but she intended to.

Several more moments passed with no sound in the room other than her ragged breath. Or perhaps his, too. She wasn't entirely sure.

"Are you certain?" His smooth growl fluttered over her ears, and she trembled. He seemed dangerous.

Why couldn't he just start? The anticipation was bound to be worse than the act.

Jane couldn't speak. Her words were stuck in her throat. She nodded.

Peter crossed the room in an instant. His hot mouth landed on hers, his tongue seeking entry through her lips. Their tongues tangled and danced. One hand fisted in her hair and pulled her closer. With the other, he felt for the open doorway leading to his chamber.

Peter's mouth left hers and he picked her up. He carried her to the huge canopied bed in the center of the room. Pulling back the counterpane, he tossed her inside and covered her body with his own before she could complain.

None of this was anything she had expected. Not that she knew what to expect.

The weight of his body pressed her down into the mattress. His musky scent invaded her, overwhelmed her. She needed to feel him. To touch him. She trailed her fingers over his chest, his ribs—feather light and tentative. Everywhere she touched, his muscles quivered.

His mouth returned to hers, then left just as quickly to slide down her neck and over her shoulders. She felt feverish in all the places his tongue traveled.

Then his hands were at the bottom of her nightrail, sliding it up an inch at a time—to her thighs, her hips, her waist, her chest. She raised her arms above her head and he slipped the gown off completely, trapping her hands in one of his own.

"I want to look at you," he said. His mouth hovered near her ear, and he leaned in to suckle the earlobe. When he nibbled on it, it triggered a liquid pull between her legs and she jumped.

He pulled away, still holding her hands above her head. She watched his hungry eyes roam over his body. They lingered on her breasts, then moved lower, lower, until he stopped at her womanhood for a moment, before returning to her breasts.

Peter's mouth came down then, laving at one breast with his tongue while he kneaded the other. He took the tip into his mouth, first sucking, then nibbling.

A deep, low sound emanated from her throat. Her legs couldn't remain still. They thrashed about her, pushing her forward.

She tugged to free her hands. Once he released her, she moved them over his abdomen, tangling her fingers in the trail of hair she found there. Heat emanated from just beneath her hands. Curiosity begged her to find the source of the heat, but she was afraid to do something wrong.

But then Peter growled and took one of her hands, pushing it lower, beneath the front fold of his breeches. "Touch me," he commanded. He raised himself up over her, staring down into her eyes. When she took his hardness into her hands and squeezed gently, his eyes rolled back in his head.

"I'm sorry," she said and quickly pulled her hand away.

He reached down and grasped her arm. "Don't stop." His eyes flashed when she took hold of him again. "Please don't stop."

Jane stroked her hand along his length. It was hot, rigid, moist. She had no idea what she'd expected, but this was an utter surprise. She circled him with her fingers, and then slid them up and down.

And she nearly came off the bed when he slipped his hand between her legs, stroking against a nub she didn't even know existed.

"Is this all right?" he asked as his fingers moved inside her.

It was better than all right; she thought she might shatter into a thousand tiny pieces. Every move he made set her skin to tingling. All she could manage was a sigh.

Just when she felt she would surely die if something didn't happen, he lifted her up and turned them both around until they were sitting, with her straddling his legs and facing him. Her breasts jiggled and she tried to cover them, but he pulled her hands away.

Again, Peter circled his tongue around the hardened nub of one breast. He blew on it then, and the cool air against the wetness had her straining against him and trembling. Peter was not finished with his exquisite torture though—he repeated the performance on the other breast.

Her breath was ragged, coming in starts and stops. When he nipped the sensitive bud, she nearly screamed.

"Do you like that?" he asked, grinning at her with the most wicked, sensual smile she'd ever seen.

Jane nodded.

"Tell me. I want to hear you say it." He bit the other one, just a bit harder.

"Oh, God," she managed. "Yes, I like that."

"Good," he said, then lay her back with her legs open before him.

Peter leaned down and she gasped. He couldn't do that, could he?

But he did. He kissed her and used his tongue like he had used his fingers before. It was sinful and wanton and the most wonderful thing she'd ever known. Her hips rose up to meet him, almost of their own volition.

Jane gripped the sheets in her hands—she needed something to anchor herself against.

When his teeth scraped across her core, she felt like she split in two.

Peter left her momentarily, then was between her thighs. The tip of his erection pressed where his lips had just been and she felt herself open to him. Slowly, he drew closer, deeper. He slid in and out, creating a wonderful friction. Leaning over her, he kissed her, mimicking the movement with his tongue.

And then he stopped, still inside her. Did he not realize she would die if he didn't finish? Not that she knew what he needed to finish— but something felt very incomplete. She shifted her hips and moaned at the lovely sensation that caused.

Peter gripped her hips and forced her to hold still. "I don't want to hurt you, Jane. But I have to." His face was strained. "It will only last a moment."

With a nod, she raised her knees, which moved him deeper inside her. He groaned and she wondered if she'd hurt him.

But then he rose off of her and came back down, much deeper than before, pushing until their bodies touched in the most intimate way. And then he froze. "Tell me when the pain is gone."

She supposed it did hurt, at least a bit. But more than pain, she felt fully alive. Aware. *Powerful.*

An instinctual need to move her hips took over, and she moved them against him.

"Are you all right? Tell me you're all right." He bit his lip in concentration and fought to hold her still, despite her constant motion.

"I'm fine," she panted. Wonderful would be more apt. Or splendid. Perhaps euphoric. But each of those took far too much concentration to vocalize.

Finally, he began to move in her again, setting a slow but steady pace. He buried his face in her neck while they rocked. Jane drew her knees up and wrapped her legs around his waist. Amazing. That drew him deeper. She had no idea he could be deeper within her womb.

She never wanted the feeling to end—being connected so intimately to the man she loved, to her husband. With languorous hands, she explored his shoulders, back, buttocks. Softness and curves met hard planes and tight muscle.

The languid pace of their lovemaking gathered momentum. Slow, steady thrusts built to rapid need. With each breath, a myriad of sensations warred for her attention—tingling breasts, intense fullness, friction.

Perhaps more intense than any of the other sensations coursing through her body was the feeling—even if only for that moment— that Peter loved her as much as she loved him.

Of course, that was mere fantasy, but she would entertain it for now.

His strokes increased to a near frantic pace. She met him measure for measure, on a quest for release.

Her inner walls tightened and released around him, triggering his own release within her. He shouted out as waves of his seed spread to fill her womb with delicious warmth.

Peter collapsed atop her. They lay together as a tangled mass of limbs, desperate for breath. Finally, he rolled to the side, pulling her along with him and drawing the bedclothes up over them both.

"Stay with me tonight," he said. He pushed the tangled mess of her hair from her face and situated her in his arms.

It wasn't an order. More a request. She could choose to return to her own chamber if she wanted—he would allow her to go. Jane knew this.

But she felt loved in the cocoon of his arms.

So she stayed, to hold on to the fantasy for just a bit longer. Within minutes, she was asleep in the arms of the man she loved.

PETER WAS STARTLED awake while it was still dark. His wife was still nestled in his embrace, her head tucked under his chin.

Jane wasn't the reason he woke. It was her cat.

The silly animal had leapt upon the bed and shoved its way between them, crawling beneath the blankets to a position surrounded by both of their bodies—Mr. Cuddlesworth must be seeking their warmth.

Peter sighed. Jane hadn't moved a muscle when the cat joined them. Most likely, Mr. Cuddlesworth had slept with her for its entire life, other than those nights it stayed with Sarah. It was extremely doubtful that her cat would stay down from the bed if he tossed it. Instead, Peter shifted so they were all more comfortable and tried to sleep again.

Jane had better appreciate the sacrifices he was continuing to make for her.

"YOU'RE SURE OF this?" Utley narrowed his eyes on the drowned rat sitting across from him. "Somerton is leaving for Wales tomorrow?"

"Sure as poss'ble. Me brother wouldn' have no reason ta lie ta me, guv."

Utley took deep breaths to slow his pulse. There was still much planning to do. These things took time.

Somerton may have run him off that night, but he would not ultimately win.

"Good work," he said. He took a sack of Somerton's coins from the inside pocket of his coat and tossed it across the table. "Thank you for your assistance."

"Ya need me 'gain, just send for me, guv." The rat pushed away from the table, put the sack in his pocket, and moved past Utley toward the door—assaulting him with unclean odor strong enough he gagged.

"Pay for a bath with some of that."

Once the air cleared, Utley pushed away from the table as well and went outside to hail a hack. There was no time to waste.

Twenty

THE ONLY THING worse than traveling to Wales with his wife, two children, a cat, and numerous servants, was the dread Peter felt about what he would encounter when they arrived. From the accounts he'd received, both from his planted spy and from Neil, the staff at Carreg Mawr was dwindling and the estate was virtually in shambles.

Changes would have to be made. The sooner they were in place, the better.

Mr. Cuddlesworth's health continued to decline over the four days' journey. The cat rarely left Jane's side, and the stomach upset it had suffered on the move from Whitstable to London had only intensified on this journey. It slept far more than Peter thought healthy, even for a cat.

The likelihood of Mr. Cuddlesworth making a return to Hardwicke House grew slimmer by the day.

That eventuality would devastate his entire family—particularly Jane. But Sarah and even Joshua loved the animal as well. Like it or not, the cat was now an important member of his family.

Peter couldn't stand to allow anything to hurt his family. There was no possible way to prevent this hurt, though. Death had ever been and would always be an inevitable, inescapable component of life.

Still, Peter resented the fact that he couldn't protect the people he loved the most from this pain. At times like these, he had to remind himself that he was only a man. A duke, true. But still just a man.

A man falling deeper in love with his wife every day.

Since that first night that she had come to him before they set out for Carreg Mawr, he'd requested that she share his bed. Jane might not love him, at least not yet. But she freely gave of herself each night, growing not only in confidence, but in eagerness.

Even if she only came to his bed out of a feeling of obligation, the fact remained that she came. Every night. And she stayed with him instead of returning to her own bed, in her private chamber. She allowed him the opportunity to pour out his love to her, even if she didn't return it.

He had to believe she was softening toward him, that she would someday love him.

In return, Peter made an even greater effort to ensure her a life of ease. As they talked more, he was fascinated by how much work had been expected of her as a child. Jane hadn't just sewed gowns for the ladies who lived nearby in order to pay for her education, but she'd also assisted her father with the gardening and her mother with the upkeep of the house.

Peter vowed she would never have to work again.

Instead, Jane could content herself with being a mother to his children. A role for which, he was pleased to note, she was impeccably equipped. Joshua and Sarah clamored for her attention, which she eagerly gave anytime they required it.

By the time they reached his Welsh estate, he knew without a doubt: he couldn't have found a better woman to be his duchess if he'd searched every ballroom in England.

Still, she was unhappy.

Jane tried not to let him see her distress. Any time she knew he was watching, she pasted a fake smile upon her lips. But he watched her more than she knew. If she thought him asleep in the carriage, she would let down her guard and cry.

Twice, he awoke in the night to the feel of her hot tears coursing down his chest. He stayed still so she wouldn't suspect he knew. Once she finally cried herself to sleep, he wiped the tears from her cheeks.

He wished desperately to know how to make her happy.

They were drawing near Kidwelly, finally. Cottages and stables started to pop up along the landscape outside the carriage window, and the fresh scent of the sea filled the air. It had been years since Peter had been to Wales, but it appeared as though nothing had changed.

The carriage drew through the town, filled with pubs and the newer factories and the sounds of horses' hooves against the lilting voices of Welsh singers. Then they moved on toward the outskirts of town, through the woods and up over the large hill, rolling ever closer to the crags and cliffs by the sea.

Halfway up the hill, the battlements atop the turrets of his estate finally came into view. The castle, built in the twelfth century, looked much the same as it ever had. Moss and ivy trailed up the outer walls of the bailey and up the portcullis gates, showcasing their verdant greens against the drab gray stone walls.

Peter had always enjoyed his time at Carreg Mawr. Yes, the castle was dark and dank and draughty, but the relaxed attitude of the people here had always suited him. If not for his concerns for the rest of his family, he might have enjoyed spending more of his holidays here.

But his sisters required the more modern comforts of London, or the spacious grandeur of Somerton Court, where Alex and Grace had been living for the last two years. So Carreg Mawr sat alone far more than he would like, with only his servants and tenants to enjoy its history.

Jane's sharp indrawn breath as the carriage pulled into the outer bailey took him by surprise. "Carreg Mawr is a castle? I had no idea." She stared out the windows with a slack jaw. "Are any of your other properties as impressive as this?"

Peter chuckled. "This is the only castle I own, if that's what you are asking. My other properties are more like what you would be used to...country manor houses. Built much more recently than this."

"I've never been inside a castle before," she murmured. "Well, not one as old and grand as this, that is. Being presented to the Queen was something else entirely."

"Indeed," he said, stifling a grin. His wife was truly fascinating. She was more impressed by a building of stone than she had been with meeting her Queen.

She clasped her hands together tightly and turned to him, eyes wide. "Will voices echo in the halls, do you imagine?"

"I needn't imagine it, since I remember quite plainly how Richard and Alex and I would call out to each other as boys, trying to see who could make his echo last the longest."

"How lovely," she said on a sigh. "I'll have to spend some time playing in the halls with Joshua and Sarah. If that's all right, of course."

"Of course." He wished she would stop seeking his approval for every little thing involving Joshua and Sarah. Hadn't he given her the responsibility of seeing to the welfare of his children?

As the carriages came to a stop, a line of servants formed outside the castle walls to greet them. Peter recognized a few familiar faces, even though it had been years since he'd last been there. The most worrisome thing he noticed, however, was the small number of servants gathering.

Turnpenny had not only done a disservice to Peter—he'd hurt the entire town by ridding the estate of so many workers. Outside of the steel and brick industries, there were not many employers in Kidwelly.

Devil take it. It appeared he had quite the job laid out before him, and he could only hope that the people in town wouldn't hold Turnpenny's offenses against him. It was, after all, Peter's property and his money paying the wages.

Still, there was no time like the present to start.

AFTER TWO WEEKS at Carreg Mawr, Jane felt the best she'd felt in months. For the first time in her marriage, she actually believed she was needed—even useful.

She spent a good amount of time with Joshua and Sarah, taking them for promenades through the castle grounds and exploring the kitchens and chapel with them. Through trial and error, the three of them had discovered that the turret overlooking the courtyard was the best place for echoes.

But beyond her time with the children, Jane was working and loving every moment of it.

So many of the servants required to care for an estate so large had been run off by the previous steward, that things inside the castle simply weren't operating as they ought. Frankly, there was far too much work to be done in the hiring of new staff for Peter to handle on his own, especially since he had yet to find someone to oversee the estate.

The cook, Mrs. Dunstan, and the housekeeper, Mrs. Prichard, took great delight in having Jane sit in with them as they interviewed ladies to help fill in as scullery maids, downstairs maids, and upstairs maids, while Peter handled the responsibility of finding new footmen, grooms, gardeners—and of course, a new steward.

Even during those times when she wasn't busy assisting these two lovely ladies, Jane kept herself quite busy. She made certain no one, including Peter, was around to see her doing so, particularly since Mrs. Prichard and her staff would highly disapprove of Her Grace's washing windows and scrubbing floors. Peter might be more accepting of her interference in the household chores than the housekeeper would be, which was saying something, indeed.

On this particular day, the lovely summer weather they'd been experiencing had turned sour. Heavy clouds rolled in from the sea and brought torrents of rain with them, meaning the children were stuck indoors to play.

Jane had played a round of Scotch-Hoppers with them in the inner bailey. But then she had left them in the care of Mrs. Pratt so she could sneak in a bit of dusting in the main keep before anyone caught her.

Mr. Cuddlesworth had been doing rather more poorly than before they'd left London—he had hardly eaten anything for three days, and he never left his basket anymore. Yet if Jane moved out of his sight for too long, he cried out to her in loud bellows. Because of that, she simply carried his basket around with her from room to room, making certain he could always lift up his head and find her whenever he awoke.

She placed his basket on the grand table in the center of the keep and covered him with a warm, woolen blanket. Without a fire blazing in the hearth, every room in the castle had a tendency to be a bit cold and draughty, even in the summer. Mr. Cuddlesworth purred and shoved his head up into her hand, so she gave his ears a good scratch before beginning her work.

The amount of dust that gathered in this castle never ceased to astound her. Only a week ago, she'd gone through this entire room, but already a thin coating of grime covered nearly everything in sight.

Digging through another basket she'd brought with her, Jane pulled out several rags. She dipped them into her bucket of water. Then she set to work. Because of the size of the room, it would likely take her an hour to finish her task.

Halfway through, at a point when Jane was perched atop one of the high-backed chairs in order to reach beat against the tapestries decorating the hall, the children came screeching in and interrupted her work, with Mrs. Pratt following close behind.

"Lady Sarah," the nursemaid called out, "Mr. Cuddlesworth is taking his nap. As well you ought to be, I might add."

"But I only want to see him, just for a moment," Sarah said.

Jane smiled down at the children from her vantage point. "It's quite all right, Mrs. Pratt. He loves them dearly. He won't mind a bit of company while I finish my work in here."

"Very well, Your Grace. But mind you, children, we'll go up for a nap before long."

They let out delighted squeals, scurried over to climb upon the table, and started to pet him.

"Ma'am, are you sure you ought to be doing all of this labor? His Grace will be most displeased if he learns of all that you've been doing."

Before she could answer the older woman, Jane was distracted by the children.

"Wake up, Mr. Cuddlesworth," Joshua said. He reached into the basket and stroked the cat. "You can't be *that* sleepy."

Sarah took matters into her own hands—literally. She picked the cat up and held him like a sleeping baby in her arms. "Come on, now. Purr for me, silly kitty." She scratched behind his ears and beneath his chin with no response.

Jane nearly fell from the chair she stood upon. Mr. Cuddlesworth hadn't moved, not to open his eyes, not to shove his head eagerly into the little hands that were ready and willing to scratch him. Not at all.

"Help me down, Mrs. Pratt," she said, trying her best to keep her voice calm. "Immediately."

The sense of urgency in her voice propelled the children's nurse into action. She rushed over and assisted Jane to the floor, and then they both hurried to the children at the table.

"Sarah, I need to see Mr. Cuddlesworth, sweetheart." Tears stung at Jane's eyes, but now was not the time to cry. She needed to be strong for the children.

When the little girl passed the cat into her arms, she knew.

Mr. Cuddlesworth had passed on. His body hung limp, lifeless in her arms—no breath, no purring. He was simply gone.

Mrs. Pratt looked on, with tears staining her gray dress.

The children were staring up at Jane. She had to do something. She had to tell them. But how?

"Miss Jane?" asked the little girl quietly. She still hadn't adjusted to calling her by any other name. "Is Mr. Cuddlesworth all right?" Sarah's chin quivered as she looked back and forth between her step-mother and her nurse.

Jane tried to answer, but nothing came out of her mouth.

"He isn't sleeping, is he?" Joshua asked.

Jane took a breath to calm herself. She had to be strong. She was the adult. "No, Joshua. He's not asleep." Taking the boy by the hand, she led him to a seat in front of the hearth. Mrs. Pratt did the same with Sarah.

She sat with one child on either side of her and Mr. Cuddlesworth on her lap. "Do you remember how I told you that he was just like a little old man?" The children nodded their heads. "Well, he got to be too old and couldn't stay with us any longer."

"Is he dead?" asked Joshua on a whimper.

Lying would serve no purpose. They deserved to know the truth. "Yes. I'm afraid so."

Sarah fell to her knees and laid her head across Mr. Cuddlesworth's limp body, her tears wetting his fur. Josh wrapped his arms tight around Jane's neck, sobbing loudly.

She held them both, doing her best to console them, all the while wishing she could follow their example and bawl openly. But now was not the time.

"I'll fetch His Grace, ma'am," said Mrs. Pratt with a sniffle, then she pivoted on her heels and fled the room.

The force of the children's grief slowly began to subside. Thunderous sobs had faded to sniffles by the time Peter arrived, the heels of his Hessian boots echoing in the cavernous hall.

"Jane," he said softly, "are you all right?" He moved in and sat beside her, where Sarah had been, slipping his arm around her waist and drawing her near.

"Yes, of course. But the children..." She needed to know the children were well looked after. "They mustn't be alone right now."

"The children will be fine. They've loved Mr. Cuddlesworth for these last months. But you loved him for his entire life." His hand slid up and down her back, caressing and coaxing her to respond.

But Jane couldn't. She couldn't let herself cry right now. If she did, she would fall apart and might never be able to put herself together again. All she could manage was a nod.

"May I take him from you?" Peter asked. "We should bury him." Ever so gently, he pried first Joshua's fingers free from Mr. Cuddlesworth's fur, then lifted Sarah from her position at Jane's lap, and finally slipped the cat out of Jane's grasp.

"Yes," Jane finally said. "Yes, we should do that."

Her sweet Mr. Cuddlesworth was gone. Jane let Peter lead her from the keep out into the rain in the courtyard, then beside the stables. She stood with Joshua and Sarah and watched him fashion a tiny coffin and dig a small grave, holding on to the children when they cried and wiping the tears from their eyes.

Sniffles sounded all around her, from Mrs. Pratt, Meg, Mrs. Dunstan, Mrs. Prichard, and so many of the other servants of Carreg Mawr as they came out in the rain to support her.

Then Peter carefully laid Mr. Cuddlesworth's body in his coffin and placed it in the earth. When the wet dirt was tossed in atop the wooden box, Jane felt the first tear fall.

She feared they might never stop.

Until a gunshot sounded behind her.

PETER CURSED BENEATH his breath as he bodily flattened Jane and his children to the ground. "Get down! Everyone, get down."

A chorus of screams echoed all around him. Why on earth had such a crowd of his servants amassed over the death of his wife's cat? Clearly, Jane had made quite an impression upon them all. Damnation. There were too many people out in the open—too many people in danger of being shot, when an obvious madman like Utley had a rifle in his hands.

How had he gotten into the castle without someone seeing him?

He lifted his head and tried to see through the pelting rain. Utley had shot at him from somewhere in the upper turrets, but thankfully, the distance had been too great for an accurate shot. Wherever he'd gone, the bastard would have to reload.

Peter pushed himself up from the ground and took off toward the castle. "Stay down, all of you."

Jane struggled to her feet behind him. "What...? What's going on?"

Blast, he didn't have time for this. "Stay down, Jane! I need you to stay with the children." Without waiting for her to respond, he raced through the courtyard and into the castle. If fortune was on his side, Utley was not so far gone that he'd intentionally injure someone else—it was Peter the bastard wanted.

He tore through the inner bailey and up the stairs to the closest turret, cursing the noise made by his Hessians all the way. Rushing up the circular stairs, his heart felt ready to burst from his chest from the exertion. He checked every nook and cranny as he went. There was no sign of Utley anywhere.

A flash of movement brushed before him just as he stepped out onto the parapet to move to the north turret. Peter flung himself back against the wall and tried to slow his breathing. With a slow stretch, he moved his head around the stone corner.

His brother, Neil, stood across the way, holding a finger to his lips. What in God's name was his brother doing in Wales? Neil shook his head ever so slightly, just enough that Peter could make the movement out, then gestured to the left with his head.

Peter craned his head to see further along the crenellated parapet. Utley stood there, frantically trying to load another ball down the barrel of his rifle. It looked like grime might be blocking the ball's path, and try as he might, Utley was making no progress.

Neil caught Peter's eye, gestured some more with his hands, and pulled a pistol from the inside of his coat. Good Lord. This couldn't be happening. Neil stealthily climbed over the parapet and moved soundlessly down the wall, facing Utley's back.

When he finally reached his new position and climbed back over the stone, Peter sucked in a breath. He pressed his eyes closed for a moment, then took a step toward the bastard. It was time to end this, once and for all.

Utley still hadn't noticed either Peter or Neil…but he was making progress on his reload.

More footsteps pounded up the stairs where Peter had just come from.

Utley's head snapped up with a maniacal look of glee. "Finally come to pay the piper then, have you Somerton? Come to atone for your sins?"

"What sins, Utley?" Peter needed to keep him talking. "What have I done that you seem so intent on seeking retribution for?"

Jane skidded to a stop just behind the wall, just out of Utley's sight. Peter's heart thudded to a complete stop. What in bloody hell was she doing up there? He'd asked her to stay with the children. To stay where she would be safe. His gaze locked onto hers. She was terrified, yet once again she was rushed in to face her fears even when she oughtn't.

He implored her with his eyes to remain silent. She gave him a tiny nod, and pressed her back against the wall.

"Like you don't know. You've gone around most of your life, pretending you're this perfect gentleman, the ideal of honor and duty and valor." Utley's upper lip lifted in a sneer. "Where was your honor when you dared my brother to his death? Where was your sense of duty to him when you knew the challenge he was up against, and didn't stop him?"

There it was again—those same questions Peter had asked himself over and over again since that blasted day almost twenty years ago. "I did dare Rawden to jump the hedge that day. There's no denying it, not that I've ever tried, Utley. But you and I both know I'd never been on that property before. None of us knew about the cliffs."

"Lies. As usual. What else should I expect? You've been lying your entire life."

Neil took two slow, deliberate steps closer, and Peter's breath caught in his throat.

"It isn't a lie. I'd been to Rotheby's principal seat countless times, but never to any of his other estates before. It was my first time in Dover." And his last.

Utley let out a nervous laugh, one that sounded like an attempt at a cackle but which came across more as a bleat. "That old goat told you and your brothers everything about everything. Whether you'd been there before or not, you knew." He made another push to load the barrel, and then grinned as he raised it and pointed.

A second shot rang out in the stillness.

"No!" Jane screamed and dashed around the corner. Peter put his arms out and caught her, stopping her progress.

Utley fell forward as a trail of bright red blood poured from a wound in his shoulder. The rifle in his hands clattered to the ground. Neil rushed out, took the rifle, and placed his pistol back in his waistband. When Utley sputtered and started to stand, one of Neil's boots stopped him and pressed him back down.

Where on earth had Neil learned to do anything remotely like that? But he seemed to have it well in hand. That meant Peter could return his attention to his wife.

"You're shaking," he said. He took off his coat and wrapped her in it, then drew her into his arms.

"He—he shot—"

"Utley intended to shoot me. Neil shot him first."

"But…" Jane shook her head from side to side, utterly bewildered by the day's events. It had been too much for her. Far, far too much.

He needed to get her back inside. She'd catch her death if he didn't get her warm and dry soon. Joshua and Sarah, as well, for that matter.

"Neil, can you handle things from here?"

"I think I've got it sorted out," his brother called out.

Peter nodded, then picked his wife up in his arms and carried her back into the castle.

He took the stairs two at a time, when he discovered that Jane was finally crying. She wouldn't want the staff to see her in such a state. For that matter, she might not want *him* to see her that way either, but she obviously could no longer hold back.

The fire in his chamber was still burning, but low. Peter stood Jane on her own feet, then added more logs and hoped they would quickly catch.

"Take off your wet clothes," he told her. "I'll be right back."

When she meekly nodded, he rushed out the door, sent Mrs. Pratt inside with his children, sent his butler out to fetch the magistrate, and made sure the rest of his servants were all safe. On his way back up to his chamber, he stripped his own coat off. As he came through the door, he followed it with his shirt. Jane was still standing where he'd left her, fully dressed in her soaked gown, with tears pouring down her cheeks.

This was precisely what he'd wished he could avoid. Christ, she looked so fragile at that moment, and he could do nothing to take the hurt or shock away.

He crossed the room to stand before her. "Let me help you. Sweetheart, I can't have you taking ill." With one hand, he untied the sash about her waist, removing the pins from her hair with the other so it could hang loose to dry.

Jane stood still, allowing him to do as he would. After he removed her gown, she was still shivering before him. Even her shift was soaked through. He pulled that over her head and dragged a blanket from the bed to wrap her in before carrying her to the wingback chair next to the hearth.

He kicked his Hessians off as quickly as he could manage, and then his wet pantaloons and breeches. If he was going to warm her, the surest manner of doing so was with his own body heat.

"Come to me," he said, pulling Jane to her feet. He took her in his arms and draped the blanket around them both.

Jane buried her face against his chest, her tears combining with the rain water still covering them both. He held her there, stroking her back, until the warmth returned to his limbs, until her tears dried in her eyes.

"Do you want to talk about it?"

Jane shook her head. "Just hold me." She wrapped her arms around his waist, drawing closer to him.

He was hard and uncomfortable with her body sliding against him, but he'd be damned if he would take her at a time like this. She needed him. She needed his love, not his lust.

She sat there with him, using his chest as a pillow, for what felt like hours. She smelled of summer and rain and sweetness. And again, warm tears fell and gathered on his chest.

"I'm sorry, love." Peter took her face in his hands and tilted her head so was facing him. "Christ, Jane. I love you so much, sweetheart. I can't stand to see you hurting."

"You're sorry?" she demanded, standing up and allowing the blanket to fall. "Why on earth are you apologizing to me now? For holding me? For helping me to grieve?" She shoved away from him and fled to the other side of the room.

"No, that's not what I apologized for. I'm sorry that Utley tried to hurt you in order to hurt me. I'm sorry that I can't take the hurt away. That I couldn't protect you from this pain."

"I'm not finished." She punctuated each word through gritted, chattering teeth.

He picked the blanket up from where she'd dropped it on the floor and carried it to wrap around her.

She shrugged his hands away again, causing the blanket to fall to the floor. Goose flesh peppered her skin as she shivered.

"Please, Jane. I'll leave you alone, but please cover yourself. I don't want you to catch a chill." He couldn't lose her. Not for anything.

"Fine." She picked the blanket up and wrapped it around herself. However desperately he wanted to put her back in his bed or seat her near the fire, he refrained.

"Go on," he encouraged. When she neglected to immediately resume where he'd interrupted, he held his hands up. "I promise. I'll remain silent until you're finished."

His wife nodded. "You can't protect me from everything, Peter. Certainly not from life itself."

"I know—"

She gave him the fiercest glare anyone had ever dared to issue him in his entire life.

"Pets dying? That's a natural part of life. You know this. But what you don't seem to recognize is that needing to *do* something—anything—is also a natural part of life. For everyone."

Jane took a seat in a wingback chair and tightened the blanket about her shoulders. "I grew up having to work. It was simply my lot in life. We aren't all born to privilege, you know, and the rest of us have to find a way to make ends meet. So I helped around the house and the garden, and I did some sewing work for the neighborhood. Again, you know all of this. But the part you seem to not understand is that I didn't just do all of this because I *had* to do it—I actually enjoyed it. I like feeling useful—feeling needed. It gives me something to do."

"But—"

"Do *not* interrupt me." Her imperial tone impressed him. "When I agreed to marry you, I only did so because you promised me—*promised* me, Peter—that you would give me responsibilities. You have enough responsibilities to occupy three normal people, yet what have you allowed me to do? To play with your children without taking part in their rearing, to work on some mindless embroidery that no one will ever look at, and to plan the menu with Cook. I will have you know, I'm not a mindless twit. Nor am I content to live an idle lifestyle. I understand that I have a new role, but there's no reason I can't fulfill the obligations of that position and also have something meaningful with which to occupy my day."

He had a hard time thinking of the last time even his mother had delivered him such a blistering set-down. Good God. All of this time, he'd been trying to take away her burdens, to make her life easier—and all he'd accomplished was to make her feel useless and miserable. Quite the opposite of his intentions.

"If we're to make this work, Peter, there will have to be some changes. Not the least of which is that if you ever dare to apologize to me again for not being able to protect me from life itself, I will throttle you to within an inch of your life. Understood?"

"Understood. May I speak?"

"When I've finished." The passion still blazed in her eyes, much the same as it did in the throes of passion. "You also need to understand that I'm not only capable of hard work, but I need it. I can work just as hard as any man or woman in your employ. Menu planning isn't enough. I need a purpose—something more than just being your wife."

"But you *are* my wife," he growled.

"Precisely. Which is even more reason to keep me content."

"Fine."

"There's one more thing."

Of course there was. He inclined his head.

"I love you. Against my better judgment and all of my efforts, but there you have it. I love you. And how dare you tell me that you love me in the midst of issuing me the most idiotic apology known to man, burying something as monumental as that in a manner I was highly likely to miss entirely? That is unacceptable. Bloody ignorant man. It's not like I would have figured that one out on my own, since you've been determined to make me miserable lately. Granted, the way you handled burying Mr. Cuddlesworth for me when you clearly don't even like cats ought to have been a clue."

She loved him. The rest of what she just said floated away, but the one tiny little sentence stuck with him. Jane loved him.

Thank God.

Epilogue

AFTER PUTTING ERASMUS Coburn in place as the new steward of Carreg Mawr, Peter and his family had returned to London. For once in his life, Town life actually represented sanity for him. He'd never expected that to happen.

Since the day Jane's cat died and Utley made his final attack, the marriage between Peter and Jane had become much more manageable. Not that he was glad about Mr. Cuddlesworth's death—not at all. But it had proven to be a catalyst of change for the two of them.

Admittedly, he was the one most in need of changing. The next day, he'd set about making her life more livable, more enjoyable for her, by giving her responsibilities.

Since then, Mrs. Pratt had been reporting to Jane. Mrs. Dunstan and Mrs. Prichard had already been working with her in hiring their replacements—primarily in asking her opinion of potential maids' abilities—but he'd also granted her the authority to oversee and organize their efforts.

The scullery maids had informed him that his wife had been going behind his back and partaking in the household chores. At first, he'd been furious about the discovery. But then, after taking a moment to think about it, he laughed. No one but Jane would sneak about *trying* to perform hard labor. Most would do the opposite.

She truly was his equal, in far more ways than he had ever realized. And that, more than anything, was a gift.

No wonder the *ton* had fallen in love with her.

Now, back at what would be their normal, married life, they were discussing what Jane's responsibilities would be at Hardwicke House.

"I would like for you to coordinate all of the maids' duties with Mrs. Wilson," Peter said. "And Cook will report to you as well...not only for meal planning, but for all of her needs."

"Excellent. And Mrs. Pratt will continue to report to me?"

"Of course. You two have developed quite a rapport of late." He was grateful for that. In seeing to all of his own duties, Peter often felt that he was neglecting his children. Now, with Jane's help, he had more time available to spend with them.

Not only that, but they were beginning to call Jane "Mother." He had encouraged them both to do so since the day they'd married. Neither Joshua nor Sarah remembered their mother. Jane was the only mother they would ever know.

"There's something else I'd like to discuss with you," Jane broached. Never a good sign—he had come to learn this. It usually meant he'd done something wrong again.

What it would be this time?

"Even with overseeing the kitchens, the maid staff, and Mrs. Pratt, I believe I'll have a great deal of free time." Jane wrung her hands together and chewed on the stray curl that had worked itself loose from the knot at her neck. "I was wondering...well, actually, I have an idea."

"An idea?" Good Lord, this sounded dreadful.

"Yes. You see, I still have the storefront on Bond Street rented. Mr. Selwood and I agreed that I could use it for a year, to start with. After that, we would renegotiate. And it's just sitting there, empty, you see. I just can't have that."

"Of course." He knew, without a doubt, he would never understand his wife. Sometimes Peter wished she would just come out with things and say what was on her mind, instead of talking circles around them.

"So, I had noticed how the gowns Miss Bentley wears to accompany Lady Warburton to social engagements aren't quite up to scratch. She does as well as she can manage, mind you, but her pay doesn't allow her to purchase the finest of fabrics, or to pay for the most fashionable of designs."

"I have no control over how much her employer pays her, Jane." Where was she headed with this?

"Oh, no. That isn't what I meant at all. I was just...well, do try to keep up with me, dear. You remember, we were talking about my shop?"

He remembered she'd been talking about the shop until she jumped to a seemingly unrelated subject. Deuced woman.

Thankfully, she continued without waiting for his response. "You see, Peter, Miss Bentley is far from alone in her predicament. Ladies of her class run into this problem all the time. So my plan is to open up a dress shop specifically for them."

"For them?"

"Yes. For the paid companions and governesses, and other ladies who live and work for the members of the *ton* and who are expected to move in those same circles—but who can't afford to dress appropriately in order to be accepted as they ought. I intend to make their gowns for them. As a charity."

"A charity. So I suppose this will be my good deed, that I'll be paying for this expense?" It wouldn't be a bad use of his money, if it kept Jane happy. But it could still become quite a bit of money. There were many governesses, paid companions, and the like in Town.

"Not at all. There's the money I've saved from before we married. I intend to use that. And part of my pin money."

"I see." Perhaps he should have listened to her when they were discussing her pin money. She said it was far too much, that she would never be able to spend even half of it in a year. Leave it to Jane to discover a way to make good use of it all.

"So may I?" She bit her lip in anticipation of his response.

"Tell me more about the logistics of this endeavor."

He could scarcely believe he was even considering the ridiculous notion. Any other gentleman of his status would forbid it and be done.

"The shop will be open two afternoons a week—only for a few hours. During those times, I'll take measurements, perform fittings, discuss fabrics and designs—the normal needs of my customers. And then I'll bring the work home with me, and I'll sew when I'm not busy with my other responsibilities."

She had obviously spent a great deal of time thinking through all of his objections. Blast it. "And if, for some reason, you need more capital to keep up with the demand?"

She squeezed his hand and smiled at him indulgently. "Oh, you have no need to worry, Peter. Sophie is certain that she can find other ladies willing to invest in my charity. It'll actually be fun, to see who she can convince—and it will give her something useful to do with her time, too."

Fun, indeed. Thank God he loved this woman.

"MOTHER! MOTHER, PAPA said you should come quickly."

At Joshua's shouted demands and Sarah's squeal, Jane set the primrose muslin she was working on aside and headed for the front drawing room. "Coming," she called out.

"Come faster," Sophie shouted on a laugh.

Sophie was here? Were Charlotte and their mother here as well? They'd gone to Somerton Court to spend Christmas with Alex and Grace, so she couldn't imagine why they would have returned already. Christmas was still a few days away.

Jane moved through the halls of Hardwicke House at a near-run. Something had to be wrong.

When Peter's footmen opened the doors of the drawing room, Jane nearly fell over from shock. Sophie, Charlotte, and Mama Hardwicke were all present, along with Alex, Grace, and their little girl. The party wasn't complete there, however. Lord Rotheby was seated under a mound of blankets by the hearth, surrounded by Neil, Richard, newly home from the wars, and Lord Sinclaire. Her parents were there, too, seated next to the dowager, and her brothers and their families were off to the side.

In the middle of them all, Peter stood with a basket in his hands and his children by his side, grinning like an imbecile. "I asked Mama to bring you something for Christmas."

"Oh, this is lovely!" Jane said. She'd never had so many people all together for Christmas before.

Peter laughed. "Yes, having our family together for Christmas is lovely, to be sure...but that isn't what I was talking about."

"In the basket," Sarah squealed. "She's in the basket!"

Joshua admonished her. "You were supposed to stay quiet and let Papa do this."

All of the adults laughed.

Jane stepped forward, inching her way closer. The blanket covering the basket moved ever so slightly, and then a tiny mewl sounded.

"A kitten?" Could it be? Peter would never willingly allow another animal into the house, would he?

"She's a girl!" Sarah cried, bouncing on the balls of her feet. The poor little dear almost couldn't contain her excitement.

Jane smiled at her. "A girl?" Just then, a gray and white spotted kitten poked her head up from beneath the blankets and bellowed at them all. She reached into the basket and pulled the tiny thing out. Almost immediately, the kitten started purring. "And what do you think we should call her?"

"Since she's a girl," Peter interjected, "perhaps she should be Mrs. Cuddlesworth."

"Oh, yes, Mother!" Joshua and Sarah said in unison.

Jane knelt down to the floor and the children reached in to pet the sweet dear along with her. "Mrs. Cuddlesworth, is it? I suppose that's as fitting as anything."

Mrs. Cuddlesworth leapt from her arms and landed on Sarah, who fell over in a peal of giggles.

Jane caught Peter's eye. He smiled down at her and helped her back to her feet, then planted a delicious kiss on her lips. "Merry Christmas, my love," he murmured against her lips. "Is that an acceptable gift?"

She nodded. It was the best gift he could have ever given her—*his love*.

About the Author

Catherine Gayle is a bestselling author of Regency-set historical romance. She's a transplanted Texan living in North Carolina with two extremely spoiled felines. In her spare time, she watches way too much hockey and reality TV, plans fun things to do for the Nephew Monster's next visit, and performs experiments in the kitchen which are rarely toxic.

Catherine would love to hear from her readers. You can find her on the internet at www.catherinegayle.com or send her an email at catherinegayle.author@gmail.com.

Printed in Great Britain
by Amazon